SAHARA'S RANSOM

THE SILESIA CHRONICLES
BOOK 3

SHANNON BLAKE

*For Caroline and Bert
and Mary and Bill*

*Far or near, in darkness or light, in death or life —
love never fails.*

ONE

SAHARA, Jared, and Rafe stood on the landing platform in Halcyon's capital city of Aquila, surrounded by men in cream-colored suits. The leader—the man with the black beard and the glasses polarized against the sun's glare—had nearly reached the stairs leading down to the street below.

"Get moving," said the man standing behind Sahara, prodding her with the sharp point of his knife.

Sahara glared at him and toyed for a fraction of a second with the thought of relieving him of his knife and his life. But then she turned away and fell in beside Jared and Rafe.

The rest of the men formed a seemingly casual but impenetrable knot around them as they followed the bearded man across the platform. Two of the men, who seemed no more than teenagers to Sahara, elbowed each other with wide grins. They seemed intent on getting Jared's attention, and when he didn't even glance in their direction, one of them jabbed at Jared's knee with the butt of his gun.

Sahara stiffened, but Jared effortlessly skipped around the hazard.

"Are you children done yet?" he asked, finally spearing the two miscreants with a withering glare. "Or is this how you treat all your visitors?"

This sent the two boys into snorting, but stifled laughter.

"Oh," said one, recovering himself, "you will wish you'd never come to Halcyon when Azimir is through with you."

"That's enough!" The guard just in front of Sahara whirled on the two youngsters, giving the speaker a stunning blow in the jaw that knocked out a tooth and split his lip.

By now the bearded man had rounded back to see what had caused the scuffle.

"Emet!" he snapped. "You had better have an explanation for this!" He gestured to the boy, who was holding a rag to his mouth and spitting blood on the platform.

"His speech is unguarded," Emet said. His voice was steady, but Sahara could see the blood draining from his face. "He—"

"He is Azimir's nephew, you idiot." The bearded man hesitated, his eyes impossible to read behind his glasses "And Azimir will deal with you both. I have no time for this nonsense."

He turned away and descended the steps at a brisk trot. Emet blew out his breath and they moved off once again.

As they headed down to street level, Sahara glanced at Jared. He stared forward, and if he felt her eyes on him, he didn't turn. His coldness only served to feed the worm of dread coiling in her gut.

"Pretty mess we're in now," muttered Rafe on her left. "Didn't I say we were in for trouble? And who's to get word back to Askalon, if they just stuff us down some deep, dark hole...or worse?"

Sahara's eyes snapped to him. "They wouldn't do that, Rafe. We're diplomats...we have some kind of protection, don't we? And they don't know what we have to say yet." Her voice trailed off as Rafe arched an eyebrow.

"Yes, they're treating us in accordance with all diplomatic protocols," he agreed. "Marching us off like a pack of vagabonds. Or didn't you notice that these guards aren't here for our protection?"

Sahara couldn't answer him. He was right, of course.

But it's possible. Maybe it's all just a misunderstanding.

There's no misunderstanding. Jared's voice cut across her mind like the lash of a whip. *Askalon is no friend to Halcyon, not any longer. The Triumvirate didn't just burn this bridge with their betrayal...they blew it to hell.*

But...we can reason with them, can't we? she responded. *This Azimir might not be so bad. Maybe we can still make a deal?*

Jared didn't respond, and Sahara didn't press him. She didn't have the chance.

The lower streets of Aquila were swarming with activity. The busy main thoroughfare bustled with foot traffic, carts, and animals of all kinds. Sahara couldn't help gaping as a group of half-dressed boys with sticks drove a set of donkeys laden with packs down the street. And then she pulled up short, causing the guard behind her to stumble and curse at her in his foreign tongue.

A string of horses was tethered to a rail in front of a tall, sandstone building down the street to her right. Tears flooded Sahara's eyes and one slipped down her cheek before she could dash it away. She hadn't seen horses since she was a girl on Amaryl. But these were lithe and slender creatures, long-legged and jet black with flowing manes and tails, nothing like the heavy draft horses they used on Amaryl. Watching them, Sahara felt a prickle down her arms. They were more like wind and fire than flesh and blood.

"You have horses!" she said softly.

The guard snorted. "Those beasts belong to the Hazad. It's market day today. Now get moving, girl, before I slay you where you stand!"

Sahara wanted to press him with more questions, but a swift glance at the guard told her that he was in no mood to field them. Sahara bit her lip and reluctantly followed the men across the busy street, where the bearded man was waiting beside two sleek black vehicles.

As the guard pushed Sahara into the back seat, he laughed at her. "These are our horses, my girl," he said. "The horses of the Zharib!"

The vehicles sped through the twisting streets, passing more camels and donkeys as they went.

"Why are there animals in the street?" Sahara asked finally.

"They belong to the Hazad," the man answered, and that seemed to be that. He offered no further explanation, and Sahara decided it was best not to ask him any more questions.

After several sharp turns, the vehicles slowed to a halt. The men got out and opened the doors for them. They were in the center of the city now, across the street from the huge temple they had seen from the air.

Sahara turned away from the temple to stare up at the facade of the palace complex. Huge blocks of honey-colored stone formed delicate arches and colonnades, offering tantalizing views of cool shadows and green spaces within.

"Let's go," said the bearded man, starting off again. He led them straight through the main courtyard, which was overshadowed by the high walls of the palace and cooled by the plashing of a great fountain in its center. They went through another colonnade and then up a wide flight of steps. A left turn, and then up another flight of steps.

Finally, the bearded man stopped in front of a set of huge, intricately carved double doors with golden handles. He pushed these open and led them inside.

The room was long and dark and cool, and the air smelled faintly of some kind of spice. In a moment, Sahara saw why—gently smoking censers on golden stands stood in each corner of the room.

"Stop," commanded Ribaddi.

He left them standing in the middle of the room, and the men who had accompanied them formed into a semi-circle behind them, effectively blocking their way out. Ribaddi went to a side door at the far end of the room and disappeared. A few minutes later, he returned with another man dressed all in black. He settled himself into the low wooden armchair at the end of the room and waved their group forward. Ribaddi stood just behind his right shoulder, arms crossed.

"So, Askalon sends greetings," the man said. His dark eyes flashed at them, and then he fell to studying his immaculately manicured nails, as if the whole affair bored him to death.

"Yes," said Jared. "We are here to negotiate the debt."

The man's eyes flickered at them again. "I see."

Jared glanced over his shoulder at the men standing behind them. "Perhaps if we might speak more privately?" he ventured.

"You may speak your business here," the man said. "These men are my Zharib...how do you say? My retainers." He fixed them once again with those dark eyes. "So speak. What from Askalon?"

"You know that the Triumvirate no longer rules Askalon."

"We know this."

Jared took a breath. "They have made you promises...promises they never intended to keep."

The man started up in his chair. "They have lied to us?"

"I'm afraid so."

"You bring evil tidings with you," the man said, his eyes narrowing to slits of suspicion. "How do I know you to be truthful?"

"Askalon is willing to offer some compensation toward discharging the Triumvirate's debts," Jared continued, ignoring his question. "Will you discuss terms?"

"I will discuss no terms with infidel liars and traitors," the man said. His voice was calm and low, but there was a seething menace in it that made Sahara's skin crawl.

"We are willing to establish good faith with Halcyon," Jared persisted. "It was the Triumvirate that wished to deceive and betray you, not the Lords of Askalon."

"We were promised *zanthos*. And nothing else will discharge the debt Askalon owes us."

Jared sighed. Sahara could feel his frustration.

"Lord Azimir," she said, "they lied to you. They lied about the *zanthos*." And then she decided to gamble everything on one throw. "There is no more of it than what they had...and what they had is not enough to pay their debt."

A slow, cruel smile curved Azimir's lips. "Is that so? Is that what the Lords of Askalon say?"

Jared laid a hand on Sahara's arm. "The Lords of Askalon say that there must be something else...some other way to satisfy Halcyon. Is there truly nothing else?"

"No, I am interested. Let the woman speak." He leaned forward in his chair. "Tell us again. Do the Lords of Askalon say there is no *zanthos*?"

Sahara began to feel that she had stepped onto dangerous ground. There was something in Azimir's eyes...something keen and knowing. She had miscalculated. Something was wrong here.

"I-I said..." she began.

"Because," Azimir interrupted, "I want to be sure I understand you."

The men standing behind them took a step forward, and Sahara heard the hiss of steel. Nine curved blades flashed in the sunlight that filtered down from the high windows. The men placed the points down on the floor, resting their hands on the hilts. But now that the scimitars were drawn, it would be the matter of an instant to bring them to the ready and strike.

She turned back to Azimir, who was watching her with all the intentness of a bird of prey.

"I said that we do not have enough *zanthos*, Lord Azimir," she said, trying at least to speak the truth without completely contradicting herself. She did not dare look at the others for fear that she would look like she was unsure of herself.

"No one betrays Halcyon. No one." Azimir's eyes were boring into her, his voice full of quiet menace. "The Triumvirate promised us weapons...weapons powered with *zanthos*. You have overthrown the Triumvirate, you say, and this much I believe. But that the weapons and the power source are not in your possession...that I do not believe."

"Askalon wants peace with Halcyon," Jared said. "But we will no longer trade with you. We have no more need of Demon's Breath. All that remains is to settle the balance. Askalon is rich in many things—fuel, and precious metals and jewels."

Azimir leaned back in his chair. "So. You try to buy Halcyon's good will with trinkets even as you cut us off?" Sahara saw the muscles of his jaw clench tight for a moment. "The debt Askalon owes Halcyon is more than you could ever afford with your trifles. We own your damn planet, fool!"

"We were sent to ask for a reduction in the terms," Rafe said, clearing his throat.

Azimir threw back his head and laughed. "You must think me an infant," he thundered, his laughter fading to anger. "Let me understand you. You will no longer trade with Halcyon, you do not have what was promised us, and now you want us to absolve part of the debt that you owe?"

"That about covers it," Rafe replied, trying to smile. Under his breath, he muttered, "I knew we drew the damned short straw on this one."

"And how exactly does this profit me?"

"Well," answered Jared, "you could be stuck with nothing at all, if you'd prefer that option. Askalon offers you partial payment in order to maintain peace and goodwill with Halcyon. But if you will not accept what we offer, then we will withdraw and you will get nothing."

Sahara stared at Jared, and then slowly turned to look at Azimir. His face was expressionless, but his eyes were burning with wrath.

"You mock me."

"No, my lord. I do not mock you."

"Then it is too bad for you."

He lifted a finger, and Sahara heard the slither of steel on stone as the men behind them lifted their weapons.

Before she could move, three of the men had Jared down on his knees, his arms pinioned behind him. A fourth knocked the heavy hilt of his scimitar against the side of Jared's head, and he slumped to the ground, unconscious.

Then she fell violently to the floor as Rafe shoved her aside. She rolled and then rose to a crouch some feet away.

Her scream died in her throat.

Rafe was smiling at her.

"Go!" he choked.

And then he slumped forward onto the stone floor, soaking it with his blood.

The scimitar that had been meant for her was buried in his back.

TWO

SAHARA HESITATED for the barest fraction of a second. Then, as she saw the men turn towards her, scimitars raised, she jumped to her feet and ran.

Behind her, she heard Azimir scream, "Catch her! Don't let her escape!"

But she was already out the door and heading for the stairs. Her eyes were half-blind with tears, and sobs that she could not voice spasmed in her chest.

She had to get out.

She slipped and slid down half a dozen stairs, skidding to a stop at the bottom. She launched herself onto her feet again, ignoring the searing pain in her leg. She heard running footsteps behind her, clattering down the steps. Shouts from angry throats echoed around the curving walls.

She quickened her pace as much as she could, limping to the next stairwell and starting down.

The men were gaining on her with every step.

She gritted her teeth against the pain. Blinked her eyes to clear them. She couldn't afford another fall.

Carefully.

Carefully.

She stumbled again as she reached the flat, but caught herself and propelled herself forward, down the colonnaded hall toward the courtyard.

As she staggered into the warm sunlight, she saw more men swarming from the other side of the courtyard. She would have to run in earnest now, or she would be caught. She sucked in a deep, shuddering breath and sprinted for the gate. The pain in her leg was lost in the flood of adrenaline that surged through her like quicksilver.

She was out in the street.

More men, standing around near the vehicles that had brought them here, sprang into action when they heard the frenzied shouts of her pursuers. They piled into the vehicles, revving the engines and swinging them around to chase her down the street.

She ran into someone, bounced off someone else. She was in the midst of a jostling crowd before she was even conscious that it was there. She pushed her way through.

An old woman's wrinkled face turned up toward her, the cracked lips forming foreign curses that she couldn't hear or understand.

A young boy laughed as he thwacked his stick on the gray hindquarters of his burdened donkey.

A muscular youth selling silks pirouetted out of her way as she barreled down on him, and then he seized her arm, yanking her painfully around.

"Where are you going in such a hurry?" he asked. He was smiling at her.

She could find no words to answer him, but looked frantically back up the street. A knot of men with raised scimitars was racing toward them, and she heard the whir of engines in the street. Then shots rang out, bullets skittering among the cobbles of the street.

Instantly, the mob of people around her surged into a screaming, seething sea of bodies, and she was nearly pulled away from the young man who held her arm. He elbowed people out of the way, holding her against the rising tide of flesh and fury.

"Oh, you have serious trouble," he shouted, his teeth flashing in another wide grin. "Come with me!"

The silks fluttered in a melting rainbow as the rack spiraled to the ground. Then he let the crowd sweep them away, through the crowd of vendors toward a dim alleyway that opened to their left.

More shots rang out behind them, and the old man beside Sahara dropped to the ground, blood gushing from a wound in his leg. He struggled to rise, and Sahara jerked against the young man, frantically yelling something about helping him.

"No time!" he said, his face grim.

Sahara watched over her shoulder, stumbling over her own feet, as the dust and weight of a thousand trampling feet pounded the old man to death. As shots continued to riddle the crowd, the young man accelerated their pace. The crowds parted and melted together again behind them, like water before the prow of a ship. As they ran, he snatched things from vendors' tables—a yellow headscarf, a pair of sandals, a cuffed bracelet, a sand-colored robe. Then they were through the crowd and into the alleyway, which seemed suddenly dark and silent as a tomb after the glare and noise of the main road.

"Quick, quick!" he commanded, pulling her along. "Don't look back!"

He led her through the twisting network of alleys, heading always downhill and to the south. Finally, in a tiny side street no more than a man's arm span wide, littered with rotting vegetables and overhung with crisscrossing networks of clothes drying on lines, he slowed to a walk and then stopped, listening intently. After a few moments, he turned back to her.

"We lost them," he grinned, releasing his hold on her hand.

Sahara collapsed to the ground, sobbing and shaking, and crawled to the wall to lean against the cool stone. The young man watched her with bright eyes, seeming neither bewildered nor surprised.

Finally, she forced herself back under control, wiping her face with the palms of her hands. She could feel the dirt clinging to her cheeks, but it didn't matter.

Nothing mattered now.

"Thank you," she managed, her voice thick.

"Well. It's not the first time I've had to outrun the Zharib," he confessed, his face creasing again in a ready grin.

Just like Rafe...always a smile.

But she mustn't think of Rafe. The tears were already lumping in her throat, choking her.

"But you are in trouble," the young man continued, "and you are a foreigner."

It wasn't a question, so she didn't offer any explanations. Instead, she said, "I need to get back to my ship. I've got to get out of here...I've got to get help. I've got..." She stopped, catching herself before she jabbered her way back into tears. She lifted her eyes to his and asked simply, "Can you help me?"

"No."

It was like a sword-stroke, and a flare of anger scorched through her grief. "Why not?"

"Because they will have taken your ship already," he said. "Believe me, they are very thorough. There is no way home for you that way."

She stared at him for a moment. "Then where the hell am I supposed to go?" she asked quietly, her voice quavering.

He stared back the way they had come for a moment, listening intently. Sahara got slowly to her feet and watched him. After a moment, he seemed satisfied and turned back to her. "Here. Put these on."

He wrapped the robe around her, clasped the bracelet around her wrist, and wound the headscarf over her riot of red hair. Then he held out the sandals. When she didn't take them immediately, he pushed them at her again. "Put them on."

"What am I dressing up like this for?" she demanded, sitting down again and tugging off her boots and socks. As she laced up the sandals, he gathered her things together and trotted down the alley to a large pile of trash. She paused and watched him shove her boots deep under the heap of rotting vegetation, wrinkling her nose at the sudden stench that seemed to consume the street.

"You stand out in a crowd, dressed as you were," he explained, hurrying back and wiping his hands on his wide-legged pants. "Now we can move more freely, without drawing too much attention to ourselves."

"Please, I have to go back," she said. "If you won't take me to my ship, then take me back."

He offered her a hand to help her to her feet, and as she clasped it and rose, he frowned at her in bewilderment. "Why would you want to go back? You just escaped!"

"You don't understand. My friends are back there. One is hurt...the other may be...dead..." She fought through the ache in her throat and in her heart, shaking her head fiercely at him. "You don't understand. I can't leave them. I have to go back."

"Not like this," the young man said. "Not like this. Come."

He tried to take her by the hand again, but she jerked away from his grasp.

"Name," she demanded. "Name first. Then maybe I'll come with you."

"My name is Rigel," he said, bowing awkwardly and grinning at her again.

With a sigh, she allowed him to take her hand. "Lead on, then, Rigel."

It was sunset when they finally emerged from the south gate of the city. Great horns blew from the guard towers as they passed through, moving with the crowd that draggled out into the rippling green fields outside the city walls. The road widened out considerably as soon as it passed through the gates, but then, abruptly, the paving stopped and it became a dirt track winding through the tall, waving grasses. In the slanting crimson light of the setting sun, the fields looked awash in blood.

As the sun sank finally below the horizon, darkness poured slowly over the land, drowning the grasses now in cool shadows. Still Rigel trotted on and Sahara, now numb with the chill of grief, stumbled after him. A gentle breeze sprang up from the south as the full moon rose, caressing her hot cheeks and carrying the strange scent of some night-blooming flower. The further south they went, the more overpowering the scent became.

Sahara coughed, then gasped. The scent was choking her, squeezing her lungs.

"Rigel!" she croaked, but he seemed not to hear her.

She staggered a few more paces, choking and coughing, and then fell to her knees in the dirt. In the moonlight, she lifted her hands and saw that they were coated with some kind of strange white pollen. She gasped for breath and darkness clouded her vision. She never felt herself hit the ground.

———

Sahara's eyes fluttered open.

The muted light of the sun was filtering through the cloth walls of a spacious tent. She was lying on the ground on some kind of soft pelt. She pushed herself up on one elbow and listened. She could hear low voices outside, and she recognized one of them as Rigel's. Cautiously, she crept toward the closed flap of the tent and edged it aside.

"So," boomed a great, but not unkind, voice, "here is the little lady who ran away from the Zharib!"

Sahara's eyes snapped up as the flap was flung aside, revealing a huge man with a long white beard and shining eyes. She slowly got to her feet and stood, watching him with muscles tensed.

"Rigel tells me you are in a bit of trouble," he said. He took his hands out of the wide sleeves of his tunic and spread them out to her in a gesture of welcome.

"Where am I?" she asked warily. "And how did I get here?"

"Rigel carried you...or dragged you—" this with a wink in Rigel's direction— "into the village last night."

Sahara shook her head, feeling suddenly strangely muddled. "My head...feels funny. What happened to me?"

"Your body is not used to the scent of the *borracha* flower," the man told her. "It's overwhelming to one who is not accustomed to it."

Sahara rubbed her hands over her face, trying to get her mind to focus. "What's that? What flower is that?"

"We harvest it. The Zharib sell it." He shrugged. "Perhaps you know it by its more common name, eh? Demon's Breath?"

Sahara dropped her hands and stared at him. "What did you say?"

"Demon's Breath. The drug. It is refined from the *borracha* flower. The plants grow in groves not far from here, and the blossoms open at night. We travel from grove to grove and harvest the flowers." He smiled warmly at her. "You are welcome here for as long as you choose to stay. We have enough and more to share."

"I'm not staying," Sahara snapped. But the world seemed suddenly to sway, and the man caught her as she fell forward.

"You must stay until you grow accustomed to the *borracha*. Stay, heal, and take counsel," the man told her gently, propelling her back inside the tent and helping her onto her pallet. "Rigel will bring you some tea to help you."

"I can't stay here," Sahara slurred, grabbing the man's sleeve and tugging at it. "My friends...my friends..."

The man shook his head. "You are no good to your friends this way. You must heal first. Be patient."

"You don't understand!" She swore with as much vehemence as she could muster in her muzzy state. "There's no medicine that can heal me. And I have to get back to Aquila!"

But even as she spoke, she collapsed onto the pallet, too dizzy and weak to rise.

She must have slept, for when she opened her eyes, the light in her little tent was brighter. Rigel was squatting beside her, shaking her shoulder and holding a metal mug with some steaming liquid in it.

"Feeling better?" he asked, sitting back on his heels as she propped herself up on an elbow to take the drink from his hand.

"A little." She hesitated. "Maybe."

"You will feel better soon," he assured her. He stood and dusted off his pants. "Drink that and rest. You will feel better."

He smiled at her and bowed out through the tent flap, leaving her alone with her tea and her thoughts.

Sahara.

The mug fell to the ground, spilling the tea in the dirt. Jared's face blurred into view, and then she was able to focus.

His head was caked with dried blood and there were dark circles under his eyes, but he was alive.

She stared at him for a moment, scarcely daring to breathe, wondering if she were hallucinating.

Jared! You're alive?

He smiled wanly at her. *And you escaped. You're safe somewhere?*

For the moment. She gulped, desperately wanting to ask him about Rafe but not daring to frame the words.

I'll come for you, she told him instead.

But he was gone.

Strength, fueled now by grief and rage, suddenly flooded into her limbs, and she scrambled out of the tent. As she raised her head, she recoiled in sudden confusion. A large group of people stood silently around her tent—men, women, and children. The white-bearded man and Rigel stood in front of the group.

"What's this?" she demanded. "Who are all these people?"

The white-bearded man opened his hands to her again. "This is your new family," he said. "I am Jessup, and we will call you Zelie— the daughter who comes from afar."

"My name is Sahara," she protested.

"Very well, Zelie Sahara," the man said, completely unperturbed.

Sahara turned in mute confusion to Rigel, who was grinning all over his handsome young face. He spread his hands to her in that same welcoming gesture.

"Zelie Sahara," he said. "Welcome to the Hazad."

THREE

A FIT of coughing startled Jared out of a dark and dreamless sleep.

He blinked. The darkness around him was so total that at first he wasn't sure he'd even opened his eyes, and then he realized that the coughing fit had been his own.

He was alone. Utterly and completely alone.

He took a deep breath.

I'm inhaling darkness. There's no air in here. Just the dark.

The thought loosed the crawling warmth of nausea, and for a moment, he wrestled with the worm of overwhelming fear. He tried telling himself that it was nonsense, that his mind was playing tricks. But darkness shrouds the line between the real and the imagined.

He had woken into a nightmare.

Then, suddenly, he recoiled as something next to him in the dark grated painfully, a stone-on-stone grinding that gradually spilled light into the room. He blinked rapidly, his eyes blinded by the sudden brightness.

After the grating came the voices, harsh and almost guttural, speaking rapidly in a language he didn't understand. He moved to raise his arm to shield his eyes from the light and get a glimpse of his captors, and in a rush he felt the cold metal shackles around his wrists and heard the heavy clank of a chain on stone. His arms were pinioned behind him, and he couldn't move.

The guards' chatter suddenly ceased, and Jared saw a shadow pass through the light of the open door. Vaguely, he saw someone crouching in front of him, keeping close inside the shadows.

"You've got company," one of the guards said, jerking Jared's attention away from the figure in the darkness. "Have a nice chat."

They pulled the door almost entirely closed once again, leaving only the tiniest sliver of light cutting across the stone floor between Jared and his visitor.

"What do you want?" Jared demanded, surprised to hear the croak in his voice. "How long have I been in this hole?"

"Not long...yet. We brought you here after your...meeting with Lord Azimir."

"So who are you, then, if you're not Azimir?" Jared jerked at the chains that held his wrists and struggled to change his position, painfully aware now of the stones beneath him.

"We're old friends, you and I."

Jared thought he could hear the wolfish grin in the man's voice. "I don't know you."

"You just don't remember, perhaps. I am Ribbadi, chief of Lord Azimir's Zharib."

Jared stared hard into the darkness, trying to catch some glimpse of the man. "So? Why am I in chains, and where is my friend?"

"Oh, that unfortunate wretch." There was a long silence, and then Ribbadi chuckled. Jared fought his chains, straining at his bonds.

"I'll kill you," he growled, the anger boiling over as the memories flashed through his mind. Rafe, falling, with a sword buried in his back. Sahara bolting for the door. "I'll rip you apart! Let me go!"

"And why would I do that when you mean me violence?" Ribbadi asked. "But no. You will stay here until Lord Azimir asks to see you again. And as for your friend, well. Time will tell, I suppose."

Jared's heart surged, hammering against his ribs. "He's alive? Is he alive?" When Ribbadi did not reply, he shouted, "Tell me, damn you! Is he alive?"

There was a rustling noise, and Jared, staring wide-eyed as a madman into the darkness, knew that Ribbadi had risen to his feet. "We will speak again soon. In the meantime, you will have food and drink brought to you."

"And light?" Jared asked.

The door grated open enough for Ribbadi to slip out. "It will be day soon."

Then he was gone, and Jared was alone in the dark once again.

Time crawled past.

Jared sat, head bowed and eyes closed, because keeping them open was pointless. He felt his senses sharpening painfully with every passing minute. The flecks of stone underneath his fingernails sent shudderings along his nerve endings. The stone bit into his bare heels. The chill of the floor seeped into his soul. And all around him, the darkness, flooding into his nostrils with every inhale, trickling out again with every exhale. Even the rasping of his breathing seemed to echo in the silence, grating on his ears.

It was enough to drive him mad.

He opened his eyes, met only darkness.

His rasping breathing quickened as the shivers of panic trembled in his gut.

I can't do this. I'll go mad. I can't survive this. I won't survive this.

And then, as a scream was collecting its raw energy in his throat, a shaft of sunlight speared down through the darkness, rending it like a veil. The scream in Jared's throat turned into a gasp, and he came reeling back to himself again.

How stupid, to be so afraid of the dark!

He looked up as more light flooded the cell and saw that there was a window set in the wall to his left, perhaps twenty paces from where he sat. As the light grew, he could see that his prison was far longer than it was wide, and that the door to his right was nothing more than a heavy slab of stone edged with metal so that it could slide along a narrow track. Set perhaps six inches from the bottom of the door was a hole, closed from the outside by a wooden panel.

Even as he stared at it, the door was suddenly shoved back again, and two guards entered the room.

They were dressed, as Ribbadi had been, in cream-colored suits, and both carried heavy guns slung over their shoulders. More light poured in through the doorway, and Jared, eyes now adjusted to the light, could glimpse a winding stone passage outside his cell. He leaned to the side, trying to see where it led, and was rewarded for his curiosity with a sharp smack on the side of his head.

"Mind your own business if you know what's good for you," the guard snapped. "There's no escape for you that way."

Jared glared up at him and said nothing. The other guard squatted behind him and fussed with the chains that bound his hands. After a moment, the heavy manacles slipped free and Jared slowly brought his arms around and tried to chafe some life back into the stiff muscles.

"Why are you freeing my hands?" he asked.

"And not even a thank you for it," the guard behind him said, getting to his feet. "It's time for your breakfast. Lord Azimir wants you alive, otherwise he'd send you breakfast and let you eat it with your eyes."

The other guard laughed hoarsely and waved to someone outside the door.

A young woman entered, and Jared couldn't help gasping. She was barefoot, and a tiny silver bracelet around her ankle jingled faintly. The scent of spice followed her, and her cropped black pants were offset by a halter top of flaming orange silk. A dark purple scarf was wound through her masses of dark hair, and round silver earrings hung almost to her shoulders. Her eyes, which flickered for a moment at him, were a startling clear green.

"Who are you?" he breathed.

Her eyes flicked at him again under their heavy black lashes, and she slid a tray of food across the stone floor to meet his hand. And then, with a jingle and waft of spicy perfume, she was gone, and the room seemed somehow darker.

"That's Emelia," the guard said, obviously watching the girl as she disappeared down the passage. "She is Lord Azimir's."

"Lord Azimir's what?"

The guard shrugged. "She does his bidding. And she holds the keys to the household and the authority of command over the house slaves."

A hundred other questions tumbled through Jared's mind. "A woman holds power in Azimir's house?" he blurted, not even sure he understood where the question had come from.

The guard regarded him quizzically, almost as if Jared's question were senseless. "It is our way," he answered slowly, then added. "I forgot that you are an outworlder and do not know our customs."

"Where did she come from?"

"She is the daughter of Jessup, the chieftain of the Hazad."

Jared's brow furrowed. "I don't understand. I thought—"

"Enough questions," the guard said, turning abruptly and touching his partner on the arm. "If you remain here, and if Azimir lets you live, perhaps you will learn more of our ways."

The guards departed and the door slid home once more. Jared stared at it for a moment, lost in thought.

Why would Azimir keep the daughter of the Hazad chieftain as the head of his household? And if she is so highly placed, then why is she bringing me my breakfast like a common servant?

He shook his head and turned his attention to his plate. But first, there was something he had to do. He closed his eyes and reached out with his mind.

Sahara.

After a moment, her face, startled and pale, blurred into focus. She was staring at him with wide eyes, as if he had just jumped out at her unawares.

Jared! You're alive!

He smiled at her, his relief draining all that was left of his energy. *And you escaped. You're safe somewhere?*

Yes. For the moment. She hesitated, then staggered to her feet. *I'm coming for you!*

She began to fade, and he stretched out a hand, as if he could hold her that way.

Sahara, no! Wait!

Even as he called out to her, he could tell that she could no longer hear him.

Jared! Don't go! Don't leave me—

She was gone.

Jared dropped his head into his hands. He was weak, weaker than he'd expected to be. Weaker than he should be.

He pulled the tray of food toward him and picked at it. The food was good—some kind of sweetened grain that was cooked with spices and dried fruits until it was creamy, with just a hint of a bite at the center of each grain. He chewed it gratefully, surprised at the way the warm spices flooded his body with a sense of comfort. The flatbread on his tray was still hot from the kiln, and a mug of dark wine finished the meal.

They're feeding me like a king and treating me like a common criminal. Jared's bewilderment only grew as he drained the mug. *What kind of game are they trying to play?*

He set the empty mug back on the tray and stretched his arms above his head, trying to ease the cramping muscles in his back. He studied the shackles on his bare ankles and realized that he had enough chain to stand, and perhaps even enough to walk almost as far as the side wall. He pushed himself slowly to his feet, pausing often to let his muscles ease back into movement. Finally, he straightened fully and took a few hesitating steps toward the window.

As he stepped into the shaft of sunlight, Jared felt warmth wash over and through him. He realized now that what he had taken to be a blessing—the gift of light and sight—would soon become another means of torment. Already the cell was warmer than it had been, and, looking up, he noticed that there was another window higher on the wall, and still another almost in the ceiling. All these would serve to catch the sun as it continued its ascent, transforming his cell into an oven at midday. But without a fire to maintain the warmth through the night, the cell would become chill and damp again by morning.

If they don't torture and kill me, there's a good chance I'll just die of some horrible illness.

He reached out a hand and touched the wall. The stone was rough under his fingers, and as he slid his hand along the stones, he was able to feel grooves and gouges in the rock. He followed the grooves toward the window, where they stopped abruptly. Stooping, Jared picked up a large fragment of rock, its edges sharp from filing it along the stones. Its tip was wide, but when he drew the edge across the pad of his thumb, it split the skin.

He cursed mildly and resisted the sudden temptation to stick his injured finger in his mouth.

That's all I need. He shook his head with a soft laugh. *Blood poisoning.*

The lesson had been drummed into him by Childir all those years ago, when he was still a boy and Childir had still been like a father to him, not a traitor-spy for the Drakkin. The mouth was no place to clean a wound.

He sighed, tightening his hand around the stone blade, and edged closer to the window. Its ledge was at eye-level, but the stone was so thick that he could see nothing but blue sky. He was still vying for a vantage of the landscape below when he heard the door grumbling in its track.

He dropped the stone and moved back into the center of the room, clasping his hands behind his back. Two guards pushed doggedly into the cell, and when they looked up and saw him standing, they recoiled. They would have backed out of the room, but Emelia propelled them forward and then pushed them aside.

"What?" she scoffed. Her clear, low voice was like the ripple of water over stone. "He will not bite like some wild beast, you pair of cowards."

She stepped forward lightly, the tiny bells around her ankle chiming merrily, and stooped to pick up his tray.

"Who are you?" Jared asked, his breath catching in his chest as he watched her. "And why am I being kept here? What does Azimir want with me?"

"You will have to ask the Lord Azimir yourself when you see him," Emelia answered with a shrug of her sun-browned shoulders. "And I?" She straightened, holding the dull metal tray in her long, strong fingers. "I am his ministering angel."

Jared's brow furrowed and he glanced up to meet her steady gaze. There was something behind her eyes, a blaze of fierce spirit, that made a mockery of her words and the cloying smile on her lips.

"The guards have orders to bring you to the courtyard this afternoon," Emelia continued, turning from him with another tinkling of bells. "Perhaps I will see you there." She paused beside one of the guards, tossing her head in Jared's direction. "Let him loose, Ubal," she said.

"But—"

"I said let him loose!" She glanced at Jared over her shoulder, and he saw again that fire in her eyes. "He needs to refresh himself and tend his wounded finger."

Jared's mouth gaped, but she was already gone, whisking through the door and leaving the two guards to do her bidding.

"You heard the mistress, Ubal," said the other guard, prodding him forward. "Let the man loose."

Ubal hesitated, but his companion continued pushing at him. Finally, grumbling and cursing under his breath, Ubal handed his gun to his companion and edged toward Jared. He gestured for Jared to sit and unclasped a ring of small keys from his belt. Jared sat down as Ubal fumbled through the keys, finally selecting one and fitting it into the lock that secured the shackles around Jared's ankles.

When the chains dropped free, Ubal scrambled away from Jared, grasping for his weapon before he had even reached the door. He never took his eyes from Jared, who was still sitting, barefoot and completely baffled, on the floor in the middle of the room.

"What's the matter with you?" Jared asked. "I'm not going to hurt you."

"So you say. But—"

"Shut up, Ubal!" his companion snapped. Then, addressing Jared, he waved a hand toward the still shadowed end of the cell. "There's a washbasin and other necessaries down there." They sidled out the door, and he added with a harsh snort of laughter, "Don't be going nowhere, now."

But Jared wasn't thinking about the guards and their strange behavior.

How the hell did she know that I had cut my finger?

FOUR

THREE HOURS LATER, a contingent of sixteen armed guards marched Jared out of his cell and up the passage. Jared's hands were manacled in front of him, and the rough stones of the passage bit into his bare feet. After a number of turnings, they came to a rough-hewn set of stairs and sunlight flooded down onto Jared's head. He could taste the furtive breeze that drifted down the steps, scented with the heady perfume of ripening fruit and flowers. As they started up the steps, the cool gurgling chuckle of a fountain grew gradually louder.

And then they emerged into the courtyard. The guards fanned out, covering the four entrances and leaving him to stand alone at the head of the stairs.

The sun was beginning its western descent, but the majority of the square was still soaked in light. Jared moved forward, stepping out of the shadows and feeling the stones suddenly warm under his feet. He lifted his face and stood still, letting the sun drench him and burn the clammy vestiges of dark shadows from his mind and soul.

The fountain in the center of the courtyard seemed almost to laugh, and he had to smile. It reminded him so much of home.

He heard the guards at the north entrance snap suddenly to

attention, and he opened his eyes, turning slowly to face the newcomer.

It was Emelia.

"It's nice to see you again," she said, joining him. "Shall we walk? Exercise is, after all, the entire reason you're out here."

"Whose idea was this?" Jared asked.

"So suspicious!" Emelia smiled. "My Lord Azimir is not cruel, you know."

Jared laughed aloud. "After what he did to my friends and I, you actually expect me to believe such nonsense? You'll have to leave me in the dark a lot longer than one night if you expect to addle my brains that much."

Emelia frowned, a delicate downward pucker of her generous mouth. "It's true, nevertheless. He wishes you to spend your time here in comfort."

"Which is why I'm chained like a dog, then, I expect."

Again, Emelia frowned. "Come, walk with me, outworlder," she said. "Perhaps a turn in the fresh air will make you less tiresome and difficult."

Jared snorted, but followed her a few paces down the side of the courtyard under the shade of some trees heavy with fragrant white blossoms. His misgivings and frustrations grew with every step, and finally he stopped.

"I'm not going any further until you answer my questions."

"But you do not get to issue orders here." Emelia said, turning to face him. "That is for me and the Lord Azimir, not for you."

"Then take me back to my cell."

Emelia returned to his side, crossing her arms and tossing back her dark head. "Why do you spurn my kindness? Why do you not allow us to treat you as a guest?"

"You must be kidding," Jared said, staring down at her with a dark frown. "Really. You must be kidding. Your guest? After you did...God knows what to my best friend? After you nearly killed my other companion? After you've kept me chained in a hole? And you're blaming all this on me?"

Emelia waved her hand, as if she could brush aside his concerns like a dust of pollen. "You must understand," she said, "that we had to take certain...precautions with you. We had to be sure. And as we see that you are no threat to us, you will find Lord Azimir to be a most gracious host."

"How did you think I was a threat?" Jared snapped, losing all remnants of his patience. "We came here in peace! We came to negotiate for Halcyon's benefit! What about our presence here was a threat?"

Emelia regarded him quizzically. "You really don't know, do you?"

"Don't know—? Don't know what? What are you talking about?"

Emelia waved a hand at the guards. "He is ready to be taken back to his cell now," she said. With one last glance at Jared's astonished face, she turned on her heel and disappeared through the north entrance.

"I must be going crazy," Jared muttered as the guards closed in around him once more. "I must be going crazy, or this is all a really bad dream."

The guard beside him laughed harshly. "This is no dream. And I'll prove it to you."

Without warning, he smashed the butt of his gun against the right side of Jared's head. A flare of white sparks drowned Jared's vision and he stumbled and fell to his knees, shredding his pants on the stones.

As he reeled, he heard the captain screaming at the guard who had hit him.

"You don't know what you've done!" he was shouting. "God help us all...you fool!"

Jared slumped forward onto the stones, darkness drowning the rapid tattoo of gunfire.

———

When Jared recovered consciousness, he was back in his cell. The side of his face felt strangely tight. Cautiously, he reached up and felt a streak of dried blood from his temple to his jaw. It had pulled the skin as it dried. He moved his jaw experimentally and pushed himself into a sitting position. He groaned. His head was throbbing painfully, and he blinked rapidly to clear his blurring vision.

"This just gets better and better," he mumbled.

He got to his feet and stumbled to the washbasin in the corner. A pull chain filled the basin, and a small lever on the side released the water down a drain that ran into the floor. He tugged the chain and watched the water gush into the basin, then scooped it into his hands and splashed his face. The cold water refreshed him and brought his mind back into clear focus. He scrubbed at the dried blood, watching the water swirl red as he rinsed his face again.

The door behind him slid open and he turned, face still dripping, to see four guards enter and take up positions on either side of the door. Emelia slipped between them and stopped, crossing her arms lightly and doing her best to adopt a confident, even defiant, expression. But Jared could see the indentations in her upper arms where her fingers pressed into the flesh, betraying her fear.

He couldn't help the hoarse laugh. "You again."

She looked mildly offended. "I heard what happened to you." She leaned a little to her left, trying to get a look at the wound. "Do you need anything? A healer, perhaps?"

"A healer." Jared chuckled, shaking his head. "You people better figure out who I am and what I'm doing here." He stopped as he saw the sudden wash of fear drain the color from her cheeks. He frowned, then continued, "One minute you're trying to sweet talk me into a stroll, and the next minute your guard knocks me senseless just for the hell of it. So which is it? Am I Lord Azimir's guest, or am I his prisoner?"

Emelia had recovered her poise. "That guard has been removed," she said briskly. "It won't happen again."

"You mean the captain shot him dead for what he did. Don't say 'removed' when you really mean 'killed'." He paused, then spat, "Like my friend. Did you 'remove' him too?"

Emelia hesitated, twisting her fingers together. "I'm...sorry. I'm not at liberty to discuss him with you," she said finally. "I'm sorry."

A cold smile flashed across Jared's face. "Oh, you will be sorry. I promise."

Her face paled again, and he could see her swallow nervously. He stepped toward her, then stopped again in confusion and alarm as she recoiled away from him, holding up her hands as though to ward him off.

What is wrong with these people? He said aloud, his voice barely a whisper, "Why are you afraid of me? I have done nothing to you. Nothing!"

Emelia hesitated, a nervous smile dancing around her lips. "You've done nothing *yet*, you mean."

"I mean no harm to any of you!"

"You just threatened me. How can you say you mean me no harm?"

Jared opened his mouth, then snapped it shut again. *I did threaten her*, he realized with a small shiver of surprise. *Why did I do that?*

"You have no idea..." Emelia's voice trailed off again, and then she finished in a whisper, "You have no idea what you are capable of."

Jared frowned. "And you do, I suppose? You know me better than I know myself, is that it?"

"We have heard of you, Dragon-Slayer." Her eyes were wide now, her voice still no more than a whisper.

"If you thought me so dangerous, then why did you destroy my companions?" he demanded.

"The Lord Azimir must answer such questions," Emelia said. "I am but a lowly..."

Jared stepped forward, seizing her arms. "Tell me what you know!" he shouted, shaking her.

The guards jumped forward in alarm, prying Emelia out of his grip. Two of the guards held him back as the others hustled her from the cell.

"Why won't you tell me what you know?" he shouted again as the guards let him go and ran from the cell.

He crossed the distance to the door in two bounds, but the stone was already closing fast. Too fast for him to wedge himself through the gap without being crushed. Jared slammed his fists against the stone and felt it shudder under the blow. Tiny stone fragments trickled down the face of the rock and pattered softly around his feet.

Jared stepped back, alarmed, and saw the slight imprint of his fists on the door. Slowly, he dropped his gaze to his fists, turning them over.

What the hell is happening to me?

His hands fell to his sides. He stood there in the rapidly gathering gloom, staring at the closed door.]

What do they really want from me?

He spent another week cloistered in his cell, the endless round of days broken only by the slow cycle of light and darkness and the three meals a day slipped to him through a crack in the door. Emelia did not return, and no one dared open the door more than the width of his tray. His beard was growing thick, and his mind, weary from fretting over Rafe and Sahara, began to sink into a doldrums of resigned hoplessness.

He sat cross-legged in the small square of sunlight for as long as the light could pass through his window, eyes closed, drinking in the warmth and the radiance. As soon as the sun passed beyond the grasp of his window, he set himself to a series of rigorous exercises. And as he pushed his muscles beyond their endurance, gritting his teeth against the pain, the seed of vengeance that he had kept so long from taking root in his heart began to grow. He was angry, his gut burning with the bitterness of hate. Like a wild animal caged, he seemed to settle without resistance into a routine, but he began to watch for an opportunity, if not for escape, then for retribution.

At last, there came a morning when the door was pushed wide

open again. Jared scrambled to his feet, retreating out of the light to crouch in a shadowed corner as a dozen guards flooded into his cell. He watched them, silent, muscles tensed to spring, and waited for Emelia's slim form to slip through the door. His fingers searched the floor beside him and closed on the object he sought: the sharpened stone. He slipped it into his pocket.

Emelia did not come. Instead, Ribbadi entered, coiling a length of thick rope in his hands. He glanced around for a moment, his expression registering his mounting alarm. But when his eyes at last lighted on Jared, the lines of concern dissolved into one of his hateful smiles.

"We won't bite," he said.

"I might," Jared growled, his voice husky from lack of use.

This seemed to stagger Ribbadi for a moment, and he hesitated, glancing at the guards and then at the door, as if he wished more reinforcements were coming.

"Come, now," he said, turning back to Jared. "Let's not have any unpleasantness. Lord Azimir has requested to see you."

"It's about damn time," Jared said. He came forward, holding out his wrists to be bound.

The guards wasted no time, and soon not only his hands were in manacles, but his ankles too. He could only walk slowly, hampered by the heavy chain that connected his ankles together. Ribbadi threaded the rope through a ring on the handcuffs and deftly tied a knot.

"Like a lamb to the slaughter," Jared muttered.

Ribbadi waved the troop of guards out the door and followed, jerking on the rope to pull Jared after him.

They crossed through the courtyard and left by the north exit—the same way Jared had seen Emelia enter all those days ago. Once out of the courtyard, they ascended a broad flight of shallow stairs and then down a long, high-ceilinged hallway. Finally, they stopped in front of a set of double doors with golden handles.

The audience hall of Azimir.

Jared's stomach revolted at the thought of standing in that place again. As Ribbadi slammed his fist against the great doors, Jared writhed in his bonds. He could feel the guards that stood on either side of him grow tense with alarm, and their fear seemed to fuel some unfathomed well of strength within him. He felt the metal begin to stretch as he strained against the shackles. Before he could break them completely, the doors swung inward, and Ribbadi dragged him forward into the long, dark room.

Azimir, as before, was dressed all in black, lounging in his audience chair with an air of careless power. Jared's footsteps faltered as they passed the spot where he had last seen Rafe, slumped over with a scimitar's blade in his back. The floor had been scrubbed clean, and there was no sign of blood on the smooth, black marble.

Azimir flicked a finger. "That's far enough," he said.

Ribbadi halted. Jared, clanking in his chains a few paces behind the bearded man, came to stand beside him. Azimir studied Jared for several minutes, and Jared met his dark eyes without flinching. He felt the shackles around his wrists slipping loosely, and he knew that he could slip free or break them without much effort. He felt the cold weight of the stone in his pocket, and he knew, without conscious thought, that he could free himself and kill Azimir before Ribbadi could react.

"Are you ready now to discuss matters with me?" Azimir asked at last.

"What matters? You know that there will be no deal reached with Askalon, not after what has happened." He couldn't help glancing back over his shoulder at the spot Rafe had drenched with his blood.

"You're wrong there, I'm afraid," Azimir said. Jared's eyes snapped back to his face, and he saw that the lord was watching him with a mirthless smile.

"How am I wrong? You think that Aelred and the Lords of Askalon will cut a deal with you after what you've done?" Jared kept his voice cold, passionless. But he could feel the strength of anger rising in him, and he tested the shackles.

"Yes, I think they will."

Jared paused. There was so much certainty in Azimir's tone. "You're lying."

Azimir shrugged. "You can believe that if you like. But this will all be so much easier if you cooperate."

"Go to hell. Whatever you're going to do, just do it. I won't cooperate with you."

Azimir shrugged again. "I think you will feel differently when you hear what I have to propose."

"I don't care about your proposals."

Azimir sighed and rubbed a hand across his brow. "I had thought that a week of solitary confinement would have made you more...agreeable."

"Well, you thought wrong."

"You force me to try more unpleasant methods, you realize. It would be so much better for everyone if you would reconsider my offer."

"What offer? You have made me no offer."

"I ask you to discuss matters with me, that is all."

Jared threw back his head, regarding Azimir through narrowed eyes. "What do you want from me? What is this about, *really*? And don't tell me you want to negotiate Askalon's debt."

"You're right. I don't."

"Then what?"

"I will not negotiate with Askalon," Azimir said. "You are going to help me destroy them."

Jared stared at him, the heavy chain jangling harshly as he staggered back a pace. His heart was hammering, and the cold fury that had been building inside him suddenly ignited.

"I will do no such thing." He twisted his hands in the shackles, feeling them slip. He raised his eyes to Azimir's face and smiled, secure in the knowledge that he held his fate in his own hands. "Go to hell, Azimir."

"Ah, well," Azimir said. "As I said, you force me to be unpleasant."

He raised a hand and the side door opened suddenly. Two guards entered, pushing someone in front of them. Someone pale, dressed in a long black robe, his footsteps heavy and slow.

Jared stared, dragging a ragged gasp into his lungs.

The shuffling figure stopped beside Azimir and raised his head.

"Hello, Jared," said Rafe.

FIVE

The shrill voice brought Sahara suddenly out of a dark dream, and for a moment, she had no idea where she was. She rolled from the cot into a crouch, staring at the tent flap and trying to slow her breathing. The pattering of feet grew louder, and a moment later, a head of brown curls pushed through the opening. The dark eyes were dancing, and a warm smile lit up the child's entire face.

"You're awake! Zelie Sahara, you're awake!"

"I am now," Sahara grumbled, but faced with those bright eyes she couldn't find it in herself to be angry.

She straightened, her head brushing the roof of the small tent. The Hazad were a nomadic people, and their tents were designed to be spacious enough for comfortable rest but compact enough to be easily transported. There was just room inside for Sahara's cot and the small overturned crate that served as her table.

The girl slipped into the tent and stood, little hands clasped in front of her, tiny toes burrowing into the soft fur that kept the dust at bay. She wore a sage-colored halter top and black wide-legged cropped pants, and an anklet of tiny bells jingled brightly when she stepped.

"You're coming with us today, aren't you?" the girl asked after a moment of silence that only Sahara found awkward.

Sahara sighed. She had been with the Hazad for almost two weeks, and last night Rigel had told her that they would be moving to a new harvest zone today. It was three days' march south of the city of Aquila, and Sahara's gut tightened at the thought. Even though she knew she wasn't leaving Jared and Rafe behind, she would have to turn her back on Aquila. It felt like a retreat.

It felt like she was abandoning her friends.

The girl was frowning at her, and Sahara sighed again. She had put off the decision last night, but it seemed she could put it off no longer.

"Please, Zelie Sahara, you will come with us, won't you?" the girl pressed, not getting the answer she wanted the first time.

"Why do you want me along, Tessa?" Sahara asked. "I'm just a stranger here, remember?"

Tessa cocked her head to the side and regarded Sahara with those bright, intense eyes. "I know. But you're special. Grandfather says so. He says we must look after you...that you're lost, and that you need time."

Sahara arched an eyebrow at the girl. "He says that, does he?"

"Yes."

"And what do I need time for? Does he tell you that?"

Tessa shook her head. "He just says that you are lost. And he says...he says that you remind him of Emelia."

"Who's that?"

"My aunt."

Sahara frowned, mentally clicking through all the members of the tribe. It was a family tribe, and Jessup, the white-bearded man who had christened her Zelie, was its patriarch. Tessa was Rigel's sister and the youngest daughter of Jessup's son Gil. He had seven other sons, and all of them were married save for the youngest, Sardil.

None of the wives are missing. So Emelia must be Jessup's daughter. This seems such a tightly-knit group...I wonder why no one has spoken of her before this.

"Where is she now?" Sahara asked.

Tessa's voice dropped to a whisper. "Rigel says we mustn't talk about Emelia. He says that she is a disgrace to the family."

"That's not a very nice thing to say."

"Maybe, he says it anyway."

Sahara waited for a moment, but Tessa said nothing further. "And? Where is she?" Sahara prompted.

"I just told you!" Tessa shook her curls and speared Sahara with a dark glance. "I mustn't talk about her. Rigel would be angry."

"Fine. Keep it to yourself, then."

Tessa didn't say another word, and though her curiosity was frustrated, Sahara had to smile. Tessa worshipped Rigel, and the threat of his displeasure was apparently enough to keep her quiet.

"Please say you'll come with us, Zelie Sahara," Tessa begged, the frown clearing from her sweet face. "I'm tired of my aunts and uncles. And Katarina is no fun."

Katarina was the only other person in Jessup's tribe that was not a member of his extended family. She was a quiet woman who kept mostly to herself, and her tent was pitched just a few paces outside the camp circle. From what Sahara had been able to gather, she seemed to be some sort of a healer. Everyone regarded her with respect, but no one made any efforts to draw her into the tribe. Whether this was from some sort of suspicion on the part of Jessup's people or because Katarina had rebuffed them, Sahara didn't know.

"I'm not any fun, either, you know," Sahara retorted.

Oh, child. If only you knew what I am...what I've done. You wouldn't want me here at all.

Looking down into that innocent face with the eyes full of girlish spunk and impishness, the sudden fear that Tessa might find out the truth about her past made her knees turn to water. And when Tessa reached out suddenly to take Sahara's hand in both her own, the tears blurred out the vision of the girl's warm smile.

In spite of all Sahara's miserable failings, all the battles she had fought, all the lives she had taken, it didn't matter. Tessa loved her.

"I'll come," Sahara found herself mumbling, even as she tugged her hand free. "I'll come. Now leave me to gather my things."

Tessa squealed with delight and raced from the tent, calling for Rigel.

Sahara dashed the tears out of her eyes and took a deep breath. *Why did I tell her that?* she wondered, suddenly angry with herself. *The last thing I want to do is to go further from Aquila!*

She moved to the tent flap and peered out. Tessa was already halfway down the dirt lane that ran around the central area of the camp, heading for the marquee tent at the far side of the circle. Sahara sighed, checking the urge to call the girl back. She didn't want to leave Aquila, but she couldn't bear the thought of disappointing Tessa now.

The campfire in the center of the circle was blazing and breakfast preparations were well underway. For a moment, Sahara watched several women stirring the large cauldron suspended over the flames. She sniffed appreciatively and stepped clear of the tent, meandering over to the fire.

"It's not ready yet, my dear," said the oldest of the women. Sahara recognized her as Yasmin, Jessup's wife. She was thin and wiry, her face and arms browned from years spent in the sun. Her white hair was coiled tightly on top of her head, and her dark eyes were warm and kind.

"I know," Sahara said, risking a smile. "But it smells good!" She stood awkwardly for a moment, watching the two younger women take turns stirring the massive pot of porridge. "Can I...help at all?"

One of the women—a dark-haired beauty named Isis—regarded Sahara with a dark frown, but Yasmin bustled around the fire with a huge smile. "Of course! There's always work enough for willing hands!"

She took Sahara's arm and propelled her into the cook tent, where neatly scoured wood bowls and spoons were stacked neatly on shelves and where sacks of foodstuffs lay piled in a heap in the corner. Bending to reach under the shelves, Yasmin pulled out a large bucket and a small three-legged stool. She thrust these into Sahara's hands.

"The children have cream on their porridge," she said. "Rigel should have gathered the goats into the milking pen by now."

Sahara gaped at her and then dropped her eyes to the bucket and the stool. "And what exactly am I supposed to do with these?"

Yasmin laughed and turned Sahara toward the entrance. "Why, they're for milking the goats, my girl!" she chided. "Go on, now!" She gave Sahara a gentle push and Sahara staggered out into the open, clutching the pail and stool.

"But I don't know how!" she protested. "Isn't there something else I can do?"

"Fancy not knowing how to milk a goat," Isis scoffed.

Sahara's face flared suddenly in a hot blush, and Isis elbowed the other girl with a snort of rude laughter. The other girl shook herself away from Isis and smiled at Sahara.

"Rigel's there...he'll show you what to do," she said.

"Fancy having to learn to milk goats from a boy," Isis sneered. "It's almost as bad as having to do a child's task in the first place."

"Perhaps I should send you to teach her, Isis," said Yasmin, returning to the fire with a handful of something that looked like salt. "Would you like that?"

"No, grandmother."

"Then hush your mouth and leave Zelie alone."

Sahara turned away and hurried to find Rigel, fuming inside. *Of course I don't know how to milk a damn goat,* she thought. *I'm an assassin, not a farm girl.*

She found Rigel just fastening the gate to the milking pens. He glanced up when he heard her approach, and he burst into a laugh when he saw the pail and bucket.

"Did my grandmother give you those?" he asked. "And did she expect you to do the morning milking?"

"Yes, and yes." Sahara dropped both to the ground.

Rigel glanced pointedly from Sahara to the tools and then back again. "Well? The goats won't milk themselves, you know."

"You cannot seriously expect me to get in that pen and milk goats, Rigel," Sahara retorted. "I've never milked anything in my life."

Rigel's eyes were dancing with mischief now. "No time like the present to learn, then, eh?"

Sahara speared a withering look in his direction. "You do it."

"Oh, no." Rigel raised his hands. "No, no. And rob you of this incredible experience?"

Sahara stared at his laughing face for a moment, then reached down and snatched up the pail and stool again. Rigel unlatched the gate and let her inside the pen with a small bow. As he closed the gate behind her and leaned on it, Sahara plunked the stool down next to one of the goats.

"I hate you," she said to Rigel. The goat regarded her, chewing placidly on a bit of hay. "I hate you, too," Sahara told the goat.

"You can't do it like that," Rigel laughed as the goat skittered away from Sahara. "You've got to tether her to the fence first."

Sahara glared at him. "Why didn't you tell me that in the first place?"

"More fun this way."

Sahara lunged after the goat and caught its halter, then dragged it to the side of the pen and deftly tied it to the rail. She went back and fetched her stool and pail, then sat down next to the goat and slid the pail under its belly. She hesitated for a moment, then looked back at Rigel.

"Now what do I do?"

Rigel gestured at the goat. "Pinch and squeeze. That's all there is to it."

"How hard can that be?" Sahara remarked to the goat, who eyed her uncertainly. "It can't possibly be harder than killing a Drakkin Chieftain, can it?"

Gingerly, she took hold of one of the goat's teats and tried to follow Rigel's instructions. She was surprised at the incredible swell of triumph she felt when a stream of rich, creamy milk spurted into the pail. She took hold of the other teat and repeated the process, giddy as the level of milk rose steadily in the bucket. Finally, no more milk came when she squeezed, and she turned to Rigel.

"I did it! I—"

Her cry of triumph turned into a yelp of horror. The goat, spooked by her outburst, kicked suddenly, toppling the pail and sloshing the milk all over the ground and all over Sahara's feet. She grabbed for the bucket, but it was already empty. The goat danced sideways as Sahara gripped the bucket, fighting the almost overwhelming urge to fling it at the animal's head. Taking a deep breath, she turned slowly, muttering a curse under her breath.

Rigel was in fits, doubled over laughing.

"You should have seen your face!" he roared, clutching his sides.

Sahara managed a tight-lipped smile that blossomed into a chuckle in spite of herself. "Now what am I supposed to do?" she asked.

Rigel, wiping his streaming eyes and heaving a deep breath, gestured around the pen. "There are six others needing to be milked," he said. "Just start over...and this time, watch out for the hooves!"

Sahara managed the rest of the milking without incident, and Rigel had to fetch her another pail before she was through. She was surprised to find how much she actually enjoyed working with the little animals. They were calm, accommodating, and forgiving beasts, and Sahara found the fevered pace of her thoughts slowing as she focused on the task.

"You see?" Rigel said as she slipped out of the enclosure with the full pail of milk. "It's not so hard...and not such bad work after all."

"I don't know why Isis was so sour about it," Sahara said as they started back to the campfire together.

"Oh, Isis is always sour. Don't mind her, Zelie Sahara."

Sahara was about to protest that she couldn't care less what Isis had to say about anything, but she closed her mouth.

That's not really true, she thought, remembering how the girl's attitude earlier had goaded her. *But I don't know why I should care what she thinks.*

They were only just in time for the breakfast service, and Yasmin chided Sahara for taking so long. "I could have had Tessa do it and she'd have been back long ago!" she said, whisking the pails from Sahara and Rigel and sending Isis for a ladle.

Sahara shrugged, but Rigel jumped in before she could say anything. "She did her best, Grandmother. But it was her first time...and one of the goats meant mischief."

Yasmin grumbled, but left Sahara alone after that. She hurried to ladle the still-warm milk into the porridge bowls, and Rigel winked at Sahara before strolling after his grandmother. Sahara stood alone, watching the line of bright-eyed children.

"So you managed it after all. I'm impressed."

Sahara started and turned to see Isis standing beside her, arms crossed tightly across her chest. Sahara frowned. "Rigel helped me," she said.

Isis snorted. "He's always messing about with the animals."

"You say it like it's a bad thing, Isis."

Isis regarded her for a moment from under her sweeping black lashes. "Isn't it?"

"I don't know." Sahara thought about how peaceful she had felt in the company of the goats. "I don't think so."

"What do you know? You're not one of us."

Sahara's anger finally flared. "No, I'm not one of you," she said instead. "But I don't have to be one of you to see that caring for the goats helps to feed your family."

Isis snorted again. "All we ever eat is porridge. Porridge with cream, porridge with herb sauce...porridge this, porridge that. I'm sick to death of porridge."

Sahara finally turned to the bristling girl. "What's your problem? You should be thankful you have food to eat at all."

"We deserve better." She was silent for a long while, then she blurted, "Do you know the fortune that is made from the crops we harvest? Do you know how the refiners and sellers live, up there in Aquila?"

"I have a pretty fair notion," Sahara answered, but Isis seemed not to have heard her.

"We are treated like dogs," she spat. "And yet, if it weren't for us, Halcyon would be no more significant than—than Eshka!"

Sahara frowned. "What's Eshka?"

"The moon. Eshka." Isis waved a hand impatiently. "It's where Azimir and his hangers-on go during the holy season."

"And when is that?"

"When the eclipse comes. In three months' time."

Sahara's frown deepened. "And what do you do when the Zharib leave for Eshka?"

"We make a pilgrimage to Telon, to the Holy City. North of here." She sighed and shook her head. "You don't understand...how could you understand? You have no idea what our life is like. And Grandfather...." Her voice trailed off.

"What about him?"

"He's not been the same since Emelia left. I think that's why Azimir took her." She paused, but Sahara said nothing. "They hold her to ensure the Hazad's loyalty. My grandfather would do anything...anything to keep her safe."

Sahara felt the familiar burn of anger beginning in her gut. "You aren't so very different from my own people," she said. "Not really. And I know what to do with tyrants."

Isis laughed out loud. "You? What could you possibly know about such things?"

Sahara grinned crookedly at her even as she felt a well of sadness open in her heart. "You might be surprised."

SIX

IT WAS THE SAME DREAM. Always the same.

She was running, tripping down the stairs. Rafe was bleeding, dying, smiling at her, the scimitar buried in his back.

And then he opened his eyes.

Sahara woke, shaking and sweating all over. The darkness in the tent was just beginning to lighten, and Sahara rolled off her cot and slipped out into the early dawn. The clouds of white pollen had subsided, and she was able to breathe deeply. Off to the west, where the sky was still dark, thousands of stars glittered like gems, but far to the east, they were fading into gray.

The air was cold, and Sahara shivered. She wrapped her arms tightly about herself and strolled into the center of the camp. The fire had been banked for the night, and there was no sign of anyone stirring in the other tents.

Except one.

As Sahara's eyes swept past the marquee tent, they caught the glimmer of light. She frowned, her eyes swinging back to find the source. A tiny light was bobbing out of the fields beyond the tent circle, heading south toward them. A lantern.

Sahara slipped forward, moving silently on bare feet. She circled around Jessup's tent and, shrouded in its shadow, she waited and watched.

The figure slowly came into view, head bowed, lantern held aloft. It was a woman, and a dusting of white pollen clung in her tangled hair. She carried something in her other hand, and Sahara frowned, trying to make out what it was. As the woman drew steadily nearer, Sahara saw that it was a wide black scarf.

The woman slowed her pace as she came close to the tent circle and raised her head. Sahara, standing motionless in the shadows, caught her breath in surprise.

It was Katarina.

What is she doing out here? And where has she been?

Katarina hesitated for a moment, and then she raised the lantern and blew out the light. In the anonymity of the shadows, she scurried toward her own tent, brushing the pollen from her hair. And just before she disappeared inside, Sahara thought she heard a soft sob.

As soon as Katarina was safely out of sight, Sahara crept back across the circle, her mind full of questions. As she approached her tent, she glanced back over her shoulder for a moment, and then recoiled when she nearly ran into Rigel. He was planted in front of her tent, arms crossed over his chest. Even in the dim light of dawn, Sahara could see the frown in his eyes.

"What?" she demanded, her own anger rising at his expression. "I'm not allowed out for some fresh air? What is this, a prison?"

"Is that what this is about? Fresh air?"

"Yes."

Rigel measured her steadily, and Sahara stared straight back into his eyes. "Why are you spying on Katarina?"

"I wasn't spying."

"Right. Because sneaking around in the shadows and watching people isn't spying."

Sahara bristled. "And how long have you been spying on me, Rigel?"

"I wasn't hiding. I've been standing right here, watching you."

"Look," Sahara said, trying a different tack. "I came out for some fresh air. I saw her trying to sneak back into camp. That's it."

Rigel's eyes narrowed as he considered her story. "You shouldn't follow her," he said finally. "She has enough..." He stopped suddenly and shook his head. "Just don't follow her."

"Fine." Sahara made to push past him, then paused. "Was there something you wanted, Rigel? Why are you here?"

"Tessa told me that you're coming with us," he said.

Sahara's mouth quirked into a smile. "She's very persuasive."

"I'm glad to hear it."

"Well, that's—"

"But many are not so happy, Zelie. Wes and his family want you left behind, and so does Fallon."

Sahara sighed. Wes was Isis's father, and Sahara had a feeling that she had had something to do with this. "Why don't they want me to come?"

"They say you are a stranger, and that you bring trouble with the Zharib. They fear for their families, and Jessup is inclined to hear them."

"But Katarina is a stranger, Rigel! Why isn't she cast out, then?"

Rigel's jaw tightened. "Katarina has been with our tribe for more than two decades," he said shortly. "She is not a stranger. Not like you."

Sahara planted a finger in Rigel's chest. "You brought me here, remember? I didn't ask for your help. And I thought..." Her voice trailed off.

"You thought what?"

"All that business of giving me a name. Of adopting me into the tribe. Was that all just for show?"

"Jessup is a warm-hearted man, and he could see that you were in distress. He thought to make you feel welcome."

"So he could just turn around and abandon me two weeks later?"

Rigel rubbed a hand over his face. "It's complicated. Jessup doesn't want to leave you, but Wes and Fallon say you must prove yourself before you can join us."

A slow smile spread across Sahara's face. "And how do they want me to do that? Trial by combat?"

Rigel's dark brows shot up in horror. "Our women do not fight, Sahara."

Sahara's heart sank. She had no doubt that she could prove herself in a fight, but now?

If they want me to prove myself by cooking porridge, I'm going to be left behind for sure. What else do the women do around here? She racked her brains for a moment. Caring for the children, cooking the meals, milking the goats.... *And that went so well. There's no way.*

"What do they want me to do?" she asked.

Rigel's smile was as pale as the eastern sky. "They know you are not from Halcyon. They know you do not know our ways. So you must prove your value to the tribe in another way."

"What way is that?"

"You must ride with the Elenni."

Sahara frowned. "Who are they?"

Rigel glanced around, then beckoned her to follow him inside the tent. "It's best if we discuss this inside," he said.

Sahara followed him silently through the tent flap and sank down on her pallet. Rigel sat cross-legged on the fur spread on the floor. For a few moments, he said nothing, intent on studying the variegated patters of silver and black and tan in the pelt. Then he glanced up and met her silent, steady gaze.

"The Elenni are runners. Messengers. They are the only way we have to communicate with the other tribes. Their identities are known only to Jessup and each tribe's chieftain."

"Why so secretive? They're just messengers."

"Maybe, but the Zharib will hunt them down. We've lost three this season already."

Sahara's eyebrow arched in surprise. "Three out of—"

"Seven."

Sahara let out a low whistle. "Why are they hunted, Rigel? Why does the Zharib want them dead?"

"It's not that hard to understand," he said, his eyes flickering at her in the early morning gloom. "They control our lives, and they see any coordination or even communication among the tribes as a threat. They only feel secure when they have us isolated and worked half to death."

"Is it the communication between the tribes a threat, Rigel?"

Rigel dropped his gaze and studied his hands. "Well, I suppose that all depends on what you mean by a threat."

Sahara ran a hand through her hair and blew out her breath. It was better than dealing with goats, wasn't it?

"Look, Rigel," she said. "I've just fought two wars to free my people from slavery. I came here to try to prevent another one, and it looks like that's failed miserably. I'm tired of fighting. I just want to get my friends out of here and go home. That's all. So you need to play straight with me. Are the Elenni helping to start some revolution, or are they just delivering condolences and congratulations between the tribes?"

Rigel regarded her with something between surprise and awe. "I had no idea," he said quietly. "You are a warrior, then?"

"You thought I milked goats where I came from?"

Rigel chuckled. "Certainly not."

"Please be straight with me. I'm not starting another revolution, and I'm sure as hell not going to fight in one. I'll stay here to rot if that's what they want me to do."

Rigel rubbed his hands together thoughtfully. "There are no plans for anything like...that at present." He hesitated, then added, "At least, not that I know of."

"Not that you know of," Sahara echoed, and swore softly under her breath. "Where are they?"

"Who?"

"Wes and Fallon."

Rigel scrambled to his feet, holding out his hands to stop her as she rose from her pallet. "No, no! Sahara, you mustn't...they'll..."

She pushed past him and stood for a moment outside the tent. The sky to the east was tinged with pink, and golden and deep turquoise arched like a rainbow over the horizon. She took a deep breath and headed for the marquee tent, Rigel scurrying behind her.

She hesitated again outside Jessup's tent flap, then elbowed her way inside. Just as she had suspected, Wes and Fallon were there, sitting with Jessup around a small brazier, glass mugs in their hands. A pot was nestled in the coals, and a rich aroma hung in the air.

"Zelie Sahara!" Jessup exclaimed as she approached, and Wes and Fallon jumped to their feet.

"Why do they want me to ride with the Elenni?" she asked, jabbing a finger in their direction.

Rigel stumbled into the tent at that moment, breathing hard. "I didn't...you have to...she doesn't—" he babbled incoherently, waving his hands.

"Sit down, Rigel," Jessup ordered sternly, his white brows knitting together in a frown. "Sit down and be still."

Rigel sank down on a low cushion next to his grandfather, his face crestfallen. Sahara's gaze snapped back to Rigel's uncles.

"Answer me," she said. "Why? Why do I need to prove myself to you?"

"You aren't one of us," Wes said warily. "We don't know if you're to be trusted."

Sahara snorted. "If I was working with the Zharib, do you think I'd still be here? Do you think you'd still be here?" Her voice hardened. "They took my friends and tried to kill me. Do you think I would work for them?"

Fallon shrugged. "Maybe. Maybe they took your friends and forced you to come here to spy on us. Or maybe you just made that whole story up. Maybe it's your cover."

The vision of Rafe bleeding to death after saving her life, of Jared beaten down and senseless, flooded into her mind, and she felt the hot stirrings of anger.

"Or maybe," she said quietly, her eyes flashing at Fallon, "maybe you're just bored picking weeds all day, so you thought you'd harass the new girl. You don't know what the hell you're talking about...or whom you're talking to."

Wes loosened the small knife in his belt. "Was that a threat?"

Sahara's eyes dropped to the knife, and a small smile flickered around the edges of her mouth. "Don't do that. Just...trust me. You really don't want to do that."

Fallon glanced at his brother. "I think he does, actually."

Wes drew the dagger, and Sahara coiled her muscles. Almost wearily, she ticked off Wes's vulnerabilities—the way he held the dagger, the way he favored his right foot, the way he seemed distracted by Fallon's presence. And she knew that she could kill him before he ever had a chance to draw back the knife.

Jessup suddenly jumped between them, laying a hand on Wes's and holding out the other to keep Sahara at bay. "I won't have blood shed like this under my roof! Put the knife away, Wes! Put it away!"

Wes hesitated, then slowly slid the knife back into its sheath.

Sahara let her muscles relax, almost overwhelmed by the wave of relief that washed over her. "That was wise," she said. "I really didn't want to kill you. You seem like a nice person...and your children would have missed you."

Fallon let out a snorting laugh, and Sahara's gaze slid to fix on his face. The laugh caught in Fallon's throat, and he coughed.

"Please, Zelie, sit down," Jessup said, gesturing to another cushion. He poured her some of the drink from the pot in the coals and handed her the mug as she sat beside him. "Wes and Fallon do you an injustice, maybe, to suspect you of treachery without cause."

Sahara shrugged. "I can understand it. From what Rigel's told me, your relationship with the Zharib isn't exactly friendly."

"It is not our way to be suspicious of guests and travelers," Jessup continued, spearing a dark glance in the direction of his two sons, who had resumed their seats opposite him. "But we have paid the price before for our trust."

He fell suddenly silent and stared into the glowing coals, and Sahara, after waiting a moment for him to continue, glanced at Wes and Fallon and then at Rigel. And then, in a flash of understanding, she said, "That's what happened to Emelia, isn't it? Someone came here and betrayed you...and he took her to Aquila. Is that right?"

Jessup sighed heavily and his dark eyes brimmed with tears. He could not speak, so Wes answered for him.

"Yes, that's right. Azimir sent a snake among us. Some of us had our concerns about him, but before we could act on them, he was gone. And so was Emelia."

"Why do you want me to ride with the Elenni?" Sahara asked.

"Because it will keep you away from the tribe," Fallon said, his voice blunt as a dull knife. "And there's a good chance you'll be killed in the first three weeks. Most are."

Sahara nodded slowly, keeping all emotion out of her face and voice. "I see. And if I'm not killed? What then?"

"Then you are welcome to stay."

Sahara measured the two brothers for a moment. "If you think that I'm going to help you overthrow the Zharib," she said carefully, "let me tell you what I told Rigel. And I hope you hear me clearly, because if you entangle me in something against my will, it won't go well for you. I want no part of your revolution." Her voice grew harder and more intense as she continued, "I want to rescue my friends, and I want to go home. I don't want to stay here, and I don't want to be part of your tribe. I'm just passing through, you understand?"

Fallon and Wes nodded slowly, and Jessup sighed again.

"The Elenni do not ride for revolution, though some might wish that they did." His eyes flickered at his sons for a moment, then flashed again at Sahara. "But before you agree to this, you must understand the danger. We are moving camp this morning, but when we have reached the next settling ground, you will come with us to the fields. You need to know the risks, and then you can decide."

"But, Father!" Wes objected. "She shouldn't—"

"She shouldn't be forced into a decision before she knows all the facts," Jessup said, cutting him off. "You would force her into the Elenni because you haven't the courage to kill her yourself."

"He couldn't kill me if he tried," Sahara said quietly, appraising Wes. "Neither could he." She jerked her head in Fallon's direction.

"That's settled, then," Jessup said briskly. "And now it is time to be on the move. See that your things are packed and ready in two hours' time."

Grumbling, the two brothers ducked out of the tent, and Jessup glanced at Sahara with a small smile. "If it were only up to me—"

"I know," Sahara said. "Don't worry about me. I don't want to cause trouble within your tribe."

She turned on her heel and headed out into the early morning sunlight. The settlement was bustling with activity. Isis was manning the cauldron in the central square again, her strong brown arms working the long-handled paddle, her brow glistening with sweat. Yasmin was hurrying in and out of the cook tent, setting scoured bowls and spoons and a jug of thick, sweet syrup on the long board. Already the children were lining up, bouncing with excitement. Their older brothers and sisters were taking down tents, and men were loading carts.

Suddenly, there was a shout from the northern edge of the circle, and Sahara turned just in time to see a rider, bent low over the lathered neck of his black horse, gallop into the camp. He made straight for Jessup's tent, and Sahara jumped clear as his horse skidded to a stop just in front of her, showering her with dirt and small stones. The rider slid off the horse with a jangle of spurs and the creak of leather, and he shouldered his way into Jessup's tent.

"You've got to get clear," Sahara heard him say. "Now. They're coming, Jessup. And they won't leave a single one of you alive."

SEVEN

JARED STARED at Rafe in disbelief, his heart beating somewhere in his throat. Rafe was pale as death, dark circles rimmed his eyes, and his cheekbones seemed to start out of his face. But he was alive. He was standing there, and he was alive.

The tears stung Jared's eyes, and he stumbled forward a few paces.

"Rafe!" he choked.

Rafe held up a bony hand and Jared faltered to a stop. There was something different about him, Jared realized suddenly. A horrible fear washed over him, drenching his body in sweat like an icy rain. There was a hollowness in his eyes, and something like deep sadness, but there was something else too. The spark of an arcane fire that had never been there before.

"What's happened to you?" Jared asked, his voice rasping in the echoing chamber. "What have they done to you?"

"They saved my life," he answered. But his voice was like death and nothing like life.

"Yes, I see that," Jared said, a choking laugh and the flash of a smile flitting like lightning through the storm of his tears. "I see that, my friend. But—"

"You see now, I hope," interrupted Azimir, his voice as dark and cold as the stones beneath Jared's feet, "that the stakes are higher than you thought. Your friend here has only just been recalled from the brink of death, and it is only the skill of my healers that keeps him from toppling over the edge." His eyes glittered at Jared. "If you choose not to cooperate, then I will just give him a little push."

Azimir seized Rafe's arm suddenly and jerked him to his knees. Rafe fell heavily, crying out in pain as his knees crashed into the stone. Jared cursed at Azimir and sprang to help his friend, but the guards caught him and pinioned his arms behind him. Azimir drew his knife and thumbed the edge thoughtfully.

"Do I have your attention now?"

"You will pay for this, I swear," Jared ground out.

"It really doesn't have to be unpleasant," Azimir said. "I told you, I would much rather just come to an agreement with you. I don't like to threaten."

"Like hell you don't."

"We could so easily be allies, you and I, and it would be so much better for your friend here. So will you be civil, or should I let him bleed a little?"

Jared stared in horror as Azimir placed the knife against the side of Rafe's face. The edge bit into the flesh, and Rafe tried weakly to move away. But what little strength he had was already spent, and he could only groan in pain.

"Stop! Stop it!" Jared shouted, struggling against the strong arms that held him. "Don't hurt him!"

Azimir withdrew the knife, and a slow trickle of dark red blood ran down Rafe's pale face. "Will you be civil and listen to my proposal, then?"

Jared said nothing, but finally jerked himself free of the guards, sending them sprawling with a heavy grunt on the stone floor. He straightened and crossed his arms across his chest.

"Good. I see you are ready to listen." Azimir sniffed and laid the knife across his knee. "As I said, I have no desire to bargain with Askalon for baubles and trinkets. They have asked for death by betraying our contract. I will accept no substitutions. And I will not accept betrayal."

"Don't you understand? There _was_ no betrayal. The Triumvirate were overthrown, and all their works now lie in ruin. The Lords of Askalon sent us here to make peace with you, not to start a war. If they had wanted to betray you, do you think we would have come to offer new terms and payment in full for the Triumvirate's debts?"

"The _zanthos_ was not delivered to us as promised," Azimir said. "That is the betrayal."

"And do you know how the Triumvirate planned to deliver the _zanthos_ to you?" Jared asked, his voice rising. "Do you? They planned to destroy you with it! They were never going to honor your contract, you fool. As soon as they discovered the _zanthos_, they were coming for you."

Azimir measured Jared silently for a moment. "And how do you know all this?"

"What does it matter how I know it? It's the truth."

"And where is the _zanthos_ now? And all these weapons?"

Jared hesitated, feeling suddenly like a rat caught in a trap. Azimir's eyes bored into him, as if searching for his very soul.

What should I tell him? His mind raced. _If I tell him the truth, then he'll know that Askalon is vulnerable. But if I tell him something else? What then?_

"You're not answering the question," Azimir said. "Do you not know the answer, or are you just unwilling to answer?" He fingered the knife edge, his eyes hot as two live coals.

Jared swallowed, inwardly cursing Aelred for the thousandth time for shipping them out here. "The _zanthos_ is secure," he said.

"Where is it?"

"Secure."

Azimir's face tightened in a thin-lipped smile. "Such games will cost your friend his life. I hope you realize that."

"I'm not playing games. I'm telling you the truth."

"Is that so? It may be truth, but it is useless to me. And you are shrewd enough to realize the danger of a lie." He paused for a moment, considering. "No matter. I will find out where it is. I have other ways of discovering such information, if you will not tell me. But now let me ask you, what of your other friend?"

"What other friend?"

Azimir's mouth twisted in a half-smile. "Don't play stupid with me. I mean the girl. The one who got away."

Jared clenched his jaw. "What of her?"

"Where is she, I wonder?" Azimir leveled his intense stare on Jared once more, measuring him. "I have a feeling you know where she is. You do, don't you?"

"She's safe somewhere. Somewhere you won't find her."

"Another truth that is as useless as a lie." Azimir shook his head. "You shouldn't be so quick to underestimate my ability to discover such things. I want you to understand that I will find her. I will. And when I do, things will become very unpleasant for you indeed."

Jared stood stiffly, hands clenched at his sides. Rafe knelt beside Azimir, his head bowed under his dark hood.

Rafe. Jared wished that his friend could hear his thoughts. *I will get you out of this, I swear.*

"You have much to consider, it seems," Azimir said, and Jared's eyes snapped back to his face. Azimir signed to the guards. "Take him back to his cell."

As the guards seized him and dragged him out of the audience chamber, Jared saw Azimir rise and haul Rafe to his feet. Jared struggled violently, kicking at the doors as they pulled him through into the corridor. It was no use.

"Rafe!" Jared shouted. "I will come for you! Rafe!"

The doors slammed shut on Rafe's feeble cry of pain.

Darkness was crawling once more into Jared's cell, mirroring the darkness that seeped from his own soul. The door ground open and Emelia slipped inside. From the shadows at the far end of the cell, he watched her hesitate for a moment, her eyes skimming over the space, searching for him.

"What are you doing here?" Jared growled. "I'm not in the mood for visitors."

Emelia started, her eyes snapping toward him but still unable to find him. After a moment, she pushed the door shut and stood there. "I'm sorry for what they did to your friend."

"Sorry doesn't cut it, I'm afraid."

"I know you're angry. But if you would just listen to what Azimir—"

"Are you here to talk me into some kind of deal? Because you're wasting your time."

He heard her sigh. The darkness was almost total, and as his sight became useless, Jared felt his other senses sharpen. A dull chill seeped into him from the stone floor, and he could hear the rustle of Emelia's dress as she shifted her weight. The spicy scent of her perfume threaded through the shadows.

"Azimir knows what you are," Emelia said softly after a moment. "He will not let you go free until you have given your word to help him."

What the hell is that supposed to mean?

"I'm nobody," he said aloud. "I'm just a messenger...an intermediary. I'm no one that anyone would miss."

Well, maybe that's not entirely true... The faces of Arnauld and Aliya flitted through his memory. *And I suppose Aelred might be concerned that we've been captured. Perhaps.*

"That's not true," Emelia whispered. "You are more than that. So much more."

"What am I, then? You seem to have a pretty fair notion."

Jared raised his eyes and stared in the direction of the door. He blinked once, twice. Suddenly, the darkness faded into grayscale, and he could see her, fidgeting nervously by the door. He could see no color, only light and shadow, but he could see clearly.

His breath caught in his throat. Heart hammering, he swept his eyes around the rest of his cell. The barred window and the deep night outside. The washbasin on the far side of the room. The etched stone wall. It was all crisp and naked without the trappings of shadow.

He scrambled to his feet and rubbed at his eyes, but nothing changed. He staggered against the wall, then swung back to face Emelia. She was staring wide-eyed at him, but from the blank, searching terror in her eyes he knew that she couldn't see him. He dropped his hands to his sides.

"What the hell is happening to me?" he asked, fighting to keep his voice slow and level and losing. "Why is this happening? What has Azimir done to me?"

"He has done nothing. Just given you a place to discover who you were born to be."

Her hands were skittering over the stone behind her, and Jared, watching her with his monochromatic vision, suddenly felt all his pity swept away by a force of cruel mirth. It bubbled out into a laugh that made the chamber echo. Emelia froze and shrank against the rock, turning her head away from him and squeezing her eyes shut to block out what she could not see.

"Blindness is so cruel, isn't it?" Jared said, his voice edged like a sword blade. "So cruel. To be alone in the dark...or to be with something you fear and don't understand—which is worse, I wonder?"

"Let me go," she whimpered. "Let me out."

"I'm not stopping you. But you should never have come." He took a step toward her, placing his feet carefully as a cat.

But somehow she heard him move, and she spun to face the door, beating on it with her small fists. The bells around her ankle jingled furiously.

"Help!" she screamed. "Help me! Help!"

Jared laughed again, merciless, feeling a power surge through him as he watched her writhing in blind helplessness against the unyielding stone. "Who will help you now? Now that you have awakened the Dragon, who will save you?"

Emelia slid to the ground, sobbing in terror, her hands still beating the stone. "Please help," she pleaded.

Jared crouched down beside her and she shriveled away from him. "You tell Azimir," Jared said softly, "that he will regret this."

Then he stood and pulled open the door. As the light in the corridor flooded into the cell, Jared's vision suddenly faded to color and he felt a searing pain through his head. He staggered away from the door with a cry of agony, falling to his knees. Emelia scrambled out the door, screaming for help. Jared, shaking and half-blinded by the light, found himself babbling something inarticulate.

Just before the door slammed shut once again, his eyes caught Emelia's. The raw terror in their depths made his mind reel. He had seen that look before. He reached out to her.

"I'm sorry!" he cried. "Forgive me!"

The last words were swallowed by the crash of stone as the door imprisoned him once more in total darkness.

"What is happening to me?" he mumbled in the silent dark.

He saw again the abject fear in Emelia's eyes, and he bowed his head to the stone floor. And then the jagged flash of a memory cut across his consciousness.

That's where he had seen that look before.

It had been all over Sahara's face as she stood there, chained to the pillar on the mountain-top, staring into the jaws of the Dragon. Just before he drove his sword into its heart and sent it tumbling to its fiery end in the chasm below.

Jared slowly sat up, planting his hands on his thighs. The darkness fled once more as his eyes adjusted to their new power of sight.

He had spent two weeks in the darkness, and now, somehow, it was part of him.

No, that's not it. Not quite. This darkness is no longer total because there is something blacker within. It's just like the way blowing out a candle in a dark room makes the darkness outside the window seem suddenly brighter.

Something was changing inside him. He could feel it beginning to claw its way out of the depths of his soul.

"I've got to get out of here," he said aloud.

But even as he said it, he knew that there was nowhere else he could go. There was nowhere to run. He had to master this force, to conquer it before it conquered him completely.

Sahara.

He reached out to her with his mind, praying desperately that she would hear him.

Sahara, please.

Slowly, he saw her face appear. Her hair was whipping around her face, and she was staring over her shoulder. He frowned as he realized that she was astride a huge black horse, galloping through a field of tall grasses.

The sun was rising, and each grass blade seemed edged with blood. And then he heard the noise. A massive engine whirring and the rattling hum of a machine gun. Shredded grasses scattered up into the brightening sky like they had been tossed into the breeze by a child's hand.

Jared jumped to his feet, trying to hold on to the vision as it began to blur.

Sahara!

And as the vision faded into the monochrome shadows of his cell, his roar of anger and frustration and sorrow sent a small shower of stones skittering down the walls.

Jared bowed his head, and his eyes burned with hot tears.

How can I hold myself back from the abyss without her?

And then a strange voice, a man's voice, suddenly cut across Jared's consciousness.

What the hell is going on?

Jared jumped back, clutching his head, feeling the room spin around him. And then, as he recovered his balance, a face begin to materialize. Jared dropped to his knees, watching in breathless silence.

How is this possible? Jared said. *How are you inside my head?*

How are you inside mine? the voice demanded.

The face blurred suddenly into focus, and Jared found himself staring wordlessly into Deor's surprised eyes.

I really hope you can explain this, Deor said. *Because this is the weirdest thing that has ever happened to me.*

Relief swept through Jared and he began to laugh. *I can't explain it. I'm sorry. But I've never been happier to see anyone in my life.*

Me either, Deor said. *Listen, you need to get out of there. You've got to come home. Something's wrong here.*

Jared's laugh died suddenly. *What's happened?*

You have to get out of there, Jared. You've been set up.

We can't get out, Jared answered. *Or didn't you hear?*

Hear what?

They turned on us, Deor. Rafe was nearly killed...he's under Azimir's influence somehow. Something's happening to me...I don't know what it is. And Sahara's gone.

Gone? Gone where?

How the hell should I know? She bolted, and all I know is that she's safe. Shards of his vision cascaded through his mind, and he corrected himself. *Or...she was safe. I don't know if she still is. Everything's gone sideways. But Azimir is planning to come for you, Deor. He's planning an assault on Askalon, and he wants me to help him destroy you. You've got to find a way to get us out of here. Tell Aelred—*

There may not be anything left of us by the time Azimir gets here, Deor said, his voice taut. *There's no one who can come for you, I'm afraid. Not now.*

What do you mean? What's going on?

Deor studied him in silence for a moment, and then he glanced suddenly over his shoulder. When his attention returned to Jared, his brows were knitted and his eyes dark. *Look, I've got to go.* He hesitated, then added, *Someone has betrayed us too, Jared. The zanthos is gone.*

EIGHT

JARED SAT IN THE SHADOWS, his head bowed, hands clasped loosely around his knees. He could feel the rough chill of the stone worming through his shirt, and he let it coil its way through him. He kept his eyes closed against the pounding in his head, and he was afraid of seeing in the dark. His communication with Deor had left his mind reeling, and the desperate desire to get free, to get out, was almost overpowering.

But he sat, silent as a statue, holding the frantic feelings in check with an almost superhuman effort.

I never could get anyone to explain it to me, he realized. How it is that I can communicate this way with...others. He shivered involuntarily. *Why now? Why Deor?*

Keeping his eyes closed, he leaned his head back against the wall. And what did his vision of Sahara mean? What was happening to her? He felt in the very core of his being that she was in danger somehow, and he knew that she was only biding her time. She would return to Aquila. And there would be bloodshed when she did.

He sighed heavily, turning his mind away from Sahara to focus again on the mystery of Deor.

And the *zanthos*.

He had been so preoccupied by the strangeness of the communication that he had almost forgotten the message. Something was wrong back on Askalon.

Deor mentioned a traitor. But who would betray Aelred and the Lords of Askalon? And why would they take the zanthos? All the weapons were destroyed...why would anyone need it?

He rubbed a hand over his face. The pain in his head was now a constant throbbing ache, and he could barely focus his thoughts. Groaning softly, he crept to his shabby pallet on hands and knees and lay down. Perhaps morning and sunlight would bring answers.

He released himself into dreams.

———

Jared smiled up at his sister. Cassandra was chattering away, leaning out the window to watch the people meandering in the courtyard below. Their mother had bought her a new dress for the Summer Festival, and she could barely contain her excitement.

"I still can't believe that Father agreed to let me go," she said, drawing in her head and turning to him with a bright smile. "It's almost too good to be true."

He smiled and smiled, staring into those dancing silver eyes. She was so beautiful, his sister was. He felt that his heart would burst with love.

"Why are you staring at me with that face?" she asked, crossing to him and ruffling his hair playfully. "I'm sorry you can't come too. But Father says you have to be sixteen."

"You're not sixteen yet," he put in.

"I will be tomorrow!"

"I will be next year," Jared said. "If Father makes an exception for one day, why not one year?"

She stuck her tongue out at him. "Maybe he would if you were nicer looking."

Jared laughed at that. "Cassie, you deserve to go. I'm only kidding."

"So am I." She perched beside him on the settee. "Didn't you have a lesson this afternoon? Learning to plant weeds with Childir or something, wasn't it?"

Jared shrugged. "He wasn't there."

His sister frowned. "It's not like him to miss your lessons, is it?"

"It happens every now and again."

Cassie leaned over and gave him a light kiss on the cheek. "You should go have some fun, then. But don't let Rafe get you into trouble again...you know what happened last time." With a wag of her finger and a bubbling laugh that made Jared smile, she pirouetted out of the sitting room toward her own chamber.

The laugh turned to a scream, and suddenly the fury and stench of battle was all around him. Jared stared in horror as Cassie fell, her mail shirt no match for the cruel scimitar of the Drakkin she faced. Blood drenched the ground, and Jared caught her as she staggered backward.

"Don't lose hope, Jared," she murmured, trying to smile. "Someday, we will have freedom." Her breath seeped out and her eyes closed.

Jared clutched her lifeless body to his breast, a roar of grief and anger tearing itself out of his lungs. His rage was so intense that he thought it would kill him. He had no notion how long he knelt there, desperately wishing that she would open her eyes again, that she would laugh, that this nightmare would end.

"Don't leave me, Cassie," he mumbled. "God, don't leave me here all alone...I can't do it. I can't do this alone."

A cold, cruel laugh cut through his grief, and he slowly raised his eyes. The Drakkin stood there, watching him mourn.

"But you are alone. You will always be alone. The Alareth line has caused us enough trouble...and it is time to make an end."

He advanced, raising his scimitar. Jared lay Cassie down carefully, adrenaline and wrath replacing grief, and cast about for a weapon. His own sword had been broken long before, and his dagger was no match for the Drakkin's longer weapon.

As he scrambled to his feet, Jared's eyes lighted on Cassie's sword, lying beside her in the bloody sand. He seized the hilt and got to his feet. Everything inside was numb, though he could vaguely feel tears streaming down his cheeks. The noise of the battle all around him seemed to fade to silence, and the only thing he saw was the dripping scimitar in the Drakkin's hand.

Jared switched the sword to his right hand, testing the grip. Then he coiled himself and sprang on his enemy.

"You will be destroyed," the Drakkin laughed.

"Maybe," Jared said. "But not today."

The scimitar clattered to the sand next to the Drakkin's head.

———

Jared came to himself with a shuddering sigh and rubbed his hands over his face. That memory, so long buried—why should he remember it now? He didn't want to remember. He had tried so desperately to forget.

But had that been a mistake? He thought about Sahara. Ruthless, lethal, yet somehow profoundly vulnerable. She had fought for so long that she didn't know how to stop...how well he knew how clinging to past hurts could jeopardize any hope of a future.

And yet...what good had it done him, in the end? What good had it done him to bury his grief and anger so deep that he had all but forgotten them? What good had it done him to throw himself into study, into music, into herb lore? He stared up at the ceiling of his cell, arching away into shadows in the early morning sunlight. It had all come to nothing, in the end.

But in the end I destroyed the Dragon. That must count for something.

The door grated open and two guards entered, crowding each other as they both tried to stand on the threshold. In the end, the brawnier guard gave his smaller companion a rough shove, and the guard staggered a few paces into the cell.

"I don't want to see Azimir," Jared said from his pallet. "So if that's why you're here, you can turn yourselves around and get lost."

"We do not come from Lord Azimir," said the smaller guard, his voice cracking. "The Lady Emelia sends for you to walk with her in the courtyard."

Jared pushed himself up onto an elbow, brows knitting in puzzlement. "I didn't think she would ever want to see me again," he confessed.

The smaller guard cast a glance over his shoulder and the other guard nodded brusquely. "It is the lady's order that you must go bound," he said, almost as if he was asking Jared's permission.

Jared rolled off his pallet and came toward them, and both guards retreated, barely contained panic clear in their eyes. Jared laughed softly and held out his hands for the shackles. "Are you planning to bind me then? It's hard to put those on myself."

"Idiot," muttered the brawny guard, elbowing his companion forward. "Get up there and bind the man."

With a shaky smile that was almost apologetic, the guard clapped the manacles around Jared's wrists and ankles. "Let's go air you out," he said.

The plashing fountain greeted him cheerfully as he entered the courtyard, and he stumbled to a halt. The guards cursed mildly at him, but they didn't jerk him forward immediately. So many memories danced through Jared's mind like so many droplets of water or fragments of refracted light.

Aliya and Arnauld's smiling faces. Rafe's contagious laugh and dark, mischievious eyes. Sahara's ruddy hair and softly pearled skin. The sweet-spicy scent of *edulia*. The throbbing music of the Summer Festival.

But the dark shadow of anger was creeping over all of these, like the coming of night or the blotting hand of storm clouds. And Jared found himself frowning, his hands straining against the manacles.

"Why so gloomy?" asked Emelia, appearing suddenly under the canopy of the trees. "You don't look nearly as happy as I mean you to be."

"Don't play games with me," said Jared. "Why should you care about my happiness? And I didn't think I'd ever see you again, not after...what happened. I'm sorry for that, by the way."

Emelia waved a hand to dismiss the guards, who retreated no further than the doorway, gums flapping wordlessly at her brash courage. Jared shambled forward, chains clinking around his feet, and joined her in the courtyard.

"I should have known better," she said with a slight shrug. "I know what you are, and the fault was mine."

"How about sharing with me, then? What am I, exactly? Because I have no idea what you're talking about."

Emelia's smooth forehead puckered into a frown, and she turned to stroll towards the fountain, beckoning for Jared to follow her. For a long time she stood, leaning on the lip of the fountain, watching the water dance in the tiered basins.

"Why are you doing this?" Jared asked. "Why are you trying to give me comfort? And why are you working for Azimir in the first place?"

"I have no choice," she answered quietly, her voice almost lost in the chatter of the water. "My service keeps my people safe. And I would do anything—" she turned to face him, her eyes flashing with sudden fire— "*anything*, for them. And as for you...it's all part of Azimir's calculations, I suppose."

"What does that mean?"

Emelia shrugged. "He believes something about you. He believes you are more than what you seem. And what I saw last night...you *are* more than what you seem. He has been searching for you for some time."

"Why?"

Emelia hesitated, her eyes straying back to the fountain. She trailed her fingers in the water, watching the ripples race away from her hand. "Tell me about yourself," she said finally. "About your homeworld."

Jared frowned. "You didn't answer my question."

"I know."

Jared studied her for a moment, then shrugged. "I'm from Silesia. It's a desert world, in many ways much like what I've seen of Halcyon." He glanced up at the azure sky. "Sun and warmth and almost no rain."

"We are heading into the dry season," Emelia said, following his gaze. "There will be no more rain for several months now." Her voice became suddenly distant. "It's harvest season," she continued. "And nearly time for the pilgrimage."

"What do your people harvest?"

Emelia sighed. "They harvest the drugs for the Zharib."

Jared glanced at her quickly. "You grow no other crops on Halcyon? How do you eat, then? Or does Azimir import everything?"

"No. Aquila Province is entirely devoted to sustaining the drug trade. But Halcyon is divided into five other provinces, and all of these are under Azimir's rule. Each province has a purpose and they all work together so that Halcyon can be self-sufficient. We import nothing."

"*Nothing?*"

"Nothing." Emelia favored him with a small smile. "There is unbelievable wealth and plenty on Halcyon...it's just unfortunate that—" She cut herself off and shook her head.

That Azimir and his cronies are the only ones who benefit from it, I bet she would say. Aloud, he said, "Tell me more about the other provinces."

"Karbala and Ash, which lie across the Sea of Ceroul to the south, are farming provinces. They receive more rain than Aquila and aren't nearly as hot, so their growing season is far longer, and beasts have more herb for grazing. Their resources of land and workers are dedicated to supporting the rest of Halcyon. All of our fabrics come from Karbala, where the Order of Weavers has its guild. Ket, which lies to the west over the mountain ranges, is rich in resources of fuel and metals, so all the other orders of craftsmen are established there. Everything—weapons, machinery, ships for space flight, even everyday essentials—is manufactured in Ket. And then there is Perl." She stopped suddenly and turned away.

"Where is Perl?"

"It's the northern province. The river Ren flows down through Aquila from the snows of Perl, winding its way to the sea."

"What happens there?"

"Nothing."

"Nothing? But from what you've said, it seems that every province has a role to play...surely one province wouldn't get left out of such an elegant division of labor?"

"Nothing happens there any longer. It's nothing but a barren wasteland."

"What used to happen there, then?"

Emelia's eyes crept up to meet his. "Perl was the religious center of Halcyon. Its wealth was in gems and gold and precious metals...vast mines of them stretching under the mountains. It was a fitting place for sacrifices, and so the priests built vast temples to house great altars of gold and jewels. They filled treasure-houses with riches, holding them in trust, they said, for their god. They studied the stars and learned how to predict the seasons—and the people bowed low and thought they held the keys to deep and secret knowledge. And gradually, the people began to believe that they not only understood these things, but controlled them. And they were afraid of their anger, and sent many gifts and sacrifices to please them."

"What kind of sacrifices?"

"At first, only animals. Karbala and Ash provided the choicest offerings from their herds, and each of the other provinces would offer something of its own products for the temple. Aquila provided the incense."

Something in her tone made Jared suddenly suspicious. "Was it incense, Emelia? Or some kind of drug?"

Emelia shuddered. "I don't know."

"But you said that they aren't there any longer," Jared said, a vague sense of foreboding crawling through his gut. "Something must have happened."

"We of the Hazad never believed their falsehoods or followed their god. And it was not long before their malice fell upon us. Threatening the people with a drought that would consume the land, they demanded that the daughter of the Hazad chieftain be offered to them in sacrifice. The god, they said, demanded her blood in exchange for the life-giving water that Perl supplied to Aquila."

Jared felt the color draining from his face. Even as cold dread gripped him, the scholar in him rejoiced as the pieces of the puzzle he had so long struggled to untangle began to fall into place. "Was she sent to them?"

"Yes."

"Who were they, Emelia?"

"They called themselves the Order of the Dragon."

Jared stared at her in silence for a long while, and then he said, "Tell me what happened."

"Once they acquired a lust for blood, it took more and more to satiate them. Discontent was brewing and growing anger, as one by one, each of the provinces had to send their highest born lady to be sacrificed. Finally, they demanded the daughter of the King himself. But the princess was pure and kind, beloved by all the people. They rose up in her defense. The King banished the Order from Halcyon, and his armies laid waste to the province of Perl. They threw down the temples to the Dragon and flung the riches into the sea. No one goes there now. It is forbidden."

Jared stared at the chains binding his hands. "They came to our system," he said, "when they left Halcyon. They set up their base on K'ilenfir and began subjugating the planets one by one. But it was never under the pretense any longer of some kind of service to a religion. They *were* the religion."

"They did not begin as evil men," Emelia said. "As my grandfather tells the story, they began as noble-minded and high-hearted philosophers. Proud men, and wise, in their way. But, in the end, the allure of power and riches consumed them. The Dragon consumed them."

"I destroyed the Dragon," Jared murmured. "I destroyed them, Emelia."

She reached out and laid a hand on his. "I know that. And that's why Azimir has been searching for you."

Jared glanced up at her, a wry smile quirking his mouth. "What, he wants to thank me?"

"No." Her dark eyes were sad and serious. "He wants to save you."

NINE

"WHAT?" Jared jerked his hands away from Emelia's, anger suddenly clouding his mind and constricting his vision. "What did you say? He wants to save me from what, exactly? From what I can tell, all he wants is for me to destroy everything I hold dear!"

"No, that's not so. Please, you must understand...that's not true at all."

Jared stared at her for a moment. Her breast was heaving, her dark eyes earnest. *She really believes what she's telling me. How can she be such a fool?*

"Why should I believe anything you say?" Jared asked quietly. "Azimir is using you. Everything you say comes from him...and it's calculated, isn't it? You prey on my weaknesses, trying to turn me to serve his ends. Lies serve better than truth for such purposes."

Emelia's face fell. "But everything I have told you is the truth, no matter what you say," she murmured. "I don't understand why you don't believe me."

"Oh, I do believe you. I do believe that Azimir wants to save me...so that he can use me to serve his own ends." Jared stepped closer to her, anger making his voice sharp. "I will *not* be the instrument of my friends' destruction. I will not help him make war on Askalon."

Emelia's eyes searched his own, and Jared felt that she was poised on the edge of something—a revelation, perhaps, or a betrayal. For a moment she hesitated there, like a diver on a cliff edge. And then she closed her eyes and took the plunge.

"Askalon is not what you think it is, Jared," she said softly.

"You have no idea what I think it is."

Emelia opened her eyes again. "Why are you working so hard to protect a world that is not even your own?"

"Askalon is the home of my friends, as I've already told you. As such, it is my world as well. I fought beside them to save it...and I will not see it fall to ruin while I still draw breath."

She sighed. "There's so much that you don't understand...so many things you don't know! You wouldn't speak that way if you knew what I know. What Azimir knows."

"I know my friends," Jared said, his voice cutting like a whip. She winced. "And I trust them a lot more than I trust you. What more do I need to know? Take me back to my cell. And do yourself a favor. Don't bring me out here to sweet talk me any more. It's not getting us anywhere. And it might be dangerous for you."

He turned and dragged his chains back toward the guards. He heard her light jingling footsteps behind him, but then she stopped suddenly. Jared slowed his pace, feeling somehow that there was something she desperately wanted to tell him. And in spite of his doubts about her integrity and her motives, his curiosity was getting the better of his skepticism.

"What can I say that will make you believe me?" she asked softly. "Is there anything I could tell you that would make you see that I speak the truth?"

"No." But he didn't move, and he heard the jingle of bells as she took another few steps toward him.

She hesitated, then blurted, "What if I told you that there is a traitor on Askalon?"

Jared turned slowly to face her. "What?"

Her hands were still clasped, and now there were tears in her eyes. "I said, would you believe me if I told you that there is a traitor on Askalon?"

"How do you know that?"

Emelia smiled at him sadly. "The king has my ear, and he confides many things in me."

"Is that so?" Jared measured her for a moment through slitted eyes. "And how would he know that there's a traitor on Askalon, I wonder? Because he's working with him, perhaps?"

"Do you think that he is blind? Do you think that he would leave Askalon unwatched, with so much at stake? He's no fool, Jared."

She had a point, and there was no guile in her eyes. Jared felt himself drawn to trust her. And yet, wasn't that exactly how they wanted him to feel? Wasn't that why Azimir sent her to him in the first place? She seemed so innocent. But it was all a sham...it had to be all just a sham.

She serves Azimir. She's a tool, and she is here to manipulate me. How can I possibly trust her?

And yet, there was the plain fact that Deor had told him the very same thing about the traitor. If that much was true, what about the rest of what she had told him? Was it possible that she really could be telling him the truth?

"So who is this traitor, then?" he asked.

"I don't know the name. But we do know one thing for certain. The traitor is a member of the Order of the Dragon." Her voice trembled as she spoke.

Jared frowned, unable to figure out why this seemed to fill her with so much fear. "I killed the Dragon, Emelia," he said. "How can there be an Order of the Dragon when there's no Dragon?"

Emelia shook her head, and now it was her turn to look at him as if he were no more than a simple child. "You don't understand, Jared.

You destroyed the old Order, the Council. The Drakkin learned how to take the Dragon's form to serve their own ends, and that's what you killed. You destroyed the Council, not the Dragon."

"You aren't making any sense. Not even a little bit. If they took the Dragon's form and I killed it, then that's the end. Done. Finished. Right?"

"No." Emelia took a few hesitant steps toward him. "You can't kill something immortal, Jared. There will always be those who serve the Dragon. Not the Drakkin, mind you—the *Dragon*. The Order did not die with the destruction of the Council. These true believers, these members of the Order, think the Dragon will return. They watch, and wait, and pray, and work to subvert everything that is good in this universe in service to him."

"Well, they're watching and praying in vain. The Dragon won't return. I watched it incinerate itself. There is no more Dragon." He offered the words with bold certainty, so why did he feel so wretchedly unsure of himself? "And what does some strange cult have to do with me, or with Azimir, anyway?"

"Askalon owes us a great debt and the promised payment is not being delivered. Askalon is very much in the King's mind. And as for you..." She paused and came quite close to him, so close that he could feel the feather touch of her breath. "You are the Dragon-Slayer," she said. "And the Order wants you destroyed."

Jared laughed out loud. "I thought Azimir wanted me destroyed anyway. He and these cult followers should be best friends."

Emelia speared him with a frustrated glance. "Haven't you heard anything I told you of our history? That same cult all but destroyed Halcyon. The Order of the Dragon has been banished from our lands, and they are hateful to us. If Azimir wanted you dead, you'd be dead already. He does not trifle with prisoners."

"Then how do you explain what he's doing to Rafe, then?" Jared snapped. "And he told me he wanted me to help him lay waste to Askalon."

She looked puzzled. "How does that mean that he desires your death?"

"Because I won't help him, and he'll have to kill me. I'm a dead man either way." He tried to grin, but the look in her eyes killed it as soon as it reached his lips. "Whether he does it himself or leaves me to the Order, it amounts to the same thing."

For a long time, Emelia looked up into his eyes, and Jared found himself growing more and more uncertain. There was something there, behind her gaze, and Jared knew that there was something she wasn't telling him.

What am I missing? He almost begged her out loud. *Tell me what I'm missing.*

"I can't say any more than I already have," Emelia said with a little sigh, turning away from him. "And I've probably said more than I should. You'll have to ask Azimir to explain."

She began to walk away, but he reached out and caught her hand. The guards started forward when she uttered a little cry of surprise and alarm.

"Emelia!" he said, then stopped in confusion. "I don't understand. Why does Azimir keeps me in chains if he wants my help? I don't understand why he threatens my friend's life. And I don't understand why he sends you here to tell me secrets. Your confidences suggest that he wants to trust me." He held up his hands, showing her the shackles. "But this doesn't show trust."

"No, it doesn't."

Emelia took his arm, leading him out of earshot of the guards. When they stood once more by the fountain, she gestured for him to sit on the edge of the basin. He obeyed, and she sat down beside him. For a long time, she didn't speak. She kept her eyes fixed on the branches of the tree across from them, and after a moment, Jared followed her gaze. He started with surprise when he realized that there were several small birds in the branches. They didn't warble or sing, but their plumage was bright. Jared felt at once that there was something wrong with them—birds so colorful should have a song.

"What are those birds?" he asked. "I've never seen anything like them...and why don't they sing?"

"Azimir's father brought them from the groves of the Hazad to please Azimir's mother," Emelia said carefully. "But he didn't like their song, so he muted them. Every generation of these birds since has had no voice. They just sit in these trees, and their beauty and their silence is a cacophony. They cannot go home again, for now they are outcasts. The birds of the Hazad would never welcome them."

Jared glanced at her, saw the soft tears in her eyes. "You think you'll never be welcomed by your people again because you serve here in Aquila?" he asked gently.

She took a deep breath and turned to him. "These birds are a constant reminder," she answered. "I too was taken from my home, caged, and made to serve another. And if I ever became a threat to him, I would be similarly destroyed. Muted...or murdered."

"I don't ask you to betray Azimir," Jared said.

"But now you, too, are like these birds. You asked me if Azimir trusted you. Yes, he trusts you. But he also fears you. Just as he trusts and fears me. I am no more than a slave in his house, but he confides more in me than in Ribbadi, the chief of his Inner Circle. I know more than I should. But instead of that knowledge giving me power, it only makes me weaker. It tightens my chains, pushes the knife edge that much closer to my throat."

Jared smiled wryly. "It's a dangerous business, being the confidante of a tyrant."

Emelia's eyes were earnest and she laid a warm hand on his arm. "And the same will be true for you. He will trust in you. Confide in you. Promise you worlds in exchange for your aid. And all the time he will never let you forget that he could end your life as easily as he could snuff out a candle." She smiled sadly at him. "I am too weak to run. I love him too much to run."

"But you would imply that I should run? Or that I still have a chance to escape somehow?"

She was silent, holding his gaze, wordlessly warning him to go, yet begging him to stay. Jared felt his heart suddenly twist strangely, and he shifted his gaze to the songless birds. They hopped from one branch to the next, watching him with their keen, bright eyes. And Jared knew at that moment that even if he had a chance to run, he wouldn't.

"Why does he keep me in chains if he wants my help, Emelia?" Jared asked, his voice quiet.

"Once you have learned to accept your place here—to accept that you belong to him and that your life is his to command—then you will have a measure of freedom. No more chains. Perhaps a nicer room."

"I will never accept those terms. I belong to no one, and my life is my own."

Emelia shook her head and gripped the cuff that secured his wrist. "That is why you are still bound." She lifted her eyes to his. "Sometimes the only way to be free is to serve, Jared."

Jared jerked his hands away from hers. "And sometimes the only way to be free is to fight."

"You cannot fight Azimir," she said, her voice dropping to an urgent whisper. "Can't you believe that I've tried?" Her eyes were filling now with angry tears, tears of helpless frustration. "He will win. He *always* wins. And I promise you, the cost of fighting will be higher than you would ever wish to pay. If he wants you to serve, you will."

"He might have won before, but not this time. He's overplayed his hand, and he has no idea what he's done. He's picked a fight with the wrong people, and he will pay for it before this is all finished."

Emelia studied him thoughtfully. "Bold words," she said quietly. "But I think you underestimate him."

"It goes both ways, I guess."

"He doesn't underestimate you. He knows what you are capable of...and that's the other reason you are bound in chains and kept in a cell."

Jared stood abruptly. "I don't belong to him, and I won't destroy my friends. And I won't run away from him, either. So next time, don't bother fetching me to walk me around the garden and sweet talk me into submission. Either bring me to Azimir or leave me alone."

He left Emelia sitting on the lip of the fountain and the guards led him back to his cell.

TEN

THE ARRIVAL of the Elenni rider had drawn a small throng of people to Jessup's tent. They huddled close together, whispering, but they kept a respectful distance from the tent itself. She alone stood within this all but sacred circle, and she caught several people watching her, their eyes sliding away from hers as soon as she glanced their way.

After a few moments, Jessup shouldered his way out of the tent. His eyes caught Sahara's.

"They're coming for you," he said. "They're looking for you, and they will find you and kill you. You must ride." Without waiting for an answer, he raised his voice to address the knot of people. "Run for the fields! You know your places! The Scythes are coming!"

Somewhere in the crowd, a woman screamed. And then pandemonium and panic ignited the crowd into motion. Isis dropped the wooden paddle and ran for a large bell tethered on a tall pole outside the kitchen tent. Its harsh clanging brought everyone else tumbling out of their tents and sent them running for the fields.

Must be a different sound when it's the dinner bell.

Someone seized her arm, and she jerked away and spun, startled to see Rigel standing beside her. "You've got to run," he said. "They will kill you, Zelie!"

Sahara shrugged, glancing up at the sky. "Won't they just take me back to Aquila? That's where I need to go anyway." She gave him a twisted smile. "Might as well get a ride there."

"No, they won't. The Scythes take no prisoners. They do nothing but kill." He made another attempt at her arm, but when she backed away again, he went for the horse instead. He snatched the bridle and led the horse toward her at a trot. "Brig says you must take his horse. Head east. The Scythes will follow you away from the tribe."

Sahara checked herself as she reached for the saddle. "What?"

Rigel's eyes dropped away from hers, and he looked genuinely miserable. "Jessup says you must prove yourself today. Lead the Scythes away from our people. And if you survive, you will be one of us."

Sahara measured him for a long time, then pulled herself up into the saddle. "Head east, is that it?"

"Yes."

Sahara gathered the reins into her hands, feeling the horse shift his weight beneath her. So many memories came flooding back to her —of riding her own horse bareback in the surf, of races over the downs with her friends before the days of grief. She threaded the leather straps through her fingers, then leaned down to catch Rigel's eye.

"Is there any way to outrun them? Or should I just stand here and let them mow me down?"

Rigel laid a hand on the horse's strong neck. "It's possible to outrun them." His eyes met hers. "But...not very likely."

Sahara gave a short laugh and glanced over her shoulder. She could see the last of Jessup's people bolting out of the tent circle, scattering as soon as they left the circle of the camp. Faintly, she could hear a vague sound, like the distant throaty hum of an engine. It was coming from the north. From Aquila.

"Tell Jessup," Sahara said, turning back to Rigel, "that I'll be back by sundown. Now get the hell out of here."

Rigel's sudden smile flared at her, and without another word, he sprinted for the safety of the fields.

"All right, then," Sahara said to the horse, who snorted and tossed his head. "Let's see what you can do."

She dug her heels into the horse's sides and he shot away from the camp. For a moment, Sahara felt her balance slipping, and her breath caught in her throat at the sheer speed of the animal. She closed her eyes, letting go of her conscious thoughts, and anchored herself in instinct and memory. Her body shifted, and she felt a sudden harmony with the movement of the horse. She opened her eyes again and smiled. It was exhilarating, and though she hated being sent out as bait, she was glad for the chance to ride.

The hum of engines was growing louder by the second, and she glanced to the north. Not three hundred yards away, she saw two silver shapes. They weren't large—maybe slightly bigger than her horse—and they flew close enough to the ground to shred the tall grasses with their long wings.

That's why they're called the Scythes, I suppose.

Their smooth silver bodies were windowless, and Sahara wondered suddenly how they could acquire a target. But as they came closer, she saw a long, flexible antenna extending up from the center of the drone, and she realized that they were remotely controlled.

So that's why I can outrun them. If I get far enough, then they'll be out of range of their handlers.

She slowed the horse's pace to a canter, and then brought him to a stop. The drones had not altered course—they were still bearing down on the settlement. A hundred yards and closing.

And then she heard the screams.

She spun the horse. Two little girls stood just outside the tent circle, holding each other and screaming. Sahara could tell that their eyes were fixed on the approaching Scythes, and they seemed completely paralyzed.

"No!" Sahara shouted. "No!"

Without thinking, she clapped her heels into the horse's sides again and galloped back. She leaned low over the horse's neck, urging him on. She could close the distance. She could make it. She focused on the two girls, and as she came closer, she began screaming at them to run.

They seemed to hear her, and they turned toward her. The smallest one held up her hands and cried to her for help.

A metallic whirring noise pulled her attention back to the drones. At first, she didn't know what was making the sound, but then she saw the barrel of a large machine gun drop down from the belly of the drone. As the guns dropped into position, the drones lifted higher into the air and spread out into an attack formation.

"Run, girls!" Sahara shouted. "Run!"

She was almost on top of them now, and the whirring suddenly became a harsh rattling. Bullets sprayed the area around them, tearing the ground and sending up huge clouds of dust. Sahara reined in the horse and pulled the girls up onto the saddle in front of her. She waited for a split second until the drones stopped firing in order to come around for another pass. Then she shot away eastward like an arrow.

She heard the drones circle around behind her and glanced back once. They were low again and were rapidly picking up speed.

"Listen!" Sahara said to the girls. "Listen to me very carefully! You see just ahead where the grass comes up to the horse's belly? I'm going to let you off there. Drop flat and crawl away from us, do you hear? Don't get caught under the drones. I'll draw them away from you. As soon as we're well past, run back for the camp."

"Yes, Zelie," the older girl said, smiling at Sahara through her tears.

"Get ready! We're nearly there."

Sahara glanced back over her shoulder again, gauging speed and distance. The next moment, the horse plunged into the tall grasses. Thirty strides into the meadow, Sahara checked the horse and the girls slipped down. She waited only just long enough to see them scrambling away into the grasses on hands and knees, and then she spurred the horse into a gallop once again.

The rising sun tinged the grasses like blood. Sahara bent over the horse's neck, using her connection to the horse to keep her fear at bay. She heard the rattling beginning again, and she glanced back. The drones were lifting out of the grasses, preparing to fire on her.

She checked the horse suddenly and wheeled around. The horse danced nervously under her, but she waited, eyes narrowed, counting breathless seconds.

"Steady," she told the horse softly. "Steady."

They were nearly on her now.

The spray of bullets shredded the grass around her, and the horse reared. She spun him around and they leapt away, heading south this time. The drones had to pull up and turn, and the whirring of the machine guns stopped for a moment. But as soon as they had corrected their course, they were bearing down on her again.

I hate running.

She began casting about for some way to bring the things down. If Jessup and his tribe wanted her to prove herself, she'd do it her own way.

I'm no runner. I'm a fighter. They picked on the wrong girl.

Just ahead of her rose a small copse of trees. They were dense and shaggy, and they grew so close together that their branches seemed almost to weave a net.

Works either way, Sahara said to herself as her mind clicked through possible scenarios.

As the horse closed the distance between them and the copse, Sahara saw that there was a narrow track cut through the hedge of branches, and even as she noticed it, she saw the grasses parting beneath the horse, revealing the rest of the track.

She spurred the horse to even greater speed, and heard the

drones accelerate behind her. She glanced back, saw them begin to lift out of the grass. The guns whirred, and bullets once more sprayed the ground around her. Sahara flattened herself on the horse's neck and he shot through the opening in the trees.

"Go, go, go!" she murmured, encouraging the horse to keep the pace.

The trees behind her erupted in flames as the drones, coming too close and too fast to stop, crashed into the net of branches. The horse shied and neighed, but there was nowhere for him to go but forward and out. A moment later, they burst through the opening on the other side of the copse, and Sahara reined him in. He was shaking and blowing, sweat foaming his flanks and shoulders.

"Good boy," Sahara said, slapping his neck and grinning like a fool. "Good boy!"

A secondary explosion rocked the ground under the horse's hooves, and he pranced nervously.

"You're right," she said. "Time for us to get gone."

She turned the horse northwest and cantered back to Jessup's settlement.

They were all there when she rode into the circle, all cheering and applauding. Smiling faces were everywhere she looked. The crowd parted to let her through and surged in behind her, following her all the way to Jessup's tent.

She reined in the horse and slid down, feeling suddenly wobbly on her legs. Two young boys ran forward to take the horse, and someone seized her around the waist.

Rigel was laughing, bouncing her up and down. And she laughed too, finally unable to keep the triumph from bubbling over.

"You can see the smoke for miles and miles!" he said, finally letting her go. "We all thought you must have been killed for certain!"

"Not today, my friend, not today," she said, clasping his shoulders.

"And you saved my girls," said a tall woman, coming forward out of the crowd, holding her daughters tightly by the hands. "They told me how you saved them from the Scythes."

Sahara felt the blood rush to her face, and she bowed her head. "I just..." She didn't know what to say. The girls left their mother and ran to embrace her legs.

"We love you, Zelie Sahara," the smallest said.

Sahara's eyes filled suddenly with tears, and she ruffled the girl's dark hair wordlessly.

"Well, Zelie," said Jessup, stepping toward her with Wes and Fallon by his side. "It seems that you have more than proved yourself today."

Sahara raised her eyes to Jessup's face, saw the wide grin of pleasure, and felt suddenly that he could not have been prouder if she were his own daughter.

He truly has adopted me into his heart.

"And my sons have something to say to you," he continued, prodding them forward.

Sahara had never seen two grown men look more embarrassed or uncomfortable. It made her want to smile, but she simply crossed her arms and tossed back her head, waiting. She didn't have to gloat, but she didn't have to make it easy on them, either.

"We're...sorry we doubted you," Wes mumbled.

"Welcome to our tribe...to our family," Fallon added, almost choking, Sahara thought, on the words.

She smiled at them. "Thank you," she said. "It's an honor."

"Now come!" sad Jessup. "Let us feast our victory and prepare to move camp! Zelie, come with me!"

He turned to lead Sahara into his tent, and Sahara moved to follow him, her eyes flitting over a sea of smiling faces. And then she saw Katarina, standing alone at the edge of the crowd.

There was no smile on her face, and when Sahara's eyes locked with hers, she quickly averted her eyes. But not before Sahara caught something in their depths.

Sorrow.

And envy.

ELEVEN

"COME, ZELIE, COME!" Jessup called, holding open the tent flap.

Sahara sighed and entered the tent. As she stepped into the tent, she stopped in surprise. Brig stood there, his corded arms folded across his broad chest.

"I hear you nearly killed my horse," he said.

"I—" Sahara's gaze swung toward Jessup in confusion, then back to Brig. "What?"

"If you're going to be one of us," Brig continued, "I need to know that you'll take more care of your horse than that."

"Are you...kidding me?" Sahara asked. "I just took down two Scythes...and you're worried about your horse?"

Brig took a step toward her. "They've got plenty more of those," he snapped. "But we don't get another horse. Savvy?"

Sahara frowned. "No. I won't run when I can fight."

"Then you aren't fit to be one of us." He turned to Jaffa. "I won't have her in my corps if she doesn't play by the rules. I don't care what Wes and Fallon want."

"Rules? What rules are those?" Sahara asked.

"We run," answered Brig, eyes flashing at her. "We always run.

And we don't play clever with the Scythes. That little stunt today? Very pretty. But very stupid."

"No, I suppose I should have let them mow me down like a blade of grass. I mean, that's how heroes go out, right?"

Brig glared at her. "That's not what I meant."

"If you're just going to run away, you might as well save them the trouble of chasing you down. Just stand there and die next time. Then at least you don't wear out the horse."

"Zelie Sahara," Jaffa said quietly, a warning in his voice.

Sahara glanced at him and swept on. "Maybe that's why you keep losing men. Did you ever think of that? If they lose two of those machines every time they come after you, don't you think that eventually they'll decide it's not worth the cost?"

"No, I don't think that any such notion will enter their minds. They don't care about the expense...they just care about exterminating any vehicle of communication between the tribes."

"Really? Do you know that for a fact, or is that what you want to believe? What is so important about carrying the mail that would make the Zharib hunt you down with so much persistence?" Sahara's gaze snapped from Brig to Jessup and back again. "So what exactly is it that you do?"

Jessup turned away from them with a sigh, waving a hand at Brig. "Tell her. She has a right to know." He moved to the large cushions that formed the seating area around the brazier. He took up a small brass poker and jabbed resignedly at the coals, coaxing them back to warmth.

After watching him for a moment, Sahara glanced at Brig. "So? Tell me what I want to know."

"I don't see why she has to know," Brig said to Jessup, his voice sullen. "Why do we need her anyway? She's an outworlder and doesn't belong here. Why don't we just send her back where she came from?"

"That is not our way, Brig, and you know it. While she is here, she is our guest, and I have welcomed her into the tribe as one of us. She did us all a great service today...saving Aron's daughters and destroying the Scythes before they could lay waste to the settlement." His eyes flashed suddenly at Brig. "You owe her thanks. She does not deserve your rebuke."

"I don't care what he thinks of me," Sahara said. "I've fought in enough conflicts to know that it's always better to inflict casualties on the enemy at every opportunity. Running never got anyone anywhere except further into the realm of slavery and fear."

"Though Grandfather does not wish it, there is a great desire among our people for freedom," Brig told her. "Not every message we carry is one of revolution, but some are. And since Azimir is paranoid, he hunts us down, never knowing when we might carry the word that brings him down from his throne."

"You see?" Sahara said, wrinkling her nose. "I knew it. You reek of revolution. And I already told you that I want no part in this fight."

"Azimir holds your friends captive?" Brig asked.

Sahara hesitated, thinking again of Rafe. "Yes."

"Then why will you not help us? For your friends."

Sahara laughed quietly and moved to squat near the brazier, holding her fingers out to the warmth of the coals. "I have no love for Azimir, and that damned drug you harvest has destroyed more people than you can possibly imagine. I didn't want to come here on this fool's errand in the first place. But that doesn't mean I'm ready to do this again."

"Again?" Jessup asked.

Sahara lifted her eyes to his face. "Yes. Again. I've been fighting my entire life. First the Drakkin, and then the Triumvirate." She saw Jessup and Brig exchange glances, but she continued, "And now this. I'm just not going to do it again. Find yourself another runner."

"You fought against the Drakkin?" Brig asked.

"Yes. We destroyed them."

Jessup jumped to his feet, his face white as the canvas sides of the tent. "That's impossible!"

Sahara frowned at him. "No, it's not. I watched the Dragon die."

Brig took a step toward her, his eyes shining. "Then the rumors are true?"

"What, have you people been living under a rock? The Triumvirate tried to take the power left by the Drakkin. So we destroyed them too." Sahara sat back on her heels and studied the two men. "You seem surprised. Who did you think I was?"

"I just thought..." Jessup began, but his voice died before he could finish the thought. "No, you must ride with the Elenni. You cannot stay here. Not for long."

It was an unexpected turn, and Sahara could see the growing light of fear in the old man's eyes. *Probably right*, she thought, an image of Tessa's smiling little face flashing through her mind. *I'm dangerous...wouldn't want me corrupting the young.*

"Grandfather," Brig said softly, "did you hear what she said? The Dragon has been destroyed!"

"And you did this? You destroyed the Dragon?" Jessup asked earnestly.

"No. My friend—the one Azimir is holding prisoner—he killed the Dragon." She paused, then added, "To save me. I was the blood-offering." She swallowed hard, fought down the memory of that pillar, of the mindless horror. She shook her head. "He destroyed it."

Brig turned on his heel and walked to the edge of the tent, muttering something under his breath in a language Sahara didn't understand. Jessup's face had lost all the rest of its color.

"And you brought him *here*? To Halcyon?" he murmured. "Didn't you know?"

An awful feeling of foreboding snaked through Sahara's gut. "What? What didn't we know?"

"Returning the Dragon-Slayer to Halcyon...oh, merciful gods..."

"Why should that matter?"

"Do you know where the Drakkin came from, Zelie Sahara?" Jessup asked instead. "Do you know where they began?"

"No."

"They began right here. On Halcyon. The Order of the Dragon

began in the province of Perl, far to the north. And they were banished from these lands when their lust for blood became abhorrent to the people. When they demanded the life of Azimir's grandmother."

"Azimir is a fool!" Brig's voice exploded from the other side of the tent. "He has gone too far. Keeping the Dragon-Slayer will bring nothing to Halcyon but ruin and destruction! What can he possibly hope to gain from it?"

"Perhaps Azimir thinks he can control him. Maybe he will try to use the Dragon-Slayer against us," Jessup said softly.

"The people need to know, Jessup. They need to know that he's here. That the end may be nearer than we thought." Brig strode to the tent flap, jerking it back and half-stepping outside.

"Wait, wait!" Sahara cried, holding up her hands. "What are you afraid of? Why should everyone need to be warned?" The ghost of a smile crossed her lips. "Jared's not someone to mess with, but he's not a world-destroyer."

Brig only looked at her, then ducked out of the tent. She could hear him calling for his horse as he ran. Sahara fixed her eyes on Jessup, who seemed to be watching something far away.

"Please," she said, the smile fading as her anxiety surged. "Please tell me. What have you to fear?"

"It's an ancient prophesy," Jessup said, focusing on her face with a pained expression. "An ancient curse. When Azimir's great-grandfather banished the Drakkin from Halcyon, they cursed us. And they cursed the one who would slay them."

"And?" Sahara prompted.

"The abyss will claim him...and any who aided him. And through him, Halcyon will be destroyed."

Sahara gaped at him, feeling as if he had just punched the wind from her lungs. "That's...that's not possible. That's not possible."

"I'm sorry, Zelie."

He ducked out of the tent and left her alone, staring blankly at the glowing coals in the brazier.

That means Askalon is cursed. They made the weapons that destroyed the Drakkin. How is this possible? How can one man destroy worlds? She felt some measure of comfort from the thought. It was so extreme. So exactly like the bold and meaningless curses of insignificant cults. *It must not be true. It's just a story told by old women to keep children in their beds at night.*

But there was something else...something worse. Sahara couldn't understand how one man could annihilate worlds. But she knew all too well how one man could be destroyed from within. What if that much was true?

What does he mean, saying that Jared will be claimed by the abyss? And that would mean that Rafe and Brytnoth are at risk as well...if Rafe is even still alive. They had a hand in the destruction of the Dragon, even though they didn't deal the death-blow.

She knew what it was to live under a curse...and she had only slain a Drakkin chieftain. The anger, the fear, the way those chains had tangled themselves around her heart so tightly that she was fit for nothing except war. But Jared had killed a Drakkin Chieftain, and so had Deor.

They escaped my fate. Didn't they?

Jared had once hinted that he wasn't what she thought. She shuddered, remembering how fiercely she had fought against the notion. And now...what if she had blinded herself? What if she should have believed him? What if he really wasn't what he seemed to be?

And what about her brother?

She shook her head. No. If they were bound by the same chains, then they had somehow managed to escape mostly unscathed. She had to believe that.

Sis!

Sahara scrambled away from the brazier, huddling against the side of Jessup's tent. How had she heard Deor's voice so clearly, when—

Sahara! It's me...it's Deor! Please tell me you can hear me!

And then she saw him, his face lighting up in relief as the connection was established. Sahara gaped at him, for a moment completely at a loss for words.

What the hell are you doing inside my head, Deor?

Funny, Deor said. *That's almost exactly what Jared said when I talked to him the other night.*

Sahara's mouth dropped open in shock. *What? What did you say? You talked to Jared?*

He told me you were safe...that you escaped.

Deor... Sahara shook her head, unwilling to focus on anything else he was saying. *Deor, stop a minute. Just stop.* He frowned at her and she continued, *How are you in my head, Deor?*

I don't know the answer to that. But I need help. And I don't know who else I can trust.

Trust? What do you mean? What's happening?

It was all too much. She clasped her forehead in her hands, trying desperately to make sense of it all.

We've been betrayed, sis. Something's gone wrong here. It's all...it's all wrong. And now....

Sahara's head snapped up. One tiny piece of the puzzle had suddenly dropped into place. *It's part of the curse. This mind-speech thing has always been part of the curse.*

What curse? What are you talking about?

The reason you're in my head, Deor! The reason you can talk to me, and to Jared. The reason Jared and I could communicate this way and no one else could. It's part of the curse. She paused, seeing his utter bewilderment. *We've all killed Drakkin chieftains. They were part of the collective...the Council. This was their way of communicating.* Her breath was ragged, and the vague stirrings of nausea were beginning to seethe in her stomach. *We're becoming what they were, Deor. We're cursed. And Jared... What's going to happen to him? How much worse can it get?*

Deor's face was maddeningly calm, and his tone jarringly practical. *Look, I don't know anything about any curse. And frankly, I've got bigger problems to deal with. Askalon is falling apart. The zanthos is gone. I need you to come home, Sahara. I need you to help me track down the traitor and the zanthos before he uses it to destroy us all.*

Deor, I can't! I can't leave Jared here. Not when...not when I don't know what he'll become. I've got to get him out.

But how? Are you going to break Jared and Rafe out of prison all by yourself?

Sahara started in surprise. *Rafe?*

He looked at her like she'd lost her mind. *Yes, Rafe.*

Did Jared tell you that he's still alive?

Yes.

Tears of relief and joy ran down her cheeks and for a moment she couldn't think straight. At least that much was good news out of this otherwise disastrous situation. And she knew, in a sudden rush, that no matter how much Deor needed her, she had to stay.

I can't come home, she said, wiping her cheeks with the palms of her hands. *Not yet.*

But, sis, Deor continued, *Azimir is coming for us...and we have nothing! Aelred...you don't understand. We have nothing. Either the traitor will destroy us or Azimir will.*

Then I need to stay here and stop him, Sahara said, feeling the cold steel of resolve hardening out her fear and panic. *I will make sure he can't get to you, and I'll get Jared and Rafe out of this mess. As soon as I have them secured, we'll come home. In the meantime, do what you can there. Just be careful.*

Deor's serious, steady eyes—eyes that reminded her so much of her own face in the mirror—met hers. A resigned smile flickered briefly across his lips.

Somehow I knew you were going to say that, he said. *I just hope you know you may be too late.*

TWELVE

DEOR SIGHED and ran a hand through his hair in frustration.

"No, no!" he shouted. "Stop!"

The twenty young trainees immediately sat back and took their rifles from their shoulders. A staggered clattering stuttered through the mid-morning air as the recruits set their weapons on the tables beside them. Weapons secure, they stared straight ahead, eyes locked on the targets down range. Deor strode along the line, hearing the soft exhales of relief as he passed without speaking.

He stopped at the very end of the line, just behind the youngest member of his training class. The girl's long blonde hair was swept back into an elegant twist that would have been more fitting for a ball than a morning at the firing range. Her rifle lay beside her on the table, the line of the barrel perfectly parallel to the table's edge. She never moved, but Deor saw the muscles in her neck stiffen. She was waiting for the ax to fall.

Deor sighed again.

"What's your name, soldier?" he asked.

"Aria. Sir."

Deor sniffed. "Pick up the rifle, Aria."

She obeyed, seating the gun against her shoulder and preparing to fire.

"Fire."

She hesitated, then squeezed the trigger.

"Clear it and set it down."

Aria obeyed, then sat quietly. Deor turned to the rest of the recruits, who were all watching this exchange with interest. Aria was the only girl in the group, and while most of the trainees regarded her with a kind of grudging respect, she also received her share of insults and sneers. She weathered it with grace—something she'd learned while she'd been working in Brogan's tavern. On the night they'd arrived in Askalon, she'd been in the group of women huddled under the street light. The group his sister had rescued. The memory made him smile.

As soon as the Triumvirate was gone, she'd approached Deor about being a part of the militia.

Sahara's influence again, I'd bet, he thought.

And she was like Sahara too in her unquenchable spirit. There was just one area where she seemed to have an issue.

"Someone tell me what went wrong with that little drill," he said to the rest of the troops.

Aria's face flushed scarlet and he felt a small twinge at calling her out in front of everyone. *But if she's in combat with these boys, their lives will depend on her. They've got to accept her, and she's got to get these issues worked out.*

One of the recruits raised his hand. "Sir? She missed the target."

Several of the boys sniggered, but Deor stared the speaker down. "No, she didn't. Perhaps I should send you to medical to have your eyes checked. Or don't you know a bullseye when you see one?"

The boy ducked his head and the sniggering stopped abruptly.

"Anyone have a serious suggestion?" Deor asked.

"Sir?" A tall, quiet boy near the other end of the row raised his hand. "She hesitated, sir. When you said fire, she hesitated."

Deor nodded. "That's right. Don't ever hesitate. Ever." His gaze swept over the recruits, lighting at last on Aria's upturned face. "Understand? You hesitate, you die. Your friends die. When you need to pull that trigger, you pull it. And if you can't square yourself with what happens on the other end of this weapon, then you need to walk away." He paused. "All right. Pack it up. Dismissed."

He turned away and headed back to the training pavilion some distance away from the firing range. He saw a figure standing just inside the pavilion, watching the exercise. As Deor ducked under the awning, the man came forward. It was Derrek. They clasped hands and Derrek followed Deor as he made for the refreshments table.

"I'm hungry," Deor said to no one in particular. He piled a trencher full of dried meat and bread and selected a ripe fruit from the heap in the center of the table. The he shoved a bottle of ale into one of the utility pockets of his combat pants. He carried his food to a small table in the corner of the pavilion and sat down. Derrek slid into the chair across from him.

"You've got a good class this time, it seems," Derrek said.

"I do. I do." Deor gnawed thoughtfully on a piece of jerky. "They're good kids."

Derrek snorted. "Kids? Most of them are your age, Deor."

Deor wrinkled his nose and pried the cap off the ale using the edge of the table. "I have an old soul."

Derrek laughed. "Well, they respect you, and that's what matters in these things, I guess." He paused while Deor took a draught from the bottle. "You know, I'm amazed that Brogan was able to get his brewing business back up and running so quickly. Never met a man so passionate about his ales."

"It shows. Never tasted better in my life." Deor wiped his mouth and regarded Derrek for a moment. "But I doubt you came here to discuss my recruits...or Brogan's ales."

A smile flashed across Derrek's face, catching in the scar on his right cheek. "No, I didn't."

He glanced around the pavilion, watching the recruits for a moment as they filed through the food line and filtered to the different tables scattered under the shelter of the tent. Then he leaned across the table, lowering his voice almost to a whisper.

"Something's not right, Deor. I can feel it. Where is Jared's team, I'd like to know? And where's that louse Gervais got to? Do we have answers? No. Just more and more questions." He sat back, scowling, and ran a hand through his hair in frustration.

Deor measured him as he munched his fruit. There was a traitor on Askalon. And who could be trusted? "Well, I hope you don't think I've got any answers."

"No, I don't suppose you do. But we run the damn military, you and I. You'd think they'd give us something...how are we supposed to prepare for contingencies with zero information?"

"I think," Deor answered slowly, "that we prepare for contingencies no matter what information we have. We should prepare for Halcyon to come after us...we have no reason to think they won't. We should prepare for upheaval and unrest...Kalkas is still finding pockets of the former slave population that are getting Demon's Breath off the black market." He shrugged. "What more do you want to know?"

Derrek swore softly. "Really? This is you talking to me right now? You can't tell me that you don't chafe at the way we've been pushed out of the inner circle, Deor. Especially when your sister is out there somewhere running errands for a bunch of fools."

Deor arched an eyebrow. "I'd be careful with that talk if I were you. It's usually dangerous."

"What? We don't live under the Triumvirate any longer, or have you forgotten that? Are the Lords of Askalon a tyranny now, where a man can't express his frustration?"

Deor sniffed and studied the half-eaten fruit in his hand. "I'd just be careful," he said, thoughts of the traitor turning over in his mind again. He glanced at Derrek for a moment, then dismissed the suspicion. Derrek was a hard man, a soldier. He was strong and independent-minded, a man who liked straight answers to straight questions. He was no traitor.

"What are you getting at, Derrek?"

"Like this case of Gervais," Derrek said. "We know the guy was a spy and a rat. And someone let him loose...and now we can't find him. That doesn't bother you? And shouldn't that bother Aelred, at least?"

"Maybe he has bigger problems right now."

Derrek snorted. "Like picking out a wedding dress for his daughter, you mean?"

Deor winced inwardly and sighed. Aelred had finally sent for his family three weeks ago, as soon as he felt certain that Askalon was stable enough for their safety. His daughter Genny was betrothed to one of Aelred's captains, and she had no sooner landed on Askalon than wedding preparations had begun in earnest. Aelred seemed consumed by the ceremony, neglecting many of his duties as head of the Council of Lords, leaving many of those duties to Brytnoth instead.

"I've got nothing to say about that," Deor said after a moment. "The man's distracted. It happens."

"Deor. It doesn't just happen to the ruler of a damn planet. Or it shouldn't. And if it does, well...."

"That's why there's a Council, Derrek. Brytnoth's handling things."

"Right. I forgot."

Deor glanced at him sharply, but Derrek's eyes were focused intently on the firing range. "What is it that you want, Derrek? What is it that they aren't giving you?"

"I don't want anything except some decisive leadership. We're on the brink of war with Halcyon and we keep having food shortages. Our trade routes aren't fully re-established, and I don't want to run out of bullets if Halcyon comes knocking on our door. You get what I'm saying here, Deor? Maybe it's time for someone else to run things for a while."

"You're on the Council, Derrek," Deor said. "If you have grievances, you should air them at the meeting tomorrow."

"I need another vote to carry the motion," Derrek said.

So we come to the point at last, Deor thought. "You want me to second your motion to...do what exactly?"

Now Derrek did lower his voice to a whisper. "I plan to move to disband the Council and to appoint you and I to run things until the Halcyon threat is resolved."

Deor set his bottle carefully on the table and rotated it between his fingers. "Oh, is that all?" Derrek stared at him in confusion, and Deor chuckled. "A joke, my friend. But I'm afraid I can't second such a motion. I didn't come here to set myself up as a dictator."

"You wouldn't be a dictator, Deor! We'd run things together...we're both men of action. Men of vision."

"Men of the hangman's noose for talking treason."

"Damn it, Deor, I'm not talking treason!"

"No need to get angry about it," Deor said smoothly. "I just think we're jumping too hastily to a drastic solution, that's all. Why don't you try airing your complaints first and see what happens?"

"And if nothing happens? What then?"

Deor shrugged. "Then we'll have to see." He pushed back his chair and stood. Derrek followed suit slowly, and Deor could see that he was profoundly unsatisfied with the result of their conversation. "I've got to get back to my trainees," Deor said, holding out his hand. "But I'll see you tomorrow, yeah?"

Derrek clasped his hand. "Yeah."

Deor turned on his heel and left the tent, heading back for the firing range. He tried to keep his stride even and casual, even though his heart and mind were racing.

Is Derrek the traitor? Could he be the one? Or... He hesitated, not even wanting to frame the thought into words. But he had to consider every possibility. *Or is this distraction of the wedding just Aelred's cover?*

Derrek's point about Aelred's failure to share information was a valid one. They were supposed to run things as a Council, but more often than not Aelred kept any news close to the vest. Was it just a result of incompetence or insecurity? Or was it symptomatic of a much bigger problem?

But what interest would Aelred have in betraying his own people? He orchestrated this whole thing, after all. He's the one who assembled the armies to overthrow the Triumvirate. He's the one who sent back the zanthos. It doesn't make any sense.

But at a certain point it didn't have to make sense to be reality. What if Aelred had set the whole thing up? What if he had brought them all here to get the Triumvirate out of the way so that he could establish himself for his own ends? And what if it was just a matter of time before he made good on his original intentions?

Deor shook his head and sighed. "I hate politics," he muttered. "Why can't they just leave me out of all this?"

But, as the man in charge of the citizen militia, he had to be more involved than everyone else. For a moment, he felt a flash of regret. In that glowing moment of victory, when he'd stood on the summit of Taur Isis and watched the works of the Triumvirate come down in smoke and fire, he'd wanted to be part of all this. He'd wanted to help rebuild Askalon, wanted to make himself a homeworld and a new life.

"I thought I was going to be world-building," he thought. "Not chasing after ghosts and refereeing internecine squabbles."

And he knew—better than Derrek could possibly imagine—just how badly things had gone for Jared, Sahara, and Rafe. Rafe had nearly been killed, Jared was a prisoner, and Sahara was a fugitive. And there was no way he could help them...not directly. He paced deliberately down the firing line, focusing his mind on making sure everything was in order for the next exercise. Anything else would make him mad with anxiety and frustration.

"Sir?"

Deor spun to see Aria just behind him. She was flushed and he noticed that her hands were clenched into fists at her sides. Whatever she had to say, he reasoned, it had her completely worked up. "What do you want?" he asked, his voice sharper than he meant it to be. "I'm not ready for the next drill yet."

"I...oh. I'm—sorry, sir." She hesitated for a moment, then turned to go.

"Stop. You obviously have something on your mind. Please say what you came to say."

She glanced at him, and seeing that he meant what he said, she continued, "I just...why did you have to call me out in front of the rest of the men, sir? I have enough problems with them already. They think I'm—well, they think I'm no good, sir. Because I'm a girl."

Deor sighed. "The best damn soldier I've ever known is a girl," he said. "Don't let those idiots get you down. You've got talent. You're an excellent shot—better than most of them—and you've got a clear head. I'm proud to have you as part of my corps. But you've got to get yourself straight here." He pointed to his breast. "You second-guess yourself and hesitate when you should charge."

"No one thinks I should be here, sir," Aria said, and Deor could hear the tears straining her voice. "Maybe I should just...you know. Quit."

Deor studied her thoughtfully. "Is that what *you* want? Or do you imagine you'd be gratifying me and everyone else if you drop out?"

Aria dropped her eyes, digging in the scraggly turf with the toe of her combat boot.

"Cut that out," Deor snapped. "I'm asking you a direct question, soldier."

Aria jerked her foot back and stood a little straighter, but she still did not raise her eyes to meet his gaze. "I...really don't know, sir."

"I'll give you until the end of the day to figure it out," he said. "If you haven't made a decision, I'm kicking you out. Is that understood?"

Aria nodded mutely, and Deor left her standing there. *She has so much potential. If only she'd stop caring so much what other people think about her.*

He couldn't help wondering if Sahara had ever struggled with self-doubt. He had missed her entire childhood—hell, he had missed his own childhood. He couldn't remember their parents. But from the little that Sahara had said, he knew that she had worshipped their father. And she seemed to be able to bury whatever insecurities she had underneath that strange mixture of bad temper and rage.

He smiled in spite of himself.

"Sir!" someone called from behind him.

"What now?" Deor muttered, turning to see who was pursuing him.

It was a page from the Great House, not one of his trainees. Deor stopped to let the man catch up to him, then waited while he sucked wind and tried to get enough breath to deliver his message.

"Maybe you should start jogging a little every day," Deor remarked, watching him with amusement. "It's good for the health, you know."

The page glared at him as he straightened. "Lord Aelred has asked for the Council to assemble this afternoon," he said, his voice still a bit breathless. "He asks you to report in one hour."

"I thought the Council was meeting tomorrow."

"No, sir. This afternoon."

"Did he give a reason for the meeting?"

"A message has come from Halcyon."

THIRTEEN

AS DEOR ENTERED the council chamber, he nodded to Brytnoth, who was already seated at the large round table. Kalkas and Brogan were already there as well, sitting across from Brytnoth and looking thoughtful, as if they had just finished a conversation with a question to which that neither knew the answer. Deor realized with a jolt of surprise that he had barely seen any of them except at these few meetings. Aelred kept them all incredibly busy...so busy that they never had time to meet.

Is that orchestrated on purpose? What is he afraid of?

He slid into the chair beside Brytnoth and smiled at him. "How are you?" he asked. "Haven't seen much of you lately."

Brytnoth shook his head, glancing surreptitiously around the room. "Things aren't going well, my friend. Not well at all."

He snapped his mouth shut again as Derrek entered the room, and Deor saw that Brytnoth's eyes followed Derrek wherever he went. He did very little to conceal the dark light of suspicion in his eyes, and Deor frowned.

"What's with you and Derrek?" he asked in a low whisper. "Something I should know about?"

Brytnoth's gaze swiveled to his face and he gave a curt shake of his head. "It's nothing." Then, after a moment's hesitation, he added, "Not now. Not here."

Deor sat back in his chair, stifling a sigh. He didn't have time to contemplate the fissures that seemed to be widening in the Council, for at that moment Aelred entered the room. He looked grave, and his hair was almost completely silver now. Deep lines had weathered his features and made him look even older, and Deor noticed that there were dark circles under his eyes, as if he weren't sleeping.

The job is taking its toll. That, or guilt is eating him alive.

"My friends," Aelred said, clearing his throat once or twice. "After a long period of no news from our team deployed to Halcyon, we have finally received word."

Kalkas sat forward eagerly. "From Sahara?" he asked. "How are the negotiations progressing?"

Aelred's face lost the rest of its color. "No. Not from Sahara."

"Who sends us word, then?" asked Brogan.

"Lord Azimir," said Aelred.

"But why should he communicate with us directly when we have representatives on Halcyon already?" Derrek demanded. "What's going on here, Aelred?"

Deor clenched his jaw, knowing very well what was coming.

"Let me share his message with you," Aelred answered. He cleared his throat again. He took a small cartridge from the sleeve of his tunic. He pressed a small button on the side of the table and fed the cartridge into the slot.

A hologram of Azimir flickered into view on the tabletop, and the image bowed. "From Azimir, Lord of Halcyon, to Aelred and the Lords of Askalon, greeting and good health to you."

"Pompous ass," muttered Brytnoth.

Aelred glanced at him in some exasperation as the hologram continued, "We would have you know that we have rejected utterly the terms which you propose for the mitigation of the Triumvirate's contract and debts. We find your offer repulsive and insulting. Until such time as you make payment in full per our original agreement with the Triumvirate, we will hold Jared Alareth and Rafe Margolis in custody. Your failure to comply will assuredly result in their deaths. You have six weeks to deliver our weapons and the *zanthos* as promised. If, at the end of this time, you have not delivered our payment, we will deliver the bodies of your friends with our armada. Peace be to you."

The image bowed again, flickered, and disappeared. For a few moments, no one said anything at all.

"He didn't say anything about Sahara," Brytnoth said finally. "What's happened to her?"

Deor bit his lip and said nothing. Aelred, he noticed, was looking more and more wretched, and though he could easily relieve him of his discomfort by sharing what he knew, he decided that such information was better kept to himself. He wanted to see how Aelred would handle things.

"I don't know," Aelred was saying. "Azimir doesn't mention her, and it's impossible to know what that means. But I have to believe that if she were dead, he would have taken the opportunity to use that as a further goad to our cooperation. No, it's my guess that she managed to escape somehow."

"He's going to regret that," Kalkas said, a small smile flickering around his mouth. "She's not the kind of girl to take kindly to her friends being held hostage."

"But if she has escaped," Derrek protested, "then why hasn't she found a way to get home again? Or at least to send word that she is alive?"

Aelred shook his head. "I don't know the answer to that. But who knows what her circumstances might be? It's possible that she may not have access to communications equipment at all...and she may have had no way to get back to the ship."

"Believe me," Deor said, "if she felt the need to send word, she'd have found a way to do so. Maybe she just wants to lay low for a while."

"So what are we going to do about this, Aelred?" Derrek asked. "Leave Sahara out of this for a moment. He's still holding Jared and Rafe hostage. What are you willing to give to save their lives?"

Aelred hesitated, and then said, "I don't know, Derrek. I just don't know."

Deor felt the slow burn of anger begin to course through his veins. *The man can't make a decision to save his life right now...not to mention anyone else's. What the hell has happened to him? Maybe Derrek is right...maybe it is time for a no-confidence vote.*

"Well, you can't hand over the *zanthos*," Brytnoth said, cutting through Deor's thoughts. "It's gone, as you told us last week. And we destroyed the weapons. So it seems to me that we've got six weeks to figure out how to tell Azimir to go ahead and kill our friends."

Deor was surprised by the sharpness in Brytnoth's voice, and he realized that his friend was probably even more disillusioned in Aelred's failure to keep things together than everyone else. The problems went beyond the disappearance of the *zanthos* and the rogue behavior of Halcyon—though these were bad enough. But food shortages in Pentapolis were starting to cause unrest, and a vigorous black market trade in Demon's Breath had sprung up in the aftermath of the revolution. Pockets of petty gangs threatened the peace and disrupted the operations of the city. And Aelred, it seemed, was doing nothing about any of it. He just sat there.

If he put half as much energy into fixing these problems as he did into pretending they didn't exist, we'd be well on our way, Deor thought, shaking his head. But then Aelred had to open his mouth.

"Maybe there's still hope for negoti—"

"Are you kidding me?" Derrek snapped. "Jared and Rafe are being held hostage, Sahara is God only knows where, and you think these people will listen to our excuses and our pathetic groveling and sniveling and begging for leniency?"

Aelred stared at Derrek for a moment, looking thoroughly taken aback. "I only meant that perhaps we'll think of some way to extricate ourselves from this mess and save their lives in the process," he said.

"I think the time for negotiations is over, Aelred," Brogan said.

"Then what would you have me do?" Aelred's temper at last gave way, and his voice rose as he slammed his fists down on the table. "What would you have me do?"

"We need to get our armies ready for war," Derrek said, folding his arms across his chest. "They give us no alternative. And we need to turn Deor's militia on these street gangs who are trafficking drugs and disrupting the food supply. Lethal force will get things in order."

"What about Jared and Rafe?" Kalkas asked. "Would you just prepare for war and abandon them, then?"

"No. But if Sahara did manage to escape, then I'll leave the rescue operation in her more than capable hands. She's resourceful enough; she should be able to come up with something. And there's nothing we can do about their situation from here. Sending another team to Halcyon after what's happened is unthinkable. Whoever else goes will suffer the same fate, if not worse. Azimir is no fool. He'll be expecting us to send a team in to rescue them. He'll be waiting for them."

"You're very quiet, Deor," Aelred said suddenly, rounding on him with a fierceness that made Deor flinch. "It's your sister we're talking about here...have you nothing to add to our discussion?"

Deor sat quietly for a moment, considering possible responses. "Based on the message from Azimir, I agree that Sahara probably escaped. And I agree that it's foolish to send another team to Halcyon to rescue Jared and Rafe. If I know my sister, she's gnawing on that little problem already, and she's more than capable of getting them out of harm's way. I also agree with Derrek that our best strategy right now is probably to prepare for a direct assault on Askalon. We have nothing to offer Azimir that will be acceptable, and he doesn't seem like the type to simply wipe the slate clean for the sake of cama- raderie. We should accelerate the training programs for the militia and begin evacuation drills of Pentapolis."

Beside him, Brytnoth was nodding slowly. "I second that," he said. "I'd just add that we should step up our initiative to find the traitors who stole the *zanthos* before we find ourselves thoroughly double-crossed."

"And how do you suggest we do that?" Derrek asked, leaning back in his chair and folding his arms across his chest.

Brytnoth's eyes flickered at him. "No need to get testy," he said. "Someone let that rat Gervais out of prison, and someone must have seen him. That's where we should start, I think."

"Good, good," Aelred said. "Brytnoth, you'll head up the task force to hunt him down and find out who stole the *zanthos*. Whatever you need, you have it. This is a top priority."

Deor fixed his eyes on the table. Why did Aelred's words sound like those of a man desperate to look in charge of a situation that had spiraled completely out of his control? It was tragic and laughable all at the same time.

"Deor," Aelred continued, "whatever spare time you have, I want you helping Brytnoth. Derrek will oversee military operations and put together an evacuation plan for the city. And Kalkas, I need you and Brogan to investigate the causes of these food shortages. Where are the supply caravans, I should like to know? Do we need to increase our imports from neighboring planets? What can be done to mitigate the effects of this growing famine?"

Kalkas muttered something under his breath about being a healer, not a grocer or a civic leader, but Brogan nodded his head. "Consider it done, Aelred."

"Good. We'll meet again in three days. I want progress! I expect progress." He swept his eyes sternly over the assembled group, and then he strode out of the room.

There was a collective exhale as soon as the door closed behind him.

"I told you, Deor," Derrek said, jabbing a finger in Deor's direction. "I told you. The man's lost his grip. He doesn't deserve to lead Askalon. He never did."

Brytnoth started in surprise. "Treason, Derrek? Is that what we've come to, and so soon? You miss the old Triumvirate days, do you?"

Derrek glared at him. "What do you know?"

"I don't understand this!" Kalkas put in. "What are you saying, Derrek? What else would you have the man do?"

"He's not *doing* anything, Kalkas," Deor said quietly. "That's the problem."

"He is, though," Brogan argued. "He's delegating tasks and following up...that's what leaders do, isn't it?"

Deor laughed grimly. "Oh, well, it would just be nice to see him out there taking some initiative, that's all. Take this food shortage problem. It's gotten worse these last two weeks, and what has he done? He calls meetings. We discuss the problem. 'Look, Aelred, people don't have enough food to eat.' 'Oh, study that problem and find out what's going on. Then report back to me.' Where's the drive to solve the problem? We don't need scholars or researchers. The people don't have enough food to eat. The *zanthos* is missing. Our friends are being held hostage. And Halcyon is preparing for war. How damned complicated is this?"

"Right," Derrek said. "That's exactly what I mean. We need a leader, someone who will take initiative."

"And you think you're that person, do you?" asked Brytnoth. "You want to tear him down and prop yourself up in his place, is that it?"

For the first time since Deor had known him, Derrek actually looked flustered. "No. No, that's not what I want at all. I just want what's best for Askalon. You know that."

"No, I don't. Because it seems to me that what Askalon needs most right now is stability. And throwing Aelred out is not fostering stability. That shows division and projects weakness. How are we supposed to make a convincing stand against Halcyon if we're squabbling among ourselves like this?"

Derrek scowled at the table. "Deor knows my mind on this," he muttered.

"Derrek, look," said Deor. "While I sympathize with your impatience, Brytnoth's right. We've got to throw our support behind Aelred, at least for the moment. Once this situation with Halcyon is diffused and Askalon's on the road to security and prosperity, then we can discuss changes to the leadership. But if we have to prop Aelred up a little longer for the sake of Askalon, then we need to do it."

Derrek shoved his chair back from the table and stood abruptly. "And what if he's the traitor, Deor?"

Deor heard the others' sharp gasps, and he sighed and shrugged his shoulders. "Well, then that's a different story, I suppose."

"Do you have any evidence for that, or are you just flinging accusations?" Brytnoth demanded. "You know, you're really starting to wear on my nerves."

"Like I care," Derrek fired back. "What are you, an old grandmother with a kerchief tied around her stringy gray hairs? Just make sure you're prepared to investigate thoroughly, no matter where the trail leads."

Without waiting for Brytnoth's response, he stalked out of the room. Kalkas and Brogan trailed silently after him, leaving Brytnoth and Deor alone.

"What an ass," Brytnoth said, shoving back from the table. "What did Sahara ever see in him, anyway?" He swore under his breath. "I can't stand the man. He's insufferable."

"He's definitely challenged in the tact department, I'll give you that," Deor agreed. "But he is one hell of a military commander, Brytnoth. I think that must be what she saw in him."

"He always did have an insubordinate streak. I just thought he would have a little more loyalty. But men like that..." He shook his head. "They're great for overthrowing regimes, not so much for establishing them."

"Do you think he's dangerous, though? Really?" Deor asked.

"I don't know." Brytnoth's face was grim. "But there's someone out there who is."

"He is right about one thing," Deor said, lowering his voice, "We've got to find that traitor...no matter who it is or where we might find him."

"I have some ideas on where we can start looking. Whoever let

Gervais free is probably also tied in with the disappearance of the *zanthos*. It can't be coincidence that he went missing and then the *zanthos* was stolen. And there weren't that many people who knew that it was secured on Perseon." He paused and then added, "Do you remember Dirk, Alberic's brother?"

"That nasty fellow on Perseon? Yes, I remember him. And I remember Gwyn warned us about him. She said he had a lot of dangerous friends on Askalon and elsewhere." He rubbed his chin thoughtfully. "Do you think he's involved?"

"I think it's a good place to start asking questions."

"Won't he be long gone by now? If he had anything to do with the theft of the *zanthos*, I can't imagine he's still hanging around on Perseon."

"He might be gone already. But maybe someone there knows where he might have gone. And anyway, we won't know until we get there."

Deor smiled up at him. "So when do we leave?"

FOURTEEN

SAHARA HUDDLED on the fur rug, staring at the cold ashes in the small brazier that warmed her tent in the evenings. She had her blanket wrapped tightly around her shoulders, arms hugging her knees to her chest. The dawn had come an hour ago, but she hadn't moved all night. She had watched the coals burn to ashes as the light around her grew, and as she took a deep breath and stirred, she felt her muscles cry out in protest.

A light tapping came from the tent flap, and she ran a hand though her tangled curls. "Yes?" she called.

Rigel poked his head through the opening and frowned when he saw her sitting on the ground. "What are you doing?" he asked. "Can I come in?"

She made a half-hearted gesture of welcome and he slipped inside, crouching on his heels as he always did. He sat silently for a few moments, an expression of expectation on his face. When she said nothing, he leaned forward to catch her eye.

"Zelie? Why are you on the floor? Have you been here all night?"

Sahara stretched her legs, groaning softly at the stiffness in her muscles. "Yes."

"But why?"

"I was trying to think." She flashed him a wretched smile. "Not succeeding much, but trying."

He frowned and nodded, concern in his eyes. "Are you unhappy here? Is Iris nagging you?"

Sahara laughed. "Oh, Iris. She never stops nagging. But it doesn't bother me...not much, anyway."

"She's been worse since we moved camp," Rigel observed. "Since you saved Aron's daughters from the Scythes." His eyes flickered at her, and there was a mischievous teasing in their depths. "I think she's jealous of you."

Sahara snorted. "I'm nobody that anybody should envy. Ever. And if they do envy me, it's because they have no idea..." Her voice trailed off, and she rubbed her legs slowly.

"No idea what?"

Sahara met his gaze. "What it's like to be cursed."

Rigel's face paled slightly, and Sahara noticed that he shuffled ever so slightly away from her. "What curse? Why should you be cursed?"

Sahara shook her head and tried to smile. She didn't know how she could even begin to explain something she barely understood herself. Instead of answering his question, she decided to change the subject. "Isn't Brig supposed to be bringing my horse? What's taking him so long?"

"We get our horses from the south, Zelie. From the farming province of Ash. Since Azimir found out that the Elenni use horses, he's tried to restrict the trade. We only get a very few, and most are stocky, shaggy beasts only fit for pulling wagons. Market day in Aquila was yesterday, and Brig said that he was promised a horse. Don't worry. I'm sure he'll be here soon." He studied her quizzically. "Why did you agree to do it? To ride with the Elenni?"

"What else am I good for?" Sahara asked, winking at him. "You saw how good I was with the goats."

"But that can be learned, Zelie! I could teach you to care for the livestock. I could teach you to harvest—"

Sahara felt her stomach turn. "I want nothing to do with that foul business," she snapped. "I've seen first-hand what it does to people, and I will have no part in it."

Rigel shrugged, seemingly unperturbed. "Then learn to tend the cookfires with Yasmin!"

"And work all day with Iris?" Sahara asked. "Are you kidding me?"

"Well...there is one other thing." He shifted, looking suddenly uncomfortable. "Perhaps Katarina would take you as a student."

"Oh? And what could she teach me?"

"She is a skilled healer."

Sahara swallowed hard. A rush of so many confused emotions flooded over her, and she felt her throat constrict suddenly. Rigel, watching her closely, peered into her face.

"Are you all right, Zelie? Is it something I said?"

"N-no," Sahara managed. "It's just...it's nothing. I didn't know she took apprentices."

"She doesn't. Well, not usually. But perhaps she'd make an exception for you. You could ask her."

"I thought you told me to stay away from her, Rigel."

"I did not. I told you not to spy on her. You haven't been spying on her again, have you?"

Sahara laughed. "No."

"Good. Then go and talk to her. Tell her you want to learn the healing arts."

"Why don't you want me riding with the Elenni?" Sahara asked. "Why are you so keen to keep me away from them?"

Rigel flushed. "I don't care, really. You'll do as you wish, I'm sure. And you didn't die on your first day, so you obviously have some skill. Or just dumb luck. Not sure which. Anyway, I just...they're mixed up in things. Grandfather tolerates them, but they always bring trouble. You seem to have enough of that already." He paused, then cocked a bright eye at Sahara. "You never told me why you were sitting on the ground all night."

"No, I didn't." Sahara grinned at him. "I'm just...I don't know what to do. I'm worried for my friends, and I'm afraid of what's happening back...back at home. And Jessup said something about some kind of prophecy. Something dark and terrifying, and I don't know what to believe any longer."

Rigel rubbed his jaw. "It seems you need some breakfast," he said matter-of-factly. "I find that most times a crisis of faith is a sign of an empty stomach."

Sahara stared at him, then broke into a laugh. "Are you serious?"

"Well," Rigel answered, "in a way. You'll see things more clearly with food in your belly. And you should go see Katarina." He got to his feet. "Go and see her. After breakfast. Which is ready, by the way."

He ducked out of the tent, leaving Sahara thoroughly bemused.

Crazy kid. He reminds me of Deor.

The thought of her brother brought all her confusion and misery rushing back, and she pushed herself to her feet and into a stretch. She folded her blanket on her pallet and pulled on her boots. She tried to comb out her hair with her fingers, but gave up after a short struggle. She tied it back in a loose knot and dragged her jacket over her halter top. Then she fastened her tent flap open and made for the porridge line that wound around the center of the camp.

This new campsite was in the middle of a series of undulating hills. There were several copses of trees within a few hundred yards of their position, and Sahara wondered for the second or third time since they had arrived why they didn't make camp under the shelter of the trees.

Especially since it looks like rain.

Sahara glanced up at the lowering clouds. Rigel had told her that it didn't often rain in Aquila, especially now, as they were heading into the dry season. But it rained just enough, apparently, for the Demon's Breath plants to thrive.

"Why aren't we camping under the trees?" she said, turning to the person standing behind her.

She almost recoiled. Katarina stood there, her face placid, but her eyes hard and glittering. Sahara was not easily intimidated by anything, but something in that woman's eyes made her cringe inside.

"Sorry," Sahara gulped. "I didn't know—"

"So you just start talking before you have any idea who is there to listen?" Katarina said, her voice as hard as the edge in her eyes.

"No, not usually," Sahara mumbled. "I was just trying to make...small talk." She hated how insignificant this woman made her feel.

Why does Rigel think studying with her would be a good idea?

"Small talk. A nice way of trying to excuse the fact that you're bothering everyone around you with your ridiculous comments."

"If I'd known you were standing there, I wouldn't have said anything at all," Sahara flared back. "God forbid you might actually have to speak to another human being."

A sudden and breathtakingly beautiful smile flashed across Katarina's face. Sahara's brows knitted in confusion. She had to hurry to catch up to the person in front of her, but then she turned back to Katarina.

"What's so funny?" she demanded.

"You have a lot of spirit," Katarina answered. "Not like most of these girls. They wilt if I frown at them. But you...there's something different about you."

"I'm not from around here."

"So I noticed."

"And I don't scare easily, either." Sahara hesitated, then decided to plunge ahead. "Rigel tells me that you're a healer. I used to be—I studied with someone once." She faltered as she thought of Jared and Aliya and the Halls of Healing in Albadir, but then she took a breath and added, "Would you teach me?"

Now it was Katarina's turn to look completely surprised. "I've never taken an apprentice," she said thoughtfully, and she measured

Sahara with a sharp and critical eye. "Do you know anything of the art?"

"I can tie a mean field dressing," Sahara said. "And I know a little of herbs...but not as much as I'd like."

"You carry much pain with you," Katarina said suddenly. "Much sadness."

"How do you know that?" Sahara snapped, folding her arms across her chest.

Katarina laughed quietly and gently uncrossed Sahara's arms. "I won't attack you, so you needn't put up your defenses. To answer your question, I see it in your eyes. Believe me, I recognize a wounded soul when I see one." She looked over Sahara's shoulder and nodded her head. "It's your turn," she said.

Sahara turned and saw that she was holding up the entire line. She darted forward, snatched her bowl and trencher from the long table, and scurried to the cauldron. Isis was manning the ladle as usual, and Sahara felt her nerves crawl.

"Holding up the line again, I see," sneered Isis. "What, Yasmin didn't have you milk the goats again this morning?"

"No," Sahara said, biting her tongue on the rest of what she wanted to say. But she couldn't stop the thought. *While you stand here and stir mush, I'll be riding with the Elenni.* "No, I'm no good at such things," she said, angry with herself for letting Isis annoy her so thoroughly.

"Yes, so I heard. Destined for better things, are we? Well. Let me give you a piece of advice." She slapped the porridge into Sahara's bowl, then raised her fierce dark eyes to meet Sahara's own. "Milking goats has a longer life expectancy than riding with the Elenni. So I hope you're ready to die."

Sahara lifted her chin. "Been ready. Don't burn yourself."

Behind her, she heard Katarina chuckling, but she didn't dare turn around. She marched out of the tent circle and made her way to the shelter of the nearest group of scrubby trees, dropping cross-legged under a wide branch. To her surprise, Katarina joined her with her own bowl a moment later. She gestured to the open space beside Sahara.

"Mind if I join you?" she asked.

"Suit yourself."

Katarina arranged herself on the ground, and Sahara was struck suddenly by the other woman's elegance. Her dress was as rough as anyone else's in the Hazad tribe, but she wore it with astonishing grace.

Almost as if she weren't born to this.

"Where are you from?" Sahara asked. "You don't belong to Jessup's tribe."

"No, I don't," Katarina said, her voice wistful. "Or, I didn't. Not until he took me in. Originally I was from another one of the Hazad tribes. But I spent most of my youth in Aquila, in the Great House."

That explains her bearing. She's spent too much time among the nobility.

"And when...when it was time for me to leave the city, I wanted to stay close by. Jessup's tribe is the closest to Aquila, and he let me join his family."

"Why would you want to stay close to the city?" Sahara asked through a mouthful of porridge. "Most of the Hazad seem to hate the very name of the place."

"It was my home for so long, and...I had other reasons."

Sahara's memory flashed back to the morning of the Scythe attacks, when she had seen Katarina returning from the direction of the city. *What was she doing that morning, I wonder?*

"Doesn't Jessup forbid his people from going to the city?"

"Yes."

Sahara turned and fixed Katarina with a piercing stare. "Then why do you go?"

Katarina's trencher clattered in her bowl, and she carefully picked it up again. "How do you know that I do?"

Sahara grinned. "I saw you coming back from the north the other morning. Before the Scythes attacked. I didn't know for sure that you had been to Aquila, not until you just confirmed it for me right now."

Katarina's face grew suddenly pale. "You think you're very clever, don't you?"

"Not particularly. But I've got a nose for trouble, you might say. And I can put two and two together. What I can't figure out, though, is why. Why would you go in the first place, and why would you sneak off at night?"

Katarina studied her. "I don't sneak. Jessup knows that I go."

"So why the need for so much secrecy, then?"

"To protect the rest of the tribe." She turned her gaze on the knots of families scattered around the camp. "I would not bring harm to them for all the world. And they fear Aquila. Fear it and hate it. But I don't. I can't."

"Why not?"

Katarina swung around to meet Sahara's gaze. "Perhaps someday I might tell you that," she said. "But not yet."

"Does Jessup know why?"

"Yes. But he keeps my secret for me." She smiled fondly. "He is a good and generous man. I've never known a better. You should feel blessed that he has welcomed you into his tribe and his family so readily. Not all have been so fortunate."

"Look," Sahara said. "Jessup may have welcomed me, but that doesn't mean the rest of his family likes it. Iris hates me, and so do several of Jessup's sons. That's why I'm riding with the Elenni. That...and other reasons."

"What other reasons could there be?"

Sahara glanced at her. "Maybe someday I'll tell you that. But not yet."

Katarina's face broke into a slow, bright smile and she rose. "Come to my tent this afternoon for your first lesson," she said.

FIFTEEN

SAHARA SQUATTED DOWN near a small patch of ugly brown weeds and sighed. She wondered if Jared had ever rebelled against Childir's attempts to teach him herb lore.

Rebellion never really seemed to suit him. But maybe I was wrong about that too.

She prodded the little plants and detached two of the milky white buds, then moved for a third. She swore when the entire third plant, roots and all, came up with her gentle tug. She sat back on her heels and flung it as far across the plain as she could manage. She saw the small spray of earth as the clod exploded on contact with the ground a short distance away. Her horse, placidly cropping the short grass nearby, lifted his head and snorted.

"What are you looking at?" she said, frowning at him. He snorted again and went back to his lunch. "Well, two will just have to do," Sahara muttered, thrusting the pods into the small pouch she wore at her belt. "There aren't any more of these stupid plants around here."

She rose and shaded her eyes, looking toward the north. Far in the distance, the rays of the setting sun glistened from the towers and minarets of Aquila in a golden shimmer. Her horse butted her shoulder affectionately, and she absently patted his strong neck and ruffled his dark mane.

In the week since Katarina had taken her as an apprentice, Sahara had managed to find a delicate balance between her duties as an Elenni runner and her studies of healing. She had shown Katarina that she wasn't afraid to work hard, and Katarina had rewarded her with more and more difficult tasks. Hunting down this tiny flower had taken her the better part of the entire afternoon, and it had brought her closer to Aquila than she had been for weeks.

She knew that Katarina still left the camp every night and headed for the city, but she hadn't impressed the woman enough yet to learn the reason why.

She sighed and rubbed the horse's head, just under his shaggy forelock. She had a sudden and almost overpowering urge to try to contact Jared, but she checked herself. She had spoken with him several times in the last week, and each time, he seemed to be spiraling further and further into some kind of dark humor. Deor had noticed the same change, and it worried her. She thought about what Jessup had said about the curse, and she heaved a deep sigh.

"I've got to get them out of there," she muttered to the horse.

If that would even make a difference now. Perhaps it's already gone too far. Perhaps there's nothing I can do.

Disconcerted by the thought, she swung up onto the horse's back and urged him into a canter. She had only gotten halfway back to camp when she spotted another rider heading in her direction. She rose in the stirrups and drew her own horse to a stop. The other rider was coming fast, and Sahara felt her pulse quicken in anticipation. As the rider drew nearer, she saw that it was Brig.

In another minute, he reined in his horse beside her. He was sweating and his horse was trembling and his shoulders and haunches were white with lather.

"What's happened?" Sahara said, catching the look in his eyes. "What's wrong?"

"They came for the settlement again," he grated. "Sahara...there are casualties this time."

Sahara felt her stomach drop as a chill iced her veins. "The Scythes? But why? Why would they come back so soon?"

"Maybe Azimir's stepping things up," Brig said with a shrug. "It doesn't matter. But you've got to come back now. And I'm riding to Zinta's settlement. Enough is enough."

Sahara seized his arm as he moved to wheel his horse to the east. "No, Brig! Think before you do this thing. Think of the lives that will be lost...so many more lives. You have no idea what this will cost you."

"And you do, I suppose? You and your damned heroics. This is what comes from standing when you should run, Sahara. They come back and kill those you love."

"Brig, he will destroy you all if you rise against him," Sahara said, searching Brig's eyes earnestly. "If you told me to run, then why are you preparing to attack?"

"Because enough is enough," Brig snapped. "We live in terror of the Scythes...of his retributions. If our production isn't up to quota, if we don't deliver fast enough, if the drones pick up an Elenni rider...they come for us, Sahara. They pick off a few and leave us cowering. We can't live like this. It's bad enough we have to harvest their damn drugs in the first place. But they try to break us because we do not believe as they believe."

"You're telling me this is about religion, now?" Sahara said. "Why should Azimir care how you worship?"

"Because we never believed in their gods, Sahara. One of our people who was the first to be given to the Drakkin in sacrifice. The hatred between the Zharib and the Hazad runs deeper than you can possibly understand."

"But it was the Zharib that banished the Drakkin, Brig. They may have sacrificed you first, but they ended it. And now...you shouldn't do this."

"He has the Dragon-Slayer, Sahara," Brig cried, pointing toward the north and the glittering golden spires. "Do you think Azimir will not twist that power to his own purpose?"

"Why would he kill you off? You harvest his drugs...you fund his empire. Think about it, Brig! He can't exterminate you without jeopardizing everything. The Scythes are just to intimidate you into doing what he wants! You've got everything to lose by challenging him."

Brig's eyes narrowed. "We're no better than slaves," he said. "We live and die at the mercy of a tyrant, and you sit there and tell me that life is better as it is? Azimir will destroy us all—not just the Hazad, Sahara. He will destroy Halcyon. He has to be stopped."

The irony of the situation hit Sahara like a blow to the gut. All those months ago, when she had arrived as a convict and a fugitive on Silesia, revolution was all she wanted. Retribution. Payback. She remembered telling the men in the tavern almost exactly what Brig was telling her now. And now here she was, counseling him to live with slavery and oppression and fear. And why? Because she was tired. Because she didn't want to fight.

Does that mean his people shouldn't be free? Just because I want out?

"I...don't know what to say, Brig," she mumbled, letting his arm drop. "I understand, believe me. I know what it is to live under oppression. The Drakkin made our lives hell too, you know."

"Then you understand what we have to do. You understand why we won't live like this any longer."

"But Brig...what hope do you have? You have no weapons. All the technology belongs to Azimir...all the advantage is on his side! What do you have that can defeat those odds?"

"We have a will to fight," Brig said.

Sahara laughed sadly and shook her head. "That's not enough to win. And that doesn't mean anything unless you also have a will to die."

Brig started in surprise and his face clouded in confusion and anger. "What's that supposed to mean?"

"You have to be prepared to lose everything. If you're going up against Azimir on his terms—in an out-and-out frontal assault—then you have to be prepared for it to end in slaughter. Trust me on this, and think about it."

Brig dropped his head and sat silently on his horse. Sahara could sense his disappointment, the flare of impotent rage. And with the recognition came a sudden rush of sympathy.

"You know what?" she said, marveling even as the words came tumbling out of her mouth. "Let me do it."

I can't believe I'm saying this. I said I wasn't going to do this again...and I'm doing it anyway.

Brig raised his head, something like a sneer ever so slightly arching his lip and his brows. "You? What can you do that I can't?"

"I'm an assassin," she answered. "You want to be rid of Azimir? Then let me do it. Alone. Quick and quiet. Once he's dead, I'll disable the drones. Then you'll have a fighting chance."

Brig regarded her with some skepticism. "I don't know if I believe you."

Sahara sighed. "What proof can I offer you?"

Brig adjusted his grip on the reins and considered for a moment. Then he met her gaze with a slow smile. "Well, there is one thing. Another job. Smaller. But one that would prove your skills and loyalty."

Sahara felt a slow sinking feeling in her gut, and she suddenly wished that she could take back her offer. Looking at Brig's smiling face, the recognition that she had just been duped into mopping up someone's mess dawned on her.

"And if I refuse?" she said carefully.

"You don't want to do that. I'll tell Jessup what you are, and he'll have you expelled from the clan. He might even have you executed."

"For what crime?"

"Killing for hire is punishable by death according to the laws of the Hazad," Brig told her. "And you offered to do just that for me."

Sahara measured him for a moment. It occurred to her suddenly that she could kill him right now and blame it on Azimir's drones.

Being an Elenni runner, no one expected him to live very long anyway. She didn't have to go through with this, and she didn't have to listen to his miserable threats.

"What makes you think," Sahara said quietly, "that I won't just kill you right here?"

Something in her tone made Brig's face pale suddenly. "You wouldn't do that."

"Wouldn't I? Why should I listen to your pathetic threats on my life? I told you what I am. I told you that I will help you even up the odds against the Zharib. And yet you still try to blackmail me into settling your scores for you under the pretense of proving myself."

Brig's jaw flapped open, but he had nothing to say. Sahara snorted in disgust and gathered up her reins. "Just as I thought. We're done here. When you're ready to trust me, let me know." Just before she spurred her horse, she hesitated. "Just out of morbid curiosity, whose life did you want me to take?"

Brig laughed. "As if I would tell you that now. You'll just report me to Jessup."

"Maybe I'll do that anyway. I never liked you, you know."

She cantered away, leaving him sitting in the middle of the plain. *The man is dangerous. Sooner or later, he's going to do something stupid. I just hope the only one he gets killed is himself.*

———

She could see the smoke long before she could see the camp itself. A single stream of black curled its languid way into the air, tinged with the light of the setting sun.

At least he was telling the truth about this anyway. Sahara urged her horse into a gallop.

She heard the sounds of grief as the camp came into view. She checked her horse and sat for a moment, head bowed. She felt the familiar rush of anger, but she caught hold of it, molded it, shaped it. It didn't drown her, and it didn't crush her under its roaring weight as it used to do. When she lifted her head, the anger was a knot of hard resolve deep in her gut.

She cantered into the settlement and slid off her horse next to Katarina's tent. It was the outlier, as usual, and completely untouched. Not far away, two tents were in smoldering ruin, and a third was partially scorched. Three bodies lay shrouded in the central square, and Sahara saw Katarina kneeling beside two other prostrate forms. Her medicine bag was open beside her, and Sahara watched as she skillfully wound a clean cloth around a woman's forearm. Sahara frowned. She didn't recognize the woman, and she thought she had learned everyone's faces by this time.

She led the horse forward, making for the small enclosure where the livestock were kept. Rigel had made a makeshift lean-to for the horse on the far side of the paddock, and Sahara took off the horse's bridle and saddle and let him loose. She carried the tack to her own tent and left it there, and then joined Katarina in the square.

"What happened here?" she asked in a low voice. "Brig said you were attacked."

Katarina glanced up at her. "Hand me that poultice mixture," she said instead, gesturing toward her bag.

Sahara obeyed, rummaging through the assorted packets of aromatic herbs until she found the one Katarina wanted. She watched as Katarina sprinkled the herbs into a shallow beaten copper basin of boiling water. The water swirled dark red, and Katarina dropped a clean cloth into the water, allowing it to soak up the mixture. Then she removed it with a clean spoon and laid it in a second basin to cool.

"Keep preparing these poultices until there's no more liquid," she instructed, her voice crisp. "I must attend to the others."

Sahara scooted over to take her place as Katarina rose. "What others?" she asked, her hands poised over the bowl.

"The others who were caught in the fields," she answered. Her eyes were dark and fathomless, but Sahara caught the gleam of heavy sorrow in their depths.

Three of Jessup's people had been killed, and half a dozen more burned or otherwise injured. Jessup's son Rush had lost his wife and eldest son, and Emil's daughter had been killed. At sundown, they were laid to rest in three graves near the copse of trees. As Sahara stood among the veiled and weeping women and the silent, angry men, listening to Jessup's resonant voice speak words of blessing on the souls of the departed, she thought about what she had said to Brig.

Jessup's voice rose and fell, and it was choked now with unshed tears.

Don't they deserve to be free? She turned the knot of anger over inside like a smooth ball between her fingers. Considering. Contemplating.

As they laid the bodies of Jessup's grandchildren in the earth, he bowed his head and wept, his voice breaking and finally dissolving in his tears.

They deserve to be free. They deserve better than this.

The sight of the funeral was consumed suddenly by the vision of Jared, sitting alone in his cell. His knees were drawn up, his head hanging down. But his voice was clear in her mind, and it arrested her own musings.

Don't do it, Sahara. He'll kill you. He's looking for you anyway...don't give him a reason to come after them. If he knows where you're hiding...you'll destroy those people if you show yourself now.

And what am I supposed to do, then, Jared? she asked, tiny flares erupting from that knot of anger. *Just sit here and do nothing while he murders women and children? You know me better than that. I'm not good at watching people suffer.*

Don't do it, Sahara. I'm begging you. He lifted his head at last, his dark eyes pleading.

Why? I can handle myself.

Because, he answered, *if you do, I'll have to kill you.*

SIXTEEN

ICE SHIVERED through Sahara's veins as she stared at Jared. She wasn't even sure she'd heard him properly. The connection was beginning to waver.

What did you say? Who would force you to kill me? And who could force you?

Jared shook his head. *Something's happening to me. And he's using me. I'm losing control. I don't know how much longer I can hold out. The darkness is claiming me...just as I always feared it would. But I'm not alone—he's waiting for me on the other side.*

You can't mean that, Sahara protested, feeling her whole body shaking. *You can't. You have to fight it! You can fight it, Jared. Fight it! Please...for me...don't lose yourself. Not after all we've been through...not after everything you've done!*

He was gone.

Sahara came back to herself with a heady rush and a gasp, only to find that she was alone. She raised her head and stared around, and realized that the others had left her to what they must have assumed was her grief. The earth was mounded over the graves, and a strange symbol was drawn in the dirt. With a choking gasp, Sahara stumbled forward to look at it more closely.

It was a strange mark, but Sahara would have recognized it anywhere. The circle inscribed with the small figure of a three-petaled flower. It was same figure that was tattooed on her own back...that the Drakkin had tried to mar with their lash strokes.

She turned and ran, heading not for Jessup's tent, but for Katarina's. She didn't want to bother Jessup with her questions when his mind was overwhelmed with grief, but she had to know.

"Katarina!" she cried, ducking through the flap of the healer's tent. "Katarina!"

Katarina's tent was larger than her own, and it had two small rooms. The front of the tent was like a sitting area, with cushions and a small brazier. There was no fire lit, and for a moment Sahara wondered if Katarina had returned from tending the wounded. But then the curtain that divided the sitting area from the sleeping quarters rustled, and Katarina slipped through.

"You needn't shout," she rebuked, her mouth quirking into a smile. "I'm not so deaf as all that."

"Sorry. I just—I was in a hurry, and I didn't think...I wasn't sure you were home."

"I have done all I can for the wounded," Katarina said, sitting down on one of the cushions and gesturing for Sahara to join her. She coaxed a small fire into life in the brazier and sat for a moment, staring into its bright warmth.

"Why do they visit destruction on Jessup's people, Katarina?" Sahara asked, pulling her knees up to her chin. "Why do they send the Scythes? If Azimir needs the Hazad to harvest the drugs, then why does he terrorize them?"

Katarina sighed. "You ask difficult questions."

"I'm not done yet," Sahara said, grinning at her. "What is that mark on the graves of the fallen? What does it mean?"

Katarina's eyes flickered at her. "Why should you care about our customs? Why should that concern you?"

Sahara scooted around wordlessly and lifted up the back of her shirt. She felt the warmth of the fire caress her skin, and heard Katarina's sharp gasp.

"Where did you get that mark? And those scars?"

Sahara dropped her shirt and turned around again. "The mark I have had since I entered training as an assassin. And the scars? I had those off the Drakkin, when they arrested me for killing their Chieftain on my homeworld of Amaryl."

Katarina's face blanched. "From the Drakkin?"

"Yes."

"And your homeworld...Amaryl? Who trained you as an assassin? And why?"

Sahara laughed. "I'm not sure how this got turned around so that I'm answering all the questions," she said. "But my father trained me because the Drakkin were exterminating the men. There was no one else left to fight."

"And your father? Who was he?"

"Anwar Acwellan. Before the Drakkin destroyed us, he was a prince."

Katarina was staring fixedly into the fire, her breathing shallow. Sahara could sense her tension, and she frowned. She waited as the seconds dragged into minutes, and finally she grew impatient. "What? What is it? What aren't you telling me?"

"When the Order of the Dragon still occupied the province of Perl," Katarina said slowly, "and when they began their blood sacrifices, many of our people fled this world to escape. The mark you bear...the mark that we etched on the graves of our beloved dead...that is the sign of our people. The three-petaled flower is the mark of the Hazad."

"How can that be?" Sahara murmured, staring at Katarina with wide eyes. "How can I bear the mark of the Hazad? It's the sign of the Shell..."

"My guess? This organization you call the Shell—it was a remnant of our people who formed a resistance to the Order of the

Dragon. And when the Drakkin themselves were expelled from Halcyon, they no doubt tracked down all those who were descended from our people in order to have their vengeance."

It all made sense, and Sahara smiled at her. "So Jessup was right after all," she murmured. "I really am 'the daughter who comes from afar'."

Katarina smiled then as well. "Yes. Jessup has a way of seeing these things. It's a gift, I think."

"I need the answer to my other questions," Sahara said. "Why does the Zharib attack you if they need you so badly?"

"He never kills enough of us to really jeopardize things," Katarina said softly, her voice sad. "Only enough that we cower in fear before him. But his will is arbitrary, and nothing we do ultimately guarantees his pleasure or our safety. The tensions between the Zharib and the Hazad stretch back for generations. They hate our faith, and they hate that we stood against the Drakkin when they did not."

"They did eventually, though. So why should that matter?"

Katarina shrugged. "I don't know. But it seems to matter to—to Azimir. That the Hazad, who for so many centuries had been no more than slaves, should raise their heads and show such strength...perhaps that's why. I don't know. I don't know why he hates us so much."

"Katarina," Sahara said carefully. "The Elenni are more than just messengers. You know this, don't you? They will start a revolution."

"I know. That's why Jessup doesn't really approve. There's a delicate balance right now that he's trying to preserve. Azimir and the Zharib tolerate us...and we tolerate them. Sometimes some of our people die...but that is the price we pay for something like peace."

Sahara felt a choking sensation in her throat. "Then they're really no different from the Order of the Dragon, are they? Taking lives with the promise that blood will bring peace."

"No," Katarina sighed after a moment. "No, they're not. They've become...monsters." She seemed suddenly sad, and she turned back to the fire, her eyes misting with tears.

Sahara sat for a long time in silence, and Katarina did not move. Finally, Sahara leaned over and touched Katarina's arm. "I'm not sure I can continue our lessons," she said.

Katarina stirred and drew a deep breath, coming back out of herself and focusing on Sahara's face. "What? Why not? You are making progress...slow progress, but measurable."

Sahara's smile felt more like a frown. "Thank you...I think. But it's not from discouragement. It's just...I think there may be a job for me to do, and..." She hesitated, fighting down tears. "And, well...it's dangerous. And I may be gone for a while."

Katarina studied her in silence for a moment. "This job," she said slowly. "Is it Brig's idea?"

Sahara shrugged. "Sort of. I volunteered."

"You volunteered." Another pause, and Katarina's eyes were suddenly hard and bright. "And what is the job?"

"I can't say."

Katarina's eyes bored into hers. "Can't? Or won't?"

"Both." Sahara shook her head. "I'm not really like you, you know. I'm not a healer...I just play at being one. I belong with the Elenni. I'm one of them."

"Are you? Are you really?"

"I'm an assassin," Sahara said, feeling suddenly miserable. "What else am I fit for?"

"You are also a healer," Katarina murmured, laying a hand on her arm. "I know you say you aren't, but it's not true. You are skilled, Sahara. You have gentle hands and a caring heart. You fight because you love fiercely. If you didn't give a damn about anyone other than yourself, you would never have earned those scars."

Katarina's face blurred out of focus as tears filled Sahara's eyes. "I had to do it," she choked. "But they never told me...they never said what it would do to me to become this."

Katarina smiled sadly and squeezed her arm. "I know."

Sahara bowed her head, but even as the tears flowed and her

shoulders shook with grief, the strangeness of Katarina's words resonated somewhere in her consciousness.

She thought about them again later, when she was back in her own tent, breathing life into a small fire to banish the dark.

There was so much to process...so much to piece together and consider. Her own lineage, strangely, meant that coming to this hateful place meant returning home. And it explained in part the way that she had slipped so easily into life here, becoming a part of Jessup's tribe as she had never been able to adapt to life on Silesia or on Askalon. There was something comfortable about this life, and though they were wary of her —and though some of them were downright hostile—there was respect, and a willingness to find a way for her to fit in and serve the tribe.

She poked at the coals and then settled back to enjoy the warmth and unsteady light. *Well, if this fight doesn't end every world I've come to know and love, maybe I can finally come home.*

She heard a soft rustling at the tent flap, and she sat up, hand moving to grip the hilt of her knife.

"Can I join you?" came Brig's muffled voice from outside.

"Come in," Sahara called softly.

Brig pushed open the tent flap and stooped under it. He stood for a moment, looking almost awkward, then sat down on the fur rug and sighed.

"What are you doing here?" Sahara asked.

Brig was hard to figure out. At times, he was brash and impulsive to a fault, ready to tear down Aquila's walls stone by stone by himself if it would mean freedom for his people. But other times he seemed incredibly unsure of himself, as though everything else were just an act. Sometimes the mask came off...and this was one of those times.

"What's on your mind?" Sahara prodded when Brig didn't answer her first question.

"Nothing. Well...not true. Lots of things. Too many things." He ran a hand through his hair. "I've been thinking. About what you said. Your offer."

"And?"

"Are you willing to do the other job? The smaller one?"

"The mess you need cleaned up, you mean?"

"That's right. Are you in?"

Sahara measured him steadily, her eyes narrowing slightly. "What aren't you telling me, Brig?"

He started, and Sahara's suspicions were confirmed. "I don't know what you mean."

"Yes, you do." She smiled, but there was no joy in it. "I don't agree to hits before I know the target. So either tell me exactly what you want or get out."

Brig rubbed his hands together slowly. "You're sharp. I like that. I like that about you."

Sahara swallowed the first thing she wanted to say to him. "Get to the point."

"Jessup thinks you might be dangerous for the tribe. I don't see that. I think you're what this tribe needed, you know? A breath of—"

Sahara leaned forward suddenly, grabbing Brig by the collar of his tunic and jerking his face toward hers. "Who is the mark?"

She felt Brig swallow and could see the sweat begin to bead on his forehead.

Damn coward...reminds me of Kirin, she thought, the memory of her first meeting with Kirin flashing through her mind. It almost made her smile, remembering how he had tried to shove the spoonful of honey in her mouth and how she had nailed him to the wall with a knife at his throat. As her focus snapped back to Brig, and she tightened her grip on his collar.

"It's...it's Katarina." His voice was almost a squeak.

Sahara froze. "What did you say?"

"Katarina."

The knife was in her hand and against Brig's throat before her conscious mind even registered the thought. She felt Brig try to squirm away, but she held him fast. "You want me to kill Katarina?" she repeated, her voice low and dangerous. "Why?"

"S-she's a traitor. That's to say, we think she's a traitor." The words came tumbling out now, tripping over themselves. "There's something strange about—"

"You don't have any idea what you're talking about," Sahara snapped. "That's nonsense. She's no traitor. And traitor to what exactly, anyway?"

Sahara shook him free and sheathed the dagger. Brig shrank away from her, his eyes never leaving her face as he nervously smoothed his collar and the front of his tunic. Something like resentment glowed in his eyes.

"She leaves camp every night and heads back to Aquila," Brig said. "What's she doing, I'd like to know?"

"And you think she's a traitor because you don't know what she's doing?"

"We only go into Aquila on market days. She goes every night, near as we can tell."

"We? Who's *we*?"

"Me and...and some of the others."

Sahara held her impatience in check with an extraordinary effort, but she couldn't help swearing under her breath. "What others?"

"You know."

"No, I don't. If I knew, I wouldn't be asking you, would I?"

Brig rubbed his jaw with his thumb. "Yeah, well, it's probably better if you don't know."

Sahara sighed. She took a small poker and prodded the coals in the brazier, watching as tiny tongues of orange and red flame licked around their edges. The chill thread of her own suspicion snaked through the heat of her fierce denial of Brig's accusation. *Where does she go?* she found herself wondering. *And why?*

Brig licked his lips nervously, and the motion brought Sahara's attention back to him. "I won't kill her," she said. "But since you have such a pathetic amount of information, I will follow her. How does that suit you?"

"And if she is meeting with the Zharib? If she is dealing falsely with Jessup and the tribe?"

Sahara held his gaze with her own as the assassin in her wrestled with the love and respect she felt for Katarina. "Then," she managed, "we'll have a different conversation next time."

Brig nodded curtly and scrambled out of the tent.

SEVENTEEN

JARED HAD BEEN in solitary confinement for a week. He hadn't seen so much as a guard's face since he'd left Emelia sitting on that fountain, and as the morning sun filtered through his barred window on the morning of the seventh day, he wondered if this was Azimir's attempt to torture him into submission.

His mouth twisted into a wry smile.

He doesn't know I can communicate with Sahara and Deor. If he thinks being alone will break me, he'll have to figure out a way inside my head.

The thought was vaguely disconcerting. He remembered how effectively Ergeron, the slick-tongued, ambitious leader of the Triumvirate, had been able to cut Sahara off from communicating with him. That proved that it was possible to disrupt their ability to communicate telepathically. It would make his life far more difficult if Azimir ever found out that he still had ties to the outside world...and more so still if he discovered how to cut them off.

Not that he'd been in constant contact with either Sahara or Deor...quite the contrary. When he had spoken to Sahara the night before, she'd been vague and distracted. Something was obviously on her mind, but she hadn't shared it with him openly. He had a notion that it was connected to a problem with the people who were sheltering her—that tribe called the Hazad—but he didn't know enough about them to make a guess.

Why would she distance herself from me now?

The thought wouldn't be silenced. He felt that same shaft of disappointment again as he considered the reasons for her unwillingness to open her thoughts to him.

Doesn't she know how much I need her?

That thought, too. He didn't want it to surface. But it wouldn't be suppressed. He dropped his head into his hands, rubbed his palms over his shaggy dark beard. He was able to keep himself tolerably clean thanks to the wash basin, but they had certainly not left him a razor. He moved under the window and groped along the base of the wall. After a moment's search, he found what he was looking for: the sharp stone that had cut his finger all those weeks ago. He turned it over in his hand, flicking his thumb along its edges. It could cut flesh, but he didn't know if it would cut hair as thick as his beard.

And if I try and fail, I'll just look ridiculous. Better to keep the beard and save this for something else.

He slipped the stone in his pocket, feeling the cold weight settle against his thigh. He tried for the hundredth time to see out the window, and for the hundredth time he failed.

His sense of abandonment continued to bubble to the surface and grow, but now it brought with it a flood of anxieties and fears that he would not name and dared not voice. In the wake of that flood came the darkness. That pit of darkness opening up within his own soul that frightened him more than the dark night of his cell or any torments Azimir could dream up.

In a sudden flash, he watched himself in his mind's eye. He saw himself breaking free of the cell. Tossing the guards aside like crumbling parchment. Bodies laying in his wake, mangled and broken. Finding Azimir...and Rafe.

It always ended here. With the vision of Rafe, standing like a wraith beside Azimir's chair. Hollow, pleading eyes. Swaying there on the edge of death.

He slammed his fists into the stone floor. Chips of rock danced up and sprinkled his hands with a fine dust. With a growl that was something between frustration and pain, he blew the dust away and got to his feet. He crossed to the basin and splashed some cold water on his face, blowing the droplets away from his mouth and shaking his wet hair back from his eyes. Then he leaned forward, gripping the edges of the basin, watching the water swirl down the small drain hole.

As long as Azimir held Rafe in this hideous stasis of death-in-life, he could do nothing. Rafe's life was the chain that held him in check. Ironically, though Azimir had brought him here and pushed him to the edge of the abyss, it was Azimir too who held him back. Rafe's life, Sahara's love, the love of his friends...these were the only things that kept him from tumbling over into the worst nightmarish version of himself.

But Sahara's love had never been certain. It was fragile, but he knew in the deepest core of his soul that it was real.

He corrected himself.

Had been real.

He hoped that it still was.

His friends were worlds away, and his connection to Deor, his link back to Askalon and home, was unpredictable.

But Rafe was here. In this very building. And Azimir held his life gathered like water in his cupped hands.

As if on cue, the stone door suddenly grated back and two guards appeared. Jared turned slowly, warily.

"Lord Azimir will see you," the larger of the two men said, stepping a few paces into the room with a set of manacles.

"Are those really necessary?" Jared asked. "I'm not planning to run."

The smaller guard guffawed. "They never plan to...but then they do. Hold out your hands before I make you hurt."

Jared complied, biting back the grunt of pain as the manacles rubbed the sore places on his wrists. Then he followed the guards into the corridor.

It was all familiar to him now. He studied it carefully every time he had the chance, committing the winding passages and sweeping stairs to his memory, filling in bits of his mental map with anything new that he noticed.

They tugged and jerked him up the final set of steps. Jared wondered, as he always did at this moment, how Sahara had managed to find her way out and escape.

She either had an incredible memory or incredible luck. He shook his head and smiled to himself. *Or both.*

The guard rapped twice on the heavy doors to the audience hall and then entered, snapping Jared's chain to catch his attention.

"Move it, you."

Jared stumbled forward, blinking at the sudden change in the light. It was just as he always imagined it—Azimir sprawled in his low chair, Rafe standing, hooded and cloaked, beside him. But as Jared approached today, Rafe slid back the cowl of his cloak and met Jared's concerned gaze. There was a dullness in his eyes that had to be drug-induced, and Jared felt a sudden surge of panic.

They've doped him up on that cursed Demon's Breath! That's why he—

"So, my friend," Azimir said. "How do you like my establishment, eh? Nice? Comfortable? Good food?" He laughed and gestured to his own face. "Perhaps if you cooperate, I can set you up with my personal attendants for a shave."

"How kind."

Azimir laughed again. "I see you are warming up to me, my friend. But your stay has not been so pleasant as I mean it to be! It is all in your hands to—how shall we say?—graduate to better accommodations?"

"To hell with your accommodations."

Azimir turned to Rafe, tsking softly. "So uncivil. Really, his manners are as rough as his beard."

"Yes, my lord," answered Rafe, his voice as dull as his expression.

"What have you done to him?" Jared asked.

"I told you! We saved his life, that's all. Can I help it if he feels such a debt of gratitude that he wishes to serve me now?"

"That's a damned lie." Jared pointed at Rafe, his chains jangling harshly. "He's been drugged. On Demon's Breath."

A look of surprise crossed Azimir's face. "Who told you—"

"No one has to tell me. I can see it in his eyes. I saw enough of it on Askalon to recognize it."

"Ah, well. It's true. I won't try to deny it. He was very difficult. Made such a fuss, you know. So it's happier this way for everyone."

Jared sucked his breath in through his teeth and clenched his fists. Azimir's eyes dropped to Jared's hands, almost as if he were checking to be sure that he was bound.

"We're getting nowhere with this, you and I," Jared said. "I won't serve you, and you're killing my friend. Slowly but surely, you're killing him."

"Well, you seemed to need some prodding." Azimir leaned forward. "And, just between you and me, he's on a triple dose. So whatever you've heard about the life expectancy on Demon's Breath...well, you can do the calculations, I'm sure."

Jared felt ice shiver through his veins as his eyes snapped to Rafe's face. "You've made a serious mistake," Jared said. "Trying to blackmail me this way."

"Oh, but it will work, I'm sure." Azimir's smile broadened. "You're that sort of man."

"You have no idea what sort of man I am."

"But I do! I've heard stories about you, my friend! Emelia tells me all sorts of delicious things about you after she comes back from your walks together. And besides that, Dragon-Slayer, I know what you have been."

Jared raised his head. "Is that so?"

"I know that as soon as you set foot on Halcyon, the darkness inside of you began to grow."

Jared swallowed hard, feeling a cold sweat slicking his clenched palms.

Azimir nodded slowly. "Yes, I can see that you understand my meaning. Do you know why this is happening to you, Dragon-Slayer? I do. It will be a narrow path for us to take, my friend. Your friend here will help you along. As long as he lives, you will be able to fight the abyss. But refuse to help me, and he dies." Azimir's eyes hardened. "And the abyss will claim you."

"You're forgetting—"

"The girl?" Azimir laughed. "Ah, love is such a pretty thing. Like a flower, the poets always say. But you know what? Flowers are so fragile. Blast the root, and the flower dies along with the tree."

He's prepared to exterminate the Hazad if I don't cooperate, Jared realized, horror clouding his vision.

"I can see the turning of your thoughts," Azimir continued. "And you will see that I have planned for every contingency. The girl will die along with her...protectors. They have been a pollution for long enough. And you think that I won't do it because they harvest my drug for me, is that it? My craftsmen in Ket have built me a mechanized army of harvesters. They will replace the Hazad and my harvests will triple." He rubbed his hands together. "I can hardly wait. But, let's focus on you, my friend! With the girl gone, your friend here is all that will keep you from toppling over the edge into darkness. And I control him. Completely. You know how it works already, so I don't need to demonstrate."

Jared felt himself shaking. Even as he felt the net closing around him, trapping him completely, two thoughts flashed through his mind.

I have to warn Sahara. And he doesn't know about Deor...if Askalon doesn't fall like he expects it to, then perhaps I have a chance.

"So you see," Azimir said after a brief pause. "You really don't have any choice at all. If you don't cooperate, then you will destroy yourself."

"How exactly is it that I'm supposed to help you, anyway?" Jared asked. "Why do you need me?"

"Now you're asking the right questions! This is progress. As I said before, I am going to help you walk the narrow path. The power that you assumed when you slew the Drakkin has awakened—you have returned to the source of their power. Didn't Emelia tell you? They began in the province of Perl, north of here."

"She told me."

"You are powerful, Dragon-Slayer. More powerful than you realize. And when I place the weapon in your hands, you and I will remake the universe. Starting with Askalon. They have forfeited their right to exist in my new universe."

"Because they defaulted on a debt?"

"No. Because they betrayed my confidence. I will not tolerate betrayal. Defy me to my face if defy me you must. But do not double-cross me."

"What's the weapon?"

Azimir smiled broadly. "That's a good question, but not one I will answer."

"I've told you before. My friends are on Askalon. I won't—"

Azimir arched an eyebrow and jerked a thumb at Rafe, who hadn't moved the entire time they were talking. "I'm sorry, you were saying?"

Jared clenched his jaw. "You heard me well enough the first time."

"But this is the wrong way to go, my friend! You were making such progress! Don't turn back now. That road is closed to you. You will destroy Askalon. Indeed, you must. I will provide you with the means...and you will execute."

Jared studied him for several minutes. His tongue felt like lead in his mouth. He twisted his hands, feeling the manacles around his wrists bend and stretch under the force. He felt the weight of the cold, sharp stone in his pocket.

Something snapped inside him.

With a roar of rage and hatred, Jared snapped his bonds and pulled the sharpened stone out of his pocket. He lunged forward, seeing only the edge of the stone and Azimir's bare throat. In a moment, it would be over. He would be free—Rafe would be free. And Sahara would be safe.

A cold steel point nestled itself just between his collarbones, and he froze, one hand gripping the arm of Azimir's chair, the other reaching for his throat. Slowly, he lowered the stone and raised his eyes, following the line of the knife, hand, and arm. It wasn't Azimir. It was Rafe, his eyes still dull and blank, but the knife point solid and steady.

"What are you doing?" Jared whispered, searching his friend's face. "Put it down, Rafe! Let me end this!"

Azimir's laugh echoed in the chamber and Jared winced. "There is only one end to this, Jared. He's my most loyal bodyguard—he will kill you without even realizing what he's doing. He has no will, no remorse, no judgment. He does what he is commanded to do—and I have commanded him to kill you if you make any attempt on my life."

"Then why hasn't he done it?" Jared gritted, his eyes never leaving Rafe's. *Come on, Rafe,* he pleaded silently. *Fight it! Remember who you are...and remember who I am!*

Azimir said a word quietly and Rafe stepped back, slipping the knife back into the sheath he wore at his waist. "You see? He does my bidding. There is nothing for it. The drug has claimed him, and he is mine to command for as long as he survives."

Jared straightened slowly, his gaze finally returning to the leader's face. He was trapped. He could feel the heavy lead of it sinking into his soul—the recognition that he had no choice and no way out.

"So," he said. "What would you have me do?"

EIGHTEEN

THEY WERE TRAITOR'S QUARTERS.

Even in the growing darkness of his soul, Jared felt the soil of his betrayal on his fingers, in his mouth, griming his hair like oil or ash. He slouched in the ornately-carved wooden armchair, frowning blackly at the cold fireplace across from him. The room was chill, even in the heat of the afternoon, and it had taken Jared a full two days to get used to the light. During the day, the room was awash in the gold rays of sunshine, and at night, the soft silver moonlight filtered through the latticework on his window.

He rubbed a hand over his face—now smooth, since they had furnished him with a heavy silver shaving razor, rich cream, and a horsehair shaving brush.

A gentle knock on the door stirred him out of his miserable thoughts.

"Come!" he called.

The door opened and Emelia entered, followed by a lesser house slave. Emelia, looking fresh and cool as a dew-laden blossom, motioned for the slave to make Jared's bed and gather his clothes for washing.

"I trust your new quarters are more comfortable?"

Jared's scowl deepened. "I paid too high a price for them."

Emelia laughed and shook her head, setting the silver hoops dancing against her slender neck. "That's nonsense."

"Really? Tell me. How well do you sleep at night, knowing you serve the man who will destroy your family and your people?"

Emelia's face fell. "That's not...the same thing."

"What do you want?"

"My Lord Azimir will see you shortly."

"Well, I won't see him." Jared's eyes flickered at her. "I want to see Rafe. Where is he?"

"He's on an errand."

"Errand? What errand?"

Emelia shrugged evasively. "Escorting a visitor to the palace."

Jared's heart surged into his throat. "What visitor?"

"The visitor my lord wants you to meet in his council chambers." Emelia smiled and ducked out the door. Her voice floated back to him, "Half an hour, Jared!"

Jared glanced over his shoulder at the servant. She was pulling the soft sheets and rich coverlet over the bed as fast as her shaking hands could manage. She kept her eyes fixed on her work, and Jared could feel that she dared not look at him.

"You don't have to be afraid," he told her. "I don't bite."

The maid's hands fluttered faster, fluffing pillows and setting them properly. "Yes, sir."

Jared felt that queer surge of power that always seemed to come in the presence of weakness or fear. He rose slowly from his seat and crossed to the end of the bed.

"Do I frighten you?"

The maid swallowed hard. She half-turned to go, but hesitated. Jared could see the vein in her smooth throat pulsing rapidly, and she still kept her eyes down. She didn't answer him.

"You are right to fear me," he said, moving behind her and cutting off her escape route to the door. "Even Azimir fears me."

"Yes, sir." Her voice was barely a whisper.

"Now, take me to him."

The maid darted around him and fled into the hall. Jared turned and followed her. By the time he emerged into the hallway, she halfway down the corridor. He set off after her, breaking into a jog after a few paces in the attempt to close the distance. She disappeared down a flight of stairs, and Jared bounded after her. She kept just close enough to him so that he wouldn't lose her, but well out of speaking distance.

Jared was almost breathless when he saw her stop and turn toward him. She raised her arm and pointed to her right, then pattered away down the hall. Jared dropped to a walk.

What's the matter with her? I didn't touch her!

He reached the place she had indicated a few moments later. He didn't recognize this area of the palace—he'd only ever been taken to the council chamber. This must either be Azimir's personal apartments or a more intimate study. A heavy wooden door, bossed with silver, sat on his right, and a wide balcony opened out on his left. He stepped out onto the marble shelf and leaned over the balustrade. Two stories below lay the courtyard and fountain where he had walked with Emelia. He wondered briefly if Azimir had spied on them from this spot, then dismissed it. Who cared if he had? What difference had it made, in the end?

He returned to the door and rapped twice. Strange that there were no guards posted here. Was it so easy to earn the man's trust?

All I had to do was agree to murder my own friends.

The door swung open. Ribbadi stood behind it and flashed a smile at Jared.

"So the mighty Dragon-Slayer does come when he's summoned," he said.

"Get out of my way."

Ribbadi's smile vanished, and resentment burned in his eyes. "Azimir may want to keep you for a pet, but you have no such favor with me."

Jared's eyes swept over him. He could taste the man's fear. "Is that supposed to mean something to me?"

Ribbadi didn't answer, but stood aside for him to enter the chamber. To Jared's surprise, the room was airy and illuminated by a row of large windows. The heavy door had made him expect thick carpets and dark curtains, but there was nothing of the sort here. Wooden latticework filtered the light into a hundred shapes on the stone floor, and Azimir sat behind a long wooden table. There was nothing on the table save a small, rectangular device. Another man stood in front of the table, his back to the door. He didn't turn as Jared approached, but Jared felt there was something vaguely familiar about him. Rafe stood just behind Azimir's right shoulder, but his dull stare was fixed on the wall. If he noticed Jared at all, he didn't show it.

Jared's heart lurched at the sight of the emptiness in his friend's eyes. As he did every time he saw Rafe, he swore a silent oath to rescue him somehow.

He glanced away and focused his attention on the stranger. The heavy, fur-lined boots and thick pants were not fit for the warm climate of Halcyon. The man had obviously come from somewhere else.

Somewhere cold.

"Jared!" Azimir cried. "You're right on time. So glad you decided to join us. Emelia said you were out of temper. I was sorry to hear it."

"Who's this?" Jared asked. He came level with the other man and looked him over. The sense of familiarity was even stronger now. "I know you," he said to the man. "Why do I know you?"

The man's sneering face turned toward him. "You don't know me."

Jared frowned. "Who is this, Azimir?"

"A friend of mine." Azimir sat forward, lacing his fingers and resting his elbows on the table. "We were just discussing the status of things."

"He's not from around here."

"Not too bright, is he?" the man asked Azimir, jerking a thumb at Jared.

Before Azimir could react, Jared had the man's arm twisted behind his back. The man squealed in surprise and pain.

"It's not polite to talk about me when I'm standing right beside you," Jared said in the man's ear.

"Jared, let the man alone. He's an idiot."

Jared dropped the man's arm and moved away. The man nursed his sore hand and glared at Jared, shuffling a few steps further away from him.

"This is my friend Dirk, from Perseon," Azimir continued. "Since you insist on doing him violence, you might as well know his name."

Jared's head snapped up. *Dirk. From Perseon. The little rat that Gwyn warned us about.* "What the hell is he doing here?"

"He's here to tell me how things are going with my *zanthos*."

"You!" Jared turned on Dirk again. "You're the traitor!"

Dirk scrambled away from Jared as he advanced. "Not just me! It wasn't my idea anyway! It was—"

"That's enough," Azimir said. "We don't need to tell him all that just yet."

"Get him away from me!" Dirk squeaked. He'd reached the wall by this point, and he watched Jared with wide eyes. "Tell him to leave me alone!"

"Weren't you just telling me something about a delay?" Azimir asked. "I seem to recall something to that effect."

Dirk's eyes snapped to Azimir. "W-what?"

"Let me see if I remember your exact... Something like, 'Lord Azimir, it's not here.'"

"It's not."

Azimir's mouth curved into a cold smile. "Exactly."

Jared ignored Azimir and advanced on Dirk, his hands knotting into fists. "Who are you working with? Who's the inside man on Askalon?"

"I-I'm not telling you that."

"Don't hurt my man, Jared," Azimir warned. "Come back here."

Jared swung around to face him. "You think you control me? Just because I've agreed to help you doesn't mean you can order me around like..." He stopped suddenly, his eyes shifting to Rafe's still and silent form. A well of anger opened within him and he turned and slammed his balled fist into Dirk's nose.

The man crumpled to the ground, blood running down his face and soaking his shirt. He groaned softly and his eyelids fluttered.

"Well," Azimir said archly, "that wasn't very nice."

"Next time," Jared said, shaking out his fist, "that will be you. And I won't just break your nose."

Azimir's face paled slightly and he coughed once. "Let's try not to have such unpleasantness, shall we?"

Jared glanced down at Dirk and shrugged, then crossed the room and planted himself once more in front of Azimir's table. "You knew this whole time, didn't you? About the *zanthos*, about Askalon, about everything."

"Yes."

"You played us for fools."

"No, no. This was all arranged. You were in the way, you see. Very inconvenient, having people like you around to prop up weak leaders. My friends on Askalon and I just happened to have a mutual interest in having you here on Halcyon for a little while."

"So we were set up."

"You were...repositioned to everyone's mutual advantage."

"We were set up."

Azimir shrugged. "Have it your own way."

Jared leaned across the table, planting his fists on the glossy wood. "Who is the traitor on Askalon?"

Azimir chuckled quietly. "Now that would be telling, wouldn't it? No, I think it's better that I keep that information to myself at present." Azimir met Jared's gaze, and Jared saw the barest flicker of doubt, the briefest waver.

"Do you really think that's wise?" Jared asked.

Azimir glanced at Rafe, then back at Jared. "I think you have no say in the matter whatsoever. And if you so much as raise a hand to strike me, he will kill you. Remember?"

Jared straightened, hands clenched into fists at his sides. "Why did you send for me? Obviously you didn't want me roughing up your errand boy over there, so what is it you want?"

"I just wanted you to know how beautifully our little plan is coming together. It is, isn't it?"

"Except for the fact that they're stalling you, it's working beautifully."

Azimir's eyes flashed at him suddenly and his body stiffened. "What do you mean? It's a simple delay...nothing that won't be resolved soon enough."

"Well, if you're of a mind to trust a traitor..." Jared shrugged. "I suppose you can keep telling yourself that."

"You don't think my men are trustworthy? They have kept their end of things very nicely so far."

"Getting my friends and I shipped over here was child's play," Jared said. "We were coming anyway, with or without their push. But stealing the *zanthos* when everyone's keen to protect it and keep it hidden just now is something else again. And who knows? Maybe they've got other plans...plans that don't involve you except as a pawn and a tool."

Azimir's eyes narrowed. "You think me a simpleton?"

"I think you're blinded by your own ambition."

Azimir stood abruptly, the legs of his chair grating on the stone floor. "It isn't ambition. It's destiny."

Jared laughed and shook his head. "Call it whatever you want. It amounts to the same thing."

"When I put the *zanthos* in your hands, then you'll understand. It will make us utterly powerful, and we will be free."

"Free from what?"

Azimir didn't answer, but his lips curved into a smile. Jared felt himself suddenly sucked into the vortex of a whirling vision. Scenes flashed before his mind, gone before he could understand their meaning. Golden light seeping through his fingers. Sahara, kneeling before him, her eyes resigned and sad. Rafe's face, deathly pale and still. And a woman he did not recognize, tears running down her cheeks.

With a shuddering gasp, he jerked himself back to the present and Azimir's cruel, triumphant, smiling face.

"There is still time," Jared said.

"Time for what?"

"Time to stop all of this. Time before you destroy yourself...and everyone else."

Fear flickered for an instant in Azimir's eyes, like a flash of lightning in a darkening sky. "No. It's not me who will be destroyed. It is the Hazad. When the *zanthos* arrives and they gather in Telon for the holy days, you will destroy them all. And then you will be mine utterly...and nothing will stand in our way."

"And if the Dragon consumes me utterly and beyond hope of recall," asked Jared in a low voice, "who will be there to save you?"

NINETEEN

"DAMN, IT'S COLD HERE," Deor said.

He stamped his feet and blew into his mittened hands, trying to chafe some warmth back into them. Brytnoth glanced over his shoulder and smiled. He pulled his furred hood more closely about his face.

"The settlement's not far," he said. "Just be glad you didn't have to come over the ridge like Jared and Rafe did the first time we came out here."

Deor lifted his eyes to the rim of craggy peaks that surrounded the crater. Steam seeped from a vent north of the settlement, and it curled its way like a lost cloud into the ice-blue sky. The settlement itself huddled in the center of the crater under a blanket of wind-swept snow. As another gust of bitter wind lashed around him, nearly pushing him off his feet, he mumbled a string of curses and hurried as fast as he could after Brytnoth.

He remembered Jared telling him about that trip. If he could feel anything other than cold, he'd be glad that Brytnoth had set them down at the landing site inside the crater.

How is he not frozen to death like me? Brytnoth was steadily outpacing him, and Deor staggered after him like a drunk man. *I can't even feel my feet!*

He toiled on for what seemed like an eternity, dragging his leaden boots through the drifts of snow, slipping on hidden patches of ice. He felt a surge of hot triumph as he reeled up to Brytnoth and realized his friend had stopped. And then he realized that he'd stopped because there was another person present.

"He was here two days ago," the person was saying. "But I haven't seen him since."

Deor's head snapped up, and he met the bright eyes and soft smile of a beautiful young woman. The black fur of her hood caressed her cheeks, the cold wind kissing them into ruddy warmth. Her eyes were a blue like Deor had never seen before. She was dressed in a pearlescent silver coat and snow pants, but even with all the bulk he could tell that she was slender as a sapling. His breath caught in his throat and he found himself grinning like an idiot through his half-frozen lips.

"Oh, so you finally made it," Brytnoth said, turning to him and shattering the moment. "I thought you'd given up back there."

"Nice of you to wait up for me," Deor managed. Then his eyes flicked back to the girl. "Who're you?"

"I'm Gwyn." Again, that smile, like summer sunshine. "I don't recognize your face."

"Deor Acwellan."

Gwyn's smile faltered and a strange look came into her eyes, but she asked no more questions. "It's too cold to stand here talking. Come inside and warm yourselves."

She turned and led the way toward a large building that hunched in the snow like an old grandmother over a kettle. Gwyn pulled open the heavy door and stood aside. They stamped their boots and ducked inside the large mess hall, empty now save for a few small children playing a dice game in a corner. Gwyn shoved the door shut behind them and then slipped across the room to the children. They paused their play and glanced up as she approached, then scattered at a word from her.

"You didn't have to kick them out," Brytnoth said as she returned.

Gwyn pushed back her hood and smiled. "Jactus is a game that can quickly get out of hand. The boys usually end up in a fist fight. It's better this way. Trust me." She gestured to a smaller table on the far side of the room. "Please make yourselves comfortable. I'll fetch some hot drinks and some food."

Brytnoth immediately made for the table at the far side, threading his way through the rows of tables and benches that lined the hall. Deor followed more slowly. He peeled off layers as he went, dropping his mittens, scarf, hat, and finally his parka on benches as they passed.

"I hope you're planning to pick all that up," Brytnoth observed as Deor slid into a chair across from him.

Deor blew into his hands and chafed some warmth back into them. "Of course. Later."

"Because Gwyn will do it for you if you don't get on it. And that would just be embarrassing."

"How is that embarrassing? If she likes cleaning—well, who am I to deny her the pleasure?"

Brytnoth frowned at him. "You better clean it up or I'll make you hike the ridge."

Deor grinned at him. "She makes you feisty!" he said. "I love it."

"Shut up. You're obnoxious. Like the annoying little brother I never had."

Deor laughed. "Sahara's not around, so I have to be someone's annoying little brother." He felt a strange thrill in the pit of his stomach as he thought of his sister and his newfound ability to connect with her and with Jared. "Listen, there's something I have to tell you. I know what's happened to them."

"Who?"

"Sahara, Jared, and Rafe. I know what's happened."

"So does everyone. Jared and Rafe are being detained by Azimir, and Sahara's on the run somewhere."

Deor waved a hand. "I mean I know what really happened. Jared's not just in custody, Brytnoth. And Rafe was nearly killed. And I know exactly where Sahara is."

"How do you know that?"

"Because I can speak to them, Brytnoth."

Brytnoth stared at him long and hard, his frown deepening. "You mean speak to them with that weird mind-link that Jared and Sahara share?"

"Yes."

"Okay, that's just strange. Not to mention totally awkward."

Deor ignored the half-smile that was quirking the corner of Brytnoth's mouth. "Sahara thinks it's part of a curse. We each killed a Drakkin Chieftain. And since the Drakkin acted as a Collective and used telepathy to communicate, she thinks that we accidentally tapped into that power when we killed the Chieftains."

"What, so you're your own little collective now?"

"Sort of. I think that's what she was getting at."

Bryntoth let out a low whistle and shook his head. "Weird, man. Just weird."

"But something's happening to Jared. Some kind of evil has a hold on him, Brytnoth. He's the Dragon-Slayer, and it seems there's some kind of curse. Going to Halcyon...woke it up. Or something like that."

"Woke it up. A curse."

Deor frowned, realizing that the story was sounding crazier by the moment. "Yes. Or something."

Brytnoth snorted and leaned back in his chair, staring up at the ceiling. Deor thrummed his fingers on the table and waited, but Brytnoth said nothing. Deor sighed.

Can't blame him. It is a new level of crazy, even for us.

He unzipped his battle dress jacket and dropped it onto the chair beside him. The room was pleasantly warm, though there was no fireplace that he could see. He noticed the strip of softly glowing yellow stones set in the wall around the perimeter of the room and got up to investigate. The stones were radiantly warm to the touch, and the heat flowed through his fingertips and coursed down his arm.

With the warmth came a strange sense of power. Deor closed his eyes as the heat of the stone thawed something he'd thought he'd buried deep in the darkest dungeon of his soul.

"That's *zanthos*," Brytnoth said.

The moment shattered around Deor like glass, and he jerked his hand away from the stone. His heart was pounding, his breath coming in ragged, shallow pants. "What?"

"*Zanthos*. They use it here for light and warmth. Not just for weapons." Brytnoth hesitated as Deor turned to him. "What the hell's wrong with you?"

"What is this stuff, Brytnoth?" he asked, brushing the question aside. "What is it really?"

"I don't understand."

"Why did the Drakkin want it so badly? And why does Azimir want it now? I want to know what the hell it really is."

"How do the Drakkin come into this? How do you know they wanted it?"

"They did. That's why they came to Askalon in the first place." He waved a hand impatiently and returned to his seat. "There's something...unnatural about this stuff, Brytnoth. Why were they after it?"

"It's a power source."

"It's not just a power source. Or...not in the way you mean."

"Isn't it enough for Azimir to want it for the weapons? He seems like the kind of person who would enjoy destroying things. Why do we need to dig any deeper than that?"

"Aelred talks about it like it's sacred or something."

"I think that's because of its incredible power," Brytnoth said, "not because it actually has some kind of mystic significance."

Deor drummed his fingers on the table with a dark frown. "Maybe. But I'm not so sure."

At that moment, Gwyn returned with a contingent of armed

guards. Brytnoth jumped to his feet, knocking over his chair, as the guards seized Deor's arms and jerked him up.

"I'm sorry," Gwyn said, her eyes fixed on Brytnoth's stunned face. "I'm sorry."

Deor thrashed in the iron grip of his captors. "What the hell is going on? Let go of me!"

"Deor Acwellan?" A raven-haired man stepped forward and confronted him. "Commander of Askalon's militia forces?"

Deor frowned. "That's right."

"You are under arrest for theft and treason...and for breaking faith with Lord Alberic."

"What?" Brytnoth cried. "Lies! Who told you such lies?"

The captain glanced at him, then turned back to Deor and his guards. "Take him away."

Deor struggled violently as the guards twisted his arms behind his back. He jerked his right arm free and decked one of the guards. The man reeled backward, stumbled over Deor's overturned chair, and fell sprawling across the table. Two more guards jumped to take the fallen man's place. They wrenched Deor's arm around and snapped heavy metal cuffs around his wrists. Deor strained against them, but they wouldn't yield.

"Brytnoth!" Deor cried, planting his boot in another guard's chest, sending the man crashing to the floor. "What's happening? What did I do?"

Brytnoth rounded the table and started for the guards, hands balled into white-knuckled fists. He stopped short when the captain pulled a *zanthos*-pistol and placed the muzzle against his forehead.

"Not another step," he said. "Alberic wants to talk to this one. And I'd hate to kill you just now."

Brytnoth slowly raised his hands and backed away, but his face was dark. "There will be hell to pay for this," he growled. "You're making a terrible mistake."

"Not my problem" the captain said, holstering his pistol. "Let's go."

The guards propelled Deor through the back door and into the kitchens. Deor caught the surprised stares of the cooks, the flash of white stone and radiant yellow light reflecting off the steel counters. Then they were out in a wide, white-tiled passage that curved and then ended at a set of doors with a keypad beside them. The captain punched one of the buttons and the doors slid back, revealing a lift lined in the same sterile white tile. The guards pushed Deor inside and the captain punched another button. The doors slid shut and the elevator dropped.

"Where are you taking me?" Deor said.

"To the prison bay," the captain answered.

"Great," muttered Deor. "Back in the slam." He jerked his arm out of the grip of the guard beside him. "Get off me. Where the hell am I going to run in this box?"

The elevator slowed to a stop and the doors slid open, revealing another white hallway lit with a strip of glowing golden stones.

"Move it," the guard snapped, giving Deor a shove.

He stumbled out of the elevator, spearing a withering glare at the guard. "You're going to regret that," he said.

"I wouldn't be making threats if I were you," the guard answered.

The troop moved down the hallway, and after about twenty yards, Deor saw cell bays opening out on either side of the passage. The captain turned and led them down the third passage, then stopped at a cell and tapped a code in the panel. The double doors slid back and the guards pushed Deor inside.

"Alberic will come to see you shortly," the captain said, flashing him a smile. "Enjoy your stay."

The doors slid shut, and Deor was alone.

"Nice of them to uncuff my wrists," Deor mumbled. He crossed to the low bench on the far side of the cell and sat down. One glance around the room had told him that there would be no breaking out of this place. A small camera mounted in the corner watched his every move, and there was no apparent way to open the door from the inside. He glanced up at the ceiling. The white tile was interrupted at regular intervals by patches of *zanthos*, so there was no weak point for lighting.

These people know how to build a prison cell. Too bad they couldn't keep their zanthos locked up this well.

But Dirk had been there to give the thieves an all-access pass to the *zanthos* storage facility. He must have known all the security protocols and codes, and if Alberic didn't trust him, others must have.

So how am I going to convince Alberic that I'm no thief? What can I say that he will believe?

He held onto the thread of a hope that Brytnoth might somehow be able to reason with him. Brytnoth knew the truth.

Didn't he?

What if Aelred sent me on this mission just to deliver me over to Alberic? And what if Brytnoth's in on it?

The thought iced his veins and he lifted his head, staring at the blank tile wall as his mind worked over the possibility.

Aelred had obviously developed a case of spinelessness since the overthrow of the Triumvirate, and it was clear that someone influential had access to his confidence. Deor had a strong suspicion that whoever was deepest in Aelred's confidence was also the one at the center of this plot...and he had clearly landed on someone's blacklist.

If the mastermind behind the *zanthos* theft had taken the trouble to frame him here on Perseon, Deor was sure he wouldn't be content with half measures. He would have planted those seeds in Aelred's mind as well, making sure his web was tight enough to catch Deor and keep him caught. Even as he felt his certainty grow, he felt the ground slipping from beneath his feet. His mind returned to his own predicament and his own stunning lack of evidence that might prove his innocence.

What am I going to say? 'No, I didn't do it, Alberic' isn't going to cut it. But all I have is my word...and Brytnoth's.

His suspicion that Brytnoth might be in on the whole thing surged again, but the shock written all over his friend's face when he'd been arrested had been completely genuine. The jittery feeling of panic subsided slowly, and he took a deep breath. Brytnoth could be trusted.

He turned his attention back to the door. He started to stand, but the door slid open. A tall man entered the cell, flanked by two guards. After one look at Deor, the man flicked his fingers at the guards.

"Leave us," he said. His voice was warm and resonant, but the eyes that fixed Deor now were hard as ice. As soon as the guards took up their post outside and closed the door, the man clasped his hands behind his back. "So. You are the one we have to thank for the mischief that's been done here."

"No," Deor said, shuffling around on the bench so that he could face the man. "And who are you?"

"I am Alberic."

"Look, I didn't arrange for the *zanthos* to be stolen. That's a lie...someone wants me out of the picture. Probably out of the picture permanently. But I didn't touch the stuff, and I certainly didn't order anyone else to do so."

"And why should I believe you?"

Damn. Was it better to fumble for words or say nothing at all? He tried words. "Brytnoth can vouch for me."

"Perhaps."

"The longer you keep me sitting in this cell, the longer it's going to take for us to track down the real thieves and traitors," Deor said. "Let me go."

Alberic chuckled. "Nice try. Your earnest desire to right the wrong that has been done to my people is commendable...but a bit thin, don't you think?"

"Thin? What the hell are you talking about? Brytnoth and I came here to find the thieves...the real thieves. Starting with a little rat named Gervais and your sneak brother Dirk."

Alberic frowned. "What's my brother got to do with this?"

"Everything. How do you think the thieves got access to the *zanthos* in the first place? They needed an inside man." He arched his eyebrows when Alberic said nothing. "That would be Dirk."

"My brother is many things, Deor Acwellan. A traitor and a thief are not among them."

"So you say. But you and I both know that it's not much of a stretch to imagine him crossing that line."

"You know nothing about my brother."

"No, but I know sneaks and rats pretty damn well. And from all I hear, Dirk's the sneakiest rat on this frozen rock. Doesn't take much for men like that to be bought, Alberic." He paused and measured the man. Alberic's face was working, and Deor knew that he was trying to choke down his suspicions. "But you already know all this. So why am I here?"

"Why are you here? If you orchestrated the whole affair, why did you come?"

Deor grinned, suddenly seeing his way out of the trap. The relief made him almost giddy. "You're right about that. If I'd orchestrated the whole affair, do you really think I'd be dumb enough to come here myself pretending to help?" he asked. "I realize you just met me five minutes ago, but please do me the courtesy of assuming I'm an intelligent life form."

Alberic rubbed his jaw thoughtfully, but a smile quirked his mouth in spite of himself. Deor's spirits soared. "Well, if you did set this all up and then come here to survey your handiwork...you'd have to be the dumbest criminal mastermind I've ever met. But if you didn't set it up, then who did?"

"I don't know yet," Deor said. "But it wasn't me. I promise you, it wasn't me. I'm not that reckless...and I sure as hell am not that stupid."

Alberic held his gaze for a few moments, then sighed. "There is complete honesty in your eyes...which is more than I can say for my brother most of the time." He moved to Deor's side and unclasped the cuffs from Deor's wrists.

"So now what?" Deor asked. He rubbed his chafed wrists and eased his stiff muscles.

"You can't go back to Askalon," Alberic said after a moment's silence. "Our law is very clear. Treason is a capital crime on Perseon, as it is on Askalon. And whoever did this knows that. They framed you for this so that you would be executed if you were caught."

"Lucky for me you're a reasonable man."

Alberic arched an eyebrow at him. "Lucky for you that you're a more honest man than my brother."

"I just don't see why I'm so important. I mean, why go through the trouble of setting me up?"

The ghost of a smile haunted Alberic's lips. "My dear fellow," he said. "Whoever did this has much bigger designs than a simple theft. Whatever they're planning to do with the *zanthos*, they didn't want you around on Askalon to get in the way."

TWENTY

DEOR SHOULDERED his way back into the mess hall. The rush of the evening meal was over and the place was all but deserted. He made his way back to the small table, where Brytnoth sat hunched over his mug and a half-eaten meal. As Deor approached, he glanced up, and his face creased in a wide grin.

"So they finally let you out, did they?" he asked. He stood and clasped Deor's wrist, then gestured him into a seat.

"I guess I look like an honest man."

"Honest fool, maybe."

"Maybe."

A slight movement at the end of the table drew Deor's attention. Gwyn had crouched down beside his chair, her elbows resting on the table. When he caught her gaze, her eyes brimmed with tears.

"I'm so sorry," she whispered. "I was just trying—"

Deor laid a finger on her lips and her eyes widened in surprise. "I know," he said. "It's fine. No harm done...I'm still in one piece, and so is Alberic. So no regrets, okay?" She nodded, mute. Deor moved his finger away from her mouth and smiled. "Well, I do have one regret," he said. "I missed dinner."

"I can fix that," Gwyn said, a smile blossoming in her eyes. "I'll be back...with food this time, not guards."

"Thank you."

Gwyn rose and vanished into the kitchen. Brytnoth was chuckling and Deor turned to him. "What's the matter with you?"

"Nothing. Nothing at all."

"You worried I'm going to steal your girl, is that it?"

"What?" The sudden flush that flamed in Brytnoth's face made Deor laugh. "Stop laughing at me! She's not..."

"Look," said Deor, "Althea's waiting for me back on Askalon...assuming I can ever get home again. You don't have to worry about me."

Before Brytnoth could respond, Gwyn returned with Deor's food. She set the plate and steaming mug in front of him, then slipped into a chair across from Deor with her own mug. As the tantalizing smell of hot spiced meat and warm bread wafted into the air, Deor's stomach growled. He hadn't realized just how hungry he was until that moment.

He shoveled several bites into his mouth before he became conscious of Gwyn's amused gaze. He paused, loaded fork halfway to his mouth, and glanced up at her. Her slender fingers cradled her mug as she sipped her tea, her eyes smiling at him over the rim.

"You aren't hungry?" he asked.

Gwyn shook her head and set down her mug. "I ate earlier. But don't let me stop you."

"Don't worry. He won't," Brytnoth said with a grin. "But we have a lot to discuss, and Deor's run-in with the law has cost us precious time. You said that you last saw Dirk a couple of days ago. Did he seem like he was up to something?"

"He's always seemed like he's up to something," Gwyn answered. "He might have been a bit shadier than usual, but nothing that would have drawn anyone's attention."

"Except yours, apparently," Deor said.

"Except mine."

"And where is he now?" Brytnoth asked. "I'd very much like to speak with him."

Gwyn's delicate face gathered into a frown. "I told you. He's not here."

"Then where the devil is he?" Deor asked. "Perseon's not the kind of place where people just wander off, is it?"

"No, but people come and go. Dirk especially." Gwyn shrugged. "How should I know where he went? I don't spy on him."

"Why not? He seems like someone who deserved to be spied on. Nasty skulking fellow."

"I don't spy on people for no reason, Deor," Gwyn replied, her mouth quirking in a smile. "And even if I had a reason, I really don't shadow them...I just notice things, that's all."

"Well, did you notice him walking off with a huge stash of *zanthos*, by any chance?"

The blood drained from Gwyn's face. "No."

Brytnoth sighed and rubbed his hand over his face. Deor sipped at his tea, letting the warm, fragrant liquid slide down his throat and warm him all through. He knew Brytnoth was frustrated, but he couldn't feel the same way when he was finally thawing out.

"If you saw anything else, Gwyn..." Brytnoth began, but stopped as her face suddenly lit up. She gripped his forearm and gave it a little shake.

"I did. I saw something else. Or someone else, rather. He came here a few weeks ago. A huge man."

"Fat?" Deor asked. Brytnoth favored him with a long-suffering glance and Deor shrugged. "What? It's a legitimate question."

"Not fat. Solid...and round." She shivered. "I didn't like the looks of him. He wasn't like...well, he wasn't like you two. Can a man that huge try to hide in his own skin? I don't know."

"Did you recognize him?" Brytnoth asked.

"I've never seen him here before," she confessed. "He came in a small shuttle, so I know he wasn't a trader."

"Trader, no...but traitor, maybe," Deor put in. "I have a pretty fair notion who it was. Can you tell us anything else about him?"

"I managed to overhear part of his conversation during dinner," she said. "He was talking to Alberic and Dirk about setting up a shipment of something. That's what made me think he was a trader."

Brytnoth frowned and rubbed his jaw. "What did this sneaky fellow want to ship?"

Gwen shook her head. "I don't know."

"Well, that's just completely frustrating," Deor said. "But I'm sure he wouldn't have come here to announce his intention to run off with your stockpile of *zanthos*. He probably came under some other pretense...acting official and flashing some kind of credentials, perhaps?"

"He told Alberic that he was here on behalf of Askalon's militia forces. And that's you, I expect."

"That's me."

"You know, I still don't understand why they would bother to frame you," Brytnoth said. "Why go through the trouble?"

"I've been puzzling over that as well. But if you were a traitor intent on overthrowing the government and propping yourself up, wouldn't you want the militia commander conveniently shuffled out of the way? Less resistance to a power grab that way."

"Yes, I see what you mean."

Deor pushed back his chair and ran a hand through his hair in frustration. "But one thing's certain. Now that I've been framed for this dirty little trick, we can't go home. At least, not yet. And no one can know that I'm not dangling at the end of the hangman's rope. They wanted to send me on the long journey by the shortest road...I need to make them believe they've succeeded."

"That shouldn't be too hard," Gwyn said. "Most people who come to Perseon come here to disappear. We're good at that."

"I'm counting on it."

"We can't just sit here forever, Deor," Brytnoth said. "Sooner or later, Aelred's going to start asking questions."

Deor frowned. "I don't know about that. I think he might have signed off on this whole thing—I think someone got to him and convinced him that he needed to get rid of me...and maybe you, too."

"Then our mastermind is someone high-ranking and influential," Brytnoth said. Then he added, "What are you thinking? I know that look."

"What look?"

"That one." Brytnoth gestured to Deor's face. "It's the same look Sahara got every time she came up with some mad scheme."

"Must run in the family," Deor answered. "I was just thinking that we should turn this right back at whoever did this. If they think they can frame me, they'll get more than they bargained for. Silent, swift, secret. That's the plan."

Brytnoth grinned. "You really do remind me so much of Sahara."

"I'll take that as a compliment."

"You should."

Deor was silent for a moment, his thoughts returning to his sister and the mess she was in. But he knew he had to focus and finish the task in front of him first. He was enough of a soldier to grit his teeth and see his mission through, but he was enough of a brother to regret it.

"There's one thing about all this *zanthos* business that I'd like to know," he said, forcing himself back to the problem at hand. He leaned across the table and lowered his voice. "Where's the rest of it?"

"It was all secured here, wasn't it?" Brytnoth turned to Gwyn. "Wasn't it?"

"No," she answered.

Brytnoth slapped a hand on the table. "Then where the hell's the rest of it?"

"I don't know. But Alberic says that the Drakkin turned Askalon over to the Triumvirate and followed that second shipment. I don't know how much was actually in the shipment, but it was enough to work very nicely as a decoy."

Deor planted his finger in the table. "We have to find that second stash. We know for sure that the Drakkin never found it...they would have used it if they had. They must have been still hunting for it when you brought them down." Deor shook his head, feeling once more the pull of the stones. "I'm telling you, Brytnoth, whatever this stuff is, it's not just an energy source. The Drakkin didn't want it to light their Council Hall. They wanted it for some other purpose."

They sat for a while in silence. Brytnoth leaned back in his chair and Deor rose and resumed his pacing, while Gwyn cleared their plates and hurried them back to the kitchen. Deor's gaze was drawn again and again to the softly radiant stones, and each time he glanced at them, the desire to touch them surged up inside him. He turned on his heel, swearing under his breath, and walked away. But twenty seconds later, he was back, and his steps brought him closer to the wall at every turn.

"These things," Deor gritted at last. "These things are driving me mad. How can you just sit there?"

Brytnoth let his chair down with a thump and frowned. "What things?"

"These damn stones! What do you think I'm talking about?"

Brytnoth stared at him, and Deor realized in a rush that his hands were clenched into fists and that he had shouted at his friend. Deor drew in a shaking breath and ran a hand through his hair.

"You see what I mean?" he said, forcing his voice to remain calm. "*Zanthos* is for more than just building high-tech weapons, Brytnoth. You don't feel the draw? You don't feel it at all?"

Brytnoth shook his head slowly, eyes still wide with surprise, and Deor sighed. "Well, then I don't know what the hell's wrong with me. No one else seems bothered by them at all."

At that moment, Gwyn hurried back into the hall. She had her heavy coat on and was pulling on her mittens as she approached.

"Come!" she said. "We've talked enough for tonight. Let me take you to a room where you can rest and take counsel. Tomorrow you can decide what you need to do."

The two men rose without a word, wrapped themselves against

the cold, and followed her back outside. Deor pulled his hood well over his face and kept his head down, following in Brytnoth's footsteps to avoid running into anything. He heard Gwyn's cheerful voice greet someone, then saw a cluster of boots tramp through the snow past them. He quickened his pace.

The residences were pods that circled the central cluster of buildings, and they were all connected to one long hallway. Gwyn slapped a button on the wall and the door to the hall slid open. She motioned them inside, and they found themselves in a small vestibule. Warmth radiated from the stones on the floor, and Deor clenched his fists.

"Why do we have to track down any more of this *zanthos*?" he muttered. "We could just pull this floor up and we'd be set."

"These stones are keyed for architectural use," Gwyn said. "They won't power weapons in their present state. They would have to be recalibrated first."

"How do you do that?" Brytnoth asked.

Gwyn moved to a small control panel near the door and pressed a button. Deor felt the temperature rise as a gentle whirring sound came from under the floor. The snow on their boots melted and ran in small rivulets toward the edge of the room, and he realized that there were small drain vents at the base of the wall. Once their feet were dry, Gwyn pressed another two buttons. The whirring stopped and the inner door slid open.

"Follow me," she said. "I'll explain when we get to your room."

She led them briskly down the wide, curving corridor. When they were about halfway around, she turned left and led them down a smaller hallway that ended at a door. She tapped a code in the silver control panel on the wall and the door slid open. She ushered them inside and closed the door.

"Is that more *zanthos*?" Deor asked, heading for the small table and chairs in the center of the room. A tiny cube of *zanthos* in a glass bowl filled the room with its quiet radiance. "It is. Not good. Not good at all. Don't you use anything else for light around here?"

"No."

Deor walked away from them toward the sleeping quarters, lacing his fingers behind his head and sighing.

I don't know how Brytnoth can stand it. There's either something wrong with him...or something wrong with me.

"To answer your question about the *zanthos*," Gwyn said to Brytnoth behind him. "There's a lab in the old mine that has the technology to convert it for safe domestic use like this."

"I don't think this stuff is safe. At all," Deor said from the other room. There was no *zanthos* in the sleeping quarters, which filled him with relief.

At least I don't have to sleep with it, he thought as he wandered back to join Gwyn and Brytnoth at the table.

"You wanted to know where the rest of the *zanthos* is, right?" Gwyn asked, turning to Deor. "I think Alberic might know. I'll see if he will come and speak with you a little later. In the meantime, please make yourselves comfortable. If you need anything—" She moved to the door and gestured to the control panel. "Just press the green button to call one of the servants." She opened the door and stepped into the hallway beyond. "I'll come back in the morning. Sleep well."

The door slid shut and they were alone.

TWENTY-ONE

Sahara turned and shaded her eyes, a smile blossoming on her face before she could stop it. Tessa was running toward her, dark curls bouncing, and Sahara sighed. She knew how much Tessa loved her, and though she basked in the warmth of the child's affection, she still felt wretchedly undeserving.

The girl's legs pumped with effort as she scurried across the central square, skirting the constantly smoldering remains of the cooking fire. Sahara walked slowly to meet her, and Tessa slowed her pace as she drew closer. Sahara carried an empty basket, and she shifted it to her left hand and held out her right to Tessa.

"Where are you going, Zelie?" Tessa asked, breathless. "Can I come too? Mama says I may if I stay very close to you."

The corner of Sahara's mouth tipped up as an intense wave of satisfaction washed through her. Since she had destroyed the two Scythes, the mothers of the tribe had settled on her as the chief protector of their children. She could hardly move about without at least two or three of them tagging along, and mothers would loiter around the breakfast line, waiting for her to appear. The only way to escape them was to promise to take their children for an hour or so.

Tessa was her most constant companion—the only time the child wasn't by her side was when her mother called her in for her lessons or her chores. Even then, Sahara suspected that she had a bolt hole somewhere because the girl wouldn't spend more than ten minutes at her task before she was chasing Sahara down again.

Initially, she'd thought it was just the novelty and that they'd weary of her as they might get tired of a too-familiar plaything.

But they didn't. If anything, they were growing more and more attached to her. Two weeks ago, a small group of girls had seen her spit a poisonous lizard to a tree with her knife. Since then, she'd been teaching them how to throw a knife. She glanced up at the sun. She had another class that afternoon, just after the noon meal. The group had doubled in size since she started, and she was going to have to find a way to get more knives.

She frowned slightly. The oldest girl in the group—a slender thing named Zinna—had snuck three knives out of her father's tent for the last class. But they couldn't keep sneaking things. It wouldn't sit well with the parents, and it certainly would make her uneasy relationship with Jessup that much more fragile.

Tessa tugged at her hand, and Sahara sighed, pulling her mind back into the present.

"Zelie! Where are you going?"

"Katarina wants something from the fields," Sahara answered. "See my basket? I have to go and gather for her."

"Can I come with you? Please?"

Sahara hesitated, her eyes scanning the fields beyond the little camp. Everything was quiet. A furtive, scorching breeze trembled the long grasses and set them rippling like waves. Still.

Too still, perhaps?

Sahara's hand tightened around Tessa's. "Not today, Tessa sweet. Not today."

Tessa's face crumbled. "Why not?"

Sahara smiled and crouched down in front of her. "Tell you what. You stay here and do your lessons while I finish this for Katarina. Then you can come later and help me with my class."

The girl tipped her chin, eyeing Sahara suspiciously. "Really? Do you promise?"

"I promise." Sahara squeezed her hand again, then let her go. The girl turned in a flurry of curls and a tinkle of bells and skipped away. Sahara glanced up at the sky again, then out at the fields. Vague worry clutched at her gut, and she called, "Tessa!" When the girl turned back to her, Sahara added, "Watch the skies."

Tessa immediately scanned the empty sky. She frowned at Sahara, shrugging her shoulders. Sahara shook her head. She had no explanation for Tessa, no rational reason why. "Just watch."

"Okay."

Sahara watched her until she vanished into her family's tent, then turned back to the path leading out of the camp. She regarded the basket in her hand with resentment as she pushed her way through the tall grasses. When she reached the end of the narrow dirt path at the edge of the camp, she hesitated, shifting the basket again. She glanced back at the camp, feeling the iron fist of fear closing around her lungs. It was drawing her back to the camp, and she knew that if she continued to walk away, it would press her into the ground with every step.

What is it? Why do I feel this way? Like I felt when... She felt an icy sweat slick her hands. *When I was chained to that pillar. When I was waiting for the Dragon.*

She dropped to her knee and laid her palm on the dirt, steadying herself. Something was wrong. Something was very wrong.

And she was utterly alone.

No one in Jessup's tribe understood the danger. The Hazad would be destroyed, and though Azimir would preside over its funeral rites, he would not be the one to deal the killing stroke. There was something else at work here, something beyond the tyrannical whims of a despot. She felt the menacing evil growing, but she couldn't figure out what it was...or how to fight it.

We should never have come here. I hate this place.

But what was the use of thinking that way? She knew better. Sahara pressed her palm into the dirt, gritting her teeth against the panic and the turmoil. She would not fall apart now. She had a mission.

Even if it was just gathering a bunch of damn herbs.

Maybe I can stop it. This evil, whatever it is. Maybe there's still time.

Time.

She glanced up at the sun and frowned. She hadn't heard anything from Jared in days, and she was still no closer to a plan to getting him and Rafe out of Azimir's clutches. The sand was slipping out of the hourglass, and she felt paralyzed by inaction and indecision.

Perhaps there was still time, even so.

Jared. She squeezed her eyes shut, the ghost of a prayer in her heart. *Jared. Please.*

The world rushed to black, and she found herself staring at Jared's bowed head, dark hair slickly parted down the center. Her breath caught in her chest as a sudden overwhelming sense of dread gripped her. Every fiber in her being screamed at her to flee, to sever the connection, but she was already trapped. It was as if he had seized her in a vise-grip. She tried to pull her mind away, but she felt his hold on her tighten.

Powerless, breathless, she waited.

He raised his head, slowly, dark hair falling to frame the face she loved so fiercely. His eyes—black now as marble or the void of space—bored into hers, and they weren't the eyes of the man she loved. Something had changed, something horrible had happened.

The Jared she knew was gone, and she couldn't find breath to scream.

You.

His voice rolled through her mind like thunder. She curled away from him, scrambling, desperate, with nowhere to hide and nowhere to run. He was inside her, consuming her, squeezing the very life out of her.

He smiled, as if watching her writhe amused him somehow.

Sahara felt the burn of two hot tears as they coursed down her cheeks.

Jared. She didn't know how she managed it. She reached out to him with a fragile tendril of her mind, desperate to soothe away the darkness, to bring back the man she loved.

You. You should know better than to call on me now. You will know better.

Another tear fell, then another. In a corner of her soul, the tiniest flare of anger sparked, but she wasn't angry with him. She hated herself for crying, hated herself for cowering away from him.

What's happening to you? she asked, trying again to reach him. *Jared, what's wrong?*

The barest flicker of memory or regret crossed his face. *Azimir is teaching me to be the man I was destined to be.* When she shook her head, he threw back his head. *What? You don't recognize me? You should.*

How could you listen to him, Jared? How can you, after what he's done to us? She gathered everything that was left of her courage and her strength and poured it out, twining herself around his thoughts like a warm embrace. *Listen to me. Come back to me. You have to fight! I need you...I need you to fight it. Fight him. Come back.*

Jared lifted his chin, his jaw a hard line of stubborn cruelty. *And what is it that you can offer me instead, you pathetic, broken girl?*

Sahara recoiled into herself, her breaths ragged and shallow. He had cuffed her away from him, as a cruel master might kick the dog who adores him.

He smiled slowly, as if he was savoring her wretchedness. *You're weak and scared. I see inside your soul, and I see doubt, fear, hatred, anger. But all these I have already, and more. Azimir has given me power beyond imagining. He has opened the door, and I have stepped over the threshold. There is nothing now that can hold me back. Least of all you.*

You're a monster, Sahara whispered. *You're dancing with dragons, Jared.*

Oh, no. A ruthless smile darkened his face. *I am the Dragon.*

And with that, he released her, letting her slump half-unconscious in the dirt.

She had no idea how long she lay there, sobs racking her body. Inside, she crawled through the shards of her shattered soul, everything that she thought she was and everything she thought she had a wreckage around her. She had no strength to move, and for a moment she wished she could just dissolve into nothing—to be at peace under the dirt.

She raised a shaking hand to smooth the hair away from her face. As she did so, she felt two strong, warm hands grip her shoulders, felt someone kneeling behind her.

"Sahara! Sahara, what happened to you?" It was Katarina's voice, and Sahara slumped in relief.

"I don't know," she moaned. "I can't...I don't think I can get up. I just...I want to die. I just want to die."

"Nonsense." Sahara could hear the frown in the healer's voice. "Pull yourself together, my girl. Come on."

"I can't! I can't. I'm so broken everywhere...everything is broken. There's nothing to hold me together anymore."

Katarina's expert hands ran over her arm, her leg, her back. "There's nothing at all broken," she said. "What happened? Did you trip?"

Sahara managed to shake her head. Something that was half a sob and half a laugh bubbled out of her, horrifying her with its mad sound. With a superhuman effort, she clamped it down and got control of herself.

"No. I didn't trip."

Katarina took hold of her shoulders again and gently rolled her onto her back. The older woman's face was smooth, but there was a warm light of concern in her eyes that Sahara hadn't seen before.

"What happened to you?" she repeated slowly. "Tell me."

"There's nothing you can do," Sahara said. "There's no way to heal what's broken in my soul, Katarina."

Katarina sat back, placing her hands on her thighs, looking for all the world like the statue of a healing goddess Sahara had seen in the market on Agora. "That's nonsense too." Katarina cocked an eyebrow at her. "And you know it is."

Sahara blinked at her, then closed her eyes. She was tired beyond exhaustion...more tired than she'd ever been in her life. Her mind was already blank...there was nothing to do but slip away.

"That won't do at all," Katarina said crisply. "Let's go."

"Go where?" Sahara's voice sounded like it came from miles away, drifting like the breeze across the plains. She vaguely heard a shuffling noise, then felt herself seized by the arms and jerked upright. She grunted in protest and tried to open her eyes, but her lids were so heavy. Too heavy.

Katarina hefted Sahara up onto her shoulder like a sack of grain, groaning softly with the effort.

"Thank goodness you decided to collapse just outside the camp," she muttered. "Or I'd never get you home."

When Sahara's eyes fluttered open, she was lying on something soft, with a warm coverlet over her. The scent of a sweet spice filled the air around her, coaxing her soul into warmth. Through the hole in the tent's roof, she could see a riot of stars. When she turned her head, she saw the shadowy figure of Katarina in the next room moving back and forth between her and a small fire.

Sahara licked her lips and swallowed. She was incredibly thirsty, and her head was pounding so that she could barely move. She tried to call out to Katarina, but her tongue seemed to stick to the roof of her mouth, and all that came out was a tiny croak.

It seemed to be enough, though, for she saw the healer stop suddenly, head turned toward the room where Sahara lay. Encouraged, Sahara croaked again, managing to do it louder this time. And that was enough for Katarina to push aside the flap of canvas that divided the tent's rooms.

"Did you make that froggish noise, or should I send for Rigel and his weapons?" Katarina asked, a smile pricking at the corners of her mouth.

"Water," Sahara managed.

Katarina slipped to her side with a cup. She helped Sahara to raise her head, then tipped the cup just a fraction. The cool liquid, lightly flavored, slid down her throat and cooled her. As she settled back onto her pillow, the throbbing in her head lessened a bit.

"How do you feel?" Katarina asked after a few moments.

"Better, I think," Sahara said, managing a crooked smile. "My head hurts like the devil."

Katarina nodded slowly. "Did you hit it when you fell?"

"I told you. I didn't fall."

Katarina jerked a small stool toward her and sat on it, taking one of Sahara's hands in both her own. "Then what happened to you?"

Sahara sighed. "It's...going to sound crazy."

"Try me."

Sahara closed her eyes, feeling weariness beginning to lap against her consciousness again. "Jared and I...we can communicate by speaking into each other's minds. And my brother too. But that's a different story." She opened an eye, saw the fierce look of concentration on Katarina's face, and continued. "Something's happened to Jared. Something horrible. He...he...it felt like he would squeeze my mind into oblivion. Like he was trying to destroy me. And he said things..." She stopped, a sudden flood of tears overwhelming her voice.

Katarina patted her hand gently. "I know. I understand. I understand how much it hurts when the one you love most in the world turns on you."

"It was like it wasn't even him anymore," she sobbed. "Like he's been ripped out and replaced with something...evil." She shuddered. "He said as much. He said he's the Dragon now."

Katarina jerked away from her as if she had suddenly turned into a serpent. "He said what?"

"He's the Dragon-Slayer. Didn't I tell you? And Azimir wants to use him somehow. It's all so confusing. But now it's like he's given into some kind of power...like Azimir has made him become something else. I don't understand how, and I barely understand why. But he nearly destroyed me." Sahara's eyes closed again, and she felt herself drifting toward sleep.

Just before she lost consciousness again, she heard Katarina whisper, "Azimir, you fool! What have you done?"

TWENTY-TWO

TWO DAYS LATER, Sahara sat in the warm sunshine outside her own tent, eyes closed, drinking in the warmth of the light and the breeze. Her recovery had been slow, and she'd found it hard to drag herself out of the sluggishness that mired her thoughts and actions. She still felt like she was walking with chains on her feet, and her mind was leaden. Yesterday, she'd been able to tell Katarina a bit more about what Jared had done, and Katarina had mixed a special tincture for her to take. It was helping. Just not fast enough.

The sun helped most. There was something about the light that teased her heart into a smile in spite of itself and seemed to breathe life back into her mind.

"Glad to see you on your feet again."

And just like that, the light was gone, and so was the joy.

Sahara opened her eyes and scowled. Brig was standing there, his dark shadow falling across her like a bad omen.

"What do you want, Brig?" she snapped. "Get out of the way. You're blocking my sunshine."

Brig snorted, but stepped to the side. "What's the matter with you? You smoke some of that Demon's Breath by accident or something?"

"No."

He watched her in silence for a moment, waiting for her to offer an explanation. When she said nothing, he prodded, "So what's the matter with you, then?"

Sahara sighed, wishing he would just leave. "I've been...ill."

"Ill?" He squinted at her, then frowned. "That's not true."

"Yes, it is. Go and ask Katarina yourself if you doubt me. I've been unconscious in her tent for the better part of two days." *Idiot*, she thought. But she welcomed the fire inside her that he'd stoked with his annoying questions. It made her feel more like her old self again, and that was a relief.

Brig hesitated for a moment, then squatted in front of her and lowered his voice. "You've got to do what you said you were going to do. And you've got to do it tonight."

Sahara straightened and studied Brig's earnest face. "Do what?"

"Follow Katarina. Tonight." His eyes glittered at her. "Or one of my boys will kill her, with or without your permission."

"He can't do that." Sahara's hands balled into fists, and the haze clouding her thoughts was scorched away by the fire of her anger.

"Yes, he can. And he will. Our spies have reported some suspicious movement of Azimir's forces in the last couple of days. He's planning something. Something big. And soon. We need to know if she's feeding him information."

Sahara pushed herself to her feet. "Keep your man on a leash," she snapped. "I'll see what I can find out." Brig rose and started to turn away, but Sahara added, "And Brig? No one touches her before I give the word, or I swear to God that I'll kill every last one of you."

Brig's face paled slightly, but there was venom in his voice. "Fine. Just see that you keep your end of the deal, or you might find a knife in your own back one of these days."

"Don't threaten me," Sahara said. "Save your dignity and get out of my sight."

Brig hesitated, as if he couldn't bear to leave without having the last word. "See you do it, then."

"Get out of my sight. Now."

Brig moved away as quickly as his pride would allow, and Sahara sighed.

Back on the job. Maybe it'll do me good.

She ducked inside the tent to make her preparations for her journey back to Aquila. Rigel had given her a small canvas knapsack to carry her few belongings when they moved camps, and she pulled it out from under her cot and threw it on the bed. She paused, considering.

I want to travel light, and it's only for tonight.

She frowned and got down on her hands and knees, reaching further under the bed and pulling out a slightly larger canvas bag. Inside were her old clothes—the ones she'd been wearing when she'd escaped from Azimir's palace. Her black battle dress pants and shirt would make moving in shadows much easier. And the large pockets in the pants would make it possible to carry what she needed without the added bulk of the knapsack.

She slipped out of the cool, comfortable clothes of the Hazad and back into her old things. Then she frowned down at her bare toes, curling them in the soft pelt. Rigel had thrown away her boots, and now she had nothing but sandals to wear. And sandals would never do for this job.

Sahara ran a hand through her unruly curls and sighed. She really had no other choice. It was sandals or bare feet.

A soft noise behind her startled her, and she whipped her head around to glance over her shoulder. Rigel stood just inside the tent, a sheepish look on his handsome young face.

"Don't you knock...or whatever?" Sahara said, taking a breath to slow her pulse back to normal. "It's not wise to frighten me like that, you know."

Rigel swallowed hard, his eyes fixed on her right hand. Sahara glanced down at the cruel knife she held at the ready. Carefully, meticulously, she sheathed it again and took a deep breath. "I could have killed you, you idiot."

Rigel sniffed. "Old habits?"

"Instinct."

Rigel stood silently for a moment, watching her. Sahara arched an eyebrow at him and sat down on her cot, slipping her feet back into her sandals.

"That looks strange, you know," Rigel commented when she stood again, shaking out the wide cuffs of her pants. The leather-thonged sandals peeped out from underneath.

She shrugged. "I don't know," she said. "It could work."

"No. It couldn't. It doesn't."

Sahara felt her temper flare. "I'm not wearing this to impress you, and I'm not putting on a fashion show where I'm going. And, anyway, since you junked my boots, this disaster is all your fault."

Rigel whipped his hand from behind his back with a sudden grin, and Sahara realized that he'd been waiting to set this moment up since he stepped inside her tent. He looked so ridiculously pleased with himself that she couldn't help a smile. And when she saw what he held out to her, the smile became a gape of surprise.

Her boots, socks stuffed in their tops, dangled between his thumb and forefinger, and Rigel's grin widened.

"Where did you get those?" she asked. "You threw them out! I saw you do it!"

"You didn't see me get them back." He hesitated. "Well, actually, it wasn't me. It was a friend of a friend...we stash things there sometimes. Things we mean to smuggle out of the city without the Zharib noticing."

"You mean that trash heap was a drop point?"

"Yes."

Sahara took the boots from him and sat down again. She kicked off the sandals and pulled on her socks and boots, grunting in satisfaction as she tightened the laces and knotted them.

"Where are you going, Zelie?" There was a vague note of warning in his voice, and Sahara glanced up at him.

"What business is that of yours?"

His eyes flickered at her, hurt, and she realized that the words had come out more harshly than she'd intended.

"You're up to something," Rigel said. "I want to know what it is. Where are you going?"

"There's just something I have to do. You wouldn't understand."

"I would, if you'd just trust me."

Sahara shook her head. "I don't trust you, Rigel. Not with this. Not with this." She stood again and pulled her hair back and knotted it. Then she met his frustrated gaze and shrugged. "You'll just have to let me go. Just like that."

Rigel stepped close to her and seized her arm in a grip that was much stronger than she expected. "If this is about Katarina, you need to let it go," he murmured. "Leave her alone, Sahara. She's been through enough."

Sahara jerked her arm out of his hand. "I can't leave her alone. If I leave her alone, Brig will have her assassinated."

Rigel recoiled, stunned. "What?"

"You heard me well enough. Now let me finish getting my things together. I'm leaving as soon as it's dark."

"Why in Ata's name would Brig want Katarina dead?" Rigel demanded, his voice hard and keen as a knife's edge.

"Because he and his crew think she's a threat to the Hazad. They think she's a spy for the Zharib." She paused, but seeing that Rigel was speechless, she added, "It's not hard to see why, Rigel. She sneaks back to Aquila every night. She never tells anyone that she's going. It's all very suspicious. Anyway, Brig wants me to follow her and find out what she's doing. Maybe it's all harmless, you know? But if I don't follow her and find out for sure, they'll kill her." Seeing that nothing she said was taking the edge off Rigel's anger, she laid a hand on his wrist. "It's the only way to save her, Rigel."

"And let's say you find out what she does in Aquila. What if it's not harmless? Then what?"

Sahara sighed, her hand dropping to her side. "Then I'll do what I have to do, Rigel."

He stared at her, horror creeping over his face until Sahara couldn't stand to look at him any longer. "You can't...Sahara, you can't," he breathed. "Please!"

Sahara swallowed, strangling the worm of doubt and dread that coiled in her gut. "Then pray to your god that she's not up to anything treacherous," she said.

"I don't understand why. Please just tell me why. Why Katarina?"

"Brig doesn't believe that I am what I say I am," she answered slowly.

Rigel made a strange choking sound. "So this is about proving something to that wretched piece of horse dung? You would kill a woman just to show the world that you can?"

Sahara winced in spite of herself. "Of course not. I'm not a monster, Rigel."

Rigel arched an eyebrow at her. "Then why?"

Sahara pressed her lips together and crossed her arms across her chest, not sure how much she wanted to tell him. But as his face grew hard and cold, Sahara felt that old wound inside rub open and begin to weep. She wanted to justify herself, wanted to say anything to make him understand what she had to do. But all she could do was stand there, mute and rigid and despairing.

"You have nothing to say to me?" he said, his voice husky. "Nothing at all?" When she didn't answer, Rigel planted a finger in her chest. "Then stay away from Tessa. And if you harm Katarina, don't ever come back here. Because I'll kill you myself."

Sahara felt the tears brimming in her eyes, and she shook her head. "Oh, Rigel," she laughed softly. "Rigel. You wouldn't. You can't. Please...I don't want to hurt Katarina. I love her...she's like the mother I never had! But..."

"But nothing. Nothing. There is no reason that could justify what you're planning to do."

He spun on his heel and ducked out of the tent, swearing under his breath as he went. Sahara's breath came in a ragged sob, and she whispered, "I hope someday you'll understand. And then maybe you won't hate me any longer."

———

The night was dark. The moon Eshka was just a sliver, and Sahara, looking up into the sky, thought that even the stars, scattered like crumbs on the table of heaven, seemed somehow dim and sad.

What a stupid thing to think.

She dropped her eyes to the path leading out of the camp. From her position in the shadows under the trees at the northern edge of the camp, she had a clear line of sight along the path to Katarina's tent. She'd been there for the better part of an hour, and still the lantern light illuminated Katarina's tent.

The hushing night breeze was laden with the now familiar and no longer dangerous scent of the Demon's Breath flowers. Sahara forced herself to take a deep breath. Even now, after so many weeks with the Hazad, she still had to force herself to take that first long, slow breath. But once it was done, her anxiety about the drug vanished, and she could focus on her task.

At last. A dark figure with a veiled lantern emerged from Katarina's tent, and Sahara's muscles tensed. A wordless prayer was in her heart, and she loosened her knife in its sheath. Katarina hurried past her, the spicy sweet scent of the perfume she wore mingling for a moment with the scent of the blossoms in the breeze. And then Sahara slipped into the shadows in her wake, matching her strides to Katarina's, stepping as quietly and swiftly as a prowling animal.

The journey toward Aquila was a silent one, and Sahara couldn't help thinking how pleasant it would have been if they'd been going together. She shoved the thought roughly aside. She couldn't afford sentimentality. Especially if things turned out worse than her hopes.

Sahara had scouted this path a number of times in the last week, and she knew which gate Katarina would use to enter the city. As the walls loomed into view, Sahara felt her throat tighten. This was the one part of this mission that she hadn't quite nailed down. Katarina had her inside man and a bag full of coins. But Sahara, trailing after her in the darkness, had nothing.

She thought about knocking out the guard, but that wouldn't work. Katarina would leave the city by the same gate, and if the guard were slumped against the wall, she would know something was wrong. Sahara didn't want her to suspect anything. If this was all for nothing, then she didn't want Katarina to realize she'd been followed.

Sahara had a length of rope with a grappling hook coiled around her shoulder, and she reached up to check it now. *Maybe up and over the wall is my safest bet, then.*

And without a second thought, she left the path, which was now curving to the east, and headed straight north for the city walls. If she could get there before Katarina, she could position herself inside the walls near the eastern gate and wait for the healer to enter the city. As soon as she was a safe distance from the path, she broke into an easy jog, a pace that she could maintain without breaking a sweat for the rest of her journey to Aquila.

The terrain under her boots was smooth at first, but it inclined steadily. The city was situated on rising ground, and the closer Sahara got to the massive walls, the rockier the ground became. Sahara's pace flagged as her footing became increasingly unsteady, and she finally had to slow to a creeping walk, feeling her way forward in the dark like a blind beggar. She cursed softly as she turned her ankle on a stone and stopped, measuring the distance she had left to travel. It wasn't more than a few hundred yards, but picking through this ruinous mess would take far longer than she could afford.

Keeping on as straight as she could, Sahara tried to increase her pace. The scrap of moon was already setting, and whatever tiny light it had given was slipping away.

Suddenly, Sahara dropped into a crouch behind a boulder. A searing ray of light swept across the rubble just ahead of her, and a moment later, Sahara heard the whirring of engines above her in the dark. She looked up and saw the dark shape of a Scythe slide by, blotting out the stars as it went. It hovered for a moment, its searchlight sweeping the area between her and the city walls once more, and then it moved off to the west.

I wonder what other security measures they have in place.

She shifted positions and peeped over the top of the boulder. She couldn't see anything moving along the walls. Her initial surge of triumphant relief was almost instantly drowned by her overwhelming sense that something was very wrong.

Azimir's not the type to leave his city vulnerable. Not in any respect. So what's the danger here? Besides the Scythes...what is it that I'm not seeing?

And suddenly a hail of bullets shattered the silence around her.

TWENTY-THREE

SAHARA CURSED and ducked behind the boulder, covering her head with her arms as the bullets continued to rain down around her position.

That's what I missed. Gun turret.

She swore again. The spray of bullets stopped, and Sahara could hear the vague whirring of the barrels as they hummed to a stop. Slowly, ever so slowly, she uncurled herself and shifted around so that she could see over the boulder once more. She wished that she had her night vision gear. In the almost total darkness, she strained her eyes until they watered, but she couldn't make out anything along the wall above her. Frustrated with her blindness, she closed her eyes and took a deep breath. Then another. And another. Then she simply let herself breathe and listened.

At first, all she could hear was the sound of her breath and the thumping of her heart. But then, other sounds began to catch her attention.

The distant hum of the Scythe out to her west.

She listened to it for a moment, and when she registered that the sound was receding, she let it go and returned back to her state of awareness.

Some small animal or large insect nosing through the scraggly undergrowth just in front of her position.

The chuckling of a night bird to the south.

The shushing breeze that slipped through the grasses and between the rocks to curl around her.

She opened her eyes. She hadn't heard what she'd expected to hear.

She hadn't heard voices.

That meant that the gun turret wasn't manned. It was a drone, like the Scythes, probably activated by a motion sensor. Sahara shifted again, trying to get a better look at the stretch of wall before her. As soon as she moved, the turret exploded into life, peppering the front of the boulder and everything around it with bullets.

Sahara froze for an instant, finding the spot on the wall where the turret stood, finally revealed as it vomited its arsenal in a halo of fire. Then she slid back into cover as the turret whirred and slowed to a stop. As she moved, she heard a click, and the firestorm ignited once again.

Sahara looked down at her boots and brushed frantically around her right foot. A small pressure plate, almost invisible to the untrained eye, was perfectly positioned to catch anyone who might be trying to use the boulder as cover for their approach to the city.

So it's not a motion sensor...it's a pressure switch. She swore and crouched further behind the boulder as several bullets ricocheted off the top and came close to nicking her in the face.

As soon as the turret wound down once more, Sahara began to search around her position for something to weight down the switch. It operated like a mine, she realized. Stepping on it had activated the turret, and any release of pressure on the plate caused the turret to shred the area. She was trapped here unless she could find a way to trick the turret into thinking she was still behind the boulder.

How much weight will that take? Her hand found a large stone just close enough for her to roll it into the shelter of the boulder. The stone was sizable and weighed as much as a small animal. *Guess I won't know until I try.*

She set the stone next to her foot. She took a deep breath and slowly edged her boot out of the way as she slid the stone to take its place. After a breathless moment, her foot was free, and she withdrew her hand, leaving the stone on the plate. The turret was silent, and the wall dark.

Sahara let out her breath in a rush and wiped the sweat from her forehead with the back of her hand. With one last glance to be sure there was no movement from the city, Sahara ran forward in a crouch to the base of the wall. She dropped the rope from her shoulder into her hand and deftly sent the grappling hook whizzing into the night air. She heard the satisfying scrape of metal on stone and then it caught and held fast. Sahara tugged experimentally twice, and then, satisfied that it would hold her weight, she jumped and caught the rope and began to climb.

The wall wasn't particularly high—maybe only thirty feet— but Sahara went carefully and slowly, watching for any sign of men patrolling the wall. But she saw nothing, and as her hands closed around the parapet, she breathed another sigh of relief.

They trust their technology too much. It will be their undoing.

She pulled herself up and over the edge and fell noiselessly onto the walkway. She crouched there for a moment, shrouded in shadow, and studied her position. The turret was ten feet away on her right, cold and silent in the pale starlight. Sahara considered disabling it, then decided against it in case it might trip the alarm.

She turned her attention away from the wall and fixed her position. She needed to make her way to the gate to intercept Katarina, and she prayed that she hadn't lost too much time. She was on the northern wall, halfway between the northern gate and the east wall. Now that she knew which direction to go, she studied the skyline of the city, an irregular stain on the sparkling dome of heaven. If she ever wanted to find her rope and her way out of the city, she would need to memorize this vista. Finally satisfied that she knew where she was, she ran silently along the wall toward the eastern gate.

The wall began sloping upward the closer she got to the gate, and Sahara checked her pace, then stopped altogether. She slid to the parapet and peered between the crenellations. She could vaguely see the road snaking away to the west and south, but she couldn't see anyone moving along it. She cursed and crept along the wall until she could go no farther. The high sides of the gate thrust up from the wall, arching away into darkness high above her. She glanced back the way she had come and spotted a wide set of steps cut into the face of the wall. They led down into the courtyard below, and Sahara slipped down them, keeping as close as she could to the wall on her left.

Now she heard voices.

Sahara froze in place, heart hammering.

There was someone at the postern gate. She could make out the husky masculine voice of the guard, but the voice of the one speaking to him was too low for her to hear. The gate rasped on its hinges, and Sahara waited, eyes riveted on the space just within the gates.

A hooded figure with a shrouded lantern hurried across the court-yard, and Sahara closed her eyes in relief. She'd made it. Barely.

She watched as Katarina made for a narrow street leading west into the heart of the city, then turned her attention back to the gate. The guard had slumped down near the postern door, head sagging on his chest, his weapon across his knees. After another moment, seeing that the guard made no movement, Sahara lowered herself over the side of the steps and dropped to the courtyard below. Then she slipped silently after Katarina.

Katarina moved like a shade through streets as dead and deserted as a crypt, her feet making no noise on the cobbled street. Dark build-ings hunched beside the road, wrapped in grim shadows. Sahara wondered who or what was inside, but she had no time to stop and consider them closely. Katarina's pace was swift, and Sahara almost had to jog to keep her in sight. She took alleyway after alleyway, winding her way ever closer to the city center and the palace. As they went along, Sahara's curiosity flared. Questions burned on the tip of her tongue, and she had to fight down the urge to catch up to Katarina and demand explanations and answers.

Before she could blow her cover, though, Katarina stopped abruptly across from a tall building. Sahara ducked into the doorway of a building as Katarina checked over her shoulder. She stood for several moments, seeming to consider her approach. Sahara's breaths came shallow and fast. The building was directly opposite the palace, and Sahara struggled to keep from drowning under the weight of the flashbacks that flooded her mind.

A sudden fear turned her knees to water.

What if he finds me? What if he can see me? What if he knows I'm here?

Sahara stared at the palace, unable to tear her eyes from its facade. Time seemed to drag to a halt, and Sahara felt a vague uneasiness grow within her, as though fingers of darkness were searching the night for her. She ripped her eyes from the palace and shrank back in the shadows within the doorway. She felt the ravages of panic shredding her nerves, and for a moment it was all she could do to keep herself from screaming.

She forced herself to take a deep breath, then another. Slowly, she regained control of her shattered nerves. After another moment, she was able to peer out into the street, just in time to see Katarina slip inside the building and someone close the door behind her.

She's meeting someone here. They're expecting her. And even as her mind framed the word 'traitor', she thought, *I've got to get inside.*

Without another moment of hesitation, she darted across the street, making her way from shadows into shadows, gliding silent and sure-footed now toward the building. She paused once more, considering it. Going through the front wasn't an option. She didn't have a death wish, and there was no telling who was inside with Katarina.

The building was separated from its nearest neighbor by a narrow alley. The darkness seemed to pool between the buildings, and in her black gear, Sahara would be almost invisible. She was a good climber, and she began to get the inklings of a plan.

After one last glance to left and right, she slipped across the street and let the shadows of the alley swallow her. She ran the fingers of her left hand lightly along the wall, using it to guide her footsteps. When she estimated she was almost halfway down the alley, she turned to face the wall. She edged sideways, searching for a place where she could climb. But the wall was smooth.

Stone by stone, Sahara, she told herself, echoing the words Jared had said to her all those many months ago. It brought the sting of tears to her eyes, and she shook her head angrily. No time for such nonsense now. She could get sentimental when she was safely back in her tent.

Her fingers brushed metal and she stopped. She explored the structure to her right with her hands, building a picture of it in her mind. It seemed to be a sort of ladder with widely placed rungs. Her mouth twisted into a grin, and she eased her way up onto the first rung, then the second. As she felt more secure, she swarmed up the ladder. As she ascended, the light around her grew. She saw the darker shapes of windows as she passed the first floor. Then, just as she reached the second floor, a light flared in the window on her left and she heard voices.

Heart hammering, Sahara stopped, barely daring to breathe. The windows were covered with an intricate latticework, and any sound she made would be audible to the people in the room.

"It's getting harder and harder for me to come, Zira," came a woman's voice. Sahara recognized it at once as Katarina's. "I think I'm being followed."

"You saw someone?" Zira asked. The woman's voice was harsh and flat, as if all the music had been sucked out of her soul. Sahara winced.

"No. It's just a feeling. I'm not well liked by some in my tribe."

"Your tribe."

Silence. "The only tribe I have left." Katarina's voice was sharp and sad, proud and bitter.

I wonder if this Zira was once part of Katarina's tribe, Sahara thought, easing a little higher on the ladder. *And I wonder why Katarina had to leave.*

"They would like you even less if they knew why you came here," Zira spat.

"Some do know. Some allow it."

"Do they know everything? Do they know you come to see your son?"

Sahara's mouth dropped open. *Son? What son?*

"Yes."

"And they know who he is to the Zharib?"

Katarina's voice was barely audible. "No."

Zira's cackling laugh fired Sahara's anger. Couldn't the woman hear how much she was hurting Katarina? For a moment, Sahara forgot why she was there. All thought that she was there to spy on Katarina was drowned in the rush of her desire to protect her from anything that might cause her grief. She almost vaulted herself through the window, but checked herself just in time.

Not yet, she told herself. *Not yet.*

"I have your payment," Katarina said, and Sahara heard a tiny jingling sound. "It's all I could manage this time."

There was silence, and Sahara knew the woman must be pawing through the bag.

"It's not enough."

"But..."

"It's not enough! You know the arrangement. My fees are reasonable. Only enough to cover the bribes for the four guards at the palace, and a modest sum for my trouble." There was a harsh jangling as the woman flung the purse to the floor. "That wouldn't even cover one of the guards."

"I thought that maybe..."

"What? That I would loan you the rest? That I would risk my neck to get you in there for free?" The woman's cackle made Sahara's skin crawl. "If anything, I should raise your price. Azimir's keeping a new pet. He sees all that moves, it's said. The Slayer will destroy the Hazad, it's said. He would be happy to start with you, I'm sure."

Sahara swallowed hard.

The Slayer. She means Jared.

A thousand images of Jared's smile flashed through her mind, and she retreated from them as fast as she could. He couldn't know she was here. And she had no idea how to keep him out of her thoughts anymore.

"N-no, Zira. Azimir would never...he wouldn't ever..."

"You're a fool. You think he would spare the Hazad because of you? If he doesn't show his strength, he will have mutiny on his hands." She hesitated, her voice a grating purr. "Wouldn't you like to know who would betray him? Which of his lords holds the knife to his throat?"

"You're a snake, Zira."

"My girls know them all."

"He's in danger, then?"

"If he cannot destroy the Hazad, if he cannot control the Slayer as he says he can...they will slit his throat and take the throne." The woman's voice dropped to a hiss. "So think about it. If you take a warning back to the Hazad, he's as good as dead."

Sahara heard Katarina's strangled sob. "I hate you, Zira," she whispered. "What's in this for you? Why are you tormenting me?"

Zira cackled. "For the fun of it! Isn't it obvious? So what if I have my girls whisper intrigues to the Council?"

"You're going to get them all killed...and yourself too. You can't play those games forever. Someone will find you out. You'll make a mistake somewhere, and that will be the end of you!"

"Don't sound so hopeful. I'm careful. Oh, so careful. It takes skill to weave webs like these, but such fun to see the flies dancing in the trap."

"You're a monster."

"Take your pathetic little purse and get out of my sight. Don't you dare come back here until you have the coin...and my price is double. I'll not risk the Slayer for less."

There was a sound of hasty footsteps retreating from the window, and then the light vanished. Sahara let her breath out in a rush. Her head was spinning. Someone in Azimir's inner circle wanted him dead, and this woman was pulling the strings of some kind of scheme to get him killed. And for some reason Katarina wanted him alive, but not so that she could sell out her own people. Katarina was no spy for Azimir. If anything, she was spying <u>on</u> Azimir, but Sahara couldn't understand why.

But wouldn't I love to fix this Zira woman. Wouldn't I just love to see her get caught in her own snare.

It was something she'd have to consider carefully on her way home. Next time she came to Aquila, she'd be coming with one very specific mission. But she could take a little side trip to fix the woman who thought she was invincible.

Sahara shifted her grip on the ladder and stretched her boot down to the rung below.

Sahara.

She slipped, scrabbling for a hand-hold on one of the rungs.

Jared's face filled her consciousness. Her right hand caught a bar and she gritted her teeth against the searing pain that flared down her arm.

Jared. Don't...don't hurt me again.

There was shocked surprise in his eyes. *Hurt you? Did I...have I hurt you? Sahara...I'm falling. I'm falling. I don't know how to catch myself.*

Tears slicked her cheeks. *You don't have to catch yourself, Jared.* She smiled at him, trying to envelop him in the love that welled up in her heart. *That's what you have me for.*

His eyes were wells of shadow, and she could almost see the Jared she knew drowning in the darkness. His voice was lost, but he mouthed a single word.

Hurry.

TWENTY-FOUR

JARED CAME out of the vision shaking. He was on his hands and knees on the plush, richly woven rug that covered the floor of his sitting room. The heavy scent of spice hung in the air like a cloud, and the light of a solitary lamp threw dark shadows against the wall.

"What's happening to me?" Jared groaned, pressing his forehead into his hands. "I hurt her. Somehow. I hurt her...God, what have I done? What am I doing?"

He crept forward into the circle of light and huddled there, his knees drawn up under his chin. The vision of her hanging there, one hand gripping the metal rung of the ladder, tears sliding down her cheeks, made his breath catch in his throat. But already the darkness was swarming over it, twisting it, distorting it. Her face was the first thing to go...her smile vanishing in shadow. Jared's breath came ragged, tears spilling over. He stretched out a hand, wanting to hold her, to catch her. But something went wrong.

She lost her grip, and he never heard her scream.

"No!" he cried. "Sahara! No!" A flood of curses broke through his tears, and he slammed his fists into the floor. The wooden planks splintered with a sickening crack.

"You really should try not to break the floor like that," came an oily voice from just behind him.

Jared jumped to his feet and spun, hands balled into fists. "Don't sneak up on me, Azimir," he growled. "One of these days, it will be the death of you."

Azimir speared a pointed glance in the direction of the floor. "This is the third time this week that I've had to repair something in your chambers," he said.

Jared caught him by the jacket, dragging his face just inches from his own. "Where's your assassin, Azimir? Left him behind this time?"

Azimir's face paled, and Jared felt a surge of triumph. "So who will save you? Who will even hear you scream?"

A stunning blow to the back of his head made him drop Azimir and fall to his knees with a grunt. Azimir backed away from him, coughing and rubbing his throat.

"I didn't leave him behind. I never leave him behind."

Jared glanced over his shoulder. Rafe stood there, a jagged, heavy-handled knife in his hand. A stab of sorrow cut through the darkness in Jared's mind. Rafe's eyes were utterly blank, his motions stiff and mechanical. He would kill Jared without a second thought. Without pity. And without regret.

"Rafe," Jared whispered. "Look at me."

His grief threatened to overwhelm him, and for a moment he hung there, suspended above the floodtide of his wrath like a raindrop trembling on a leaf's edge. His eyes swung toward Azimir, who was standing with his arms folded across his chest.

"What?" said Azimir with a short bark of laughter. "You will not harm me. You dare not lift your finger. But I will show you where you can loose your fury."

Jared lost his hold and slipped once more into the abyss. Each time he clawed his way up again, but each fall into darkness carried him further and further down. Soon he would not be able to see the light at all, no matter how far he climbed.

"Azimir," he said, just before the shadows claimed him once more. "You have no idea what you are playing with. It will destroy you."

Azimir's face paled slightly. "So you say. But you're always a bit doom and gloom when the mood takes you."

Jared dropped his head and closed his eyes. "Don't say I didn't warn you," he said softly.

———

When Jared opened his eyes again, Azimir and Rafe were gone. A pale streak of early morning sunlight was warm on his face, making the lamplight look sickly. He drew in a deep breath and rubbed a hand over his face.

"I need a shave and some breakfast," he mumbled and pushed himself stiffly to his feet.

"I've brought your breakfast."

Jared spun around and saw Emelia. She was standing next to the window, her hands folded in front of her. Beside her on the small, round table sat a tray with a steaming pot of the dark coffee the Zharib took with their breakfast. A cut glass bowl of berries and a plate of sweet breads studded with nuts and dried fruit rounded out the offerings.

"What are you doing here?" he growled. He ran a hand through his hair. "Don't you knock?"

"You didn't hear me."

Jared grunted and moved to the table. He selected a berry and popped it into his mouth, feeling the juices explode against his tongue. It was like eating sunshine, and he smiled in spite of himself.

"Doesn't that feel better?" Emelia asked, smiling at him in return.

Jared took another berry from the bowl and moved to the window, staring out over the sharply canted roofs of the city. "Emelia," he said slowly, "I don't know how much longer I can hold out."

Emelia's face was drawn, and she moved to stand beside him with a soft jingle of the bells around her ankle. "I know," she murmured. "I know." She hesitated, then drew something out of the sash that encircled her slender waist. "That's why I brought you this."

She held it out to him, hilt first. She bowed as his hand clasped what she proffered to him.

It was Sahara's dagger.

His breath caught in his throat.

"Where did you get this?" he demanded. When she merely looked mutely at him, he repeated, "Where?"

Emelia moved to the window and pointed. Jared joined her and followed the direction of her finger. Across the wide avenue that encircled the palace was a tall building, perhaps five stories high. Even in the bright morning sun, the alley that separated it from the nearest building was black as pitch.

"I found it in that alley," she said. "And I was told..." She stopped suddenly, choking on her words.

The dagger fell to the floor as Jared seized both of Emelia's shoulders in a vise-grip. "Told? Who told you?"

Tears spilled onto Emelia's pale cheeks. "She wanted you to have it. As a promise. She told me...she told me to give it to you."

"Who?"

"The red-headed girl who loves you, Jared."

He reeled away from her. "You saw her? When? Where?"

"I met her outside that house. She was here on some kind of mission...she didn't say what." Emelia clasped her hands. "She said you needed this. That it would give you strength and courage...and that she would come for you."

Jared found that his hands were shaking. In spite of everything—in spite of the fact that he had hurt her somehow—she was here somewhere close by. She knew what was happening, and she had refused to abandon him.

"She could have been on the other side of the system by now," he murmured, stooping to pick up the knife. "But she stayed." He lifted his eyes to Emelia's face. "Where is she now?"

Emelia shook her head. "She wouldn't tell me that, in case..." Her voice trailed off. "She wouldn't tell me. But she said to tell you that she won't be far."

"She's in danger. Does she know? Does she know how great and how close the danger is?"

Emelia shrugged. "I don't know. But she seems...she seems to understand such things, Jared." The ghost of a smile touched her lips. "I think she knows. And I think she doesn't give a damn."

Jared had to smile. "No," he said. "She wouldn't."

He knelt there on the floor, turning the dagger over in his hands. It was almost a prayer, and he felt his heart reaching out to Sahara, though his mind was strangely silent.

I hope you know I love you. I don't want this. I don't want to hurt you. I don't want to hurt anyone.

He drew the knife slowly, the sunlight catching on its keen edge. Sahara had carried this knife since he had brought her to Albadir out of the desert. He ran his thumb along the blade, then pulled the knife apart, testing the weight of the double blades in his hands. He could feel the heaviness of Emelia's gaze on him, could almost taste her quivering fear.

These blades had slain a Guardian—a hell-hound of the Drakkin. They had slain many men on the porch of their shelter that rainy night on K'ilenfir. And before that, in the battle against the Drakkin on Silesia, how many had it sent to the afterlife? More than he could count, but death was heavy on their edges.

He took a deep breath, turning the blades slowly in his hands. The call of blood was strong.

The fire of hate flickered, then flared.

He hated Azimir.

He hated the cold blankness of Rafe's stare, the weight of the blade in Rafe's cold hand.

"I could kill them both," he said, hardly aware that he spoke aloud. He turned the thought over in his mind as he rose to his feet. "What is Rafe to me now? He has turned against me and does the bidding of that pathetic worm who calls himself lord of the Zharib. Why should his death stop me? Why should I hold back for his sake?"

Emelia's sharp intake of breath caught his attention.

He swung around to face her.

"Why are you still here?" he asked, his voice low. "I wouldn't stay, if I were you." He flipped the knife in his right hand. "I would go."

Emelia swallowed hard. "And if I stay? Will you kill me too?"

"You shouldn't say such things. Not to me. Not right now." Vaguely, he could feel part of himself recoiling, part of his mind screaming at him. But the darkness was building within him, and soon that voice was lost in the swirling shadows.

Emelia's eyes shifted over Jared's left shoulder and fixed on the door. Jared knew that she was calculating the distance, the time, the obstacles between her and safety. Jared took a step forward and she instinctively backed away. Her hands twined themselves in the latticework of the window.

"You shouldn't back away," Jared said, his voice still low. "There is only death for you that way."

"Remember," Emelia whispered.

She darted forward and grabbed the small table. The crystal and china smashed to bits on the floor. Jared sprang at her, slicing downward with the knife in his right hand. It caught in her forearm and tore. Her scream of pain was drowned in the sickening splintering of wood as she flung the table through the latticework.

Sunlight poured into the room.

Jared crossed his left arm over his right, preparing to deal the death stroke.

At the last second, her eyes caught his.

"Remember," she whispered. "She loves you."

And then she flung herself out the window.

TWENTY-FIVE

A LIGHT TAPPING on their door roused Deor from his dark and troubled thoughts. In the time it took him to raise his head, Brytnoth was already at the door, and a moment later, he stepped aside to let Alberic enter the room. Deor got to his feet and crossed his arms over his chest.

"You're not here to fling me back into prison, I hope," he said.

Alberic managed a smile. "Didn't I apologize for that little misunderstanding already?"

"No."

"Well, I'm sorry, then. But you have to admit, it was understandable."

"Not from my perspective."

Brytnoth stepped between them and frowned at Deor. "Let's focus on the problem at hand instead of past mistakes, shall we?"

Deor spread his hands and flung himself back into his chair, glowering at the sliver of *zanthos* in the glass on the table. "Whatever you say."

Brytnoth showed Alberic to a chair and then joined him at the table. "We need to know what you know, Lord Alberic, about the rest of the *zanthos*. It's critically important, and...."

"And if I tell you what I know, what do you plan to do with it?"

Brytnoth sat back, then muttered, "This again?"

At the same moment, Deor slammed his fist down on the table. "I'm going to use it to annihilate the bastards who are messing with my militia, my planet, and my sister. Is that good enough for you?"

Alberic regarded him with something like amusement in his eyes. "You know my philosophy about the *zanthos*."

"No, I really don't."

"He wasn't here last time," Brytnoth said, then turned to Deor. "Lord Alberic isn't keen on people using the *zanthos* for weapons."

"You're kidding me, right? Right?" Deor glanced from Brytnoth to Alberic, then back again. "That's..." Catching the warning in Brytnoth's eyes, Deor swallowed the rest of what he wanted to say. "Very nice," he finished lamely.

"My lord," Brytnoth said, "you made allowances for us before."

"Yes, and look where that's gotten us," he snapped. "My *zanthos* is gone...and my people are completely vulnerable now. Our existence is known now. Our secret is revealed. And what's to stop the people who stole the *zanthos* from using it to destroy Perseon utterly?"

"Nothing." Deor crossed his boots on the table and his arms across his chest. "Which is why we need to know where that other stash is located. Askalon is compromised. And if Askalon is compromised, then Perseon is vulnerable. You know as well as we do that the people responsible for this aren't the kind to move by half measures. If they think you are a liability, then you are all dead. All of you."

Alberic sat in silence, his index finger tracing tiny circles on the table. His eyes were fixed on the *zanthos* in the glass, and slowly, he began to nod. Deor felt hope surge up inside him, and he glanced at Brytnoth. His friend sat, muscles tense, watching the leader consider his situation.

"All right," Alberic said finally. "I know it isn't your fault that the *zanthos* is gone. Power like this is difficult to hide, and once it's revealed, it's even more difficult to protect." He heaved a sigh. "And I will do whatever it takes to keep my people safe."

"So where is the second stash?" Brytnoth pressed.

Alberic raised his head and took a deep breath. "It's on Silesia."

———

Deor stared out the gallery window as their ship descended through Silesia's atmosphere. As the re-entry flames dissipated, the searing blue curve of the Silesian sky and the shimmering expanse of red, rolling sands and granite-colored hills opened out below them.

"So this is where Sahara spent all those months," Deor said, watching as the dunes became more and more defined. To the east, he could see a splash of vivid green against the sands, setting off a cluster of bright white buildings that seemed to smile in the sun.

"That's Albadir," Brytnoth told him, gesturing toward the settlement. "That's Jared's home...and Rafe's."

"And Sahara's," Deor said. Out of the corner of his eye, he could see Brytnoth's puzzled frown, but he didn't elaborate.

In another few moments, the ship settled onto the small landing platform just west of Albadir and Deor slapped the button to lower the ramp.

As they stepped down onto the platform, Deor saw a man hurrying toward them.

"Arnauld!" Brytnoth called.

"It's good to see you again," Arnauld said, a smile spreading across his face. He clasped each of their wrists in turn. "Your trip was uneventful, I trust?"

"About as uneventful as it gets," Deor answered. "You've done a good job eliminating raiders and pirates, Lord Arnauld."

The leader's grin widened at the praise. "We do what we can. But I don't have the manpower to police the system. All I've done is gather some like-minded leaders on nearby planets— they're providing the ships and the men to see the job through."

"Well, it's a damn good job anyway," Deor said. "You're to be commended. I wish Askalon was doing more to hold up its end...but we've got our own problems now."

Arnauld's face gathered into a frown. "So I hear." He clapped them on the shoulders as the ship's engines wound down into silence. "I'm glad you could come. I just wish it could be under a different set of circumstances."

"Likewise," Deor said. "Have you been able to do any investigating at all? Have you found what we're looking for?"

"Oh, haven't we just. But come. Refreshment first, then you're free to head out on your scavenging mission."

Arnauld stepped aside and gestured for them to head off the landing platform. Deor ground his teeth in impatience, but he followed Brytnoth off the platform. As they reached the ground, Brytnoth turned to Arnauld.

"This is new," he said. "You've been busy since you got back!"

"Besides fixing what the Dragon destroyed, we desperately needed to make some improvements," Arnauld said. "Adding a formal landing platform so that we could once more be a power in this system was just one of the many things on my list."

Brytnoth nodded his appreciation as they gazed down the wide avenue leading into the white-walled city of Albadir. "It's as beautiful as I remember it," he said, a smile creasing his face. "It's like coming home."

"I think you'll find much more to like about the city now," Arnauld answered. "And, Deor, I hope you enjoy seeing the place where your sister spent so much time."

"It certainly gives me a new perspective on her sufferings," Deor muttered, swiping a hand across his brow. "I don't know which is worse...this inferno or the deep freeze of Perseon."

Arnauld laughed and led the way into the city. Albadir was bustling with activity, and Deor found his spirits lift in spite of the shimmering heat. Cool fountains and the swift river, the deep shadows under the green trees, and the glistening white stone of the buildings seemed somehow clean and full of vibrant life. Everywhere he looked, he saw smiling faces and heard laughter.

"This is what I've been missing all my life," he murmured to Brytnoth. "No wonder Sahara loves it so much here."

Brytnoth turned to him in surprise. "You think so?" he said. "You said as much earlier. But I'll be honest...I thought she wanted to go back to Amaryl with you."

Deor snorted. "Are you kidding? And leave Jared? Not a chance, my friend. Not a chance. You wait and see. They'll come back here for good someday, if we all make it out of this colossal mess alive."

"I don't know, Deor." Brytnoth's face creased in worry. "I don't know if..."

"If what?"

"If he will."

"Who? Jared?"

Brytnoth nodded. "Has Sahara given you any more news about him and Rafe?"

"No. I haven't heard from her in days. It's making me nervous, to tell you the truth." He sighed. "I just hope she doesn't do something stupid."

"She can handle herself all right."

"Sure. But something's changed, Brytnoth. She's changed." He shrugged. "I don't know. I can't explain what I mean, so don't ask. I'm just worried about her, and I wish there was more I could do."

Brytnoth nodded. "I can appreciate that, and I'm with you. If it wasn't suicide, I'd be the first to charge in there and try to get them out. But we have to take a different road. The best way for us to help them is to figure out what the hell is going on back on Askalon. It's all tied together somehow."

"I know. You're right. And that's why we're here. I just hope we didn't come all the way across the system for nothing."

"Did you see the grin on Arnauld's face? I don't think we're here for nothing."

In spite of Deor's impatience, it was the next day before they could sit down and discuss matters with Arnauld. He insisted on pampering them, showing them the best of what Albadir had to offer. Brytnoth called it his famous hospitality. Deor called it damn annoying.

But true to his promise, Arnauld welcomed them into his chamber immediately after breakfast the next morning, and even Deor's sour expression couldn't poison his mood.

"You know," he said as they settled into comfortable chairs in the sun-soaked room, "we had always wondered what the Drakkin were doing in those labor camps. I'm glad we had the chance to delve into the mystery." He glanced at Deor. "You know that those camps were supposed to be your sister's future, right? She was headed there to serve a life sentence when her ship crashed and Jared brought her to us."

"You don't say."

Arnauld frowned, then turned to Brytnoth. "What's his problem this morning?"

"He doesn't like delays." Brytnoth speared a withering glare in Deor's direction. "But that's no excuse for his atrocious manners."

"I don't have atrocious manners. I'm just not sitting here while our planet goes to hell so that I can fill my scrapbook with family memories."

Arnauld chuckled. "He really does remind me of her, you know," he remarked. "You're so much like your sister when she first came to us," he added as Deor frowned blackly at him. "She was like a wild animal."

"Can we please just get down to business?" Deor said. "She was tame compared to what I'm about to be if we don't leave off the reminiscing."

"All right, all right!" Arnauld said, throwing up his hands in mock surrender. "To business, then. As I told you when we talked, we've been able to get inside those mines and now I think we've finally discovered what the Drakkin were searching for all those years."

He reached into his pocket and pulled out a tiny yellow sphere. It glowed faintly as he turned it in his fingers, and the sunlight spilling across the floor seemed pale in comparison.

Deor and Brytnoth both gasped, and a smile quirked Arnauld's mouth. "I see you know what this is," he said. "So I don't have to explain."

"You pulled that *zanthos* out of the mines?" Deor asked. "Is that where you found it?"

"Well, it certainly wasn't a parting gift from Aelred. Yes, we found it. And I think there's more. Much more. We just haven't broken through to the lower level yet."

"I assume you're working around the clock to get there?" Deor said.

"Kirin is heading up the team up there," Arnauld answered. "And yes, he's driving them pretty hard."

Deor reached out and took the sphere from Arnauld, feeling the surge of power tingle through him. "If we're right," he said, "and there's a stash of *zanthos* somewhere in those mines, then this will turn the tables on Halcyon very nicely."

"And if there's not?" Brytnoth said. "What if what you're holding is all there is?"

Deor glanced at him. "I'm not thinking that way until we've turned the guts of those mines inside out," he said. "It's got to be there."

"You're welcome to head out there and take a look yourself if you like," Arnauld said. "I can have a shuttle ready in ten minutes."

Deor rose and Brytnoth followed suit. Deor closed his hand around the sphere and clutched it for a moment, then slipped it into his pocket.

"Make it five."

TWENTY-SIX

"I'VE NEVER BEEN OUT HERE, you know," Brytnoth confessed as they got off the shuttle.

They stood for a moment, staring around them in awe. Massive arms of gray stone surrounded them on three sides, arching up and away into the cloudless sky. Just in front of them, a maw opened into the heart of the mountain, and a rough stone path ran under their feet and vanished into it.

"Where is everybody?" Deor asked the pilot.

The man shrugged, his face a strange shade of pale. "Down there, most likely. I'm headed back to the city. Kirin can fix you up with a ride back."

Without another word, he shut the door of the shuttle and gunned the engines. In a moment, the shuttle skipped over the rim of rock and passed out of sight and earshot.

"What's he in such a hurry for?" Deor muttered. The heat was eating into him, and he felt his skin crawling with irritation. "What the hell's wrong with people?"

Brytnoth's mouth quirked into a smile. "People? He's just one guy, Deor."

"Whatever. Let's find Kirin and the *zanthos* and get the hell out of here."

They started toward the yawning entrance to the mines. As they drew closer, Deor's irritability ebbed away, and he felt the clammy breath of fear seeping into him. He glanced at Brytnoth, saw his friend swallow hard. They took a few more steps, but when they crossed the threshold into the shadows under the mountain, Deor stopped suddenly.

"Wait," he said, his voice hoarse. "Just wait. Something's not right here."

"I was thinking the same thing," Brytnoth agreed. "Do you smell that?"

Deor wrinkled his nose. Now that Brytnoth mentioned it, he did smell something.

Something decaying and rotten.

Something dead.

What is this place?

He wanted to shout it, but his words turned to ash in his mouth.

After a long moment, "Where's Kirin, Deor?"

Deor shook his head. He still had no voice.

Another long moment dragged past. "We have to go in there," Brytnoth said. "We have to find him."

Some part of Deor was laughing right now. Laughing at his fear. He had served the Drakkin. He had done things that made Sahara look like a schoolgirl. Nothing should frighten him now.

Nothing except heading down into a dark hole filled with dead things.

He shuddered and saw Brytnoth's wan smile.

"I know," Brytnoth said. "Why didn't Arnauld tell us about this place?"

Deor managed to find his voice at last. "Maybe he doesn't know, Brytnoth. Or..."

"Or what?"

Deor hesitated. *Maybe he doesn't sense the evil here.* Out loud, he simply said, "I don't know."

Brytnoth took a breath and jogged Deor's arm. "Let's go. Maybe it will get better further inside."

Deor shot him a skeptical look and loosened his pistol in its holster. "Maybe."

They moved slowly into the tunnel. The smell of damp and earth and decomp wormed its way into Deor's nostrils, nearly choking him. The uncertain light played off the irregular humpy forms of rock and earth, and Deor realized that there were other passageways leading off this main tunnel. Those blacker mouths in this already black hole made his skin crawl with fear, as though he could sense something watching him just beyond the limits of his sight. After they had gone a dozen paces or so, Deor felt a vague pain in his jaw and realized that he was clenching his teeth, as if he could ward off panic or hold himself together by biting hard enough. With a shake of his head, he forced his jaw to relax. And just as he allowed his shoulders to loosen a bit, they heard voices down below them.

"That's Kirin's voice," Brytnoth said. "Thank God at least there's someone else alive down here."

They quickened their pace. Deor noticed that as the sound of voices grew louder, the light around them grew brighter as well, and soon they could see great lanterns strung from the soaring roof of the cave ahead. The light seemed to slick the walls, and rivulets of green slime trickling down from the ceiling of rock.

"Kirin!" Brytnoth called, and Deor started. The sound echoed in the chamber, and the voices ahead died in sudden confused and surprised silence.

"Brytnoth?" And then Kirin himself came into view, hustling up the tunnel. "Brytnoth! And Deor! What the devil are you two doing here?"

Deor found himself grinning like an idiot. It was so ridiculously comforting, seeing another living person in this hell hole, that he couldn't help himself.

"What are you doing here?" Kirin repeated, staring at them as if they'd walked out of thin air. "Does Arnauld know you're here?"

"His damn shuttle brought us here," Deor answered. "Of course he knows."

"We're here to see what you've found, Kirin," Brytnoth said. "Arnauld says the search hasn't been for nothing."

Kirin studied them thoughtfully for a moment, then turned and beckoned for them to follow him. "Come and see for yourselves."

They trekked down the passageway into the large cavern. A small knot of men stood near the entrance, large, flat shovels in their hands. From further back in the cavern, Deor heard more men's voices and the sound of shovels digging into soft earth. He swung his gaze from the work crew to the center of the cavern. He started in surprise and gasped.

"What is all this?"

Kirin grinned at him. "This? This is what we found."

Deor gaped. The light, which he'd thought was from those few lanterns hanging still above their heads, was actually coming from a huge pile of *zanthos*. It was at least as tall as he was and twice as long, the stones cut into every imaginable size and shape, as if they'd been tossed into a cart and dumped here as soon as they'd come out of the ground.

"Is this stuff refined...or whatever? It looks rough." Brytnoth edged closer to the pile and touched one of the largest of the stones.

"I don't know," Kirin said. "I'm no expert. But from what I remember seeing on Askalon, this stuff is rough."

"Is this all you found?" Deor asked.

Kirin and Brytnoth regarded him in surprise. "What do you mean, is this all we found?" Kirin asked. "Isn't this good enough for you?"

Deor favored him with a lopsided grin. "Not what I meant. I was just wondering if you'd found anything to go with this."

Kirin frowned. "I'm not understanding you."

"He means weapons," Brytnoth said. "Like we had back on Askalon."

"No. Or, perhaps I should say, not yet." As Deor's brows shot up in surprise, he added, "There's evidence back there—" he gestured toward the back of the cavern— "that someone dug a fresh shaft. It's been filled in again, but none too neatly. Our boys just broke through into this room yesterday, so we haven't had a chance to investigate fully."

Deor folded his arms across his chest and strolled toward the pile of *zanthos*. The pull was so strong that it took all his willpower and strength not to run. The small bead of *zanthos* in his pocket seemed to hum, almost as if some strange cosmic concordant note were sounding just beyond the range of his hearing.

"Gwyn said this stuff had to be refined," he said thoughtfully. "That it could be weaponized or...well, domesticated, for lack of a better word." He glanced back at his friends. "Do you really think this is in its raw state?"

"Doesn't it look like that to you?" Brytnoth asked.

Deor considered, feeling the shivering in the air, savoring the power that ebbed from the stones like sunlight or water in the desert. "No."

Kirin's eyes snapped to his face. "No? But that would mean...."

Deor dragged himself away from the stones. As he passed Kirin, he said, "Get your boys digging that hole. Now."

His boots dug into the soft earth that had sifted across the stone floor, gripping and pulling him down the tunnel, away from the *zanthos* and the smell of death. He heard Brytnoth running up the tunnel behind him, but he didn't slow his pace. If he slowed down, he would never make it out.

He had to get out.

He was on his hands and knees by the time he reached the tunnel entrance. His breath was ragged in his chest, and his vision swam. The *zanthos* in his pocket felt as though it would burn through his skin, and he clawed at the dirt.

"Deor! Deor!"

Brytnoth's voice sounded like it was coming from above a great depth of water. He was drowning.

He couldn't breathe.

He couldn't see.

His hand convulsed, gripping dirt and stones until they cut into his palm.

I am alive, he told himself. The pain in his hand sliced through the darkness and the panic, a tiny shaft of light, a promise of a way out. *I live. I breathe. I see. I live. I live.*

He repeated it over and over, clawing his way up through the shadows until he broke the surface and gasped air into his aching lungs.

He rolled over, staring up at the blazing sky—blue beyond imagining. The heat nosed its way into his paralyzed and frozen limbs, thawing him from the outside in. He closed his eyes and exhaled, drinking in the heat and the light.

"Deor!"

Deor opened his eyes reluctantly. Brytnoth was crouching beside him, his face a mask of worry and even fear.

"What happened, Deor?"

Deor blinked and tried to swallow. His mouth and throat were utterly dry. He closed his eyes again, fleeing from the horror within.

"I told you before," he croaked, his eyes focusing once more on Brytnoth's face. "This *zanthos* stuff isn't what you think. It's evil." He paused, then continued, "If Azimir makes Jared use it, it will destroy him...just like it almost destroyed me."

Brytnoth sank back with a deep sigh. "How are we going to stop him, Deor? What can we possibly do to save him?"

Deor propped himself on his elbows. "I don't even know what this is. So how am I supposed to know how to stop it?"

"What do you think is buried back there?" Brytnoth asked after a long silence.

Deor pushed himself fully upright. "Well, either a bunch of dead bodies or a cache of weapons."

Brytnoth recoiled. "Bodies? Why?"

"You noticed it back there," he said. "The smell of decay."

"I know...but I thought that was just...you know. Animals or bats or something."

"No. Not animals. A lot of death went into building that holding room. But whether they were casualties of the Drakkin or the people who made this drop, I don't know." He glanced back at the tunnel and shuddered. "Let's get out of here. I'm sure they'll send word once they've broken through to the next chamber." He moved forward a few paces, then stopped. "Damn."

"What?"

"Don't you remember? Our ride ditched us. We're stuck here unless Kirin gives us a lift." He saw Brytnoth open his mouth and knew what he wanted to say. "No. I'm not going back down there. At least...not right now." He waved a hand in the direction of the tunnel. "But you can. I'll just sit here and wait for a bit. I need to think."

"You sure?"

"Of course." He managed a smile and shooed Brytnoth toward the entrance. "I'll be fine."

With one last glance, Brytnoth left him standing outside. As the shadows under the mountain swallowed his friend, Deor felt a searing pain in his head. A suffocating darkness swallowed his consciousness and he fell to his knees. Stones cut deeper and deeper into his knees, as if someone were pressing him into the earth.

"What are you doing with my *zanthos*, Deor?"

Deor scrabbled feebly in the dirt. The darkness in his mind swam and dissolved in vague outlines. And then he realized what he was seeing. The top of a man's dark head.

The throttle hold on his mind tightened.

"What? You don't know me?" the man said.

Slowly, he raised his face to Deor's stunned gaze.

It was Jared.

TWENTY-SEVEN

SAHARA SAT up and shook her head. She was reeling, and she stared up into the darkness. She blinked rapidly, and her vision cleared. The black shadows around her were less dense, and there seemed to be a tinge of light along the top of the building above her. She wondered vaguely how far she had fallen and how long she'd been lying there in the alley. At the thought, the pain came in a rush—every joint and bone seemed jarred and out of place.

He knocked me off the ladder, she realized, her breath catching in her throat.

She remembered his anguished eyes, the desperation in his voice. But something had gone wrong. She'd lost her grip on the ladder at that last moment. He'd changed in that last moment, and something like a shadow had come between them.

No...not Jared. Not the Jared I know.

She pressed the heels of her hands into her eyes for a moment, willing the tears back into the well of grief in her heart. Then she pushed herself to her feet. As she moved, she heard the clank of metal on stone, and she knelt again, groping in the pitch dark. Her fingers finally found the source of the sound: the hilt of her knife.

She clenched it in her hand and rose slowly. She stood a moment, the cold metal pressing into her palm. Then she lifted her eyes and saw, at the far end of the alley, the cold gray light of dawn spreading through the street.

She edged toward it, still clenching the dagger in her hand.

Just before she reached the corner, she heard a voice behind her.

"Wait."

She froze, then felt her muscles ready themselves. Her grip loosened on the knife, and she silently slipped it from its sheath. Soft footsteps pattered down the alley toward her, and she closed her eyes.

The next moment, she spun, catching the person by surprise. In a flurry of veils, Sahara pinned her pursuer against the wall, the knife ready for a killing stroke.

"Why are you following me?" she hissed.

The figure lifted a shaking hand slowly, silently begging Sahara to stay her hand. Then the figure pushed back the veils that shrouded her face.

"Don't hurt me. Please."

Sahara stared into the dark eyes, wide and pleading. The woman was beautiful - stunningly beautiful. Silver bracelets tinkled on her arm, and as she shifted her feet to keep her balance, tiny bells around her ankle jangled.

"Who are you? And why are you following me?" Sahara asked again, lowering the dagger slightly.

"I might ask you the same. Why are you outside this place? What business do you have here?"

Sahara frowned. "I'm not the one with a dagger pointed at my eye," she said. "Of the two of us, seems I'm asking and you're answering."

The woman took a deep breath. "My name is Emelia," she said softly. "My father..."

Sahara lowered the knife. "Jessup."

Confusion filled the woman's eyes. "How did you know that?"

"Because I'm an adopted member of his tribe," Sahara answered.

"But how do I know you are who you say you are?"

"But I know who you are," she breathed, realization dawning in her voice. "You're Sahara—the red-headed one that Jared speaks of so much."

Sahara recoiled. "You know Jared?"

Emelia pointed down the alley. "Azimir has me...I'm little more than a prisoner. I know Jared...and I know Rafe." Her voice faltered. "As much as it is possible to know one in his state."

"What state?"

"He's Azimir's puppet now. His mind is overthrown...he is totally under the influence of Demon's Breath." She shook her head. "He's the ghost of a man now. But he is alive."

Sahara's hand fell to her side and she stepped back, releasing the woman. "I followed Katarina here," she said. "You know the woman?"

"Of course I know her." Emelia tugged her robes straight and moved away from the wall. "Why should she be followed? She has suffered enough."

"Because there are those who would see her dead. There are those who suspect her of betraying the Hazad to Azimir."

"Lies!"

Sahara nodded. "No doubt. But I was sent to make sure."

"And have you?"

Sahara tilted her chin, studying the woman intently. "And how do I know that you won't rat me out? Why should I tell you anything?"

Emelia glanced over her shoulder and then stepped close to Sahara. In a low, frantic whisper, she said, "Because I will tell you something first. Jared is slipping fast. Azimir doesn't know what he's doing. He's prodded the sleeping Dragon, and he has pushed Jared into the abyss. He thinks that Jared will be able to hold himself back enough not to turn on Azimir...but I know better. He is becoming what the Drakkin were...only..."

Her voice trailed off and Sahara arched an eyebrow. "Only?"

"Only he doesn't want to be. It will destroy him either way...he will go mad, or he will fall into darkness." The tears started into Emelia's eyes. "I see it daily. His struggles grow more and more feeble, like the final throes of a dying man. Very soon now he will be lost. Unless..."

"Unless what?"

"Unless something is done. If Azimir gives him the *zanthos*, Jared will destroy us all. Not just the Hazad. Azimir can't control him...you can't control this kind of power."

"You said Jared is slipping." Sahara swallowed hard as Emelia nodded. "Why is this happening to him?"

"He is the Slayer." Emelia shrugged. "And the Dragon will have his vengeance."

Sahara was silent for a long time. She stared down at the knife in her hands, remembering the desperate light in Jared's eyes, the mad struggle between hope and hate within him.

"Can you get a message to him from me?" she asked. When Emelia didn't answer immediately, she raised her eyes to the woman's face. "Can you?"

"It's getting dangerous for me to..."

"Will you take him a message or not?"

Emelia swallowed. "Yes."

Sahara held out the dagger, hilt first. "Give him this. And tell him to hold on. I'm coming for him."

"I will."

Emelia took the dagger gingerly and tucked it into the wide sash at her waist. She turned away, then checked herself. "Will you do something for me?"

"Name it."

The woman's eyes filled with tears. "Tell my father I love him. And if I don't make it out of this alive, please tell him that I did this for my family. For the Hazad."

Sahara nodded once, and Emelia hurried away. As she watched the woman round the far corner, Sahara felt a pit of sickening dread open in her gut.

That might have been a mistake. Maybe I shouldn't have sent her to Jared...what if...

She squeezed her eyes shut and clenched her jaw against the thought. As long as there was a chance, she'd take it. As long as there was hope, she would choose to believe.

She turned back to the alley entrance and contemplated her escape. Weaponless now, she wanted to avoid a confrontation at all costs. She needed quick and quiet, and she needed to get back to camp before Brig did something stupid.

Judging by the light, the sun had only just risen, and there were only a few sleepy merchants making their slow way up the thorough-fare toward the marketplace. There was no sign of movement from the palace across the street, but somehow the quiet made Sahara's skin crawl. It wasn't a peaceful kind of quiet. More like the steady calm of a snake preparing to strike its prey.

Another vendor was toiling up the street. He balanced two long poles fitted out with fluttering scarves of every size and hue. In the gray dawn, he was a traveling rainbow. Sahara glanced down at her clothes, which were suited very well for a nighttime operation.

Not so much for prancing through the city streets in broad daylight.

Her eyes strayed back to the merchant and his scarves, and the seedling of an idea sprouted in her mind. She backed up a few paces, well into the shadows of the alley, and waited. As soon as she saw the man start across the alley entrance, she whistled.

The man stopped and turned to look down the alley. Sahara whistled again.

"Give me a hand, would you?" she barked, doing her best to make her voice low and rough.

The man started down the alleyway, his eyes fixed straight ahead. As he passed her position, Sahara jumped him, and a moment later, she leaned his unconscious body against the wall.

"I'm sorry," she murmured.

She deftly untwisted several long scarves from the nearest pole and wound them over her battle dress. She wrapped her hair in a bright orange length of silk and then kicked the poles next to the man's lifeless hand. For a moment, she hesitated, then dug in her pocket for a tiny sack of coins. She tossed two silver pennies into the man's lap and then hurried out of the alley.

As she made her way back toward the city walls, conflict began to roil within her. She wanted desperately to turn around, to track Emelia down and take back her daggers...to take them to Jared herself. A knot of fear was twisting itself in her gut. She had placed Emelia in danger. Everything the woman had told her about Jared's fall into darkness, his instability—what she herself had felt—should have warned her away from sending Emelia to give him a weapon. But she hadn't listened to the warnings in her heart...or she was too willing to trust that the man she loved would somehow find his own way through the fog and shadows.

It can't be helped. What's done is done...and there's nothing I can do to change things now. I need to get out of here. If I'm captured, all this will be for nothing anyway.

At that moment, she heard the solid tramping of feet coming up the cross street just ahead of her. She slipped into a shadowed doorway and pulled her veil up to cover her face. A small squadron of guards marched past, their heavy guns perched on their shoulders. Something about the weapons looked vaguely familiar.

A soft yellow glow seemed to seep from the barrel of the gun.

Sahara frowned and slipped back into the street. She kept close to the wall and raced on silent feet to the intersection. She flattened herself against the wall for a moment, listening to the steady tattoo of marching feet. There was no falter or change in pace, and Sahara knew that she'd escaped their notice. Taking a deep breath, she edged around the corner.

It was exactly as she had feared.

Those were Askalon's weapons, and they were loaded with *zanthos.*

The traitor had done his work.

TWENTY-EIGHT

WHEN SAHARA GOT BACK to the camp, it was nearly midday and most of the settlement was already out in the fields. As she slipped around behind the tent line and made for her campsite, no one stirred in the central square or poked a head out of a nearby tent. It was quiet. Too quiet.

What if they're all dead?

The sudden thought jerked Sahara up short. She gazed around the camp. Smoking fires smoldered in the central square, curls of grey smoke tinging the dawn with haze. Yasmin, who usually bustled in and out of the cook tent for hours—Sahara wasn't even entirely sure that she ever left— was nowhere in sight. A pail of grain lay on its side and a golden cascade of kernels lay half kicked into dust.

Sahara swung her gaze toward the marquis tent across the square. There was no sign of movement.

The smaller tents.

Sahara swept her eyes over each, feeling her breath grow more frantic with each passing second. Sweat slicked her hands.

They said they'd be heading to Telon for the holy season, she remembered as she turned slowly on her heel to study the tents behind her. Even as the hopeful thought framed itself into words, she shook her head. The pilgrimage was still a week away. And they wouldn't have left without her.

No? Why not? Maybe everyone thought you were dead or disappeared.

Bitterness surged up inside her, but a tiny kernel of certainty formed like adamant. She knew they wouldn't have left without her. They would have given her a chance.

She finished her scan of the camp and rubbed a hand over her face. They wouldn't have left without her by choice. But maybe they hadn't had a choice.

Sahara hesitated, wrestling with the choice she now faced. Should she try to track them down? Or should she go back to Aquila and finish her mission?

A hundred images spilled into her mind. Katarina's rare smile. Jessup's crinkling face and warm, weathered hands. Rigel doubled over laughing as she stood dripping with goat's milk. The sounds and smells and warmth of Jessup's tribe...the tribe that had adopted her. The home she loved.

And then, crowding everything else out, the vision of Jared's terrible eyes and ruthless smile. The feeling of being pressed into the dirt like an insect. The hollow fear in Emelia's lovely face.

Her mouth tightened into a grim line. She had no choice, really. She'd just grab what was left of her things and head back to the city. This graveyard of a camp held nothing for her now, and if they'd left without her, then they'd have to manage without her.

Fighting down the stab of sadness, she made for her tent. As she passed the last camp before her own, children's squealing laughter erupted from the tent. Sahara jumped like a startled hare and stared in surprise the children themselves exploded from the tent with their mother after them.

As she watched the three pairs of short brown legs and three pairs of tiny feet pumping vigorously across the square, relief turned her knees to water and washed away whatever decision she thought she'd made to abandon her people to their fate.

Smiling to herself, she slipped inside her own tent and blew out her breath. She collapsed onto the cot, burying her face in her small pillow. She moved to unsheathe her knife from the scabbard she wore at the small of her back. Then she checked the motion, remembering that it wasn't there any longer.

I'll have to do something about that. She felt strangely vulnerable. *Until Jared can return mine.*

She pasted a smile on her face and tried to pretend optimism for a moment. But the thought of Jared and a happy ending to this mess felt like a glaring lie, not a promise. Her stomach did a flip and sick dread trickled through her.

Jared needed her. Badly. Based on the information Emelia had given her, things were slipping much faster than she'd expected. And she wasn't even sure now that killing Azimir and pulling Jared and Rafe out of Aquila would fix things. It seemed more and more likely that it would only do more harm than good.

She rolled over onto her back, clenching her eyes shut as if that could blot out reality along with the sunlight.

Sis.

Sahara's eyes snapped open and she propped herself up on one elbow. *Deor?*

The next moment, her brother's face filled her mind's eye. He looked pale and desperate, and Sahara swallowed hard. The last thing she needed right now was another crisis, but it looked like she was about to get one anyway.

What's going on? Has something happened? She had to ask, even though she was almost sure she didn't want the answer. She gritted her teeth and waited.

No, it's just... I need to talk to you. To someone. And you need to know.

Need to know what?

Sahara frowned. Deor was usually so clear. Now he sounded confused. Lost. She felt a surge of fear, and realized in that moment just how much Deor had anchored her. Now the anchor was slipping. Sahara clenched her hands into fists until the knuckles showed white. Panic was beginning to clutch at her. She couldn't slip. She wouldn't slip.

There's something weird about this zanthos stuff. It's not just an energy source. Not just a natural energy source, I mean.

What's that supposed to mean? What else would it be?

I don't know. Deor's voice was rough, and he ran a hand through his ruddy hair. *But there's something wrong with it. It's driving me insane...like I'm drawn to it. Like a magnet. I don't know why. No one else seems to feel it. Brytnoth doesn't. There's something about me...some reason why it's calling to me.*

You know how strange that sounds, right?

Deor's eyes flashed at her. *This whole damn thing is nothing but strange. But that doesn't make it any less true.*

Fair enough. She'd entertain the notion and humor him, if it would make him feel better. *What do you think it is?*

I'm telling you I don't know. But there's some reason why the Drakkin needed this. And if Azimir thinks he'll be able to give this to Jared and control him—and it—then he's a damn fool.

He's a fool...and he's weak, Sahara said. *He's a weak man who is trying to appear ruthless. He's afraid of his own people. My sources tell me that he's almost out of the nobility's good graces. This stunt with Jared and the zanthos is supposed to be his grand moment—the proof that he's a bigger man than all of them. That he's worthy to be lord and ruler on Halcyon.*

He's going to destroy his entire world, Deor said. *And I'm not convinced he won't destroy all worlds.*

That's a bit dramatic, isn't it?

Maybe. Maybe not. I'm telling you, sis. Something's changed with this stuff. When we used those zanthos-pistols on Askalon, they didn't do a thing for me. But ever since you landed on Halcyon, every time I get near some, it's digging its fingers into my soul.

Sahara arched an eyebrow. *Deor. Honestly. I never figured you for the hysterical type.*

Go find some and see for yourself. I think it has something to do with our past. Because like I said, Brytnoth doesn't feel it at all.

An interesting theory. But what in our past would—

Sahara stopped. She felt like she'd just been broadsided.

Jared was the Slayer. And she and Deor had both assassinated Drakkin Chieftains. That was why the three of them could communicate mind-to-mind. Somehow, they were being manipulated into becoming the new Collective. And what if the Drakkin knew that the *zanthos* was a source of some kind of dark energy—the same dark energy that gave them their own power?

Then all of this would make perfect sense.

Jared was being consumed from within by the Dragon. And, as the Dragon, he craved the *zanthos*. The Drakkin had served a power of darkness. Of annihilation. And in service to that power, they exterminated worlds. But slowly. Too slowly.

That's why they'd needed the *zanthos*. It had the power to annihilate life—maybe even all life—in their hands.

In Jared's hands.

Sahara swallowed hard. Everything inside of her was shaking. Deor was nodding, as if he had read the progress of her thoughts as she connected the pieces together.

What are we going to do? she said. *Deor, how can we stop it?*

I don't know if we can. But I have a very strong feeling that... His voice trailed off.

Just say it.

That we won't survive this. You and I. How can we? We're part of the Collective, Sahara. We're doing his work now.

Sahara pushed herself to her feet, hating how the ground seemed to pitch and roll underneath her.

No. Like hell I am. And like hell you are. We're going to stop this, you and I. Together. We're going to save Jared and Rafe. We're going to make this right.

Deor arched an eyebrow. *I wish I could believe all that.*

Sahara wanted to shake him. *You have to believe it. Otherwise you are doing his work, Deor! Fight it! You have to fight...I need you to fight. I wish you could know how much I need you...I can't do this all alone.*

Tears were knotting in her throat. Deor straightened, and the ghost of a smile flickered across his mouth. *Don't you get all emotional on me. I don't think I could take that. You're the tough one, remember?*

Sahara shook her head violently. *Not so much. Not anymore.*

Deor took a deep breath. *Well, if we're supposed to fight this damn thing, then you have to tell me what to do with all this.*

He gestured vaguely behind him, and Sahara shifted her gaze to study what she could see of his surroundings.

Where are you? That doesn't look like Askalon...or Perseon. Sahara frowned. *That looks...Deor, that looks like Silesia.*

It is. We've been following the stolen zanthos. So here we are, at the site of the Drakkin labor camps. I'm sure you remember those...you were supposed to live the rest of your life in one.

Sahara swallowed hard and repressed a shudder. Memories of the burning ship and burning bodies and burning sands threatened to overwhelm her. *And did you find what you were looking for?*

Yes, and more than that. We found weapons.

Sahara started. *Weapons? How could there be zanthos-weapons on Silesia, Deor?* And then understanding suddenly dawned, and the chill horror of it all flooded through her. *Oh...Deor...*

What?

It's a trap. You're being set up...you have to get out of there. Leave it. Just leave it there. Leave it all there.

Deor didn't blink, but he arched an eyebrow at her, and something like laughter flickered in the depths of his eyes.

You've got to be kidding me. Not again.

TWENTY-NINE

DEOR SAT with his back against a stone, knees drawn up and arms hanging loosely. He held the sphere of *zanthos* between his fingers and rotated it slowly, contemplating it. It was altogether beautiful, warm and golden like a tiny, benevolent sun.

Sahara thinks I can just walk away from this. She doesn't know. She hasn't felt its power. She doesn't understand.

She'd told him this was a trap. The *zanthos* and the weapons—someone had put them here. Someone had laid his path, tugging him along it like a wretched blind man. At every crossroads, they had collected him and propelled him along, like the inevitable hand of fate or destiny.

Surely, if it was a trap, he should walk away. He should leave the stash of *zanthos* and all those weapons here. Bury them. Pretend they'd never been found...or buried there in the first place.

He was being played. He knew it beyond any shadow of a doubt. Someone was setting him up.

And now, like a dupe, he would cart this stuff back to Askalon, and he would be arrested. He saw it all unfolding, rippling out in front of him like the unfurling of a dark flag. They would stand him up in the public square as Threat Number One to the regime. They would proclaim him the thief who had ferreted these weapons away until Aelred was weak and vulnerable, only to return for them under the guise of serving the lord he meant to trample. They would grind him into dust in front of the people, and then they would hang him as a traitor. He saw his lifeless body dangling from the rope, a crow's feast, while his brave militia was scattered or arrested or executed by firing squad beneath his bloodless corpse.

And then, once he and his militia were out of the way, the real traitor would seize the weapons and destroy Aelred and the Lords of Askalon. Everything they had worked so hard to build was already crumbling into dust. They had tried to chisel a statue out of a block of sand, and it was all running like so much water through their fingers.

Deor clenched his jaw, surprised by the hot tears that burned behind his eyes.

And now it's too late to turn back. Everyone knows it's here. The traitor on Askalon knows. He swallowed hard. *And Jared knows. If Jared knows, then it will just be a matter of time anyway until this all ends in flames. Might as well take my chances.*

He turned the sphere again, and now anger flared through him. *I'll make him pay. Whoever it is on Askalon who thinks he can push me around and set me up. By God, he's going to pay.*

As the thought occurred to him, the sudden sweet desire for vengeance intoxicated him. He wasn't some child, some errand boy who could be sent to fetch and carry, only to be disposed of like so much garbage when he'd served his purpose. He was worth more than that.

He was capable of so much more than that.

He was on this mission because he—he alone—was the single greatest threat to the traitor's plans.

It was time for him to rise up, to throttle this upstart who thought he was fit to rule. Deor would strangle the traitor with his own net.

What does he know, after all? Another turn of the sphere. *It would serve him right—*and the thought made him smile—*it would* *serve him right if I brought these weapons back and blasted him to hell with them. After all, I know how to use them. I know what they're for. And I'd do a damn sight better against Jared than some ignorant backwater slug with illusions of grandeur.*

He rotated the sphere again and savored the thought. He would have a triumphant return to Askalon—the captive and the dupe turned victor. He would rain fire down on those who threatened everything he had worked to build.

Askalon would be his.

And then, with Sahara by his side, they would destroy Halcyon.

Deor hesitated.

Sahara will never strike Halcyon while Jared is there. Frustration swept through him for a moment. Then he shook his head and smiled.

She just doesn't understand. But I will make her understand.

How could she? She didn't know how powerful she could be. Everything they had ever fought for—everything they had ever suffered for—it could all be theirs now. The miserable unraveling of their lives, the slow martyrdom of slavery and loss, it would all end. And it would end in triumph.

Jared is already lost to her anyway. She has to face that reality. He had to make her see the truth. *Jared is the real threat now. The Slayer has become the Dragon, and he has to be destroyed. It's the only way to save everything we love most.*

He sighed. It was tragic, but true. She would have to face it before the end. Alone, she would never make an end of Jared. She couldn't possibly do it. But what could they not accomplish together?

They would set their people free at last and rule with benevolence and justice. They would take the weapon of the enemy and shove it down his throat, and then they would stand back and watch him burn.

He turned the stone in his fingers again.

It was right here. It was so close that he could almost taste it.

He closed his eyes.

A sudden shard of a vision stabbed through his mind. Dark eyes, deep wells of hate, bored into his mind.

Jared's eyes.

The unspoken words held him fast for a moment. The hatred, the power, the terror, the warning, the promise. Deor was lashed to a mast and the ship was sinking. He was drowning in dark water, and there was no one to hear his last gurgling scream.

Deor's eyes snapped open. His heart was pounding, and the metallic taste of fear was thick in his mouth. A sudden sweat washed him in a bone-icing chill even in the shimmering heat of the Silesian desert.

But even as the terror swelled within him, something else overtook it and then swept it utterly away.

I hate him. I hate him. And she will have to choose.

Deor clenched the sphere of *zanthos* in his fist.

If Jared wants it, let him come and take it.

He got to his feet, slipped the sphere in his pocket, and headed back inside the cave, basking in the warmth of power and the call to war.

THIRTY

"DEOR!" Brytnoth exclaimed. "I thought you were going to wait outside."

"You thought wrong."

Deor strode through the cavern, the lurid glow of the hoard of *zanthos* shimmering on the bare rock walls. The sphere was heavy and warm in his pocket. The wheels were in motion. It was time to jump aboard or be shredded.

He stopped beside Brytnoth and studied the work going on at the far side of the cavern. Men were shifting stones like so many ants at work and Kirin stood on a boulder, shouting directions to his crew.

"Never figured him for much of a leader," Deor said, jerking his head in Kirin's direction. "Guess he found his calling."

Brytnoth glanced at him. "What's the matter with you?" he asked. "You look...different somehow."

Deor turned to his friend. "Do I? Nothing's the matter. But I've made a decision. We're taking all of this and we're heading back to Askalon."

"Weren't we doing that anyway?"

Deor frowned. "We were. But now we're taking these back to

Askalon because we're going to obliterate whoever it is that's been jerking us around. The traitor thinks he can set us up? He thinks he can lead us along and make us do his dirty work just so we can get back in time to be hanged? Like hell. I don't think so."

Brytnoth regarded him in surprise. "You think that's what's going on here?"

"How do you think those weapons got down here, Brytnoth?"

"What—?"

At that moment, a series of loud shouts echoed up from the passage. Deor crossed his arms over his chest and threw back his head. Kirin charged out of the hole his men had made, a *zanthos*-pistol in his hands.

"Look!" he shouted. "Look at this! And there's hundreds down there...where did these come from? And who put them here?"

Deor turned to Brytnoth. "As I said."

"You knew. How did you know they were in there, Deor?"

Deor laughed quietly. "I can put two and two together, Brytnoth. Whoever stole the *zanthos* in the first place made sure he would have the ability to use it once it was found again. He moved the weapons here and hid them first. And he knew that Aelred would come up with this crusade to find the stolen *zanthos*...it was all part of the plan. Hell, he probably put that into Aelred's head in the first place."

Brytnoth's face was pale. "Deor...you realize who you're accusing, don't you?"

"Who?"

Brytnoth swallowed. "Who was put in charge of destroying those weapons after we overthrew the Triumvirate, Deor? Who is the only one who could have orchestrated all of this—who had the access to the weapons, to the ships, to everything?"

Deor's eyes narrowed suddenly. "Derrek." He slapped his forehead. "I'm an idiot. Of course. It all makes perfect sense now."

"And that's why he needed to get rid of you. Because if the militia rallied behind you, he'd have a civil war on his hands instead of a bloodless coup."

Deor flashed him a grin. "Well, guess he's going to have a bit of a surprise, then. Are you ready to put him in the ground? Are you with me?"

Kirin glanced from Deor to Brytnoth and back again. "You are aware that you sound crazy, right? What exactly are you planning to do?"

Deor swung around to face Kirin. "I plan to take the weapons and the *zanthos* and blow him and his allies straight to hell. And then I'm going after Halcyon."

"What?" Brytnoth recoiled. "You're going to do what?"

"Are you with me?" Deor repeated. "Or should I just leave you here?"

"What are you talking about? Of course I'm with you! But..." Brytnoth frowned at him, that searching light in his eyes again as he studied Deor. "Something's not right about this. I've got a funny feeling that—"

Deor turned on his heel and started back to the surface. "Just get those weapons out of that hole. And get me a ship back to Albadir. Right now."

"You heard the man," he heard Brytnoth say to Kirin. Brytnoth's firm steps hurried after his. "Deor, wait!" Brytnoth called.

Deor paused at the mouth of the tunnel and leaned his forearm against the rock, staring out at the encircling hills. "If this is the only cave the Drakkin ever dug in all those years," he said, "they didn't do a very good job managing their slave labor."

"If it was the only cave, I'd agree. But Kirin told me that there's a whole network of tunnels and caves over those smaller ridges to the north," Brytnoth said, coming to stand beside him. "This was the last place they thought to look—and it's apparently the last place the Drakkin thought to look as well. Kirin said that the entrance was cleverly concealed, and it took them two days to open it up."

"Yes, but that's recent work, Brytnoth," Deor said. "Remember? That's Derrek's doing."

"How did he know we'd find this, then? How did he rig the exploration?"

"I don't know. But I plan to ask him when we get back."

"Yeah. About that." Brytnoth sucked in a breath and blew it out slowly. "Not sure that's the best strategy. We can't just ride in there with guns blazing when we have no idea what the situation is on the ground."

"Yes, I can."

"Deor. Seriously. That's a great way to get a lot of innocent people killed. We need to get a message to someone there and find out what's going on. We can't plan our return until we know more."

"Always the prudent one. No report is going to change my mind, Brytnoth. I'm taking him down."

"And Halcyon? Why do that? Why should we care about getting rid of Derrek if you're planning to drive the ship into the same damn wormhole?"

Deor paused and rubbed his jaw. "You'd rather just sit around and wait for annihilation, then?"

"No. I never said that."

"Then we have to go after Azimir. He's unleashed the Dragon, Brytnoth. Jared is...he's becoming a monster. And it's getting worse. If Azimir puts the *zanthos* in his hands, it's curtains, my friend."

"And what do you propose we do about it, then?"

"Don't forget, either," Deor added, almost before Brytnoth had finished speaking, "that my sister is over there. I'm not going to just leave her there to rot."

"I admire your fraternal affections," Brytnoth said. "But is suicide the best way to demonstrate it?"

Deor's frustration had been building, and it finally boiled over. He rounded on Brytnoth with a flare of anger that made his friend step back in surprise. "It won't be suicide, Brytnoth! I'm going to take these weapons and this *zanthos*, and after I bury Derrek, I'm going after Azimir. With Sahara's help, this will all be over quickly and neatly. And then we can all go home and live happily ever after."

Brytnoth laughed and shook his head. "Okay, I agree with Kirin. You've lost it, Deor. What kind of crazy has gotten into you?"

Deor scowled at him, heat rising to his face. "I—"

"You honestly think she's going to do anything that would jeopardize Jared? If you believe that, then you don't know her at all. I don't care if she is your sister."

A hundred responses tumbled into Deor's mind - a hundred cutting and derisive words. Deor snapped his mouth shut and turned away to look at the hills once more. "She's going to have to make that choice," he muttered. "Either she helps me against him, or she signs my death warrant."

"It shouldn't come to that, Deor," Brytnoth said, his voice taut. "You shouldn't put her in that kind of position. What kind of choice is that for her?"

"The only one there is."

"That's a lie. You're forcing her into that corner by your own decision to go after Derrek and then Azimir. Why don't you talk to her first? See what she has to say. Maybe she already has a plan for taking Azimir down."

"And how's she supposed to do that alone, Brytnoth? I respect her skills, believe me. But that's a bit much."

Brytnoth shook his head again. "I think you're banking on some very shaky assumptions. In my experience, that usually means trouble."

The transport ship pulled into view and idled in front of the cave. Deor headed for it and said over his shoulder, "Then stay here and rot. This is my time now. Mine. So either join me or get the hell out of my way."

Brytnoth, who had started to follow him to the transport, pulled up short and stared at him. And just before he turned away, Deor caught the expression of confused alarm that washed over his friend's face. Something deep in his soul tugged at him, nagging him like a pesky insect. Deor swatted it away and boarded the transport for Albadir, leaving Brytnoth in the dust.

THIRTY-ONE

DEOR STOOD on the landing platform outside the city of Albadir, squinting against the glare of the scorching desert sun. As he stood with arms folded across his chest, he could feel the sweat beginning to dampen the back of his shirt. The glare, the heat, the slow oozing of sweat all grated on his raw nerves, and his jaw spasmed.

He couldn't wait to get off this damned planet.

He squinted harder, until he couldn't decide which made his eyes hurt worse - the glare or the squinting. He fished around in the deep pockets of his battle dress pants, silently praying he'd remembered to slip the pair of polarized glasses into one of them before he'd left the Great House that morning. He was about to give up with a curse when he discovered them. Eyes finally shielded from the punishing sun, he was able to observe his crew's progress in relative comfort.

If only it weren't so hot. What does Sahara see in this blasted place?

His foul mood dissipated as he watched the last of the crates of *zanthos* disappear into the ship's hold. In just two days' time, Kirin's crew, aided by reinforcements from Albadir, had managed to empty the caverns of the stockpiles of *zanthos* and weapons. And now, finally, they were preparing to head back for Askalon. And that thought made Deor smile.

He'd heard nothing more from Sahara, so he assumed that she was laying low. That was well enough. He had enough to worry about at the moment.

His eyes wandered over the ship and lighted on Brytnoth, who was completing a final inspection of the craft with their pilot before they left for Askalon. His smile faded.

Like friends who don't act much like friends when it counts, he thought, unable to catch himself before he framed the words in his mind. *Friends who do nothing but question and doubt.*

It didn't matter. Once he had regained control of Askalon, then Brytnoth would believe in him. Sometimes faith had to be earned.

He watched as Brytnoth shook hands with the pilot and then headed across the platform toward him.

"Well?" Deor asked. "Is she fit to fly?"

"She's fit enough," Brytnoth answered with a ready grin. "We'll make it there in one piece, I think. Whether we'll stay in one piece for long once we get there is another matter entirely."

Deor studied Brytnoth from behind the polarized lenses. "You still doubt me?"

Brytnoth sighed, lines of exasperation creasing his brow. "It's not you. It's the situation...and the crazy plan. I think that you could do what you say you want to do under the right circumstances. I'm just not convinced that these are the right circumstances."

"To hell with your circumstances," Deor said. The edge in his voice surprised him, and Brytnoth's eyes flashed. But before he could speak, Deor swept on, "We'll take the hazard and triumph, or die trying. When do we leave?"

"Two hours' time. The fuel cells have to finish charging and they're loading the last few supply crates in the hold." Brytnoth clapped Deor on the shoulder, and though his smile was warm enough, there was a new light in his eyes. "Let's go grab a bite first. You look like you could use a drink."

"That's the truth."

They headed off the platform together and Brytnoth led the way to the tavern. The sudden drop in the temperature as they shouldered inside the building made Deor shiver, and he had to stand in the doorway for a moment to let his eyes adjust to the dark. Especially during the day, walking into the tavern felt like stepping through a gateway into another world—a world of shadows and close secrets.

Brytnoth jogged Deor's elbow. "Come on," he said. "This is on me."

He moved toward the bar, gesturing Deor to take a seat in the corner booth. Deor obeyed, glancing suspiciously at the pair of wizened old men crouched over their mugs on the far side of the room. They were watching him with an unfriendly curiosity that mirrored his own.

"What's with these people?" he muttered. "Where's Brytnoth with those damned drinks?"

A moment later, Brytnoth slid into the booth across from him and set two tankards down. "What's the matter?" he asked. "You look like you've eaten something remarkably sour."

Deor jerked his shoulders in a shrug. "These people," he said. "They're getting on my nerves."

"What people?"

"Nosy yammer-jaws who have nothing better to do with their time than sit around in a foul-smelling hole of a tavern all day."

Brytnoth's brows darkened in a frown. "Deor," he said quietly, leaning forward across the table. "Are you all right?"

The calm in Brytnoth's voice cut through the chaos in his mind, and he saw himself suddenly, clearly, as if looking in a mirror.

What is wrong with me? he wondered, and a sudden fear clawed at him.

He stared at Brytnoth. "I don't know," he choked. "I don't know what..." With a shudder, he gulped several mouthfuls of ale.

"You're not acting like yourself," Brytnoth continued. "Something's happened to you."

"I don't know!" Deor slammed the tankard back onto the table. Then, realizing even without looking that the old men in the corner were frowning blackly at him, he lowered his voice and made a half-hearted attempt to mop up the spilled ale. "It's this place. I hate it here. And I don't know why, so don't ask."

Brytnoth studied him silently, and Deor scrubbed harder at the spill with the cloth he had dragged out of his pocket.

"Was it the mine?" Brytnoth said finally, his voice barely audible.

"What mine?"

"The mine, Deor. Where we found...what we found. What we're taking back to Askalon."

"No."

Brytnoth threw back his head and crossed his arms over his chest. "Not true."

Deor stopped scrubbing and raised his eyes to his friend's face. "Are you calling me a liar now?"

"Should I be?"

"Go to hell."

"That's not very nice. I'm trying to help you."

"Then mind your own damn business."

Brytnoth leaned forward suddenly, his fists crashing into the table. Then he pointed a finger in Deor's face. "You listen to me. You want to take the most powerful element known in this universe back to my home planet and play king of the mountain with a pair of bloody traitors and tyrants, and my world hangs in the balance. I'd say that makes you and your attitude my damn business, Deor."

"Is that what this is all about? You still doubt that we can take back Askalon?"

"Yes, I do. You know I do. And why you won't listen to reason is beyond me. That's what I'm trying to figure out. You weren't always so reckless."

"Being cornered makes me reckless. You can't weasel your way out of everything with diplomacy, Brytnoth. Sometimes the only way out is through."

"That I grant you. But, Deor, we have no idea what things are like back on Askalon. And without hard intel, we should proceed with caution."

Deor sat back. "Then what do you propose we do?"

"Let's go back to Perseon first. Maybe we can find out more. And the *zanthos* belongs there anyway. Perhaps, with that information, we can find out how to counter Derrek."

"I don't care about Derrek. He's a piddling little despot who thinks he's called to something greater. He's a gnat. An insect."

"I wouldn't be so—"

"No, Brytnoth. We need to keep our eyes focused on the true threat. We need to take back Askalon so that we can strike at Halcyon from a position of strength. With our own *zanthos* and our own resources, we are on equal footing with Halcyon. And with Sahara's help, we can destroy them."

Brytnoth was shaking his head even before Deor finished speaking. "No, Deor. You underestimate Derrek, and you underestimate Sahara's love for Jared. She will never strike him down. Ever."

"I think you're wrong."

"I know I'm right."

Deor stared into Brytnoth's steel gray eyes. "Well, time will tell, I guess." He gulped down the rest of his ale and sent the empty tankard spinning toward the wall at the far end of the booth. "Let's find out who's right, shall we?"

"On one condition."

"What now?"

Brytnoth extended his hand across the table. "On the condition that no matter what happens, we stick together."

Deor's mouth quirked into a smile and he clasped Brytnoth's hand. "Agreed. Now let's go take back your planet."

———

In spite of everything they had done, Askalon was still a gray world. As their ship descended through the thick clouds that still shrouded the planet's surface, Deor felt a strange crawling uneasiness in his stomach. Something was wrong, but he didn't know what. He glanced at Brytnoth, who was sitting in his flight chair with his head back and his eyes closed.

"Don't you want to see it?" Deor asked.

Brytnoth opened one eye. "See what?"

"Your home. Askalon. We're landing."

Brytnoth closed his eye again. "I've seen it. And I have no desire to see it again."

"You don't want to see Askalon again?"

"Not what I meant." Brytnoth sat up and opened both eyes. "I have no desire to see how badly she's been brutalized. It's too much. When we get our boots on the ground, then I'll look."

Deor shrugged as Brytnoth leaned back and closed his eyes again. For a few moments, he toyed with the idea of confessing his nervousness. But when he remembered how much Brytnoth already doubted him and his plan, he swallowed his words and fixed his gaze instead on watching their approach.

The uncertain light of evening made it difficult to see anything on the ground below them, but as their altitude dropped, he began to make out a small swarm of people on the landing pad. His gut clenched again in momentary panic, and he glanced at Brytnoth.

"Brytnoth," he said, the word out of his mouth before he'd even formed the intention to speak.

"What?"

"You are with me, aren't you? No matter what?"

Brytnoth sighed. "Yes, Deor. I'm with you."

The landing gear touched down with a gentle lurch, and Deor slipped out of his harness. He drew his *zanthos*-pistol and fired it up. "Then suit up," he said. "It's time."

They waited, side by side, as the ramp was lowered. Deor saw

Derrek moving toward them across the platform, hand outstretched, a smile plastered on his face.

They disembarked and the clash of their boots on the metal ramp seemed too loud in Deor's ears. He held the pistol down at his side, close to his thigh, finger pressed to the stock and ready to aim and fire.

"Deor!" Derrek called as they reached the level of the platform. He laughed as if seeing them filled him with indescribable joy. "Brytnoth! A sight for sore eyes! Welcome home, both of you! And home in triumph, I hear?"

"Triumph indeed," murmured Deor. He raised the pistol and planted the muzzle in the center of Derrek's forehead. "Stand down."

Derrek raised both his arms slowly out to his sides as if he were surrendering, but his glinting eyes said something else entirely. And it was then that Deor realized that they were already surrounded. Out of the corner of his eye, he saw the glint of weapons.

"Deor," Brytnoth whispered. "They've already taken the ship."

"How in the hell..." Deor felt panic surge through him, and he snapped his gaze back to Derrek. The warmth in his smile was gone, leaving just the empty shell.

"What? You thought you could just step off that ship and take me down, didn't you?" Derrek said. "Didn't you, you pathetic little maggot?"

Deor swallowed. In that moment of hesitation, Derrek slapped his arm aside, sending the pistol skittering across the platform.

"What have you done with Aelred and the other Lords?" Brytnoth demanded. "Where are they?"

"What should I care? Dead or hiding, it doesn't matter to me. I control Pentapolis. Askalon is mine." Derrek's eyes flicked back to Deor. "And you. You were such a good little dupe. So eager to scurry off for lord and kingdom, eh? Such a good little subject. I had no doubt you would see this through for me."

Inside, Deor seethed. "You're going to regret this, Derrek."

"Oh, am I? I don't think so." He laughed, but there was no mirth in it now. "It's really hilarious, actually. Hearing you threaten me when you're weaponless and surrounded and completely, utterly, absolutely in my power. Every breath you take is because I will you to stay alive." His arm snaked forward and coiled around Deor's neck, pulling him forward until his head rested on Derrek's chest. "I hope you understand now. I hope it's all totally clear in your mind how you have been played from the very beginning. I have pulled your strings, and how beautifully you have danced, like a little puppet in a dumb show."

"And you're being played by a power greater than you can possibly comprehend," Deor said, shoving Derrek away from him. "And I hope you realize just how much a puppet you've been before the end of your miserable life. I may have been played, but I've never been a traitor. And when Jared finishes with you, I hope you find yourself in that special circle of Hell reserved just for rotten scum like you."

Derrek's jaw convulsed in a paroxysm of rage, and for a moment, Deor thought he would give the order for his men to fire. Instead, he motioned for a small squad to come forward.

"Get these men back to Headquarters," he told the captain. "I'll deal with them later." He planted a finger in Deor's chest. "You're going to regret bringing him up," he said. "I promise you."

As Derrek pushed past them and headed for the ship, the captain slammed the butt of his rifle into Deor's back.

"Get moving," he said. "The General has plans for you."

Deor and Brytnoth, propelled by the threat of blows from the dozen soldiers who boxed them in, marched briskly toward the steps on the far side of the platform.

"Where's Headquarters, I wonder?" Deor muttered as they reached the street below.

"Shut up, you!" snapped the soldier next to him, giving him a vicious blow with his gun.

Deor stumbled forward and fell to his knees. Anger was roiling in his gut, but they were so far outnumbered that striking back would be suicide.

Well, he thought, *maybe not.*

When the soldier reached down to jerk him to his feet, Deor seized his arm and plowed him headfirst into the pavement. Then he wrenched the gun out of the man's hand and riddled him with bullets.

A chaos of shouts erupted around him. He heard Brytnoth screaming his name, heard the sharp report of gunfire somewhere to his left. But before he could get to his feet and see what was happening, something crashed into his skull and he crumpled to the ground.

Vaguely, he heard more gunfire. Someone collapsed on top of him and he grunted, but he couldn't make his body move. He blinked slowly, trying to clear his vision. He thought he heard Brytnoth screaming something again, but he couldn't make out the words. Everything seemed to be a buzzing blur of gray.

Suddenly, everything was quiet. He tried to cough the acrid smoke of gunfire out of his lungs and found that the man on top of him made it almost impossible to breathe. He made a choking sound, tried to call Brytnoth's name.

And then, blessedly, the body on top of him was hauled away. Someone grabbed his shoulder and rolled him over. He stared up into the gray haze, blinking rapidly. A face came into focus. It was smudged with dirt and had a nasty scrape across the right cheek, but he would have known that dark ponytail anywhere.

"Aria?" he croaked. "Is that you?"

Her mouth tipped in a smile. "Commander," she said, inclining her head slightly. "Welcome to the Underground."

THIRTY-TWO

SAHARA WATCHED the building in front of her, her eyes stinging with weariness and the dry night air. She'd decided to follow Katarina into Aquila one last time before giving her report on the situation to Brig, and now she was beginning to regret it. Every muscle in her body longed for the comfort of her soft pallet back at camp. She shifted her position, wrapping her cloak more tightly around her. She'd been sitting here for almost an hour—surely Katarina wouldn't spend much longer doing whatever it was she was doing in that house.

Sahara wondered at herself a bit. She sat across the narrow alley, eyes fixed on the upper floor window that peered in on Katarina's meeting place. But she was supposed to be here on reconnaissance. She should be infiltrating that house, overlistening whatever conversations were taking place. Finding out, beyond the shadow of any doubt, that Katarina was everything she said she was, and nothing of a traitor.

And yet, here she was, across the street, huddled in her cloak like an old woman begging bread.

I'm getting soft. She rubbed a hand over her face. *Six months ago,*

I wouldn't have hesitated.

But everything had changed. Her world was upside-down and inside-out, and she had enough to worry about without chasing down some fool's suspicions to prove they were ghosts.

I know she's not a traitor. So why am I going to pry into her business?

But even as the thought formed itself, she was enmeshed in doubts. *Did* she know that Katarina wasn't a traitor? Could she really trust anyone in this hellish place, where nothing was as it seemed and good men became monsters?

She squirmed again on her perch, but no amount of snugging the cloak around her would ease the chill she felt growing inside. She focused more intently on the window across the way, trying to make out any sounds or movement. But she saw and heard nothing. The curtain sighed outward as a light breeze ruffled Sahara's hair.

Dawn was coming.

Where is Katarina?

And then, as she watched, the curtain was sucked suddenly inward as the pressure changed inside the room. Someone had opened a door. Someone was coming.

The next moment, she saw Katarina's dark form emerge from the front door. She turned at the last moment and blew a kiss to the person standing just out of Sahara's view. What could it mean? That first night, Katarina was threatened here. Now she was blowing kisses? Sahara frowned. It didn't make sense.

She waited until Katarina had hurried out of sight down the narrow street, and then she uncurled herself from her position and clambered down the wall.

I need more information.

She glanced down the way Katarina had taken, caught the briefest hint of her shadowy form passing out of view around a far corner, and then made a decision. Today, she would stay in Aquila. She would find out what was going on. Brig was an idiot. He didn't understand where the true threat lay, but she did. And instead of wasting another night spying on the only mother she had ever known, she would find out how close Azimir was to having the power to annihilate them all.

It would be difficult. She could handle surveillance nets and drones and guards. But she didn't know how to keep herself hidden from Jared, who seemed to be able to sense her when she was close to the palace walls. At least, she thought he could. She always felt the creeping fingers of shadow prying at her mind and heart whenever she was in this place, and she was thankful that she had learned how to control the gateway to her mind. But she knew, too, that if Jared really tried, she had no way to defend against him. He was too strong, too powerful now.

And that decided her. She would head away from the palace, down toward the landing platforms. Scum that hung around the loading docks always knew more than was good for them. Perhaps she might pick up something useful.

She swung around and headed south, following the gentle downward slope of the street and keeping to the deep shadows beneath the buildings. She caught a glimpse of the eastern sky through a gap in the buildings to her left. The light was growing. Already the stars along the horizon were gone, their light dimmed to nothingness by the promise of the sun.

I hope Katarina gets out of the city before daybreak. She wasn't sure when the guards changed, but she knew Katarina was cutting it close this time. Too close. *When I get back to camp, I've got to tell her to stop coming. It's too dangerous now. She needs to stay away from this place.*

It would help if she knew why Katarina came at all, and once again that nagging sensation that she hadn't really done her job came over her. She shoved it away. There would be plenty of time for doubt later. But for now, she needed her wits clear.

She slipped her hand beneath her cloak to feel at the small of her back. Her knife was gone. Of course it was gone...she had given it to that woman as a token for Jared. She sighed and wished she'd given the woman something else. She hated the thought of worming her way into a den of thieves without a good knife ready to hand.

I didn't have it on K'ilenfir when I infiltrated that prison. And I managed well enough without it.

She slammed the door on the memory before she got any further than that. The last thing she needed was to attract Jared's attention by frolicking in memories.

The street took a sharp turn to the west and headed more steeply downhill. Behind her, she heard the noises of a city coming awake— window shutters being opened, sleepy voices trailing like vines down into the street below. She heard the sound of cookware rattling in one of the apartments above her, and then came the smells of exotic food —spiced meats, pungent hot drinks, and sweet breads. Sahara's stomach growled. She'd have to find food somewhere if she was going to stay sharp, and since she had hardly any money on her, she'd probably have to pinch it like some ragged little street urchin.

Remembering back to the day they had arrived in Aquila, she figured that there would soon be street vendors pushing their wares in narrow carts down the streets. There would be opportunity to lift something from one of them in the eddying currents of people. Sahara took a breath, savoring for a moment the cool of the desert dawn, then wished she hadn't. It made her realize just how thirsty she was.

Threading her way through a narrow alley, she emerged suddenly on a wide thoroughfare, and she could see down the slope all the way to the platforms at the bottom of the hill. A few motivated vendors were already pulling their carts into position and propping up samples of their wares to tempt would-be buyers. Sahara glanced up at the sky, gauging the time. The central azure dome was tinged with gold on the eastern edge. The sun had risen, but barely. It was time.

She was about to step out into the street when she checked herself. She would be conspicuous now in her dark cloak. Her battle dress was bad enough, marking her as a solider or a merc, but the cloak made her positively suspicious. She unclasped the neck fastening and rolled it into a tight bundle. Glancing back the way she had come, she noticed a tumble of crates four or five doors back down the alley. She crossed to them and wedged the cloak in among them.

Whoever finds it will be the richer for it. And who knows? Maybe it's one of those drop points Rigel told me about.

She faced the boulevard again, instinctively reaching once more for the cold reassurance of her knife hilt. And once again, she felt that stab of misgiving when her hand closed on nothing. She mumbled a curse and then a prayer and headed down the hill.

The docks were already buzzing with activity, even though the hour was still early. But many of the men Sahara passed looked groggy, swollen-eyed, and still reeked of last night's drinking. It was exactly what she had been counting on—men's heads so muzzy from overindulgence that they would do anything, and say anything, to make her leave them alone.

She passed several men as she made her way into the heart of the warehouse district, but let them be. They seemed wary and guarded, and she didn't want to engage anyone whose guard was already up. She had to find just the right mark. She swiveled her eyes from side to side, keeping her chin up and her shoulders back, hoping that she was projecting enough authority to keep unfriendly questions away.

And then she saw him. He was ten feet down a smelly side-street, heaving crates from a transport into a lopsided pile on the street. She paused to watch for a moment, a laugh catching in her throat as she saw the topmost crate slip down when he turned to reach for another crate. She heard it thud onto his foot, and the man yelped in pain. As he jerked his foot out from under the broken crate, the one he held in his hands slipped and splintered on the pavement.

The man's string of curses were loud but slurred, and Sahara nodded to herself. She'd found her man.

"What do you think you're doing, you stupid, clumsy rat-brother?" she demanded.

The man turned, limping a bit, and squinted at her. "Who're

you?"

"One of your betters. And you'd best explain how you let Lord Azimir's—" she hesitated for a moment, looking over the scattered contents of the two crates. *Demon's Breath*, she realized. "How did you let so much of Lord Azimir's valuable product be spoiled like this?"

"Just slipped," the man mumbled, nudging a bag of the drug with his boot. "'S all. Just slipped out me hands. Nothing I could do."

Sahara crossed her arms and glared at him for a moment. "And where is this bound?" she asked. "Answer quick or I'll dock the value from your pay."

"Ship's here from Askalon. This goes back tonight."

Sahara's pulse quickened. "Askalon, is it? And how will they like it, I wonder, when their shipment is short?"

The man sniffed and rolled his shoulders. "Dunno."

Sahara measured the man for a moment, then made a decision. She seized the man's arm in a vise-grip and propelled him, squawking and wriggling, into the dark warehouse behind him.

"What's this? What's this?" he kept repeating, but his reflexes and his wits were so dull that she had no trouble forcing him to go where she wanted him.

She paused for a moment inside the warehouse doorway, letting her eyes adjust to the sudden gloom. But as soon as she could make out shapes, she shoved the man towards a stack of crates along the far wall. With one last push, she sent him staggering over his own feet, and he fell in a heap in front of the crates.

"Are you going to kill me for what I've done?" he whimpered.

"Kill you?" Sahara said, edging her voice with ice. "Perhaps." The man's whimper became a miserable blubber, and Sahara added, "But perhaps not. If you tell me what I want to know, perhaps I'll let you go. And perhaps, if you're very helpful, I might not mention that you broke those crates."

"I'll be helpful. Very helpful. Just don't kill me, I beg you! Please..."

"Shut. Up." Sahara folded her arms and waited for the man's mumblings to cease. "Now. This ship that's here from Askalon. Did you see who was on it? And what was her cargo?"

"Not supposed to talk about that. The captain said we'd get fifty if we said anything about what was on that ship."

"Well, at least fifty lashes would leave you alive." The man tipped his head up at her, and Sahara could tell that he was trying to make out the meaning in her words. "If you don't tell me what I want to know, you'll be dead," Sahara explained slowly. "And if I don't kill you, I will tell your captain just how much of Lord Azimir's product is strewn all over the street because you drink too much and can't hold your liquor. And then he'll kill you himself. So take your pick."

The man hesitated, and Sahara heard the beginnings of more pathetic blubberings. "Skeleton crew was on her," he said finally. "Skeleton crew."

"And their leader?"

"Tall man. Brawny. Looks like he knows how to handle himself in a fight, that one. But shifty too."

Sahara nodded slowly, her mind clicking through various possible suspects. "And the cargo?"

"A very special something, that. Secret. Went straight to the fortress."

"What was it, you idiot?"

The man mumbled something, and Sahara sprang on him, grabbing him by the shoulders of his jumpsuit and slamming his head into the crate behind him. The man gulped and let out a gurgling howl.

"What was it?" Sahara repeated, her face close to the man's own.

"I didn't see myself," he mumbled, the words barely audible. "But I heard the brawny one tell my captain to be careful with it. That the Lord Azimir would be distressed if something happened to his *zanthos*."

Sahara dropped the man in a wretched heap and backed away.

"No," she breathed. "It's here. It's already here."

"Are you...are you going to kill me?" the man whimpered,

crawling toward her feet like a whipped cur.

"No. Not today. But breathe a word of this to anyone, and I will find you, do you understand? And then you'd wish you'd never seen me."

"I swear it. I swear." The man gulped, latching his trembling fingers around her boot. "And...and are you going to report me?"

Sahara kicked him away. "No, for goodness' sake. Get up and get out of my sight, you miserable excuse for a human being."

The man didn't linger. He scrambled to his feet and lurched out the door.

Sahara stood in the darkness, her head down, eyes closed. If the *zanthos* were already here, then they were out of time.

She had to get home, had to warn her people.

And then she would have to come back and face Jared alone.

She turned to go, then froze. She heard the man's sobbing, shaking voice wailing from outside the warehouse. The sound iced her blood and she stared at the rectangle of light that marked the doorway.

"No, please! I didn't mean...it was just an accident!"

Sahara crept toward the door, angling to the left. She reached the doorframe and peered around.

The man was on his knees and a *zanthos*-pistol was pressed to his head. Her eyes snapped up.

Gervais.

It all made sense now. His escape from that prison must have been part of the plot back on Askalon, the plot that now held her brother and her friends in jeopardy. And here he was, doing the traitor's dirty work, delivering the *zanthos* to Azimir.

She swallowed hard. Without her knives, she felt suddenly powerless to do anything for the man groveling in the dust.

Well, maybe not entirely powerless.

Taking a deep breath, she stepped around the doorframe into the light.

"Hello, Gervais," she said. "What a surprise."

THIRTY-THREE

GERVAIS STARED AT HER, his mouth flapping open. The worker wasted no time in using the distraction to scramble away from him, and out of the corner of her eye Sahara saw him crouch behind the stack of crates like a frightened rat.

"What in hell are you doing here?" Gervais choked, some color finally coming back into his face. "I thought Azimir had you under lock and key somewhere...or buried in a shallow grave."

Sahara snorted. "Guess your boss doesn't tell you much, does he?" She cocked her head and narrowed her eyes. "Makes you wonder what else he hasn't told you."

Gervais swallowed. "No, it doesn't."

"Yes, it does. And if it doesn't, then you're every bit as stupid as I thought you were. Aelred made a mistake, sparing your life. I won't be so foolish."

"What're you getting at? What's your game?"

"No game. But you've caused quite a problem for my friends and I, Gervais. And I really don't like you."

Gervais's snorting laugh was hollow with nervous uncertainty.

"What the hell should I care? You think I'm here for a popularity contest?"

Sahara smiled coldly at him, even as she felt her insides shrink. She was on that path again, that same accursed path that always ended with blood on her hands and a body in the street. The thought of Gervais' body in the dust made her stomach clench. A vision of Jessup's kind, wrinkled face and warm eyes flashed into her mind. She'd come so far from that life. So far. And yet, here she was again.

It's not going to end that way this time. I'll find another way...I don't want his blood on my hands.

And yet, she knew that her best chance of getting him to talk was to manipulate his fear of her. He knew what she was capable of. She just hoped he wouldn't call her bluff.

Gervais was watching her steadily, and Sahara could sense his confidence beginning to ebb back into him. "You planning to make me talk, then, girlie?" he jeered. "I'd like to see you try."

Sahara steadied herself inside.

Here we go.

She took a breath and looked at her hands, turning them over to study her short, rounded nails. Then she glanced up at Gervais and shook her head. "You really wouldn't. Because most people who end up on my bad side end up dead. And I think you know that."

Gervais jerked his shoulders in what was supposed to be a shrug, and his voice shook as he tried to laugh. "Go to hell."

"I hate to break this to you, friend. This is hell. Welcome to it."

Gervais measured her for a long moment, eyes narrowed. "So what are you going to do?"

"I'd be more worried about what you're going to do, Gervais. Because what happens next is completely up to you."

"What's that supposed to mean?"

"If you tell me where you've taken all that *zanthos* and who's calling the shots back on Askalon, then maybe I'll let you live. If not..." Sahara shrugged. "Like I said, it's your call."

Gervais hesitated. He spread his legs in a fighting stance, but his eyes darted from side to side, as if seeking for help from somewhere in the vacant alleyway. Sahara let her body go loose and supple. She was without her knives, she didn't want his blood on her hands, and he was calling her bluff. She would have to try to stall him.

A movement behind the crates caught Sahara's eye. The worker was holding a short knife in his hand. As soon as he caught her eye, he jerked his head at Gervais and gestured with the knife.

Great, she thought. *All I need is some amateur getting himself killed.*

But if she could get her hands on that knife...

Sahara's eyes snapped back to Gervais as he balled his hands into massive fists.

"Go to hell, Sahara," Gervais said again, finally coming to a decision. "I'm not telling you nothing."

"Your funeral," she said quietly.

"Or yours."

Without warning, Gervais sprang at her. His bulk made him slow, but he was enormous. As he stretched out his arms to seize and crush her, Sahara ducked under them. His momentum carried him past her, and she aimed a kick at his backside. He staggered forward, a growl rumbling out of his chest. As soon as he regained his footing, he turned to face her again, rage and poor conditioning purpling his face.

"I'd really prefer this not to end this way," Sahara said, backing slowly. "It'd be so much better for both of us if you would just tell me what I want to know."

He cursed at her and came at her again. She darted to the side and sent him reeling with another kick. He barreled into the load of crates, knocking two to the ground. They shattered and spilled their guts all over the street, and he swore fiercely.

"Quit dancing around and stand still!" he roared.

"There'll be hell to pay on Askalon for that," Sahara observed. "See? You don't want to go back there anyway. All that product wasted...and it's all on you. Much better to stay here on Halcyon. Make a new life for yourself. You know your bosses on Askalon would kill you as soon as look at you...so why not just tell me everything? You don't owe them."

"Shut up!" He wheeled around and stood there, panting. But for a moment, he hesitated, hands clenching and unclenching in impotent rage. "Just shut up, you!"

Sahara balanced, waiting, then decided to press him a bit further. "I don't want to kill you, Gervais. Just tell me what you know. Please."

He angled forward, keeping her at a distance, measuring her. "I already said. I ain't talking to you. And you can't kill me...'cause then you got nothing. And he's coming for you. This little shipment here? That's nothing." He started to chuckle, then his gut rolled in a laugh. "This moron thinks it's all on the up and up. What an idiot. Still wet behind the ears, is he? We've got big plans...and he's got no idea." He stopped circling and just laughed, clutching at his sides.

Sahara waited in silence. *Just a little more. Just a little. Come on. Spit it out.*

"Oh, yes," Gervais continued. "It's going to hit him hard when he realizes how he's been rolled. He'll pave the way, and then Derrek...." His face went suddenly ashen and he stood, goggling at her, mouth flapping open.

"Derrek. I thought as much." Sahara crossed her arms over her chest. "So he's planning a double-cross, eh? He told you that, did he? Let you in on all his big plans, is that it?" She shook her head. "For a back-stabbing traitor he's a pretty awful judge of character."

He was on her before she could move. The blow to her stomach made her feel like her world was going to explode, and she staggered backwards, stumbling over the mess of broken crate. Gasping for breath, she collapsed. He was on her before she could crawl away, straddling her and pinning her down. He seized her by the throat with one hand and scrabbled in the dirt with the other, looking for a shard of wood to end her.

She tried to choke something and the pressure around her throat increased. She batted at his arm, feebly. Her vision was drowning in a sea of gray.

It was over. She knew it was over.

The pressure around her throat suddenly disappeared and she gasped for air. But Gervais' bulk slumped over her, compressing her lungs even as she fought to fill them with air. She writhed under the weight of the body, her croaking voice babbling something inarticulate. She felt panic taking over and had just enough sense left to realize that her thrashing was ineffective. She gulped in a breath and strained against the body. Her hands came away slick with blood.

Her stomach lurched, and she gasped again for air.

"Help, somebody..." she wheezed. "Help me!"

She pushed at Gervais' body again, but her strength was sapped by adrenaline and lack of oxygen. Just when she thought she'd suffocate to death, the body rolled off her.

Sahara clawed herself onto her side, coughing and retching as air rushed into her lungs. She closed her eyes, tried to calm her breathing. Waves of dizziness eddied her for a moment, then passed. She took a few more shaking breaths, then pushed herself upright and wiped her forehead on the back of her hand.

"Lucky for you I stuck around," said the dock worker. "And lucky for you I know how to use a knife."

Sahara dropped her hand and looked at Gervais. The plain hilt of a short knife protruded from the back of his neck.

"I owe you," Sahara croaked. "He was going to kill me for sure." She shuddered and pressed a hand to her throat. "What's your name? Never did catch it."

"Eril. But the boys just call me Ril."

Sahara extended her hand and he clasped her wrist, helping her to her feet.

"Well met, then, Ril," she said. "And thank you."

Ril inclined his head. "Figure now I'm sure you won't be telling on me about the crates," he said, his mouth crinkling in a grin. "Insurance."

"No, I won't be telling. You have my word on that."

"Did he tell you what you wanted to know?"

"Some." She cocked her head at him, studying the man with renewed curiosity. "What do you know about that shipment of *zanthos*? Where was it headed?"

Ril's face paled slightly. "I don't think I know anything else that will help you."

"Let me be the judge of that."

Ril swallowed noisily and glanced around. "First help me get him inside before somebody sees. Then we'll talk. Here, get his legs."

Sahara positioned herself at Gervais' feet and watched Ril hitch the body under the arms. Everything about him suggested that this wasn't the first time he'd hidden a body, but Sahara was sure that he couldn't stand up to anyone in a fair fight.

He's the kind that knifes you in a dark alley. He'll never face you down...but he'll stab you in the back.

As they heaved and hauled Gervais' corpse into the dark warehouse, Sahara felt a growing sense of uneasiness about her companion. Ril had said something earlier about insurance—making sure she didn't tattle on him to his superiors about his sloppy work. Sahara wondered now if her knowledge of his clumsiness and his crime was insurance, or whether it made her a liability.

Ril kicked some sacking out of the way to make a space on the floor for the body. He jerked his head at the spot and dropped his end of the corpse. Sahara did the same, then stretched her back and arms.

"They're always heavier dead," Ril said, observing her with a sharp glint in his eye. "This your first?"

A dangerous question. Sahara was immediately on guard, her eyes fixed on the man's half-shadowed face.

"Does it look like it?"

Ril shrugged. "Dunno. First time hiding a body, maybe. You the straight-up type, then?"

"How do you mean?"

"Straight-up." He grinned at her, his sharp incisors flashing at her. "You knife 'em in the belly, right?"

"If that's the best spot."

Ril laughed. "Ah, that's what I like to hear. You know when to take advantage, is that it? Take your opportunity as it comes, right? And you'd knife a man in the back if it came to it, then."

"If it came to it."

They stared at each other for long seconds. Sahara barely dared to breathe. It was that moment—he would either decide he respected her enough to let her go her way, or he'd add her to his list and then look for an opportunity to cross her out.

And what am I doing? What I always do...measuring him, considering the weaknesses, how hard to hit and where to send him to his judgment. Enough. It's got to stop.

"You want to kill me," she murmured, "then go right ahead. I'm standing right here."

"I just saved your life. Why would I want to kill you?"

"We both know the answer to that."

Ril shrugged again. "If I'd wanted to kill you, I'd have let him do it." He jabbed a toe into Gervais' shoulder. "He'd have smothered you nice and good. But that's not my way." His wolfish smile flashed at her again, and he bent suddenly to cover the body with the sacks.

Sahara eased her breath out of her lungs and felt her hands begin to shake. She needed some of Katarina's hot, fragrant tea.

And suddenly, she had an almost overwhelming desire to dash out the door while Ril was stooped at his work. She could run, she could get back the the Hazad and never come into Aquila again.

Can't do that. Can't run away from this. Azimir's going to destroy the whole damn planet...running to the Hazad isn't going to do anybody any good.

She clenched her trembling hands into fists. "You done?"

"It'll do for now," Ril said, straightening. "The boys'll come by later and take care of the rest of him." He grinned at her and jerked his head toward the door. "Go on. Ladies first."

For the barest fraction of a second, Sahara hesitated. Then she steeled her nerves and stalked outside. Ril followed her with a strange shuffling gait. When Sahara reached the crates, she turned and saw what he was doing. He was scuffing dirt over the trail of blood.

"Does this kind of thing happen a lot?" Sahara asked. "You're quite professional about the whole thing."

"Well, there's times when things need sorting out. And there's times when they can't be sorted. And we've got a long leash here."

"So it seems." Sahara glanced toward the main street and saw with some surprise that it was bustling with activity. "No one cares whether there's a brawl and someone gets killed?"

"Life's short. It happens." He shook his head and planted his fists on his hips. "But this now." He gestured to the broken crates and spilled drugs. "This is a damn tragedy."

Sahara turned back to him, studying him. His callousness iced her veins, and she suddenly wanted to be done with him. "That's your problem," she said hastily. "When did that shipment of *zanthos* leave the dock?"

"Few minutes before you got here," he said as he squatted in the dust beside the pile of bagged product and shattered wood. "It's to the fortress by now, I'm sure. Why? You keen to go get you some?"

"Don't be a moron," she snapped. "Do you know what it's for? Do you know why it's here?"

"All I know is Lord Azimir wants it," Ril said with a roll of his shoulders. "Why should I care what he's up to?"

"Because he's meddling with powers he doesn't understand and can't possibly control," Sahara said, keeping her voice low. "And he will destroy Halcyon with them."

Ril's eyes widened at that. "Serious? On purpose?"

"Probably not. But it doesn't really matter whether he means to do it on purpose or not." Sahara paused, then said, "I need to know about him, Ril. What can you tell me?"

"No one knows much. But there's been rumors lately. The lords of the other houses don't like him, that's plain."

"How do you know that?"

"We dock workers report directly to House Dracor. They control the transportation and shipping in Aquila. Powerful, get it? They get to call a lot of the shots, because if Lord Dracor doesn't like something, he tells us to stay home. We stay home, nothing gets moved. No product gets shipped...and no money gets made."

Why in hell would you outsource transportation? Sahara wondered. *That's just stupid politics.*

"How did Dracor end up in charge of such a big sector of Aquila's economy?"

"That's Azimir's father's doing. When they discovered the Demon's Breath drug, Aquila exploded. Everyone flooded into the city, hoping to get rich. So Azimir's father seized control of the drug trade for his family. They have a new name under Azimir—that's the Zharib. But Azimir's father had enough sense to know that the other lords would band together and overthrow him, so he invited each House to meet with him over some fancy plated dinner. He cut deals with each of them, seduced their support with promises of wealth and power beyond imagining." Ril chuckled and shook his head, returning to his painstaking task of cleaning up the spilled drug.

"You know an awful lot," Sahara commented.

"I keep my ears open is all," Ril said, not even bothering to glance at her. "I may just work the docks, but I'm not stupid. And my business depends on sharp ears."

"Your business?"

Ril grinned at her again, flashing those sharp teeth. "My business. You know, people say and do a lot of things when they're getting off a ship after a long journey," he said. "Things as maybe they don't want spread around."

"You mean the sort of things people would pay handsomely to keep quiet?"

Ril winked at her. "Anyways, Dracor got handed the transportation guild. While the old man was in charge, Aquila was stable. Everyone minded his own business and the system worked. But once

Azimir took over, there's been rumblings. And everyone knows that Dracor despises Azimir. Calls him a half-breed. Says he doesn't deserve to rule."

Sahara glanced at him quickly. *Half-breed?* "I don't understand. Isn't Azimir a good ruler?"

"Dracor says he's not. Dracor says he's soft. Too soft on the Hazad especially. Most of the Houses want the Hazad destroyed once and for all, especially now that the new shipment of drone harvesters has been delivered from Ket."

"Come on, Ril. Is the Hazad really a threat?"

He shrugged. "How should I know? But rumor on the street has it that there's a big party up at the fortress tonight. And the Guildmasters are going to lobby for exterminating the Hazad once and for all." He glanced around, sniffed, and scratched his chin. "Leastaways, that's what I heard Lord Zin tell his mistress this morning."

Sahara swallowed hard. "And it's tonight? This party? You're sure?"

"Sure, I'm sure." Ril glanced around again, then lowered his voice so much that Sahara could barely hear him. "But I know something most don't," he said. "Something that Azimir isn't supposed to know."

"And what is that?"

Ril licked his lips. "How much is it worth to you?"

Sahara measured him, her mind clicking through a series of increasingly unpleasant scenarios. "What's your price?"

Ril wiped his nose on the back of his hand and sat back on his heels. "Well, I was going to report all this here as I'm supposed to do. You know, repackage it and bow and scrape and all that. Hope for a flogging and keep my job, like. But you made me go and get blood on my hands this morning, and I didn't have plans for that today. You've cost me, girl. You've cost me quite a bit. And now you want my information. My little tidbit that I was saving for just the right moment, and just the right price."

"Just tell me what you want."

"Well, in spite of the trouble you've caused me, I kind of like you."

Sahara stiffened, her eyes riveted on his face. She said nothing and waited, her breathing shallow. Ril seemed to guess something of her thoughts, for he grinned and winked at her.

"I'm willing to cut you a deal," he said. "You let me keep all this here—" he gestured to the drugs at his feet— "and I tell you my secret."

"Those aren't mine to give."

"No, but they're yours to take away if you report me."

"I already told you that I wasn't going to—"

"Well, and when I tell you my secret, then you have that much more reason to keep your mouth shut, don't you?"

Sahara frowned. The man's reasoning was sideways, but she wasn't about to argue. "Fine. Deal. Tell me what you know. And hurry up about it."

Ril beckoned for her to squat down beside him. She crouched and he pulled her close so that he could whisper in her ear. His breath smelled of liquor and pickled fish, and she had to steel herself against a shudder and a gag.

"It's just this. Dracor's got an army of drones hidden in three warehouses on the far side of the landing platform. And my crew captain is the one who's looking after them. He's been smuggling them in from Ket a few at a time, hidden in the shipments of harvesters."

"Is that so?"

Ril nodded, a grin creasing his face. "That's so. And the shipment of *zanthos* has come in just in time for the Hazad's pilgrimage to Telon. The time is almost here."

Sahara pulled away from him. "Time for what?"

"War."

Sahara stared at him for a moment. "So Dracor is planning a coup," she murmured. "Azimir is planning to annihilate the Hazad. And Ket's running armaments to Dracor. Why?"

"I'm not especially savvy in things political," Ril said, "but even I can see that. With the Hazad destroyed, Ket holds the key to Aquila's power. Influence, girl. And money. Because they supply all the harvesters...and without the harvesters..."

"No Demon's Breath."

Ril closed his mouth tight and winked at her.

Sahara's mind worked feverishly. Azimir meant to take out the Hazad, but she was sure now that that wasn't all he was planning. He had to know that he was vulnerable. He had to realize that his throne was in jeopardy.

What would I do if I had unlimited power at my disposal? Would I just appease my petty lords and hope they patted me on the back for it?

Even as she framed the question in her mind, she knew the answer.

Of course not. I'd destroy them all, and then I'd take out the Princes of all the other provinces too, just for good measure. Especially if I knew that Ket was working with Dracor to subvert me.

She scratched in the dirt with a shard of wood, feeling that there was something she wasn't seeing. There was a piece missing.

Dracor can't know what Azimir is planning. He's so confident that his smuggling has gotten him the edge, so confident in the support of the other Houses. And he's written Azimir off as a half-breed fool. He's so blinded by his hatred and prejudice that he doesn't realize just how much he's left out of his little equation. And he's probably convinced the other provinces that he can take Aquila. And Azimir would know that there's been dealing behind his back. That's why he can't leave the provinces intact. Except...

"What about Perl?" she asked out loud.

"Eh?" said Ril with a shudder. "Good God, girl. No one talks about that accursed place. And no one goes there, either. It's for the damned."

And clarity suddenly crystallized everything in Sahara's mind. She pressed the point of the stick into the earth as though it was the only stable point in her universe.

So that's the answer to all the riddles, she thought. *That's where*

Azimir is hiding everything he needs. And if he's preparing to unleash Jared...then he will retreat to Perl as his stronghold. And that means....

Sahara felt her hands begin to shake and she clenched them tight. "Not that you're asking for my advice," she said, "but I'd clear out of town if I were you."

"Why's that?" Ril asked, eyes suddenly narrowed in suspicion.

"Because war is coming," she said. "You said so yourself. And I wouldn't want to be here when it does."

"Lots of opportunity to profit off wars," Ril said. "Don't you worry about me."

"I wasn't planning on it."

Sahara got to her feet and headed back into the city at a run.

THIRTY-FOUR

"I HOPE this will show you how beautifully I have everything worked out," Azimir said as he led the way down the expansive colonnade to his council room. He chuckled to himself, then glanced at Jared over his shoulder. "Really, Jared, I think even you will be impressed."

Jared said nothing. Through the black haze that seemed to cloud all his thoughts and vision, he felt only revulsion for the man. Nothing Azimir could do would impress him. He was petty, concerned with the spinning of a petty little world. Jared threw back his shoulders. There were larger things in motion now—things Azimir hadn't foreseen.

As they reached the heavy double doors, the two guards snapped to attention. The naked blades of their scimitars caught the westering sun and glinted like fire. They never moved a muscle, but Jared saw them eying him out of the corners of their eyes. He smiled to himself as he caught the scent of fear.

"Open the doors, you fools!" Azimir snapped.

They jumped to obey like a pair of whipped dogs, flinching away from Azimir as they pushed the doors inward. Azimir muttered a curse at them as he and Jared entered, but he was rubbing his hands too excitedly to pay them any more mind than that.

"It should have been here an hour ago," he murmured. "What can be the delay?"

"Perhaps you should speak to Dracor," Jared said. "Ask him why he's allowing it."

Azimir seated himself in his low throne, fixing Jared quizzically. "Allowing it? I have no doubt it happens without his knowledge or permission."

Jared shrugged. "Suit yourself."

Azimir regarded him for a long moment, and Jared met his gaze steadily until Azimir looked away. That gloating feeling of triumph welled up in Jared again. His power over Azimir was growing by the day. It wouldn't be long now.

"I don't know how it is you suddenly think you understand everything there is to know about ruling here," Azimir said. "Or why you think I want your advice. You are here for one reason, and one only. I don't need your help otherwise."

"Suit yourself."

"Stop saying that!" Azimir slammed his fist down on the arm of his chair. "I order you to silence!"

Jared folded his arms across his chest and threw back his head. It was laughable, really—this little man and his impotent rage. Like a kitten giving orders to a mastiff. But Jared could bide his time. Let him think he was in charge. The truth would be clear soon enough.

Azimir glared at Jared for another moment, then rang the small silver bell beside his chair. The door behind the dais opened and Rafe shuffled forward. Jared's heart twisted as it did every time he saw his friend, and for a moment, the darkness lifted. But in its place hate rolled in, a hatred that burned in his gut and made him want to tear Azimir apart with his bare hands.

"Tell your friend here to be silent," Azimir ordered Rafe.

"Silence," said Rafe. His voice, as listless as his eyes, was little more than a hoarse whisper.

"I hope you understand," Jared said to Azimir, "that you have traded your life for whatever political advantage you're playing for here." He snapped his gaze to Azimir's face. "I will make sure of it."

Azimir waved his hand. "You obey, or I hurt him. You will do nothing unless I order it."

"And if your leash breaks?" Jared asked, his voice low. "What then?"

Azimir opened his mouth to respond, but at that moment one of the guards stepped into the hall. Jared turned to see the man bowing low over his scimitar.

"My apologies, Lord Azimir," he said. "But Ribbadi is here."

Azimir's eyes flickered at Jared. "Don't think we're through here," he murmured. Then, loud enough for the guard to hear, he said, "Show him in! Don't stand there scraping in the doorway."

The guard vanished, and a moment later, Ribbadi strolled into the hall. His cream-colored suit was impeccably fitted as always, flowing with his lithe steps. The man always reminded Jared of a serpent.

Azimir was standing, and when Ribbadi reached the dais, they clasped hands at the wrist. Ribbadi's dark eyes fixed on Jared for a moment, then slid to Rafe.

"All well here, Excellency?" he asked.

"Of course," Azimir replied. "You have word?" He turned to Rafe. "Bring my friend a chair. And you—" he addressed Jared as Rafe moved away— "go stand over there." He pointed to the censer that stood smoking at the far edge of the dais. "And keep your mouth shut."

Jared took up his new position and closed his eyes. His hearing, like all of his senses, was sharper now. If Azimir hoped to keep his plans secret, sending him ten feet away wasn't sufficient.

"Is it here?" Azimir asked Ribbadi as soon as he thought Jared was out of earshot. "Have you seen it?"

"It is here, and I have seen it. They are bringing it now."

"Has it all been accounted for? Did you see to it personally?"

Ribbadi bowed slightly. "Personally. All accounted for. Derrek and his crew have more sense than the last lot."

Rafe returned with the chair and set it near to Azimir's. Azimir gestured for Rafe to join Jared, then motioned for Ribbadi to sit.

"And they have proved invaluable allies indeed," Azimir said, glancing up in Jared's direction. "They have given us everything we need."

"You mean to go forward with the plan, then?" Ribbadi asked, his voice so low that Jared, even with his heightened senses, could barely make out the words. "Tonight? You mean to make a trial?"

A cold smile spread slowly across Azimir's face. "Timing is everything, my friend. With the Hazad already on their way to Telon, I need to convince the Houses that they should trust me...that they should trust in the power that has come into my hands."

"You don't think they will believe your word?"

Azimir's face darkened. "No. When Dracor plots behind my back, thinking me blind as an infant, and as stupid, I think they may need more persuasive evidence. And you know as well as I that they put no faith in the old gods."

"Or demons." Ribbadi glanced at Jared. "Are you sure..." His voice trailed off, and he turned back to Azimir, leaning forward earnestly. Again, his voice dropped to an almost inaudible whisper. "Are you sure of your control?"

Azimir recoiled slightly. "Sure of my control? Over what? Him?" He paused, his eyes fixing Jared again for a moment, then shifting to Rafe. "Yes, I'm sure."

"I thought there was an...accident."

Azimir started slightly. "Accident?"

"Emelia."

"That was no accident." Azimir's voice was short and cutting. "She threw herself out the damn window, Ribbadi. She killed herself."

"You're sure?"

"I'm sure."

Ribbadi measured him in silence for a moment, then he rose. "In that case, my brother, we are with you. Until tonight." Ribbadi clasped Azimir's hand once more, and then he turned on his heel and left the hall.

Azimir slumped back in his throne, running his forefinger idly over the rich carvings on its arm. Jared knew that look.

It was doubt.

Azimir didn't look at him, and Jared could sense that, for some reason, he dared not. As Azimir brooded, the silence grew more and more oppressive, and Jared, breathing deeply, drank it in.

When the door to the throne room opened suddenly, Azimir jumped. He cursed at the guard who appeared, and the man dropped immediately to his knees, bowing his forehead to the floor.

"Pardon, Excellency!" he cried. "But the shipment has arrived, and Ribbadi said you should be told at once."

Azimir sprang to his feet and was pattering down the length of the hall almost before the man had finished speaking. As he disappeared through the doorway, he shouted over his shoulder, "Stay there!"

The massive doors slammed to, and Jared and Rafe, for the first time since they had arrived on Aquila, were alone together.

Jared's breath escaped in a slow hiss. Rafe just stood there, swaying slightly, as if he hadn't even realized that Azimir had gone. He was staring blankly at the opposite wall, his eyes fixed on the bright blue swatches of sky visible through the clerestory windows.

"Rafe," Jared murmured.

Rafe flinched as though something had stung him. He shuffled a few paces away from Jared and then stopped.

"Rafe," Jared said again, raising his voice a little. When he still got no response, he stepped up onto the dais and confronted his friend. He hesitated, suddenly feeling awkward. Hot tears were stinging his eyes, burning away the darkness that clouded him.

"Rafe, I—" He stretched out a hand and touched Rafe's shoulder. Rafe slapped his hand away with a force that staggered him. Rafe appeared emaciated and weak, but the blow left Jared's hand stinging.

"Don't touch me," Rafe said, his voice no more than a hoarse whisper. "Don't touch me."

"Why? Why not? Rafe, we're friends! We—don't you remember? Don't you remember me?"

Rafe's eyes finally shifted from the windows to study Jared's face. There was a hollowness in them that made Jared's throat constrict. His hands balled into fists.

"Curse you, Azimir," he murmured. "I will kill you for this. I will kill you."

Rafe just regarded him steadily, blankly. And then, as if he found Jared boring, his gaze shifted once more to the windows.

"I want to look at the blue," he said. "The blue...out there."

"Look at me," Jared pleaded. "Please, Rafe, I need to know that you remember!"

But Rafe didn't look at him again, and Jared sank slowly to his knees. His grief spilled over, and silent sobs racked his body. He bowed his head in his hands and dug his palms into his eyes, as if somehow he could press out the vision of this wraith who used to be his dearest friend.

"I know you're in there," he murmured. "I know it...because somehow, even in this darkness, I know you. I need you, Rafe...I need you to be strong. I need you to fight this drug—because if I lose you like I lost Sahara, then..." His voice trailed away. "Like I lost Emelia..."

Her scream and the look in her eyes just before she threw herself out the window were seared into his memory. They haunted his sleep and hovered just outside of consciousness when he woke. He raised his head and looked at Rafe.

"I didn't do it," he whispered. "Please believe me...I didn't kill her. I wouldn't have hurt her." Confusion made him stumble over his words. "At least, I don't think I meant... But she did that. She did that..." And he couldn't bring himself to finish it aloud, but the words were in his mind.

For me. She did that for me.

"He will bring us all to grief and ruin," Rafe said suddenly, sounding like a man lost in a dream. "He doesn't know the power he has awakened." And with a sudden flash of clarity, Rafe looked at Jared. "Don't do it, Jared. Don't do it."

"Don't do what?" Jared scrambled to his feet. "What, Rafe?"

But the clarity was drowned in haze once more, and Rafe turned back to the window. "I love to look at the blue," he said.

"Don't do what?" Jared whispered, desperate to clasp his friend's hand, to force him to speak.

At that moment, the doors swung open once more and Azimir returned, beaming and rubbing his hands. As he reached the dais and saw Jared standing in front of Rafe, his smile dimmed and he jerked to a stop, muscles stiff. His eyes moved rapidly between them, and when he saw Rafe's vacant expression, his body relaxed and his self-satisfied smile returned.

"Come now!" he said. "Don't just stand there! We have a big night ahead, and we must get you ready for your debut."

THIRTY-FIVE

SAHARA WAS ALMOST BACK to the High Streets of Aquila when she checked her pace to a walk. Awareness flooded her, and she realized that she was in one of the major market squares. Vendors and buyers swirled around her in a dance of barter and trade and the loud confusion of voices thrummed in her ears. An old woman with gapped teeth was shaking her bony finger in the face of a round man in a brilliantly striped tunic. He was framed by an array of dark dried meats on sticks.

"You cheated me last week!" her shrill voice punctured the chaos of noise. "You won't cheat me again!"

"My prices go up," the man said with a careless shrug. "My prices go up, your prices go up. Simple as that. Now get out of the way, woman."

"Then I go elsewhere to spend my pennies!" she spat, snatching her faded cloth sack from the table.

Sahara turned away just in time to avoid being run over by a knot of ragged children. Their leader was a tall boy with a shock of curly black hair, and for a moment, Sahara opened her mouth to speak, then shut it again. She recognized him from Jessup's tribe, or thought she did. For an instant, his dark eyes locked with hers. Then, with a lopsided grin that convinced her that she had seen him before, he was gone, leading his merry band of thieves through the riot of colored robes and fluttering silk tents. She watched him snatch a dark, ripe fruit from a nearby vendor's stand and smiled to herself.

I don't know that Jessup likes his young ones training as thieves, but that boy's a master and no mistake.

The thought of Jessup and the Hazad finally stilled her pace. She stood for a moment in the midst of the crowd, barely hearing the curses hurled at her from surprised passers-by who nearly tripped over her and spilled their parcels.

She realized in a rush that she had chosen to return to the city instead of rushing home to warn her people. She frowned. Why had she done that?

Before she could collect her thoughts, a stout man laden with an overfull basket jostled into her. Five or six fruits tumbled into the dirt, and Sahara skipped back as he juggled the rest of his wares. As soon as he regained his balance, he began shouting at her.

"What's wrong with you?" he demanded. "Get out of the way! Look what your stupidity has cost me, girl!"

"Sorry," Sahara mumbled. She stooped to catch one of the rolling fruits and dusted it off on her pants. "Sorry." She held it out to him, but he swatted it out of her hand.

"I don't want it now," he hissed. "Get out of my sight!"

Sahara sidestepped a few paces into the crowd, feeling oddly chastened. She needed to get somewhere quiet, where she could think and be out of the way. She glanced around made out a sign advertising a tea shop in the northwest corner of the square. She picked her way carefully through the throngs of people and slipped inside.

A little silver bell tinkled as she pushed the door open. She was surprised at the relative emptiness of the shop—she would have thought that the crowds of thirsty shoppers would have filled the place to capacity. But she was grateful for the sudden stillness and shadows, and she made for a tiny corner table that promised solitude.

She heaved a sigh of relief as she sat down, and realized that she was shaking. The events of the morning had unsettled her, and she frowned.

All those weeks with Jessup's people have made me soft. It's not the first time I've faced down death, after all.

And why should she have been so cowed by the fat man in the market square? It didn't make any sense. Her frown deepened.

"Would you care for some tea?"

The deep voice at her shoulder made her jump, and she glanced up in surprise.

"No. Yes. No." She took a breath, then said firmly, "No. Thank you."

The man's eyebrow arched. "You look like you could use a cup of tea," he suggested gently. "We have many herbal—"

"Maybe later."

The man inclined his head. "A cup of tea, or I must ask you to pay for the table," he said.

Sahara snorted softly. "Pay for the table? There's hardly anyone in here!"

"Nevertheless, it is our policy," the man said. "I will come back in a few minutes." He placed a small card on the table and moved away into the fragrant shadows.

Sahara watched him go, then pulled the card toward her with her forefinger. It was a menu, written in a gorgeous script. Sahara knew many of the herbal combinations from her study with Katarina, and she decided that she might need something to get her jangling nerves under control. She fumbled in her pocket and pulled out two small coins and dropped them on the card. Then she pushed it away and rubbed her hands over her face.

She had to decide what she was going to do. The information Ril had shared with her made it abundantly clear that she was out of time. She had to save Jared, and she couldn't abandon her people to annihilation at Azimir's hands. And, strangely, maintaining the status quo for now was the surest way to keep Jared safe.

If Dracor and the other Lords are planning to stage a coup at this banquet, then they will surely take Jared out. He's a liability. And if Azimir intends to make a demonstration of Jared's power, then I'll lose him to the Dragon.

"You are ready to order something?" the waiter asked.

Sahara nodded and pointed. "Make it strong," she said.

He bowed and withdrew again, and Sahara sighed. She wondered suddenly about Deor, and realized that she hadn't heard from him in days. The realization made her frown. Last she knew, he was back on Silesia, walking into a trap laid by the traitors on Askalon. She'd tried to tell him to leave it all there...all those weapons, and the *zanthos* from Perseon. But what if he hadn't listened to her? What if he'd taken it, and tried to go back to Askalon with it?

What if he'd been caught?

What if he's been killed?

She pressed her palms down onto the smooth wood of the table to keep them from shaking. She closed her eyes, wondered if she should make an attempt to reach him.

And she knew, suddenly, that he hadn't listened to her. The *zanthos* that Ril had unloaded that morning had come from Askalon. And the only way they would have been able to send it to Azimir was if Deor had fetched it back from Silesia.

Damn, she thought miserably. *Damn his stubbornness.*

If he'd brought it back to Askalon, then he was either captured or killed. *And it doesn't really matter which at this point,* she thought, swallowing hard against the knot in her throat. *It ends the same way.*

She took a deep breath and carefully twined her fingers together on the table. She had to focus on the problem in front of her. The problem of Azimir and Jared and this damn coup that threatened to spin everything into total chaos.

What can I do, ultimately? Wouldn't it be better to just go home and die defending my people?

But she couldn't. No matter how much she might want to run, she couldn't.

Leaving Aquila now meant losing Jared to the Dragon. And once he was swallowed up, then it was finished. Everything she loved would be destroyed. She had to intervene somehow.

The waiter returned with her steaming cup of tea and set it down on an elegantly woven mat that looked like a miniature rug.

"Your tea, mistress," he said with that little bow. "Will there be anything else?"

"Thanks. And no." Sahara lifted the cup to her lips and took a sip. It was hot, but not undrinkable, and it was slightly sweet from the thick honey that laced it. She nodded to him. "It's good."

He smiled and left her alone again. As soon as he was out of sight, Sahara slammed back the rest of the tea and pushed back from the table. It was time to go.

She skirted the busy market square and headed toward the fortress. As she went, she mulled over the next phase of her nonexistent plan: getting inside. Taking out a guard was possible, but risky. She couldn't chance being discovered—if a guard were found unconscious or dead, the fortress would be on lockdown and the banquet cancelled, and there went her chance to accomplish anything.

So that's out. I'll have to find another way in.

She hadn't been in the city during the day enough to have a strong sense of the guards' patrol routes. Trying to slip through their security net unseen in the middle of the day was risky at best. And if she were caught, she had no alibi.

Then that's out too.

Sahara paused and glanced around. She was well into the High Streets now, and she could clearly see the fortress from her position. She slipped into a narrow alleyway and leaned against the stone wall. She could feel the frustration beginning to build, along with a returning sense of near panic. She had to find a way into that fortress.

And then, as she studied its massive gates and domed roofs, it hit her.

It'll be just like old times. Ironic, really. Jared always wanted me to dress up for a fancy party. All he had to do was get himself into deadly danger.

She stepped back into the street and glanced once more at the fortress. Then she turned and headed back to the market district. She had seen a dress shop on her way up the hill—she just hoped she could remember where it was, and hoped that they would have something that would fit in a pinch.

The midday heat was beginning to thin the crowds, and Sahara breathed a small sigh of relief when her way was no longer choked with throngs of shoppers and merchants. They would be back out in full force before nightfall, when the shopping usually devolved into something like a street party. It was the strangest thing Sahara had ever seen—and it always surprised her that Azimir, cruel tyrant and drug trafficker though he was, allowed his people to enjoy themselves.

Because they use more drugs that way, maybe. She pushed open the door of the dress shop. *No doubt it's all about profit to him.*

She stopped suddenly, all but gaping at the finery that surrounded her. Rich silks and brocades in every hue she could imagine hung in ordered rows along the walls. Tiny gemstones caught the light from the open door and the whole place seemed to sparkle.

"Can I help you?" a young woman with long, dark hair in a thick braid asked as she came toward her.

Sahara snapped her mouth shut and gestured to the racks. "I'm looking for...I need..."

"A dress?" The woman asked, looking Sahara up and down with a quizzical, half-amused light in her dark eyes. "We often have foreign traders coming to purchase our wares. But you don't look like a merchant."

Sahara studied her for a moment. "Can you help me or not?"

"Perhaps. That all depends on what you need, I suppose."

Sahara swallowed. She knew she didn't look like much—and she probably looked like a merc, outfitted as she was in her boots and black battle dress. She'd planned to march in here and announce that Lord So-and-so had invited her to attend Lord Azimir's banquet, but she realized now that she didn't look like she'd be anyone's choice for a date. Her red hair alone marked her as a foreigner.

"I need a dress for a party. A...a fancy party." She swallowed again and stopped, hoping that might be enough information to satisfy the woman.

"Oh? And this party—where is it? Who will attend?"

"My captain's throwing a party tonight," she lied. Then she put on her best imitation of a desperate pleading look and added, "I need to make an impression, if you catch my meaning. It's really important."

The woman smiled then. "A dress to make an impression," she mused. She walked slowly around Sahara, eying her up and down. "Not much fashion sense, eh?" she said as she came around in front of Sahara once more. She gestured distastefully to Sahara's clothing. "You always wear black like this?"

Sahara stiffened. "In my line of work, it's helpful," she snapped before she could catch herself.

The woman arched an eyebrow at her, then waved a hand to the far wall. "Those will all be your size," she said. "Or near enough. You have coin to pay?"

Damn. I forgot about money. "I was hoping..."

The woman's brow arched farther. "Hoping what?"

"Maybe I could just borrow it? You know, just for tonight?" Sahara tried to smile. "Do you do that here?"

The woman pointed imperiously to the door. "We do not lend our gowns," she said.

"Well, then how much?" She slipped to the rack and pulled out a canary yellow silk decked in peacock blue gemstones. "Like this one?"

"That is all wrong for you." The woman snatched it out of her hand and stuffed it back into its place. "No yellow."

"Why...whatever. How much?"

"That one? 500 gold."

"Five hun—" Sahara gaped at her. "Five hundred? Is that the cheapest one you have?"

The woman's mouth twisted in a smile. "I thought you wanted to make an impression."

I'll make an impression on your face. Just give me a damn dress already. Out loud, she gritted, "Yes. I do. But I could never afford something like that. Ever. So I'll just have to go elsewhere."

The woman studied her immaculately manicured nails and snorted softly. "Without the coin, don't waste your time. I'm the only merchant who is willing to make...alternate arrangements."

"What's that supposed to mean?" Sahara asked, her voice edgy.

"I have a little problem with one of my suppliers. If you take care of it for me, then perhaps we can talk about the dress."

"How am I supposed to take care of it?"

The woman glanced at her, then returned to inspecting her nails. "Since this is your line of work, I'm sure you'll think of something."

"What's the problem with him?"

"He's cheating me. I pay him a certain amount for a certain length of fabric. He's been cutting me short for months."

"How much short?"

The woman's eyes flickered at her. "500 gold."

Sahara's mouth twisted in a smile. "Is that right?"

"That's right."

Sahara's eyes strayed to the rack and fastened on a barely visible sleeve of thinnest ivory chiffon and a pale pink brocade bodice. "I want to pick out the dress first," she said. "Then I'll take care of your dirty work for you."

The woman bowed and gestured to the rack. "All of these are 500 gold," she said. "But if you want to make a pleasing impression, stay away from the yellows."

Sahara reached out and touched the delicate sleeve, then grasped the hanger and pulled the dress free. Tiny knotted silk buttons ran down the front until the dropped waist bodice flared suddenly into a cascade of brocade and chiffon. Sahara had never seen anything so lovely.

The woman was nodding her approval. "It's a good hue for you," she said. "Better than black." She pointed to a small stall curtained off from the rest of the store. "You can try it on in there."

Sahara folded the gown carefully over her arm and closeted herself in the stall. I can't very well wear these, she thought as she tugged off her boots. She discarded the rest of her garments in a pile on the floor and slipped into the gown.

Her breath caught in her throat. The fabric was unbelievably soft and delicate. She'd never worn anything like it in her life, and she wished suddenly that Jared could see her in it.

He will see you in it, you idiot, she told herself, but it wasn't the same thing. He was at least half-Dragon now, and he wouldn't care about such things.

She pushed the thought out of her mind and stepped carefully out from behind the curtain to admire herself in the tall mirror that leaned against the wall outside. It fit her perfectly, and she knew she'd found what she wanted.

"You'll need some jewels to wear this properly," the woman said. "And perhaps a clip of diamonds for your hair."

Sahara regarded her. "And how much for that?"

The woman shrugged. "You do me this favor with Nazam," she said, "and I will loan them to you."

"I thought you didn't loan things." Sahara turned slightly, admiring herself in the glass.

"For you, I will make that one exception," the woman answered.

Sahara considered the offer for a moment, then turned to face the woman. "Done. Where do I find him?"

THIRTY-SIX

SAHARA CONTEMPLATED the faded yellow door of the little fabric shop with growing distaste. She'd been revolted by Brig's suggestion that she should assassinate Katarina in order to win approval with his gang. And now the dress woman wanted her to smash some guy's face because he was robbing her. She doubted very much if the dress she had chosen was worth what the woman claimed.

But it's not for the dress. It's for Jared...and for the Hazad. Because if things go down tonight like Ril said they would, then I will lose them both.

She threw back her shoulders and slapped open the door, sending the tinkling silver bell hung over its top clattering to the floor.

An angular, bespectacled man sat behind the counter, poring over some kind of electronic tablet. As she approached the counter, Sahara could see that he was reviewing orders and receipts. He was so absorbed that even Sahara's explosive entrance hadn't distracted him.

Sahara sniffed and leaned on the counter, trying to angle her head low enough to catch the man's eye. When she finally entered his range of vision, he started so violently that he nearly dropped both tablet and spectacles onto the floor. Sahara leaned back as he juggled both.

"Are you the cloth merchant?" she said.

The man finally regained control of his things, and he pushed the spectacles up his beak-like nose to study her more intently. "Who might you be? I haven't seen you here before."

"I'm new in town."

The man nodded, his mouth open in a silent "ah." Then he frowned. "I don't sell directly to the—"

"I'm not here to buy."

Another nod, and then the man checked himself. "Then why are you here, exactly?"

"I'm here to settle a debt."

The man laughed nervously and placed the tablet on the counter, resting his bony fingertips beside it. "I see. And what debt might that be?"

"The dress merchant three streets over. Iliadora, I think she said? Her debt."

The man snorted. "I owe her nothing."

"She thinks otherwise."

"I have nothing to say to you." He flicked his fingers at her, shooing her out the door. "Go back to Ilia and tell her she can buy her cloth elsewhere if she doesn't like how I do business."

Sahara folded her arms. "Final answer?" And when the man nodded, she added, "You sure about that?"

The man sized her up again and seemed to find her not worth much. "Absolutely. I have plenty of other—"

Sahara seized the man by the collar and jerked, hard. The man's face smashed into the smooth wood of the counter, leaving him with a bloody nose and broken spectacles. The tablet slipped out of his hands and shattered on the floor.

He howled and his hands flapped around his face, feeling his spectacles, his nose, trying to assess the damage.

"You sure you don't owe her something?" Sahara repeated coldly.

"Because we can do this all day. Although," she paused and glanced out the small front window of the shop, "I do have an engagement this evening, so if you take too long in coughing up the money, I'll just truss you up and take everything you have. Unless you'd rather I ended your life instead?"

The man stopped his spastic movements and stared at her through bleared eyes. "You can't...you wouldn't..."

The fear in his face made her insides hurt. But she steeled herself and said, "I can and I would. I just smashed your face into your own counter. Don't make me break your neck."

The man hesitated. "Guards!" he said suddenly, trying to edge out from behind the table. "I'll call the guards!"

Sahara moved to cut off his escape. "I really wouldn't do that if I were you. Because then you'll have a pile of bodies in the middle of your shop, and yours will be the one on top."

The man's mouth gaped open, and he squinted at her through the broken lenses of his spectacles. "I don't believe you," he said weakly.

"Really? You need another demonstration?" She lunged at him and he recoiled, huddling against the wall behind the counter.

"No!" he squeaked. "No! I'll pay! I'll pay! Just let me...here, let me..." His bony hands gestured wildly at the drawer behind the counter, and Sahara stepped aside. He jerked open the drawer and seized a wad of paper. He thrust it at Sahara.

"What the hell is this?" she said.

He withdrew his hands slightly, frowning at her. "It's...money. 750 gold. It's not enough?"

"Doesn't look like gold to me," Sahara muttered, then shrugged. If these people paid each other in bits of paper, that was their affair. Sahara held out her hand and he dropped the packet into her palm. "Nice doing business with you," she said. "Have a pleasant day."

She turned on her heel and left the shop, feeling a small thrill of triumph. She hadn't killed the man, and she'd come out 250 ahead.

That might just be enough for some accessories.

The palace was a blaze of lights. From where she stood, just inside the shadowed archway of the temple across from the palace, Sahara had a clear view of the arriving guests. The gates stood wide open, and liveried servants stood at intervals along the edges of the central courtyard. The huge fountain that Sahara remembered so well from their arrival in Aquila shimmered from a series of underwater lights.

The wealthy Lords of Aquila and their consorts arrived in those same sleek, black vehicles that had belonged to the Zharib, flags blazoned with the signs of their Houses standing out stiff as pokers, even though there was no breeze. As she watched their slow parade into the drive, Sahara wondered if the vehicles had been gifts from Azimir's father to the various Houses. With all the vehicles the same, they were at once a status symbol and an equalizer.

Everybody's equal at a round table except the guy giving out the seats.

Another car purred up the street, and Sahara studied it intently. With some of the extra money she'd squeezed out of the cloth merchant, she had paid Ilia to fill her in on the different Houses, their emblems, and what each controlled in Aquila. In the course of the conversation, Ilia had let slip the all-important fact that Lord Nazari, whose House managed construction and public works for the city, had a son.

A young, handsome, unattached, son who often frustrated his father by insisting on going alone to functions like these, event though he was the most sought-after bachelor in the city.

"The children of all the other Houses are all married already," Ilia had told her. "And Azimir has no child. That makes Tesla Nazari the most courted man in Aquila."

Sahara smiled to herself. *He might like to attend these functions alone, but he won't tonight.*

She just had to look for the black hammer on a white field.

Two more vehicles passed her position. House Sarraf's pillar of gold on a green field and Antar's crossed gold scimitars on a black field—symbols of the Houses of Finance and Security. Ilia had told her that although House Antar controlled the policing of the city, Azimir's Zharib managed security within the palace complex itself. Azimir would trust his safety to no outside House, and Sahara couldn't blame him for that.

She'd lost count now of how many vehicles she'd seen. Had Nazari arrived early? She thought she'd planted herself here well ahead of time, but perhaps not. She squatted down in the shadows, her silk dress pooling around her, and started to pull of her jeweled slippers. She'd stashed her black battle gear behind a pillar just inside the archway, and if she had to make a stealth entrance, gaudy silks and gems wouldn't do.

She got one slipper off when she heard the hum of an engine. She shoved the slipper back on her foot and rose. Finally, the House Nazari vehicle purred up the avenue to the palace.

Sahara smiled to herself as she gauged the closing distance between herself and the vehicle. It was already slowing, preparing to make the turn into the palace courtyard. And just before it did so, Sahara stepped directly in front of it.

She caught the impact on her right side and crumpled into the street, a mess of silk and brocade and jewels.

The driver slammed on the brakes and the vehicle skidded to a stop. Sahara heard curses and shouts, and then a young man's voice came close to her ear.

"Are you all right? God, are you hurt?" The voice was deep and pleasant, but there was a slowness to it that suggested either a lack of wits or overbreeding.

Sahara had added plenty of dramatic flair to the impact, but in reality her hip and side were bruised where the car had bumped her. This was her chance.

She groaned and turned her head so that she could look up into the man's face. He was immaculately dressed in a cream silk suit with a dark gray necktie. Polarized glasses framed his face and set off his dark curls. His beard was trimmed into a goatee—not unlike Azimir's, Sahara thought with distaste. But he was handsome enough, and seemed concerned enough. He'd do for tonight.

"I-I think I might be," she said softly, grasping for her right thigh. "I didn't see you coming at all. I-I'm so sorry!"

"Not your fault. Ven's a reckless brute." He held out a hand and helped her to sit up. As she pushed her curls out of her face, she noticed with satisfaction that Tesla was making no secret out of admiring her. "Were you going to the palace?" he asked.

"I was, but I timed my visit ill, it seems," she said. "I didn't know there was a party tonight."

"You're here to see Lord Azimir?"

Sahara made her best effort at a flirtatious flutter of lashes and smiled at him, cocking her head to one side in that idiotic way that seemed to make men lose their wits. "Come, my lord," she said, rebuking. "I don't even know your name, and you want me to tell you all my business?"

He laughed, and the sound rolled like dark honey off the edge of a silver spoon. "I like your spirit," he said. "But since we've hit you with the damn car, the least I can do is offer to take you to the party. If you've never been to one at House Azimir, you've never been to one at all, I always say. He throws such monstrous good soirees."

Sahara arched an eyebrow. "Is that so?"

"Yes, it's so. Come. You won't regret it. I promise." He got to his feet and dusted off his trousers. Then he reached down a hand and helped her to her feet. "And since you're keen on names, it's Tesla Nazari." He smiled at her, but Sahara wondered if his eyes were smiling behind the glasses that reflected her mussed hair and shy smile. "And you are?"

"Calypso," she said without thinking. "Calypso Acwellan."

"Calypso," he repeated slowly, as if savoring it. He took her hand and led her toward the car. "A great pleasure, I'm sure. And now—"

"Is everything all right, my boy?"

Sahara glanced up to see a severe, silver-haired man in a black suit standing by the open door of the vehicle. Tesla waved a hand at him.

"Yes, Father, everything's all right. And look—I found a date for the party! Now you don't have to be mortified."

Nazari muttered something inaudible, but given the vinegar in his expression, Sahara was sure it wasn't very nice. She hesitated, wanting to snap something at him that would rattle his teeth, but decided that a smile and a deferent little bow of the head was a better fit for her current role.

"I've heard of you," she said. "It's an honor to meet you."

"Well, if Tesla insists on bringing you, get in," Nazari snapped. "We're late." Nazari disappeared into the vehicle and Sahara glanced at Tesla.

"He's in a foul humor, I guess," Tesla said with a shrug. "Damned politics always gets him so worked up these days. That's why I don't bother much with this sort of thing. Let these biddies peck each other to death. In the meantime, life in Aquila rolls on, and I intend to roll right along with it."

Is that so? How very philosophical.

Tesla held the door open for her and she slid into the dark leather seat across from Nazari. He looked her up and down twice, sniffed as though she stank of the street, and then turned away to look out the window.

"Didn't know exotic was to your taste," he commented to Tesla as his son got into the vehicle and closed the door. "Don't know if I want you seen with a redheaded doll like this. She looks foreign. You need to think more carefully about your prospects."

"Father, we almost killed her with the car," Tesla said. His voice was worn like a rug that had seen too much traffic, and Sahara wondered how often he'd had this same conversation. "I'm just trying to make it up to her."

"I don't know if it will play well," he said. "I don't want you to spoil things with Kalah with one of your stupid stunts."

Tesla snorted. "Kalah's your idea of a good match, not mine," he muttered. "She'd be a lovely choice if I wanted to marry a mouldy old rock with moss on it."

The sudden flash of humor caught Sahara by surprise and she stifled a laugh. Some of it escaped in an indelicate snort before she could stop it, and Nazari glared at her. Sahara met his piggish gaze steadily, then reflected that Calypso really wasn't the type to stare men down. She dropped her eyes and smoothed her face into a lady-like frown. For a few breathless seconds, she sat under Nazari's gaze. Then he released her and shifted his attention out the window once more.

"Who's Kalah?" Sahara whispered to Tesla, leaning close to him and hoping he could smell the atrociously expensive perfume she'd spritzed on before leaving Ilia's shop.

"Some fossil Father's dug up over in Ket. He thinks that since we're in the construction business, perhaps his son should marry building materials."

Sahara choked on another giggle and gave him a nudge. "Stop! That's not nice...poor girl, I'm sure she's very fine."

"Fine as a chisel," he said. "And just as sharp."

"Will you stop?" Sahara hissed, pinching herself to keep from laughing. "You'll make your Father angry with me, and I want so much to make a good impression!"

"Oh, you are. You are." Tesla favored her with a slow, warm smile. "I'm sure you'll be the talk of the party."

The sudden reminder of her true errand made Sahara suddenly sober.

That's truer than you could possibly imagine.

THIRTY-SEVEN

JARED SAT at the head of the long banquet table and thrummed his fingers on the polished wood. Candlelight and the delicate creaminess of china dishes warmed the rich wood, and the flickering light glowed in the cut crystal goblets half-filled with claret wine. All down the long length of the table, small bowls filled with *borracha* flowers filled the air with a hint of spicy sweetness.

Azimir had certainly spared no expense on the sumptuousness of the evening. A small orchestra of exotic wind and string instruments wove their gentle melodies in the far corner of the hall, and there was a large space at that end left clear for dancing. Jared doubted that it would ever be used, but it kept up appearances.

Servants in wide-legged white pants and broad black sashes welcomed Azimir's guests and showed them to the table. Elegant place cards written in gold flowing script sat above each plate, and there was a good deal of excited chatter as gorgeously dressed lords and ladies filtered into the hall.

Jared's mood darkened. They wouldn't be smiling and laughing if they knew why they were really here. He hoped they'd all kissed their children good-bye before they came.

"Isn't this splendid?" said an older woman dressed in peacock blue silk.

She poured herself into the seat beside him, and Jared studied her for a moment. The neckline of her gown was cut far too low for her age, and if she was trying to mask her sagging skin with ropes of sparkling jewels, it wasn't working.

After a moment, she registered that he was watching her, and a sudden flush warmed her hollow cheeks. She held out a bony hand to him. "Lady Bata," she fluttered. "And you are...?"

Jared swung his gaze back to the flow of guests coming through the west doors of the hall, debating whether he should trouble with an answer.

"Jared," he answered finally.

The woman seemed determined not to be put off by his unfriendly manner. She touched his arm as though she had something very important and very secret to tell him. He glanced back at her.

"What?"

"I hear Azimir's new pet will be here," she whispered. "Never seen him myself, but I hear that he is quite something." She suddenly drew in her breath through her teeth, a soft hiss escaping through her rouged lips. "Is that him?"

Jared glanced over his shoulder, following Lady Bata's wide-eyed gaze, and felt a sudden stab of sadness. Rafe, looking like a wraith in his black silk suit, hovered mutely just behind Azimir's chair.

Jared shook his head once, feeling the sudden swell of anger drown the sadness in his mind. But Lady Bata seemed not to care. She'd already lost interest in Rafe and was scanning the rest of the assembly.

"Azimir always did meddle with powers that were better left alone," she commented conspiratorially to Jared. "Even experiments with the occult, it's said. Of course, Lord Bata and I do not approve. It's all highly irregular. We wish he would come to temple and set the example for his people, but..." She left the statement hanging and shook her head sadly. "Well, some are enlightened and some aren't, I guess."

Jared cocked an eyebrow at her. *Stupid woman. She has no idea who I am...or what I am.*

He was saved from her tedious conversation by the arrival of Lord and Lady Ridwan. With a little squeal, Lady Bata heaved herself out of her chair and hurried to meet them. Lady Ridwan was a severe looking woman, and her black silk with its wide green sash did little to soften the edges. She looked like something poisonous. And Lord Ridwan was little better. He must have cut a fine figure in his younger days, but his muscular stature was eroding now in folds of flesh. His eyes, Jared noticed, were sharp—and not so much with intelligence as with cunning.

Jared drummed his fingers on the table more insistently. The evening was already a bore, and they hadn't even served the soup yet.

The servants began pulling out chairs and escorting Azimir's guests to the table. Lady Bata caused a minor fuss by insisting that Lady Ridwan be seated on the other side of her husband, requiring place cards to be exchanged. Finally, she was content and settled in her chair once more, and Jared clenched his jaw, waiting for the onslaught of tedium. But she was more interested in leaning over her plate to chatter with Lady Ridwan.

Lord Bata, Jared noticed, seemed profoundly uncomfortable with the arrangement. Something in the stiff way he held himself together now that Lady Ridwan was beside him made Jared suddenly suspect that they spent far too much time in each other's company when no one else was watching. Lord Bata sat fidgeting with his pocket watch, then suddenly interrupted Lord Sayed and Lord Sarraf, who were disputing some obscure point in Aquila's legal code.

Jared tuned them out and glanced around the table. Two places were conspicuously empty, and Jared wondered why.

"Nazari can never be on time for anything," Lady Bata commented to her husband, who was paying her no attention. "Why, do you remember last month when we invited them for breakfast after service? They were an hour late, and no explanation. Everything was cold. Such bad form."

Lady Bata seemed to realize suddenly that her husband wasn't listening to her, and Jared braced himself.

"Such bad form," Lady Bata said, turning to him and never losing a beat. "I told Lord Bata it would be the last card they would ever receive from me. And now he's late again. It's probably on account of that worthless son of his. Just last evening as we took tea, I told Lord Bata that he would come to no good end. If his poor mother were still alive, well, perhaps she might have made him into something fine. But Lord Nazari never looks at his son if he can help it. I'm afraid he's becoming quite wild."

Jared's hand spasmed into a fist. *The woman doesn't have a clue what a bore she is. I'll never make it through all five courses sitting here. I'll put her out of my misery before dessert.*

At that moment, a hushed buzz of excitement drew several servants to the entrance of the hall like a swarm of flies. Jared glanced up with interest, relieved that something had distracted Lady Bata's attention for the moment, even if he was condemned to listen to her commentary afterward. For now, she was craning her vulture's neck to see who was at the door.

"It's him!" she fluttered. "I told you he would be late. But who is—"

Azimir was at the door now, stooping low over someone's hand. A young woman, strikingly lovely, was on Tesla Nazari's arm. A clip of diamonds set in her dark, ruddy curls sparkled like the smile she was wearing. Her face was fresh, and the palest pink silk of her gown was elegantly understated compared to the gaudy peacocks already assembled in the hall.

Azimir waved one of the servants toward the kitchen—to set another place for the unexpected guest, no doubt.

Lord Nazari gestured imperiously for his son and the lady to be seated. Jared saw Nazari's lip curl as he indicated to Azimir that he would wait for another place to be set. Azimir inclined his head and returned to his seat beside Jared as a servant showed Tesla and the lady to their places.

"Who is she?" Jared asked in a low voice.

"No idea. Never seen her before," Azimir replied.

Jared watched her intently, unable to take his eyes off her as she leaned over to murmur something in Tesla Nazari's ear. And when she pulled back with a slow-blossoming smile, Jared could almost feel the heat of the sudden flame that lit deep in Tesla's eyes. There was something at once completely foreign and totally familiar about her. But his memory failed him.

Look at me, he thought. If he could just catch her eyes, he might remember.

But she was at obvious pains not to look in his direction. He frowned and vowed to make her look before the end of the evening.

Moments later, Lord Nazari was seated and the servants brought the first course. The clatter of spoons in soup bowls mingled with the swirl of insipid small talk. Not even the thin veneer of carefully culti-vated smiles could hide the growing nervous energy in the room. Lord Sayad glanced across the table at Lord Bata, and something in his eyes said something completely different than the words coming out of his mouth. Lord Dracor, who sat opposite Azimir on the other end of the table, continued to fix Jared and Azimir with a hard stare, as though he was measuring something.

When the soup course had been cleared and the servants were setting delicate pink and orange ices in cut glass bowls in front of the guests, Azimir rose and tapped his goblet lightly with his fork.

"Lords and ladies," he said, clearing his throat. "I have not just asked you here tonight to enjoy your brilliant company. We have business to discuss, and I am confident that, together, we will decide what is best for the future of Aquila...and Halcyon."

There was a smattering of polite applause, mostly from the ladies, Jared noticed. His mouth quirked into a smile. If they'd had any clue about the political game Azimir was playing, they wouldn't be clapping.

"The question before us is the question that has plagued our city for generations. For months now, you have been asking me for a solution to the problem of the Hazad. I have spent many weeks pondering my answer, and I am now ready to present to you my solution."

Jared found himself staring once more at the fascinating woman sitting beside Tesla. As Azimir spoke, she stiffened almost imperceptibly, and he wondered why she should take so much interest. A swift glance around the table revealed that all of the other ladies were watching Azimir with polite but vacant expressions on their faces. All, that is, except Lady Bata, who looked as though she were preparing to dive into deep water.

"What solution is that?" asked Lord Sarraf. "We have discussed before the financial implications of drastic solutions. I hope—"

"You can rest easy on that point," Azimir said. "The last of the drone harvesters has been delivered, and ahead of schedule, I might add. We owe our gratitude to the persistence of Lord Dracor, who has ensured that the shipments from Ket have been timely."

"But what can that mean?" demanded Lady Bata. "Drones?"

"Drones," echoed Azimir, nodding slowly. "Drones that can harvest the *borracha* without threatening revolution. In a word, ladies and gentlemen, we have no more need of the Hazad. And so, I propose to you that we put into action the plan that we have so long delayed: their annihilation."

"The sooner the better," said Lady Bata, surprising Jared with the sudden detached cruelty in her voice. "They are heretics and unbelievers...they are a pollution and an abomination."

Lord Antar waved a hand to silence her. "All that aside, really," he said. "They're a liability. We've lost more drones in the last six months to the Hazad than in the last five years combined. They are clearly mobilizing something...and they've found an ally who knows how to disable our tech."

Jared's eyes fixed once more on the lady in pink. She was carefully eating her ice, eyes downcast. And yet, there was something about her posture that told Jared that she was listening intently. He wondered again why she should care so much about Azimir's political machinations. He found it utterly boring. He was here for one purpose...and he couldn't give a damn who approved.

"Listen to Antar," agreed Lord Sayad. "There is nothing in our laws that protects rebels. If they are committing acts of aggression against Aquila, then they have placed themselves outside the right of law...if they ever had claim to it in the first place."

A burst of side chatter greeted this statement, and Azimir seemed content, for the moment, to let the excitement ride.

"So what is it you propose to do about the problem, Lord Azimir?" Dracor asked, his deep voice cutting suddenly through the discussion. In the silence that followed, he continued, "What's your solution?"

"In a week's time, all of the Hazad tribes will be gathered in the city of Telon for the annual pilgrimage," Azimir said. "And I propose that we send them all to meet their God."

There was no flurry of conversation this time. Jared's mouth twisted into the barest hint of a smile.

"How?" pressed Dracor after a moment. "Do we have enough drone power for a strike like that?"

Jared glanced up at Azimir. The moment had come at last.

"Oh, we don't have need of drones," Azimir answered quietly. "We have something much more...potent. Much more efficient. We will strike them with the thing they fear the most...and through their sacrifice, we will solidify our power for generations."

"Sacrifice?" said Lord Bata, alerting on the word. "Killing a thousand men, women, and children is—"

"A fitting sacrifice," Azimir murmured, turning to face Bata down. "When much is asked, much is required in exchange."

"A sacrifice to what?" Lord Ridwan demanded. "What in hell are you getting at, Azimir? Just come out and say it plain."

Azimir pressed his palms into the table. For a moment, he stood with head bowed and eyes closed. Then he lifted his gaze to meet the wide-eyed stares of the assembly.

"The Dragon has awoken," Azimir said, his voice low and terrible. "I have called him, and he has come. And he is here among us tonight."

There was a sudden swell of nervous voices as the ladies gripped each other's hands and shook their heads. Jared could feel disapproval seeping from Lady Bata as she leaned across her husband to tell Lady Ridwan what she thought of such apostasy.

"Do you still believe in those fairy tales?" Dracor asked, his voice cold as the ice that sat untouched on his plate. "You think you can call up some demon and that it will somehow protect you from what you know is coming?"

Jared's hands clenched into fists. Azimir had told him to watch Dracor, and Jared suddenly understood why. Dracor had his own cards to play tonight. He glanced at Azimir for a cue, but the drug lord was chuckling and shaking his head. Slowly, he rotated the intricately worked ring on his finger.

"You have no idea," he said, "what you are talking about. You have no conception of the immensity of what's at stake here. And you blaspheme in your unbelief. The Dragon is here, I tell you. He needs just this."

And he slipped off the ring and set it down on the table.

At the heart of the twining silver strands sat a tiny sphere of gold. As it caught the light of the candles, it seemed almost to breathe and take on life. Everyone at the table was suddenly quiet, every eye riveted on that tiny object.

Almost every eye.

Jared glanced up and found the strange woman staring straight at him, her deep green eyes as intense and deep as other green eyes he knew and loved so well....

The spark of recognition flared in his mind, but she looked away before he could fix the memory.

"What is that?" Lady Bata breathed beside him.

"This?" Azimir said. "This is *zanthos*. And with it, the Dragon will destroy the Hazad. And once we are rid of them, then we will destroy anyone—and any world—that stands against us."

"You are mad," Dracor spat suddenly. "Utterly mad."

Azimir threw back his head and laughed. Jared saw the strange woman start in her seat at the maniacal sound, and then watched as her entire body coiled itself once more.

He could feel the fear growing in the room, and he smiled to himself. As much as they wanted not to believe Azimir, they were terrified by the possibility that he could be telling the truth.

"You doubt me?" Azimir said, recovering himself. "You doubt the power I hold? Please, allow me to demonstrate."

He turned to Jared and gestured to the ring. Jared stretched out his hand and took the band. He heard Lady Bata's squeak of surprise beside him as he slipped it onto his index finger.

His world swirled into darkness.

These people doubted him. They laughed at him. They would pay for their unbelief.

He rose from his seat and waited for Azimir's word.

In the breathless silence, Jared could sense the swelling of fear. Lady Ridwan looked faint, and she was clutching at her husband's silk waistcoat as if he could save her from what was coming. Lord Leil had knocked over his ice, and it was melting all over the table, but not one of the servants dared to move from their places along the wall to mop it up before it dripped onto his silk suit.

And Tesla Nazari was whispering to the lady in pink, saying something urgent. With his suddenly sharpened senses, Jared could just make out the words.

"Let me get you out of here," he was saying. "I didn't know...I'm sorry...let's go. Let's go now, before this gets any worse."

The woman said nothing in reply. Jared, eyes fixed on her straight and silent form, noticed that she alone of all the party seemed utterly calm.

"I said you were mad," Dracor said again, his voice laced with disdain. "You come here with fairy tales and magic tricks and pretend you have a plan. I say it is no plan, and I say again that you are mad. And so, we depose you from your leadership."

Azimir began to laugh again, the sound chasing the dancing shadows in the honeycombed dome of the ceiling. Dracor stood and slammed his fist on the table, setting the china rattling.

"It's unanimous, Azimir," he said. "You're finished. We can either do this without a fuss, or we can do it the old-fashioned way." He drew his dagger and drove it point first into the wood of the table. "On a knife's edge."

"You are a bigger fool than I had imagined, Dracor," Azimir said. "You think you can just send me to my room like a naughty child? You think you can sneak in here and surprise me with a bloodless coup, as if I had no idea it was coming? Did you think I didn't know about your plans? Did you really think I wouldn't be prepared for this?"

Dracor stiffened. "What?"

"You think me a child, soft-witted and naive," Azimir went on. "You think I am weak because I do not act when and how you wish. You think you know so much more than I about the ways of the world...about running the world. And yet, here you are. You have walked right into my beautiful trap and handed me exactly what I wanted."

Dracor's face drained of color, and his eyes, too bright now in his livid face, were riveted on Azimir. "What?"

Azimir opened his arms as if to envelop them all in an embrace. "My lovely and stupid people," he said, "I wanted you to be the first to witness the power that I have harnessed. Unfortunately for you, you won't be able to see how everything turns out. I gave you the chance, and...well, you've declined."

"What are you going to do?" gasped Lady Sarraf. "Azimir...please don't—"

Azimir glanced at Jared and raised a finger to point down the length of the table at Dracor. "Him first."

Jared closed his eyes, feeling the darkness open like a chasm within him. Feeling the heat of the *zanthos* seep into his finger and creep up his hand and into his arm, firing his veins.

He concentrated on it, drew the heat into himself to nourish the swelling darkness.

And then, suddenly, there was a shattering scream and the crash of toppling chairs as people sprang to their feet.

Jared's eyes snapped open.

Dracor lay on the table in a welling pool of blood, the china plate shattered beneath him, eyes wide and blank. blood from his slit throat.

Behind him, the dripping knife still in her hand, stood the lady in pink.

Their eyes locked, and in that instant Jared knew her.

Sahara.

"Assassin!" shrieked Lady Bata, her shrill voice slicing through Jared's consciousness. "Assassin! Azimir! Do something!"

"*You!*" roared Azimir, and Jared knew that he had recognized her too. "Guards!"

"Sahara!" cried Jared at the same instant, his voice breaking, everything else forgotten. "Sahara!"

Sahara flipped the knife in her hand, her stance fluid and ready. But Jared knew that she would be no match for the swarm of guards who poured suddenly into the hall. He watched her take three of them down before the rest managed to pinion her arms behind her back and drive her to her knees. The knife clattered to the floor and one of the guards kicked it and sent it spinning across the hall.

"What?" Tesla was saying, his voice frantic, his hands balled into fists at his sides. "Calypso? I thought... Who *are* you?"

Sahara ignored him. "Azimir! she shouted. "Consider this a warning. You'll never win this fight....not while I'm still alive."

"I should have put you down the moment I laid eyes on you," Azimir growled. "It's not a mistake I will make again."

Sahara raised her chin, defiant just as Jared always remembered her.

"Go ahead," she said. And then her eyes locked with Jared's. "If you dare."

Azimir flicked a finger at her and one of the guards lifted his scimitar, ready to deal the death stroke.

Jared raised his hand and leveled the *zanthos* ring at Azimir, his eyes never leaving Sahara's face. Through the darkness that was clouding all his vision again like a gathering storm, he could see her eyes riveted on him, wide with horror.

"No!" she screamed. "Jared, don't! Don't!"

"Let her go, Azimir," Jared said, his voice rolling through the room, deep and terrible.

The guard hesitated and for a moment, everyone stood still.

"Are you mad?" Azimir said, turning on him. "Are you—?"

"Let her go, or I will end you," Jared growled. "Let her go!"

The pitch of his voice dropped suddenly and the command thundered through the hall. Every glass on the table exploded. Through the shower of crystal shards, Jared saw the lords and ladies stampede for the door. The guards holding Sahara dropped their scimitars to cover their ears.

Sahara sprang to her feet and moved to head for the door. One of the guards kept his wits enough to clutch at her, and she slammed her jeweled slipper into his nose.

The man howled and dropped away from her, but now the other guards had recovered themselves. Sahara cursed as two of them gripped the hem of her skirt and dragged her down to the floor again. She flailed and cursed again as her legs became hopelessly entangled in the yards of fabric. She managed to catch another one of the guards on the outside of the knee and he buckled. His scimitar clattered to the floor and she lurched for it, but the guards hauled on her dress before she could reach it. She heard a seam rip, and she tried flailing again. The guards were savvy now, though, and were swiftly twisting the fabric of her skirt around her legs.

Even as her lower half was immobilized, the guard with the

blown knee regained his weapon and limped toward her head, preparing to send her into oblivion with the butt end of his scimitar.

Azimir's voice suddenly rang out over the chaos of screams, and Sahara heard the edge of panic in it.

"No!" he shouted. "Let her go!"

The binding around her legs was suddenly loosed, and Sahara scrambled away from the knot of guards, catching a glimpse of their stunned faces as she regained her feet and pelted for the door.

Jared watched as she slipped outside, and then he lowered his hand and pulled off the ring, tossing it onto the table. He shook his hand absently. The darkness within him receded, and he slowly registered the bloody table, the shards of glass, and the desperate hate in Azimir's eyes.

"You will pay for this," Azimir growled. "I will find a way to make you pay for this."

"You've already made me a monster," Jared said slowly. "What more could you possibly do?"

THIRTY-EIGHT

DEOR HUDDLED in the folds of a rough blanket, staring into the glowing ashes of the meager fire. He should have been grateful for the privilege, since Aria had told him that no fires were permitted in the Underground. Instead, he shrank further into the blanket and scowled. The scowl turned into a wince and a curse as his movement jarred his sore shoulder.

"Well, that went well," remarked Brytnoth placidly.

He squatted beside Deor and nudged the fire with a length of sapling wood. Sparks leapt up, and by their furtive light Deor caught a glimpse of the sea of small faces peering at him out of the shadows.

"Shut up," he growled. Then he shrugged off the blanket, cursing again at the shooting pain down his arm. "Look at this place, Brytnoth," he said. "We left and the whole place has gone to hell. Those kids look like no one's fed them for a week."

"I know."

Deor's face hardened. "Derrek's going to pay for this."

"I know. But not yet."

Deor snorted. "Not yet. Is that your response to everything? These are your damn people, Brytnoth, not mine. If anyone should be hopping mad right now, it's you. Everything we fought for...everything we went through, and it's all been undone."

"No, it hasn't. It's just been moved underground."

"Very funny."

"I wasn't joking."

Deor measured him in silence for a moment, then shifted his gaze back to the fire. "Well, I do have to admit one thing," he said. "You were right about the circumstances. We never even had a chance."

Brytnoth wedged the fresh wood into the embers and wiped his hands on his pants. "It was a brave thought," he said.

"You've got to be joking now," Deor said, staring at his friend. "Either that, or you're patronizing me. I'd rather think you were joking."

"I'm doing neither! Look, it was a brave idea. Come in here, guns blazing, take down the guy who set you up before he even knows what's hit him. It was a brave idea...stupid, but brave."

Deor opened his mouth to snap something back, then caught the glint of a smile in Brytnoth's eyes. "Well, in retrospect, stupid's a better word for what that was," he said. "I don't know what came over me."

"I do," Brytnoth said. "It was that *zanthos*. The minute you got near it on Perseon you started acting buggy. And when we found that stash on Silesia, you went positively nuts. Why do you suppose that was, Deor?"

Deor glanced at him. "It's because I killed one of the Drakkin," he said softly. "Just like Sahara did. And just like Jared...but because he killed the Dragon, the Dragon is consuming him. Sahara and I are just part of the Collective. But Jared...Jared's the Slayer, Brytnoth." He shook his head. "If he gets hold of that *zanthos*, he will destroy...everything."

Brytnoth took a breath to speak, but a hand dropped onto his shoulder. He glanced up in surprise and saw Aria.

"Lord Aelred wants to see you both," she said. "Follow me."

Brytnoth rose and held out a hand to help Deor to his feet. Deor groaned softly and stretched—his muscles had taken a beating, and sitting hadn't done him any favors.

"You all right, Commander?" Aria asked.

"I'll live. Just lead on."

She turned on her heel and led them through the gloom. Deor tripped over several odds and ends of broken pulleys.

"Does anyone else find it highly ironic that the Underground is actually housed in an abandoned warehouse?" he said, aiming a vicious kick at the latest hazard in his path. "Who thought this was a good idea?"

Aria glanced at him over her shoulder and smiled. "It keeps us in the city," she said. "Close enough to the action without being too close."

"And how is it that Derrek's men haven't found you out?"

"They don't come into this district," she said. "It's slated for demolition, and with the supply problems and everything else, he just hasn't gotten around to tearing us down yet."

Deor snorted. "Plotting world-domination has a nasty way of screwing up your priorities," he said. "No time for practicalities like providing food for your people, for instance, when you're hellbent on destroying someone else's planet." Out of the corner of his eye, Deor caught a glimpse of Brytnoth's smile, and he grinned too. "You know, maybe you and I should just retire," he said. "We could find some little trading moon somewhere and set up a tourist stand. Let's leave all this business of dragons and politics to these idiots who like to play with fire."

Aria glanced back at him again. "Commander," she said, "you and I both know that you could never actually walk away from a fight."

"No...but a guy can dream, can't he?"

Their walk through the old warehouse took them past the medical wing, which was curtained off from the main floor by sterile drapes.

"Kalchas is running things over there," Aria said, pointing a finger at the drapes.

Deor couldn't suppress a shudder. In the gloomy light, the drapes looked ghostly, as if slipping through them would bring you suddenly into the afterlife.

"That's nice," he said.

"It is...when you hear what's happened," Aria replied.

Deor and Brytnoth exchanged glances.

At the far side of the warehouse floor, they came to a series of interconnected rooms—what used to be the foreman's office and the workers' break room and locker area. Aria opened the door to the office and showed them inside.

"Here they are, Lord Aelred," she said. She pointed Deor and Brynoth into the two rat-gnawed chairs in front of the heavy wood desk and then left with a smile.

Lord Aelred slouched on the other side of the desk, his back to them. After several long minutes, Deor cleared his throat.

"You wanted to see us, sir?" he said. He shifted his weight in the chair, trying to escape the uncomfortable sensation that there was nothing supporting his seat.

Aelred didn't turn. "Yes. I did."

"Why?"

"Do you know why Derrek has done this?" Aelred asked after another long silence. "Do you? And do you know how he's done it?"

"With all due respect, does any of that matter, my lord?" Brytnoth asked.

At that, Aelred rotated his chair on its squeaky hinges. "Yes, it matters. What follows next directly flows from the origins of all of this."

"Maybe he's just an opportunist," Deor suggested. "He served the Triumvirate until he saw a way to get on top of them. Then he put you under when the time was right. In a manner of speaking."

"Oh, no question. He has been biding his time. They all have."

"They? Who's they?"

"The rest of his inner circle." Aelred studied them for a moment over the pyramid of his fingers. "You know, when the Order of the

Dragon was banished three generations ago from Halcyon, they consolidated their power on the moon of K'ilenfir. Then, when they were secure and had discovered how to take the form of the Dragon to subjugate worlds, they went on their search for *zanthos*. They knew it could give them the power not just to subjugate, but to annihilate. They came to Askalon looking for it. We hid it from them on Perseon and shipped some to our sisterworld of Silesia.

"Their anger was swift and terrible—and that story you know already. How our people were banished, how the Triumvirate was set up to rule and to harvest the energy they needed to continue their search and tighten their control over this system. Then the Drakkin pursued the *zanthos* to Silesia, establishing the labor camps in the wasteland and importing slave labor to dig for it even as they pursued their program of gradual subjugation through fear and blood sacrifices."

"That's all very interesting history, my lord," Deor said slowly. "But how exactly does it relate to our present circumstances?"

Aelred favored him with a long-suffering look. "You are a man of many gifts and talents, Deor Acwellan," he said. "Sadly, patience is not among them."

Deor grinned and glanced sidelong at Brytnoth. "Well, it runs in our family."

"Here's how it relates. The cult of the Order of the Dragon has been growing. Those who followed the Drakkin undermined and helped to overthrow worlds. They allied themselves with the dark power. And the point, Deor, is that Derrek is one of them."

Brytnoth sat forward suddenly, and the front leg of his chair bent crazily to one side. "He's a member of the Order of the Dragon?"

"Yes. And they've never given up the search for the *zanthos*...not even after the Dragon was destroyed on Silesia."

"By Jared."

Aelred's eyes glinted at him. "Yes."

"So now they have the *zanthos*...and Azimir has Jared. How does this work?"

"Wait, wait," Deor said, waving his hand. "Wait. Before we get to all that...how do you know that Derrek's a member of this cult?"

Aelred heaved a sigh. "I should have seen it right away. But in my eagerness to take back Askalon from the Triumvirate, I wasn't careful enough. The Drakkin were careful, Deor."

"I'm well aware of their throughness," he said dryly.

"Then you won't be surprised to learn that they made sure to populate the Triumvirate's ranks with some of their own followers. If the Triumvirate ever stepped out of line, they would be there to reset the system, so to speak. Derrek was one of those followers. And when the Dragon had been slain and the Triumvirate looked like losing, he decided it was time to move on."

"But what tipped you off?" Deor pressed. "How did you find out?"

Aelred shook his head and swiveled around in his chair so that he could face out the grimy window that peered over the warehouse floor. Deor followed his gaze. A few grubby looking children were kicking a small ball, trying to get it through a pair of rusted barrels. Every once in a while, they could hear muffled shouts of triumph through the heavy glass.

"Oh," Aelred said at last. "Don't give me credit for the discovery. It didn't take any sleuthing or spying to find it out. He told me."

"Why would he tell you that?" Brytnoth asked. "A bit too eager to show his hand, I'd say."

"Well, when you're beating your enemy to a pulp, I guess there's a moment when you just get some insatiable desire to explain yourself...to let your enemy know just how stupid he is, and how smart you are. So, as I lay bleeding on the floor, Derrek paused. He revealed himself. And in that moment of hesitation, my men were able to get me away...at great cost of life, I might add."

He fell silent for a long time, watching the children at their game. A dispute seemed to have broken out, for two of the boys were circling each other, small hands fisted at their sides. Aelred shook his head and sighed, and Deor grinned at him. Brytnoth, who had paid no attention to the little vignette out the window, slumped back in his chair, scowling.

"We invited him in through the damn front door," he muttered. "And now he has the *zanthos*...he has everything."

"Yes. And now they will take the *zanthos* to Halcyon," Aelred said. "Back to the place where they began, where the dark power of the Dragon is the strongest. They will allow Azimir to use Jared to destroy the Hazad—whom they hate. They will sacrifice Jared and release their god, and they will destroy..." His voice trailed off.

"What?" Deor asked, his voice barely audible. "Destroy what, Aelred?"

Aelred did not answer, but he pressed his fingertips together until the nailbeds showed pale. "We can't let them get that far," he said instead. "We have to do something. Azimir doesn't understand what's really happening here. He thinks he'll be able to take the *zanthos* from Derrek and then turn around and stab him in the back, using Jared to annihilate Askalon and prop himself up. His ambitions are petty, and his vision myopic. He thinks only of his own insecurities, and of the promise of power to make himself secure. He has no idea of the true stakes."

"So what do we do?" Brytnoth asked. Deor shifted his gaze to his friend and saw the horror in his eyes."What can any of us do to stop this?"

"Well, we can't stay holed up here like a bunch of rats, that's for sure," Deor said. He turned back to Aelred, his mind was working feverishly. "Listen. I've got a mad idea..." He glanced at Brytnoth, then continued, "And I know I haven't had a great track record on those lately. But when Derrek and his Order leave for Halcyon, then we have to take back Askalon. And Brytnoth and I will need a select strike force and whatever *zanthos* we can scrounge up. We're heading for Halcyon."

"How is Derrek controlling the army?" Brytnoth asked suddenly. "How did he convince them to turn on their own people?"

"Oh, did I forget that little detail? He's been importing Demon's Breath from Halcyon, and he's got the army doped up on it."

Deor's eyes widened and he thought back to the curtained-off medical wing. "Is that what Kalchas is really doing over there?" he said. "Is he making that surrogate?"

"As fast as he can."

"Great." Deor rubbed his hands thoughtfully along the rough wood arms of his chair. "Now...if only we had some *zanthos* of our own. We could have a real party then."

Brytnoth jerked up straight in his chair and he gripped Deor's wrist. "We do. We do have our own." His entire face lit up in a smile. "And it's right under Derrek's nose."

Deor frowned and thought for a moment, and then his shoulders slumped. "Oh, hell," he said. "I've got to freeze again, don't I?"

"What are you talking about?" Aelred interrupted.

"On Perseon, my lord. They use *zanthos* for everything. And, more importantly, they have the technology to repurpose it...to weaponize it, or domesticate it."

"It's brilliant," Aelred said, a slow smile creasing his face. "Derrek will never see it coming..."

"So, once he and his minions head offworld for Halcyon, we sober up the military and then fortify Askalon with a new stockpile of weapons-grade *zanthos*. And then Brytnoth and I will follow him."

Aelred tapped his fingers together. "No," he said. "You won't have time. Any delay could put you on Halcyon too late. You'll have to go immediately."

"They'll track us, Aelred." Deor said.

"No, they won't. Because you'll be on board their ship."

THIRTY-NINE

DEOR AND BRYTNOTH made their way back through the dimly lit warehouse. Even in the late afternoon, the grime that coated the high windows filtered out most of the light. The air was close and laden with the damp smell of mildew and dirt and the very faintest hint of decomp.

"This is a disgusting place," Deor observed.

"Come on." Brytnoth glanced at him with a grin. "It's not nearly as bad as the hole we dug you out of all those months ago, remember?"

Deor thought for a moment. The prison of K'ilenfir had been no paradise...and the food had definitely been worse. "True," he agreed. "But this seems worse somehow. Maybe it's because I'd gotten used to not living like a worm."

Brytnoth waved a hand in the direction of the children, who had resolved their differences and were now whooping with delight as a teammate charged ahead with the ball. "They don't seem to mind it."

Deor snorted. "Kids don't mind anything. I know...I was one."

Brytnoth's eyes lit up. "Really?" he breathed. "You were? Really?"

"Shut up." Deor shoved him and Brytnoth laughed out loud. "You know what I meant. There was a time when I didn't care about anything either. All I needed was someone to smile at me." His face hardened suddenly and anger burned in his throat. "Kids can be joyful without sun, without more than a mouthful of food at a time, without clothes or warmth. All they need is someone to smile at them once in a while. To show them a little bit of love."

Deor jerked his head toward the group, where several solicitous mothers were now watching from the sidelines. As one little boy slammed the ball through the barrels, one of the mothers beamed and clapped her hands. The boy turned around, his face radiant.

"See?" Deor said. "That's what I mean."

"And that's what we're going to save," Brytnoth said. "These children deserve sunshine and all the good things in life...and no fanatical, dragon-worshipping freak of nature is going to keep my people from having what they need to be truly happy."

Deor regarded him with a half-smile. "Glad to see you finally fired up," he said, his voice lightly teasing. "So let's get ready. We've got some sneaking around to do."

They passed the medical wing and made their way back to the camping area. Deor realized now just how many cots and blankets were scattered on the warehouse floor. There must have been hundreds, some grouped for families, some laid singly around the perimeter. Deor reasoned that those who were here alone were pegged for guard duty, and their position around the rest of the camp made it easy for them to rotate shifts without disturbing others.

"Aelred organized all this?" he murmured, glancing at Brytnoth. His friend chuckled.

"Why are you looking at me as though I had an answer? We came to this party together, remember?"

They sat cross-legged on the floor on their blankets. Deor stared at the charred remains of his little fire and poked at it half-heartedly with the scorched end of a stick. It crumbled into black chunks and dust, and he tossed the stick aside.

"How in hell are we supposed to sneak onto that ship, Deor?" Brytnoth asked after a long silence. "Derrek knows us too well...we'll be recognized in five minutes. And I don't know about you, but I can imagine all kids of awful ways to be executed in space."

"Well, we'll just have to get low and stay that way," Deor answered. "Avoid Derrek's line of sight at all times. I figured we'd show up and volunteer for cleaning duty or something similarly low and dirty and absolutely unappealing to Derrek. He'd never look twice at a cleaning crew. He's just not the type to give a damn about those who serve him."

"It's not a bad idea," Bryntoth said slowly, rubbing his chin. "But still, this is incredibly risky."

But Deor was grinning. "Oh, it's risky. But I've been thinking something. If Jared can use the *zanthos* because he's the Dragon-Slayer, then what about Sahara and me? Why couldn't we use it too? Maybe we wouldn't pack the same punch, but...you saw what it did to me, Brytnoth."

"Yeah. I did. It turned you into the absolute worst version of yourself. A mini dragon."

Deor made a face. "Mini? Me?"

"Yeah, you. The stuff is pure evil, isn't it?"

Deor rubbed his chin thoughtfully and swept his eyes over the camp. A young mother with two tiny children sat near them, her face streaked with dirt and tears. She held the youngest—a baby no more than a few weeks old—cradled against her chest and was trying to coax her other child to nibble a hard chunk of bread. The little child, a girl with wispy blonde curls, was gathering herself together for a storm of temper. Deor saw a tear slide down the mother's cheek, and then another. They dripped onto the soft head of her infant.

"Deor?" Brytnoth asked, leaning forward.

"Just a minute."

Deor rose and approached the little family. The mother looked up, startled, her tears forgotten, as Deor crouched down beside her. He smiled at her, then turned to the little girl. Her wide gray eyes reminded Deor of clouds heavy with cleansing rain.

"I'm Deor," he said. "What's your name?"

The girl blinked at him for a moment and twisted her fingers together. Her eyes sought out her mother's, and seeming to find reassurance there, she answered softly, "Tryss."

"Well, Tryss, aren't you hungry?"

"No. Least not for nasty bread like that."

Deor glanced at the girl's mother, whose desperate and pleading eyes told Deor that the girl had been refusing food for some time. He turned back to Tryss. "How old are you, little lady?"

"Four."

"Four! So big! And you help your mother with your baby sister?"

"Yes."

Deor leaned forward and dropped his voice to a whisper. "Your mother needs your help, Tryss. It's a very big job...and it will take a big, strong girl to do it. Are you ready, do you think?"

"Yes."

Deor shifted his eyes to the mother's face and held out a hand. She placed the hunk of biscuit in his palm and he winked at her. Then he turned back to the girl. "Your mother needs you to eat so you can be big and strong. Do you think you can do that?"

The girl hesitated, her eyes shifting from Deor's face to the bread he held out to her. Finally, she shrugged, snatched the bread like a little bird pouncing on a crumb in a busy street, and disappeared into the tent.

Deor smiled and brushed the crumbs off his hand.

"Thank you," the young mother whispered.

Deor looked up and was surprised to see tears running down the woman's face. "I hope...you don't mind I intervened?" he said.

She managed a smile through her tears. "Nothing's been the same since..." Her voice broke, and she swiped at her cheeks with the back of her free hand. "Since we had to come here."

"Things will soon be right again. I promise you."

"Things can never be right. Not until you bring Dale back."

Deor guessed that Dale must be the woman's husband. He didn't want to ask anything further because he was afraid of the answer, but he felt awkwardly that there was no polite way to just walk away now. "Where is he?"

"He was conscripted into Derrek's crew," she said. "He and my brother Liam both. And God knows if they will ever make it back alive."

Deor frowned and sat back on his heels. "Conscripted? Didn't Derrek have enough men in the army?"

The woman shook her head. "My husband works at the docks," she explained. "He's got a special skillset. Derrek threatened all our lives if Dale didn't agree to serve as chief engineer on his ship. And Liam is a weapons specialist." Fresh tears were flowing now. "I know that Derrek has something horrible planned," she said. "And I know it has to do with Halcyon somehow. I just want my family home safe."

Deor glanced over at Brytnoth and beckoned to him. Brytnoth's face registered confusion, but he rose and threaded his way through the other little camps toward them.

"Listen," Deor said, dropping his voice. "Brytnoth and I have to get onto that ship. Can you describe your husband and brother for us? If you can help us get on board, I promise you that we will keep them safe."

The woman arched an eyebrow at him. "You can promise that? Who are you, anyway?"

Brytnoth crouched down beside Deor. "What's going on?"

Deor ignored him for the moment. "My name is Deor Acwellan," he said. "Before the coup, I ran Aelred's militia."

The woman's eyes widened. "I remember you," she said softly. "I remember Dale telling me about you. You and—" Her eyes turned to Brytnoth and she studied him for a moment. "And you. And a few others. You helped to overthrow the Triumvirate."

"That's right," Brytnoth said. "I still don't understand why—"

"Her husband and brother are crew on Derrek's ship," Deor interrupted. Then he addressed the woman, "So, can you help us? We have to get onto that ship."

The woman snuggled her baby close, watching them intently for several long seconds. "You swear to me that you will see them both home safe?"

"As far as is in my power," Deor answered earnestly, "I swear. We both do."

The woman took a deep breath. "Dale is tall...taller than Lord Aelred by half a head at least. He has fair curly hair like my Tryss. And you'll likely find him on the docks. He has a burn scar on his left hand, just between the thumb and forefinger. Tell him Alison sent you. And..." She stopped, hesitating. But then she seemed to come to a decision. "Please give him our love, when you find him. And tell him if he doesn't come back, I'll never forgive him."

"We'll tell him," Brytnoth said. "And Liam?"

Alison smiled suddenly. "He's a firebrand. And he's got the scars to prove it. His nose has been broken I don't know how many times— it's crooked now. And he's broad-shouldered and has a chest like an ale barrel. He just looks like the sort who'd get into a fight in a bar. But he's got a good heart."

Deor rose and Brytnoth stood with him. "Thank you," Deor said. "We'll bring them home safe."

Alison smiled at them. "And if you happen to kill that bastard Derrek," she said mildly, "you'll be doing me a kindness."

Deor and Brytnoth exchanged glances, and Deor fought hard to keep from smiling.

"We'll do our best to take care of that too," Brytnoth said, seeming to sense that Deor couldn't speak at the moment.

With a wave at Tryss, who was peeking out of the folds of the tent flap, Deor and Brytnoth picked their way back to their own campsite. After standing for a moment and contemplating the cold ashes of the small fire, Deor turned on his heel and headed for the door of the warehouse. Brytnoth sprang after him.

"Where are you going?"

"We need to gather some supplies," Deor said over his shoulder.

"We shouldn't go out there," Brytnoth protested. "What if we're caught?"

Deor turned to face his worried friend. "We won't be caught. I have an idea."

He started moving toward the door again and recoiled as Aria stepped directly into his path and crossed her arms over her chest. Her ice blue eyes were intense and her dark ponytail danced as she threw back her head to look at him.

"Where are you going, Commander?" she demanded. "Sneaking out, are we?"

Deor arched an eyebrow at her. "So what if we are?"

"It's not allowed."

"You have no say about that, I'm afraid. We're going on Aelred's orders."

"Sort of," muttered Brytnoth, half under his breath. Aria's eyes flashed at him, then snapped back to Deor.

"If you're going, then I'm coming with you."

"Oh, no. No, you're not. You're staying here. And there's another thing. I'm not Commander any longer. You are."

Aria's arms slipped to her sides and her mouth dropped open. "What?"

Deor placed his hands on her shoulders and gave her a gentle shake. "You're head of the militia now. Just until I get back." He gave her a crooked smile. "Can you handle it?"

"No! I mean...I can handle...but where are you going?"

Deor glanced at Brytnoth. "We're going to Halcyon," he said in a low voice. "On Derrek's ship." He gave her another gentle shake. "And that's why you can't come with me. I need you here. Aelred needs you here."

Aria's jaw tightened, and Deor wondered for a moment whether she was fighting back tears. "I won't let you down, Commander," she said softly.

"I know that. I wouldn't have recommended you as my replacement if I thought you'd muck it up." Her eyes widened, and Deor found that he was taking absurd pleasure in surprising her. "Just remember," he added, releasing her shoulders, "don't hesitate."

He hardly had time to register the light of mischief that sprang into her eyes before she'd taken his face in her hands and pressed her lips to his.

"I won't," she promised, pulling back and flashing a smile at him. Then she slipped past them and headed for Aelred's office. Deor watched her go, his mind reeling.

Deor jumped when Brynoth dropped a hand on his shoulder. "Well, that was unexpected," Brytnoth observed. "You can close your mouth now."

Deor turned stunned eyes on his friend. "What in hell was that about?"

Brytnoth shrugged, and his face broke into a broad grin. "You obviously overwhelmed her with your ravishing good looks."

Deor scowled at him. "Right. I'm sure that's it."

"Come on, Deor. Does a girl need a reason? I wouldn't be complaining."

"I'm her commanding officer, Brytnoth," Deor said. "Makes things just a little bit complicated."

"Actually, she's your commanding officer now. And maybe you'll just have to ask Aelred for a promotion or reassignment."

"To what?"

"Well, if things go according to plan, he'll need a commanding general for the military, since Derrek will be permanently retired. That's tailor-made for you, I'd say."

"Are you trying to work out a way to get me into trouble with women, Brytnoth?" Deor asked. "Some friend you are!"

Brytnoth slapped him on the back and laughed. "Come on," he said. "If we survive this, I guess you'll have plenty to look forward to."

They circuited the last few campsites and made their way across the smooth concrete floor toward the massive doors. Huge rusted chains dangled from their pulleys high above their heads like the memory of a tortured past or the ghost of a machine that had long since crumbled to dust. The doors were no more than mouldering wooden planks mounted on metal hinges and battens, and chinks of light seeped through them and spilled on the floor like thin gruel.

"I've no notion of the time," Deor said. "By the light, I'd say it's almost dawn."

"If we're going to hitch a ride on that ship," Brytnoth agreed, "we'd better hurry."

Two men stepped out of the shadows on either side of the door as they approached. One had a crossbow, but the other was armed with a machine gun.

"Back to your camp, citizens," he said, leveling his weapon at them.

"Put that away and step aside," Deor snapped. "We're here on Aelred's orders. Let us out."

"None are permitted out."

Deor stepped up to the man until the muzzle of the gun was pressed into his chest. "Really? You going to shoot me? Go ahead."

The other man raised his crossbow, and Brytnoth held up a hand.

"Stop, he said. "This is Commander Acwellan. Lord Aelred has a mission for us. You either let us out the damn door, or you'll be dangling from those chains for your stupidity."

The men slowly lowered their weapons, and the man with the machine gun peered closely at Deor in the meager light. Recognition flashed across his face, and he inclined his head slightly.

"Commander," he said. "I didn't recognize you. Forgive me."

He jerked his head at the other man, who hurried to the door and fumbled with the fastenings. Then he pulled the door open a crack—just wide enough for Deor and Brytnoth to slip through—and stepped aside.

"It's hell out there, Commander," the man with the machine gun said. "You sure you're heading out?"

"If we don't," Deor said, "it'll be hell everywhere."

And without another word, he and Brytnoth slipped through the doorway into the empty street beyond.

FORTY

SAHARA HADN'T STOPPED RUNNING since she left Azimir's banquet hall. The streets of Aquila were steeped in shadows, and she suddenly pulled up short, terrified for a moment that she'd been running blind and had lost her way. Without the help of moonlight, everything looked the same—broad main streets branching into narrow twisting alleyways between tall, many-windowed buildings.

All those windows.

Sahara doubled over, gasping for breath. She hadn't realized just how tiring it was to run in a gown like this, and she wished suddenly that she'd had the sense to pick up her other things before she'd gone on her mad flight through the city. There was nothing to be done about it now. She couldn't go back. She didn't dare go back.

He had recognized her.

He had saved her.

She took a few shaking deep breaths and straightened slowly. It would be best not to dwell on all that right now. She'd think about it later, when she was back in her tent among her people. Right now, she needed to focus.

Somehow she had to get her bearings. She glanced around, squelching the panic that threatened to choke her. She was at the end of a narrow alley, crisscrossed with lines sagging under the weight of drying clothes. The rich scent of blossoms from climbing vines wafted toward her on the hushing of the night breeze.

She knew that scent. A slow smile spread across her face, and she turned to the wall behind her. A trellis dripping with trailing vines and soft-petaled flowers leaned against the rough stone of the city wall. And looped through the wooden frame, exactly where she had secured it, was the rope she'd used to climb down into the city.

With a whispered prayer of thanksgiving, Sahara untied the rope and jerked it clear. Then she hesitated, brushing a hand against the smooth, soft silk of her skirt. The climb would be hard enough without being hampered by yards of fabric, and she couldn't risk getting tangled up. Lovely as the dress was, it had to go. She had a shift on underneath, and that would be easier to manage. It wasn't ideal, but it would have to work.

Or would it?

She glanced back down the alley, then shrugged out of the gown and scooped the shimmering folds over her arm. After a moment's hesitation, she kicked off the jeweled slippers too and added them to the pile. Then she trotted to the nearest of the clotheslines.

It was hung with nothing but rags and a few long, trailing scarves. She didn't need anything long and trailing...she'd had enough of that for one night. She shifted her gaze over her head. The second story line had exactly what she needed...but it was too high out of reach, and there was no easy way to climb up to it. She chewed her lip in nervous frustration. Every second she lingered in the alley raised her chances of being caught. But she couldn't run all the way back to Jessup's camp without shoes and in nothing but a shift.

She slipped past the first set of lines to the ones beyond. Blessedly, she found what she needed. Clipped to the line was a pair of dark breeches and a wide black sash. A rough linen shirt hung beside them. She jerked them off the line and pinned the dress there instead.

It'll bring a fair price. Should be more than enough to pay for what I've taken.

She shimmied into the breeches and slipped the shirt over the shift she wore, winding the sash around her waist to hold the breeches up. Then she glanced around. There was no sign of shoes anywhere...and why should there be? Who would leave shoes outside overnight?

With a sigh, she dropped the slippers and stepped into them again. They were better than nothing.

She wound her way back through the shadows and took the rope in both hands. With a soft grunt, she began the painstaking process of scaling the wall. After what felt like an hour, she clambered onto the ledge and pulled the rope up after her. Glancing to her left and right to be sure there were no patrols coming, she dropped it over the other side of the wall and rappelled down. No sense in hesitating. She'd lost enough time already, and she had a long run ahead of her if she was going to make it back to Jessup's camp before dawn.

The sky to the east was just beginning to pale when she saw the soft curl of smoke from the tents of the Hazad camp. The knot in her stomach loosened just a bit. She wasn't too late. They were still here.

She picked up her pace and made straight for Jessup's marquee tent on the far side of the clearing. A soft light inside told her that Jessup and Yasmin were already awake. She was about to slip past the slumbering guard when he jerked awake, thrusting the nasty point of his spear under her nose.

"What're you doing?" he slurred, rubbing vigorously at his eyes with his other hand.

"I have to see Jessup," she hissed. "It's Saha—Zelie. Let me in."

The guard scrubbed at his face again, and the point of the spear wobbled dangerously close to her face. Then he peered at her in the early morning gloom. A vague light of recognition sparked in his bleared eyes, but then he looked her up and down and frowned, taking in her rough, oversized clothes and sparkling slippers.

"You look like her," he said slowly, his voice thick with sleep. "But what the devil is all that?"

"I don't have time for your stupid questions," Sahara snapped. "Let me in."

The guard shrugged his shoulders and held open the tent flap for her. Sahara slipped inside and stood blinking for a moment in the soft light.

Jessup was seated in the small sitting area, nursing a mug of something steaming hot. A tiny blaze burned in the brazier nearby, casting vast shadows on the tent walls. For all the commotion with the guard outside, Jessup didn't look up and seemed not even to have heard her enter.

Sahara opened her mouth to speak, then hesitated. A look of such drawn concern was on Jessup's face that she didn't know how she could bear to burden him any further. But she had no choice. The survival of the Hazad depended on it.

Clearing her throat softly, she stepped forward into the flickering circle of light. "Jessup?" she said. "Jessup? I need to speak..."

His head snapped up and he focused on her. "Who the—" Then he stopped. "Zelie Sahara? What is—?" He gestured vaguely at her strange clothes and set his mug down on a low table beside his chair. "Where in all wonder have you been?"

Sahara stumbled forward and dropped to her knees on the heavy rug under Jessup's feet. She took one of his wrinkled hands in both her own and pressed it, staring up into his kind face. "Jessup, please. You have to listen to me. You can't take our people to Telon. Not this time. Please...please just keep everyone away from there."

Jessup's frown of concern returned. "We have never missed the pilgrimage to the Holy City," he said slowly. "Not even when we were persecuted by the Order of the Dragon. Is our plight now any worse than that?" He paused, shaking his head. "I don't intend to fail in our duties to God because some upstart tyrant thinks he's harnessed the dark power."

Sahara's eyes widened, and she tightened her grip on Jessup's hand. "But he <u>has</u> harnessed it. Jessup, you don't understand. He <u>has</u>. Azimir will destroy you all, down to the last child. You cannot do this thing!"

Jessup's face softened into a smile as he gazed at her. "You are like a daughter to me," he said. "You are one of our own now. And you know enough of our faith to know that our duty to God is higher than anything...yes, higher even than self-preservation. When the Drakkin first rose in the north, only the Hazad stood against them. Only the Hazad refused to bow to their demon-god. We are enemies of old. And we are not about to run from him now, just because he has decided to manifest himself once more. We stand with the light...and we do not run from evil."

Two burning tears rolled down Sahara's cheeks. "But...but you can't do this!" she whispered, her voice hoarse with tears. "Jessup...I don't understand!"

"No, my daughter. I know you don't." He smiled down at her gently and brushed his fingers against her cheek. "How could you? Our ways are still not your ways, even though you are learning more every day. Come with us to Telon. Perhaps you will find the answers there."

"I don't need any answers!" Sahara flared, blinking hard to keep back her tears. "I've had my fill of answers...and I don't need reasons or arguments. I just need..." Her voice trailed off for a moment, and then she took a breath and rushed on. "I need you to survive. I can't lose you. I've lost everything I have ever loved...everything."

Jessup shook his head gently. "Have you?"

Sahara wanted to scream curses at him. The memories jumbled through her mind, mingling with her tears. Memories of Jared, a dark voice that wasn't his voice pouring from his lips and darkness blotting out the light of love in his eyes. Of Rafe, standing like a wraith, consumed by an addiction to a poison he couldn't refuse. Of her father, fastening a silver chain around her ankle and making promises he couldn't keep. Of her mother, grey and cold, dead from grief. And of Deor...

Her breath caught suddenly in her throat, and her eyes, swimming with unshed tears, snapped to Jessup's face. His smile broadened, and he reached out to grasp her shoulders.

"Deor," she whispered, feeling a tiny flicker of hope light in her heart. "Maybe..." She stopped, hardly daring to let the thought form.

"God has never abandoned us, Zelie. Not ever. And He will not do so now. The dark power is no match for Him. This fight is already won."

"But at what cost?" Sahara murmured. "Jessup...what if—"

"What if we all die there in Telon, you would ask?" Jessup sighed and lifted his shoulders in a shrug. "If we all die, then it is His will. And if our God wills us to die, can we escape it by running away?"

"I have to save him, Jessup," Sahara said suddenly, gripping his hands where they still held her shoulders. The tears spilled down her cheeks, and a sob caught in her throat. "I have to save him. And I don't know how. He's being consumed by the Dragon...and he will be used by Azimir as a weapon of his vicious hate." She squeezed the old man's hands earnestly. "I'm an assassin, Jessup. I'm no child of the light. I work in the dark with a knife in the throat. The only thing I've ever trusted is a hard steel edge. The only creed I've ever lived by is kill or be killed. And now..."

Jessup cocked his head at her, a smile ghosting his lips. "And yet," he said slowly, "you would risk everything, even your own life, to save the man you love. That doesn't seem to fit in your so-called creed. From where I sit, I see a woman who has spent every moment of her life fighting for what she loves. Her people, her family, her friends. That doesn't sound like a child of darkness to me." A warm light suddenly filled his eyes and he cupped her face gently in his hands. "You fight for love, Sahara. Not for hate."

Sahara dropped her hands and blinked at him, feeling suddenly as though a sweeping vista of light had opened suddenly within her soul. Her mind reeled.

"And that," Jessup added softly, "is why he loves you still."

"But it's not enough," Sahara whispered. "He's drowning, Jessup. It's not enough. Not enough to save him." Her eyes welled with tears again. "I've tried. And—"

She remembered suddenly the look in Jared's eyes when she knelt in the banquet hall, the sword raised over her head. He had turned on Azimir to save her. The spark of hope burned a little brighter. Maybe it wasn't too late for him after all. Maybe, somehow, she could still reach him...could still draw him out of the clutches of the Dragon.

But in the next instant, the spark flickered out. She felt insignificant, and she didn't know how her love could possibly be strong enough to break the dark power that held him hostage. It was all impossible...and now Jessup wasn't listening to her. He would take their people to Telon, and they would all be annihilated.

Jessup seemed to sense something of her thoughts, for he gently raised her face so that she had to look into his eyes once more. "Come with us to Telon," he said earnestly. "And then I think you'll find the answers you seek."

———

The caravan was ready to move out by midday. Sahara's tent had been collapsed and packed away with the others in the wagons, and she sat now on her horse, watching the slow procession with an ever deepening scowl.

"You don't have to look so excited," said a voice, and Sahara glanced down to her right.

"Rigel!" she said, smiling in spite of herself. "I thought you would be with your family."

The young man shrugged easily. "You looked like you could use some company," he said. "So here I am."

Sahara swung down out of the saddle and they moved off with

the last of the wagons. Sahara glanced at Rigel sidelong and grinned at him.

"Some company," she said. "Did Jessup think I needed extra penance on this pilgrimage?"

Rigel laughed, a clear, ringing laugh that was utterly contagious. Sahara found herself laughing with him, and suddenly the world seemed a bit brighter.

"You know," Rigel observed, sobering. "I haven't seen much of Brig lately. You're one of the Elenni...have you seen him?"

Sahara looked at him quickly. "No, I haven't. But I've been...busy lately."

"So I've noticed. You haven't been to milk the goats in three days. I've had to do it for you."

Sahara winced. "I'm sorry, Rigel," she said. "I didn't mean for you to be stuck with my chores."

Rigel shrugged again. "No worries. I figured you were off on some important Elenni mission or something." The barest trace of wistfulness colored his words, and Sahara glanced at him again.

"You don't mean you wish you were one of us?" she said.

"Who, me?" Rigel shook his head in the negative, but the barest hesitation in the movement told Sahara that he was bluffing.

"Look, Rigel. You may not be a rider or much of a fighter, but you may well be needed before all's said and done."

"That sounds ominous."

"I hope so. I meant it to."

Sahara looked away from him, glancing back over her shoulder at the little cove of trees and flattened grasses that marked all that was left of their camp. Suddenly and unexplainably, Sahara felt a wave of homesickness.

"It won't ever be the same," she muttered. "Even if everything comes right somehow, it won't ever be the same."

But maybe there was still a way to stop all of this before it ever got started.

She turned back to Rigel with a little sigh, her eyes dropping to his hip. She had noticed before that he sometimes carried a short, curved dagger in an elaborately tooled leather sheath. He was wearing it now, and she saw for the first time that in the center of the scrollwork design was the three-petaled flower that was the symbol of their people.

"Rigel," she said softly. "I'm going to need to borrow your knife."

FORTY-ONE

THE JOURNEY to the Holy City of Telon had been slow and uneventful. It had taken a full two weeks' time to reach the walls of the city, and even so Jessup's tribe had been the first to arrive. They had been camped just outside the gates in the shelter of a small copse of shaggy trees for three days. Every day, more tribes had straggled in, setting up tents, waiting for their brothers and sisters.

The terrain to the north of Aquila was rough and rocky and long stretches of the countryside were barren—these scrubby trees were the only things that seemed hardy enough to withstand the harshness of the terrain and the climate.

This far north, the air was always chill, even under the noon sun. And the days had been growing darker. Isis said it was the slow approach of the annual eclipse, but Sahara felt that it was something else too. The growing darkness and the chill that had nothing to do with the climate...they were from another source altogether.

Sahara didn't need anyone to tell her that they were close to the borders of the cursed country of Perl. Telon seemed to perch on its very doorstep. And the dark power, as Jessup called it, was rising. She had no doubt that it would reach its zenith with the coming of the eclipse, which Isis had told her would happen in four days' time.

Sahara slapped the rough wood of the stick impatiently against the palm of her hand. She was crouched in the sedge in front of Katarina's tent, trying to ward off the damp of the hour before dawn with a thick cloak. She jerked the cowl up over her riot of red curls and tried to huddle deeper into its folds.

There was no easy way to do what she had to do. She'd known this day was coming, They'd both known. She just wished that it hadn't come so soon.

The tent behind her was still and empty. From the shadows of her cowl, Sahara surveyed the rest of the camp, watching especially the western approach. Now that they were far from Aquila, Katarina seemed to take comfort in keeping her routine of nightly journeys. Sahara had trailed her two nights ago and discovered that she had slipped into the still and sleeping city of Telon to kneel in the dust in front of the closed doors of the Great Temple. Even from where she had concealed herself in the shadows of an alleyway, Sahara could hear the sobs that racked Katarina's body.

She hadn't followed her again.

Sahara poked at the tufts of scrubby grass with the end of her stick and frowned. She didn't really care why Katarina insisted on sneaking out of the camp every night, but she felt profoundly unsettled by it all. First in Aquila, now in Telon...there was something not quite right about it all. She'd already vouched for Katarina's loyalty to Brig, and he'd accepted her word on the matter with a grunt and a shrug. She just wished she'd convinced herself of it too.

Brig had disappeared. No one had seen him for days, and Sahara contemplated his absence with a vague uneasiness. Maybe he wasn't who he had seemed to be. But Sahara couldn't imagine how he could possibly make things worse than they already were.

She swallowed hard and jabbed the stick into the ground. The whole thing was a nightmare, and the deeper into the dream she got, the more entangled and impossible everything became.

Stay focused. I have a mission. Deviation from the plan will just get me killed. Somehow I'll figure the rest of this mess out. Just not right now.

At last, she saw the lantern light bobbing across the square. Two more steps and Katarina would extinguish the light. She always did.

One. Two.

And now the shadowy figure continued in darkness.

Sahara let her breath out in a slow hiss. Predictability got you killed. She wished that Katarina would be more careful. She didn't trust Brig, especially when she couldn't see him. And after today, she wouldn't be able to protect Katarina any longer.

"You really should be more careful," Sahara said quietly as Katarina hurried the last few steps to her tent.

The other woman recoiled with a gasp, her face suddenly ashen. She stared at Sahara for a minute, then, as recognition dawned on her face, she smoothed a shaking hand across her brow. A smile, pale as the eastern sky, touched her lips.

"I didn't see you sitting there," she whispered. "Why are you here? Is something wrong?"

Sahara rose and jerked open the tent flap. "We can talk inside."

Something in Sahara's tone furrowed Katarina's brow, but she ducked under Sahara's arm and entered the tent. Sahara followed, returning to a crouch by the entrance as Katarina shed her wraps and lit a small fire in the brazier.

As the tiny flames licked around the lacework of dried sticks, Katarina paused and studied Sahara in the unsteady light.

"Are you hungry?" she asked. "Breakfast won't be for hours yet, but I always keep a little—"

"No."

Sahara met her gaze, wincing inside as she saw the doubt in Katarina's eyes. Doubt and even fear. She could taste the question that Katarina didn't dare ask.

"I need a cup of tea," Katarina murmured.

She turned abruptly and moved to a small shelf on the opposite side of the tent. She had set up her little store of herbal medicines when they'd arrived in Telon, and Sahara watched curiously as she moved two small tins aside and reached her hand toward the back of the shelf. Katarina withdrew a small box and flicked open the lid.

"What's that?" Sahara asked.

"Something I keep for emergencies."

Sahara frowned. "This isn't an emergency."

Katarina glanced at Sahara over her shoulder, hesitating. "No? You're not here to...to kill me?"

Sahara swallowed hard, but the tightness in her throat only grew. For a moment, she could do nothing but wrestle with her tears. She wanted to run to Katarina and beg her forgiveness for everything she had ever done...to feel the balm of love and absolution flood out the dark and twisted passages in her soul. But she couldn't move. She just crouched there like an insect caught in a web and her heart wept.

"No." Sahara almost couldn't recognize her own voice. "How could you...why would you think that?"

Katarina snapped the lid shut and slipped the box back into its place. She avoided Sahara's gaze and focused intently on measuring a heap of minced leaves from one of the other tins into a mug. She placed a small rack over the brazier and placed a kettle on it. Her movements, measured as a ceremonial dance, did little to mask her uneasiness.

"How could you imagine that I would come here to kill you?" Sahara repeated, her voice stronger this time.

"Brig hates me," Katarina said. "He's always hated me. And you work for him now."

"I don't work for anyone but myself," Sahara said. "And you."

Katarina's eyes snapped to her face, but Sahara didn't waver. After a moment, Katarina laughed softly and shook her head. "You don't work for me, Sahara. You are like a daughter to me. I have tried to teach you what I know because..."

"Because?"

"Isn't it natural to want to pass down what you know? And I have no one else but you."

"And what else would you teach me, then? The secret ways into Aquila? The name of the guard who will take bribes from the Hazad? The address of the house where you can hide in the city for hours with no one asking questions?" Sahara kept her voice like ice even as she felt the burn of anger and suspicion ignite in her gut. "Are those things the reason you kneel in the dirt before the Temple and weep?"

Katarina poured the hot water over her tea, releasing a fragrant cloud of steam. She settled the little lid over the mug and placed it carefully beside her to steep. "Why should you think I know such things?"

"We both know that you know such things," Sahara said. "I want to know why."

Katarina shook her dark hair back from her face and lifted her chin. "It's not important. And I didn't realize I was being followed. I have served Jessup's tribe faithfully for years...and now he sends a foreign assassin to dog my steps and kill me in the dark?"

"You know it wasn't Jessup, Katarina. It was Brig."

"Of course. And who does Brig work for, then?"

"Katarina."

It was almost a command, and it had the desired effect. Katarina folded her hands and waited. Only at the end of a long silence did she dare to lift her eyes to Sahara's face. When she did, Sahara leaned forward.

"I spied on you to save your life, not to take it."

Katarina's eyes slid away from hers. "I wish I could believe that."

"Believe it. If I wanted to kill you, I wouldn't have to spy on you first," Sahara said, the bitterness almost choking her. "You'd never even see me coming. And I certainly wouldn't sit in the chill and the damp in front of your tent for an hour to announce my intentions to you."

Katarina sniffed. "I suppose that's so."

"I didn't come here to kill you. I came to say good-bye."

At that, Katarina's head snapped up. "What? Why?"

"It's time for me to go. It's time to end all this. And I'm the only one who can."

"That's not true! Surely...surely there's another way? Brig's always scheming, always making plans to set the Hazad free. Doesn't he have some kind of plan? Why does it have to be you?"

"Brig's out of the picture," she said. "I'm on my own now. And it has to be me. I don't see any other assassins lurking in the shadows around here, do you?"

Katarina swallowed hard, her face suddenly white as a *borracha* flower. "Why does this require an assassin?"

"I should think that was obvious."

For long seconds, Sahara held Katarina's gaze, letting the significance of it all sink in. The older woman's lips began to tremble, and tears filmed her eyes. And suddenly, Sahara wasn't sure whether Katarina was weeping because she would be in danger...or for some other reason she couldn't understand.

"Please don't do this thing," Katarina whispered, her voice barely audible. "Please, Sahara. Please don't."

"And if I don't, Azimir will not leave a single one of you—not one single child—alive. You know he won't. It's only a matter of time...and there's precious little of that left. There are things in motion..." Sahara stopped suddenly and shook her head. "Just believe me. It's better this way." Sahara opened her hands and stared at her palms, slowly closing her fingers. "It seems this is what I was made for," she murmured. "To be a *shamat*. A killer of kings."

She rose and started to duck out of the tent, but then she hesitated, glancing over her shoulder. Katarina's face was now wet with tears, and her eyes were wide with horror and grief. Sahara tried to smile at her.

"If I never see you again, I just want you to know something," Sahara said, a tear slipping down her own cheek. "For what it's worth, you were the closest thing to a mother that I've ever known. And I'll never forget you."

And before she completely broke down, Sahara pushed through the tent flap into the chill dawn, the sound of Katarina's shaking sobs filling her ears.

Sahara slipped away, heading for the city of Telon. Silently, she bid farewell to the people she loved so dearly, to the only family she had really ever known. It was all for them, what she was about to do. And she would do anything—anything at all—to keep them from harm.

But the certainty of what she had to do and why didn't make it any easier. She was sure that she would never see any of them again. She felt sure that once she raised her hand against Azimir, Jared would turn on her, and that filled her with a paralyzing fear that made her numb inside and out.

If Jared came after her, she would not defend herself against him. He would kill her, and she would die with love and forgiveness on her lips. And maybe that would be enough. Maybe, without Azimir, Jared would have no need to destroy the Hazad. Maybe her sacrifice would be enough to appease the Dragon.

It was too much to hope that her sacrifice would set him free.

Better not go down that road right now. Focus, Sahara. One thing at a time. One foot in front of the other.

She left the tent line and scurried into the barren plain at the edge of the camp. She glanced at the sky to the east, then bent her gaze on the distant crumbling gray walls of Telon. From following Katarina, she knew that the city was all but deserted. She would find the wide wooden gate unguarded. There would be nothing to stop her from getting into the city. She had already planned to hide in the Temple itself, for she had no doubt that whatever Azimir was planning, it would happen there.

But she had no idea how she would confront him when the time came.

Later. Figure it out later. She broke into a jog. *I'll figure it out later.*

The stones crunched under her boots, and the eastern sky flared into color. As the rays of the sun slid over the edge of the world, their meager warmth bathed her cold face and hands and filled her with hope. As she ran, she remembered how the sun had warmed her in her captivity in the stronghold of the Drakkin on Silesia. And she remembered how Jared's steady, unflagging love had sustained her and given her the strength to resist until the very end.

Can I do less than offer him the same, even if he despises me? Even if he would crush me into dust and scatter me to the winds? Perhaps there is a little corner of his soul that can still see light...and if there is...

Her feet pounded the ground. Steady. Solid. Determined. Like his love had been. Like hers was now.

She would reach out to him. If it killed her, it didn't matter. She was dead anyway.

Jared.

She slowed her pace to a walk, then stopped. She turned to the east, felt the light bathe her face and fill her soul. She took a deep breath, reached out with light and love and breathless hope.

Jared.

The darkness came, rolling against her like a tidal wave, but she held to the light, filled her lungs with it as she drew in her breath. The darkness collided against the light, shivering her to her knees on the rough stones.

In the black darkness she saw him, the obsidian of his eyes boring into hers. And as the sobs caught in her throat, she stretched out her arms to him.

I love you. Jared, I love you. I love you.

The darkness trembled.

Sahara, he said. It was Jared's voice, not the voice of the monster she feared. And suddenly those eyes were the eyes of the Jared she knew. *Save me.*

The darkness crashed down around him again and withdrew, leaving her crumpled and weeping on the desolate plain.

FORTY-TWO

DEOR AND BRYTNOTH crouched in the shadows at the edge of the landing platform, watching the crew perform their last-minute flight checks and rechecks. A tattered dawn was just breaking through the racks of clouds massed on the eastern horizon.

"Derrek'll be here any minute," Brytnoth murmured. "We've got to go. Now. Do you see those men anywhere?"

Deor pointed across the platform. A tall man with fair hair that curled almost to his shoulders was inspecting the craft's landing gear. "That's Dale right there. Let's go."

They slipped from their hideout and strolled across the landing pad, trying to look as though they belonged there. In the bustle of pre-flight preparations, no one paid any attention to them. Dale was focused on his task and seemed not to see them until they planted themselves next to the gear.

"Dale?" Deor asked, keeping his voice low.

Dale's eyes snapped to his face and he frowned. "Who're you? What do you want? We're busy, if you haven't noticed. I don't have time for loiterers and miscreants."

Deor's mouth twisted in a smile. "So you're Dale?"

"Of course I am. Get out of my way." He pushed past Deor to the second set of landing gear. Deor and Brytnoth trailed after him.

"Stop just a moment," Deor said.

Dale ignored him and continued his visual inspection. "Go away," he said. "Let me do my job. Is this Derrek's idea of a joke? Sending morons to harass me when we're supposed to be underway in twenty?"

"Alison sent us," Brytnoth murmured.

Dale turned slowly, his gray eyes wide in surprise. "What?"

"Your wife sent us," Brytnoth repeated. "We need your help."

"I'm the one who needs help," Dale retorted. "If you've talked to Alison, you know that damn well."

"We are here to help you. But you need to get us on this ship first." Deor folded his arms across his chest. "We're here to make sure things don't go according to plan. Savvy?"

Dale studied them for a moment in the half-light, then grinned. "Yeah. But if Derrek finds you..."

"He won't. And if he does, your name won't come up."

Dale glanced hastily around the platform, and only once he was satisfied that no one was paying any attention to them did he give a short nod of assent. "Get on board and head to the crew quarters. There's a locker room and extra jumpsuits. Engineering's are green. Get them on and then get to the engineering deck. If anyone asks, say I called up extra help for this run."

"We were told to look for Liam as well," Brytnoth said.

"I'll find Liam. You just get out of sight."

"We'll need Liam," Deor said. "We'll need access to that weapons bay."

Dale shooed them away from the landing gear. "You'll get it. But Derrek will be here any moment, and if he shows up while you're standing here, you'll be executed on the spot. Go!"

Deor and Brytnoth headed for the ramp at a jog. At the bottom, they stood aside for two men carrying crates marked with a strange symbol. Deor glanced at Brytnoth and mouthed the word *zanthos*.

Brytnoth nodded and they followed the men aboard. They watched the men disappear to the right around the wide curving hallway.

"Weapons bay's that way," Deor said softly, gesturing to a sign bolted to the wall in front of them. An arrow pointing to the left indicated the way to the crew quarters. "Let's go."

It took them some time to find the crew locker room. The ship was much bigger than either of them had expected, and they got lost more than once in the maze of interconnected passageways. Vaguely, they heard the ship powering up. As they turned yet another corner to find themselves in another high-ceilinged, metal-floored hallway, Deor glanced at Brytnoth's tense face. He clenched his jaw and quickened his pace. A final turn brought them suddenly to the door of the crew quarters, and Deor heaved a sigh of relief.

When they were finally in the locker room, stepping into the dark green jumpsuits of the engineering deck, Deor realized that his heart was pounding and his forehead beaded with sweat.

"As soon as we're official looking," he said, "we're going to get the lay of this ship. And first place I want to see is the weapons bay."

But there was no time. A sudden blaring over the ship's com system made both of them start. And before the sound had ended, they felt the ship lift off.

"Guess there's no backing out now," Brytnoth said, zipping his jumpsuit and grinning. "Let's go check out the weapons bay."

They made their way back through the now-brightly illuminated passageways to the main deck of the ship. The curving hallway brought them to a set of closed elevator doors controlled by a backlit keypad. Deor rubbed his jaw and contemplated the arrangement for a moment.

"Seems this won't get us anywhere," he said. "We need the access code."

"Get out of the way," growled a voice from behind them. "I'm headed down and I don't have time to fool with a couple of engineering pukes."

Deor and Brytnoth turned in surprise, and a slow smile spread across Deor's face. The man wasn't tall, but he was barrel-chested, and his nose was decidedly quirked to one side.

"Liam," Brytnoth said suddenly, and Deor knew that he had recognized the man as well.

"I don't know your face. You got a reason to be making free with my name?"

"Alison sent us," Deor said softly. "Didn't Dale tell you?"

Liam's eyes suddenly lit up. "I was wondering when you'd show up. Come on, then, little stowaways. Seems we have work to do, eh?"

He stepped between them and tapped a series of seven numbers on the keypad. The elevator doors slid open and they crowded inside. Liam pressed a button and a few seconds later the doors parted once more. Liam beckoned for them to follow him as he stepped out into the wide hallway. This one, unlike the passageways above, felt sterile somehow. White, curving walls, white floors, bright ambient light from the white ceiling tiles—everything felt scrubbed and suffocating.

They followed Liam's swift pace and soon the hallway opened out into a large vaulted storage room. Rows of black metal racks, stark against the whiteness, were bolted to the floor and the ceiling, and they held crates all bearing that strange insignia Deor had seen earlier. In the center of the room a strange contraption had been set up, and someone was crouched in front of the lower mechanism. As a hand reached into a nearby toolbox, Deor realized that the person was either finishing its assembly or fixing something that was malfunctioning.

Liam quickened his steps, and Deor and Brytnoth had to trot to keep up with him.

"What's wrong with the accelerator?" Liam demanded, stopping just behind the crouched figure and folding his hands across his broad chest. "We were supposed to be already weaponizing that *zanthos*. What happened?"

The figure turned, and both Deor and Brytnoth recoiled.

"Gwyn!" Deor gasped. "What in hell are you doing here?"

Gwyn's face turned ashen. "I never expected to see you again," she said. "I thought for sure Derrek had had you killed already."

"Not yet," Brytnoth retorted. "How did you get here? And how is it possibly that you're helping Derrek?"

Gwyn fiddled with the tool in her hand, looking profoundly uncomfortable. Liam nudged her with the toe of his boot.

"Tell them," he said.

Gwyn sighed and looked up. "I had no choice. He came to Perseon. Killed ten of our villagers without warning. Just lined them up and executed them on the spot. Then he asked for the person in charge of weaponizing the *zanthos*." She shrugged her shoulders. "Can you blame Arnauld for handing me over?"

Deor and Bryntoth exchanged glances.

"You?" Brytnoth said, turning back to Gwyn. "That's how you knew so much about it...I wondered."

"So here I am," Gwyn said. "Although it's all been very hush-hush. I thought I was coming to make sure Askalon's defenses were operational. Seems I was wrong about that."

"You were dead wrong," Deor said. "We're on our way to destroy Halcyon."

Sudden footsteps behind them made Gwyn start to her feet. Deor clapped his mouth shut and stood, muscles taut. Brytnoth glanced at him sidelong, and neither of them moved to turn.

"Everything in order down here?" It was Derrek's voice.

Deor cursed inwardly and squeezed his eyes shut, curses giving way to a desperate prayer. He felt Brytnoth stiffen imperceptibly beside him.

"Yes, Commander," Gwyn said, gesturing to the machine. "We're a go down here."

"Good. Then get started. We'll be in Halcyon in four days. I want this *zanthos* fully weaponized and ready, understood? Your people are counting on you."

"I understand. We'll work around the clock."

"See that you do." The footsteps began to recede, then suddenly halted. "Why are there engineering bay drones in the weapons hold?"

Deor saw Gwyn open her mouth to answer, but Liam cut her off.

"I brought them," he said shortly. "Damned weapons techs didn't show on time, and I needed a hand. Dale said he could spare them."

There was a long pause, and Deor steeled himself not to turn. Finally, Derrek said, "Let me know if the techs don't show in an hour. I'll have them executed."

"Yes, Commander."

The footsteps receded in earnest now, and as soon as they had faded away, Brytnoth blew out his breath. Liam clapped Deor on the back and laughed grimly.

"Thought our number was up, did you?" he said. "We've got work to do. I had Dale send those techs packing before they ever got on board. After we're done here for the morning, I'll take you back to the crew quarters and get you some weapons tech jumpsuits. That way you won't come under suspicion again."

Gwyn crouched and carefully replaced the tool in the box, her hands visibly shaking. "I hate him," she said. "He rigged our mess hall and dormitories with explosives and left a detachment of men there to blow our settlement to hell if I ever stepped out of line. I hate him."

"Then help us," Brytnoth said, crouching beside her. "Help us. We're here to stop him before he destroys everything...help us. You know how this stuff works...so help us render it useless to him."

Gwyn shook her head. "I don't understand. If I mess this up, he'll kill my people. I have to comply, Brytnoth. I don't have a choice."

Deor was tapping his fingers against his mouth, and suddenly he snapped his fingers. "I've got an idea." His face broke into a wide grin. He gestured to the machine. "This is to weaponize the *zanthos*, right?"

"Yes," Gwyn responded slowly. "But it's also used to deactivate weapons-grade *zanthos* for use in domestic applications."

Deor's grin widened. "Perfect. Then we give Derrek exactly what he wants. We weaponize that crate there. And the rest we turn into light bulbs."

They all stared at him, and then Liam began to laugh. "I like you, kid," he said, slapping Deor on the back again. "I like you a lot."

But Brytnoth was shaking his head. "What if he finds out we're duping him?" he said.

"That's a chance we'll have to take."

Gwyn got to her feet, brushing off her jumpsuit. "It's the only way to prevent him from being able to activate the entire stockpile," she said. "If he did that..."

"It's not him that I'm worried about," Deor said. "It's the Dragon waiting for us on Halcyon."

FORTY-THREE

SAHARA WOKE with a start to the sound of many tramping feet. She was huddled in the darkest corner of the Great Temple, knees drawn up to her chest, her face buried in her crossed arms. The last thing she remembered was trying to mumble her way through some kind of prayer to a God she barely knew but desperately wanted to love.

I must have fallen asleep...and I have no idea of the time.

She had been lurking in the city for the last three days, watching it slowly come alive as the tribes of the Hazad gathered for their great feast. Every tribe had its role, she had learned. Some operated the taverns, bringing with them livestock and great stores of grain, and the scent of baked flatbreads and spiced meats soon filled the dry, dusty air of the ancient city.

Sahara had mingled with the crowds who milled about the city, trying to learn more about the ceremonies that would take place. But no one was willing to discuss such things with someone they didn't know. Even though she was now dressed as one of them—a long, flowing, muted green wrap over wide-legged black pants and a cropped top—her red curls seemed to set her apart too much for trust.

She had finally holed herself up in the Temple after an ancient baker woman had told her that everyone would gather there at noon on the day of the eclipse.

And now there was this steady march, and somehow, Sahara knew that this was not the pace of holy pilgrims, but the tattoo of their destruction.

She raised her head slowly. It was still dark, but she could make out the shapes of men swarming toward the high altar and raised sanctuary. She blinked rapidly, and then her vision suddenly swam and drowned as her brother's voice filled her mind.

Sahara! Deor said, and there was a schoolboy grin on his face that made her want to laugh with delight. *We're here.*

Here? she asked, suddenly sobering. *Where's here? What do you mean?*

Here. On Halcyon. In the Holy City of Telon.

Sahara swallowed hard. *Who's we, Deor?*

Brytnoth and I. And Gwyn. You remember Gwyn, right? From Perseon?

Sahara didn't answer. She listened to that death knell of marching feet. *You're in the Temple, aren't you? You brought a lot more people with you than just Brytnoth and Gwyn, from the sound of it.*

We're with Derrek and his crew.

What? Sahara almost came to her feet, but checked the motion just in time. *What? How could you sell out to him, Deor, after what he did to you? I bet you delivered that zanthos right to him, too. And now he's here...*

Inwardly, she groaned. She laid her head back on her arms and felt the tears burn their way down her cheeks.

No, of course not! Well, I did bring the zanthos, but that was.... Nevermind. But no. We're not actually with him, Sahara. We hitched a ride...and I think he'll find that not everything will go according to plan now.

Sahara raised her face once more and took a deep breath. She swiped her cheeks with the palms of her hands. *You sabotaged his mission! What did you do?*

Well, that would spoil the surprise. Deor's eyes were dancing, and Sahara wanted to reach out and hug him. *Where are you?*

Don't come to me. Not yet. Stay with Derrek and wait for my word.

You're the boss, he said. *And Sahara...*

What?

You're not alone anymore.

And with that, he was gone.

Sahara wanted to weep for joy. Maybe her feeble attempts at prayer had been heard after all. And Deor was her brother again, not that half-crazed lunatic under the thrall of whatever power was latent in the *zanthos*.

And Brytnoth is here too, she thought, gratitude overflowing in her heart.

Suddenly, everything that had seemed so impossible just a few short hours ago felt suddenly within her grasp. They would rescue Rafe, and Jared would be hauled out of the jaws of the Dragon. Everything would come right after all.

There was just one thing now that she had to do.

She considered the situation for a moment as she heard a harsh voice—so strident in the still peace of the Temple— giving orders. It sounded vaguely familiar, and after a moment she placed it.

That must be Derrek. But he's changed somehow.

Slowly, the Temple was beginning to fill with a feeble light. High windows above the altar, which faced the east, were letting in the dawn. Sahara watched the sunlight creep over the dusty stone floor, catching in little pockets between the flagstones, sending long, dark shadows of tall pillars fleeing toward the far walls. She saw now that each pillar was actually a set of stone rings laid one on top of the other. Each ring, about two feet thick, was decorated with a different pattern. Some of the artwork had faded over the years, but she saw in the center of every pillar the emblem of the Hazad —that three-petaled flower that was burned into her own flesh.

Somehow, the sight gave her hope. It was like the promise of something, the whisper of a voice that she couldn't quite hear, but could feel its stirrings in her soul.

From her position in the southwest corner of the Temple, Sahara could now see the men that Derrek had arranged. They were partially concealed along the northern wall, standing in a double row behind the pillars. The sunlight hadn't reached them there, and in their black uniforms, they were almost invisible. Derrek stood alone on the raised stair of the sanctuary, his back to the altar. He was waiting.

They didn't have to wait long. The massive doors in the west wall swung open, and pilgrims began to shuffle into the Temple. Sahara watched them, breathless. Their eyes were downcast, their hands palm up at their sides. A reverent murmuring, from a thousand voices whispering in unison a single line of text, filled the Temple. Again, Sahara felt that surge of hope.

The massive nave was filled to capacity now, and Sahara, edging her way along the southern wall toward the sanctuary, caught sight of Jessup and Rigel and Yasmin and the rest of her tribe near the center of the crowd. Glancing back through the open doors, she saw the Temple square filled with people. All those trusting hands turned palm up to give and receive from their God, all those humble eyes focused on the dirt at their feet.

And suddenly, Sahara stopped. There was a rippling and a startled murmur from the rear of the crowd in the square, and then she saw it parting like wood before the axehead.

Azimir had come.

And by his side was Jared, wrapped all in a dark cloak with the cowl drawn up over his head. Sahara shrank back against the rough stone of the south wall. And as quickly as it had come, her hope and confidence began to melt away. Maybe she was already too late.

The frightened and surprised murmuring grew more audible as the wedge of Azimir's men drove through the crowds and entered the temple. They made straight for the sanctuary where Derrek stood waiting. And now, suddenly, a heavy, expectant hush fell over the crowd. It was as if, for the first time, they noticed the man standing in the holy place, and saw, in the light that was now its strongest, the troop of soldiers waiting in the wings.

Sahara swallowed her fear and her doubt and edged along the wall again. She had to get within striking distance of that sanctuary. She was almost level with it now, and she stopped just behind the last pillar, wrapping herself in its shadow and edging around so that she could see the sanctuary.

"Well met at last," Azimir was saying, clasping Derrek's hand at the wrist. "Is everything prepared?"

"It is," Derrek answered. "We wait for your word."

Out of the corner of her eye, Sahara caught motion in the crowd. She turned to look and saw Jessup, Rigel at his heels, making his way toward the sanctuary stairs. His face was full of confusion and even, Sahara thought, fear. She swallowed hard as the crowd parted to let him through.

Jessup and Rigel reached the stairs, and Jessup extended his hands to Azimir. "My lord Azimir," he said, his voice rolling like a strong wind through the temple, "we have done you no violence. We have kept our agreement. How is it that you come here now, armed for conflict, on this holiest of holy days?"

"You have harbored our enemy in your midst," Azimir answered. "Is that not cause enough? Is that not breach enough to void our contract?"

Jessup was shaking his head, his voice earnest. "You have my daughter as surety. I have—"

Azimir's laugh rang out, and, almost as a single body, the crowd flinched away from him. The horrible sound, so startling in that quiet place, swelled until Sahara wanted to cover her ears and hide in some dark corner. Only Jessup stood unmoving, but Sahara saw the fists clench at his sides.

"Your daughter is dead, old man," Azimir said at last.

Emelia was dead.

Sahara's mouth went dry. Emelia. The woman she had met in the alleyway outside the palace. The woman she had sent to Jared with a message...and her dagger.

No...please no....

Her eyes flicked to where Jared stood, masked in his cowled cloak. Had he killed her? Had the Dragon murdered Jessup's daughter?

She glanced back at Jessup. His face was utterly pale, but now something like rage was burning deep in his eyes.

"We had a pact," he said through clenched teeth. "You were to keep her safe, and we were to keep the peace. We had a pact. Does your word mean nothing now?"

Azimir hesitated, but then a ruthless smile bared his teeth. "It doesn't matter now."

A sudden darkness seemed to spread suddenly from the sanctuary, devouring the sunlight in the nave as it crept forward. For a moment, Sahara thought it came from Jared. Her hands turned to ice, and her heart pounded in her chest. But then she realized what it was.

The eclipse had begun.

She was out of time.

FORTY-FOUR

FROM WHERE HE stood in the sanctuary, his cowl masking his face, Jared watched the pathetic little scene unfold. An old man—he guessed it must be Jessup—was trying to ward off the evil that was coming to him and all his people with his wrinkled hands.

Where is their champion? Is this all they can muster? This shaking supplication from a miserable beggar and his lackey?

When Azimir laughed, Jared wanted to laugh with him, to shake down the walls of the temple on such a fool.

And yet...

"Your daughter is dead, old man," Azimir said, his voice like a knife's edge.

Somewhere deep within his mind, a memory stirred and woke, and he watched it unfold.

Emelia's eyes, full of wistful sorrow. And her voice, gentle to the very end.

Remember. She loves you.

The darkness within him shuddered. For that instant, sunlight seeped in, and Jared caught his breath, his eyes snapping to fix on Azimir's silk-clad form.

The dagger was here at his belt. Her dagger. Sahara's dagger. Would it not be fitting to end it all right now?

His fingers closed around the hilt and twitched, but then the darkness blotted out the light. He let his fingers fall to his side.

He focused his gaze once more beyond Azimir. The pain in Jessup's face, the impotent rage in his eyes—it made Jared want to laugh again.

And then, almost as if it were welling up out of his own heart, darkness seeped through the temple.

It was time.

He felt the sudden surge of power within him as the sun began to vanish behind the moon Eshka. It was time. He was ready.

What is that fool Azimir waiting for?

He was conferring with that foreigner Derrek, the traitor from Askalon.

"When we have concluded business here," he heard Azimir say, "then we will return with you to Askalon. You have my word."

They clasped hands at the wrists.

How ironic. Why should Derrek believe anything that wretched oath-breaker Azimir tells him?

He saw the answer in Derrek's half-maddened eyes. He knew that the power Derrek craved was so close, the man could almost taste it. He was drunk with it...and he would do anything now to have it for his own. Even trust an oath-breaker.

Suddenly, Derrek's eyes fixed on Jared. "You have promised me the Slayer," he said to Azimir. "Do not disappoint me, or I will kill you myself."

"When we have concluded our business here," Azimir repeated, "he is all yours."

Jared stared back at Derrek, though he knew the other man could not see his face. There was something else now in Derrek's gaze, something more than just lust for power. There was the crazed light of fanaticism. Jared's eyes narrowed.

Perhaps I should just annihilate them all. That would solve all the mysteries.

Azimir turned back to face the crowd of the Hazad once more, and Derrek stepped to the side, folding his arms across his chest. The darkness had almost covered the sanctuary and was seeping over the steps toward the feet of the crowd.

"The darkness is upon you," Azimir said, his voice echoing through the Temple. "And the end of your world has come."

Everyone in the Temple dropped to their knees. Jessup raised his hands to Heaven, and the murmuring chanting began again. The force of it hit Jared like a blow to the gut, and it was all he could do to keep from staggering back.

The darkness was growing. They could not stop it.

Jared clenched his hand, feeling the *zanthos* ring around his finger grow warm.

Derrek snapped his fingers.

His men stepped out of the deep shadows, and each one held a *zanthos* gun ready, each one targeting someone in the crowd.

Jared threw back the cowl of his cloak and stepped foward.

"You don't need those," he said, his voice rolling like deep thunder.

And with a roar, he raised his hand to heaven.

FORTY-FIVE

SAHARA COULDN'T BREATHE.

Emelia was dead. Dead because of what she had done...and now what could she do, in the end, to save her people from destruction?

The darkness washed over her, filling her mouth and nose as she struggled to bring air into her lungs.

"No!" she screamed suddenly, her voice ripping through the chanting and Jared's inhuman roar.

Silence dropped like a curtain on the assembled crowd.

Sahara flung herself from behind the pillar, ripping Rigel's knife from her belt. She was on Azimir before he even registered what was happening. The force of her charge knocked him flat on his back, and she straddled his chest, raising the curved blade high in the air.

Somewhere at the back of the temple, a woman's anguished, sobbing cry wavered in the air, and then was drowned in sudden chaos.

A sea of bodies swarmed for the western doors, and the temple echoed with screams. The darkness seeped into the crowd, catching some and paralyzing them with fear.

Sahara stared down into Azimir's surprised face, and his face twisted into rage as he recognized.

"You!" he hissed. "Why is it always you?"

"Stop," Sahara said, fighting to keep the emotion out of her voice. "While you still have control. Spare them, Azimir...or you will die."

Out of the corner of her eye, she saw Derrek's hand fly up, silently ordering his men to hold their fire. And though she couldn't see him, she felt Jared's eyes boring into her back, waiting, watching.

The knife edged higher and she tightened her grip on the hilt.

"Call him off," she gritted. "Damn it, Azimir! Call him off!"

"Sahara!"

Sahara turned in spite of herself. It wasn't the voice she was expecting to hear.

It was Katarina.

Sahara watched in mute horror as the only mother she had ever really known dragged herself up the steps to the sanctuary. Her face was bloodied and one arm hung crazily askew by her side. Tears were pouring down her face, and gasping sobs racked her broken body.

They must have nearly trampled her to death, Sahara realized. Then she said aloud, "Katarina! What are you doing? Get out of here while you still can!"

"Don't kill him!" Katarina cried, pulling herself up the last step and easing her broken body into a crumpled sitting position. "For the love of God, please don't do this!"

Sahara's knife hand trembled.

"I have to," she whispered. "Katarina, I have to...for our people..."

"He's my son!"

The knife fell from Sahara's hand and clattered on the stone floor of the sanctuary, and all that was left of Sahara's hopes came crashing down in flaming ruin.

"Your..." Azimir choked.

His face spasmed in some kind of bewildered rage mingled with the grief of realization. Looking at his face, Sahara knew that he knew Katarina told the truth. For a moment, it paralyzed him. Then he bucked suddenly, sending Sahara tumbling sideways, her hand scrabbling for the hilt of the knife.

Just as her fingers brushed the cold metal, something rock-hard slammed into her face, sending her sliding back across the floor. Stunned, she rolled to her hands and knees and shook her head, spitting out the blood that was pooling in her mouth. Then she looked up.

Jared bent over her, a ruthless grin on his chiseled face, dark hair falling over darker eyes. He seized her by the hair on the top of her head, jerking her up to her knees.

"Did you think you could stop me?" he growled. "Did you really think killing him would stop me? You pathetic little fool."

Sahara couldn't speak. Horror closed her throat, tightened its iron bands around her chest. Her mouth and nose were throbbing, and she could feel the hot, slick blood trickling down her chin.

A single tear slipped down her cheek, and she gripped Jared's wrist with a trembling hand.

"I told you," she said slowly, her voice hoarse. "I love you. And I would do anything for you...and for them." She pointed at the maddened crowds shoving their way out of the temple.

Jared flung her away from him as if her touch burned him.

"If you love them so much, then die with them!"

He raised the ring, and Sahara saw stones begin to glow all around the temple as he called up the power that seethed within him. The air began to tremble with a vibration that she couldn't hear, but that shook the ancient walls of the temple to their foundations. Dirt and bits of stone rained down on the crowds still trapped in the nave, and the terrified screams became a long wavering wail of despair.

Of course. Azimir had already been here. He had prepared this place to be a death trap...and he didn't need Derrek's *zanthos* at all. Azimir had lured him here to die with the rest of them.

And she knew beyond shadow of doubt that the drones Azimir had secreted in Perl were even now destroying his political enemies in Aquila. Vaguely, she thought of Tesla Nazari.

I'm sorry. I'm sorry I couldn't save you.

Over the din of her people's screams, she heard Derrck's voice shouting, but she couldn't understand the words.

She turned her tear-stained face to the ceiling. And then she saw it.

The ceiling was painted over with a faded and crumbling depiction of the persecution of the Hazad by the Drakkin. In the center was a young girl, bound to a pillar. Darkness surrounded her, but a ray of light from the faded blue heaven illuminated her upturned face. Rigel had told her the story...how the daughter of the Hazad chieftain had been the first to be sacrificed to the Drakkin. The girl had been first blood offering. And Sahara had been the last...and the one that had destroyed them.

She scrambled forward and grabbed Jared's arm.

"Stop!" she cried, choking on tears. "You don't want them. You want me." She tightened her grip on his arm, holding his gaze. "You want me instead."

Jared suddenly stopped and stared down at her. "What did you say?"

Sahara knelt in front of him, hands clasped. She heard a man screaming at her, begging her to get clear.

Deor.

Tears spilled over her cheeks as she silently bid him farewell.

"You have wanted me for a long time," she said softly, addressing the Dragon who stood before her clothed in the form of the man she loved. "You were robbed of me on Silesia. And I am one of them...I am one of the Hazad. I am daughter of everything you hate, and I offer myself to you freely. My life, in exchange for my people. Let them go...and take me instead."

From behind her, Katarina's scream shivered Sahara's resolve, but she clenched her hands into fists and raised her chin. She kept her eyes fixed on Jared's, staring into the abyss within them.

The sun vanished behind the moon. The darkness was complete.

"So be it," said Jared. He lowered his hand and leveled the ring at her.

Sahara closed her eyes. "I love you," she whispered. "Never forget."

There was a blinding flash.

Sahara felt something crash into her body, bone-jarring, shattering her inner calm in a shower of pain that tingled like a million sparks. She skidded across the stone sanctuary and slammed into the far wall.

For a split second, she thought she was dead. Then she opened her eyes.

In the dwindling glow, she saw Deor and Jared both crumple to the ground.

The desperate screams of her people and the rattle of machine gun fire rolled over her like a wave. Derrek's hoarse cries rose above the chaos, and she saw his men seep out of the dark shadows along the side of the temple. A groaning roar shook the stones beneath her. She heard the crash of crumbling stone as part of the ceiling at the far end of the temple came down.

She stretched out a hand and tried to scream, but no sound came. Bullets peppered the floor around her and she curled against the sanctuary wall. Her mind was utterly numb.

As more of the ceiling came down in the nave, Sahara became aware that someone was crouched over her. Strong hands, solid and warm, gripped her arms.

"Let's go!" a voice was saying. A familiar voice. A man's voice. "Got to get you clear."

"No," she said feebly, but she was too weak to struggle. The man started to drag her by her arms out of the sanctuary, but when he pulled her over some fragments of rock and she cried out, he stooped and lifted her in his arms. He staggered behind some of the chunks of fallen roof and ducked into cover just as bullets sprayed the face of the stones.

Sahara huddled against the rock and stared at the man's dark form.

"We've got to get Jared away from Derrek," he was saying. He was crouched so that he could look over the stone at the sanctuary. "He's going to kill him."

When she said nothing, the man gripped her shoulders and gave her a gentle shake.

"Sahara."

She blinked at him in the mouldering dark, and he shook her again.

"Sahara. It's Brytnoth. Snap out of it. I need you."

"Brytnoth," she whispered. She pressed the palms of her hands to her eyes and heaved a shuddering breath. "What...? I'm not...?"

"No. You're not dead. Not yet." She heard the barest tinge of a smile in his voice. "Come on. Let's get Jared out of there."

He moved into position again. Sahara forced her muscles to work, pushing herself upright. She stared across the empty expanse of floor.

Silhouetted against the glowing embers of what was left of the *zanthos*, she could make out ten men standing in a wide circle around a crumpled form. Others stood back, weapons raised, keeping Azimir's men pinned down behind rubble on the far side of the temple. Glancing down the length of the nave, Sahara saw people scrambling over masonry to slip out of a wide gash that had been knocked in the western wall.

Her people were free.

And in a rush of adrenaline and sudden clarity, everything that had happened erupted in her mind. She gripped Brytnoth's arm, not even daring to look at him.

"Where's Deor?"

FORTY-SIX

THE HAUNTING chant wove its chill into Deor's consciousness, bringing him suddenly awake and aware. For a moment, he thought he hadn't opened his eyes at all. But then he saw, out of the corner of his eye, the sputtering glow of one of the *zanthos* stones. He rolled onto his side and saw Jared's crumpled body not three feet away.

He started to scramble forward, but a sudden cage seemed to have sprung out of the ground, cutting him off from his friend. Glancing up, he realized that it was a circle of men, closing in around Jared's body. And then he saw Derrek, standing tall in the center of the ring.

The sudden hasp of steel on stone sent a chill through his body.

Derrek was going to kill Jared...and that meant he wasn't already dead.

Deor lurched to his feet and came face to face with the business end of a nasty looking machine gun.

"Back," the soldier growled. "Get back."

Deor stepped back with his right foot, then slapped the muzzle aside and slammed his elbow into the man's face, grabbing the gun as the man fell. The man's startled squawk had drawn the attention of half a dozen other members of Derrek's guard, and Deor made a run for the south side of the temple. He dove behind a pillar as a spray of bullets sent dust and bits of stone flying in his wake.

"Who the hell are you?"

Deor turned, surprised, and found that he was crouched beside Azimir. He opened his mouth to speak, then thought better of it.

He glanced around the pillar and saw the glint of steel in Derrek's hand.

"Damn," he growled. Another hail of bullets greeted him, and he ducked into cover once more.

Azimir's men returned fire.

"He's going to kill Jared," Azimir said in the darkness beside him. "He came to kill him...and now there is nothing to stop him."

"Like hell there isn't," Deor said. "Look, I don't really know who you are, and I don't really care right now. But we're on the same side of this. If Derrek kills Jared, he will loose the Dragon. Do you have any idea what that means?"

He hazarded a glance around the pillar again, and was rewarded with another volley from Derrek's men. Without waiting for a response from Azimir, Deor made his decision.

"I'll get their attention," he said. "Break that circle. Whatever you have to do." He glanced at Azimir and saw the leader give a brusque nod. "On my mark." Deor shifted his position, preparing to make a dash for the next pillar. "Go!"

He bolted out of cover with a yell. Derrek's men opened fire, and Deor felt a bullet graze his shoulder as he dove behind the cover of the next pillar. He rolled to his feet and slammed his back against the stone, breathing hard. His shoulder throbbed, but adrenaline numbed the pain. He twisted around to watch Azimir charge through the line of chanting men and take Derrek down with a mighty spring. The circle scattered like a murder of startled crows, and Deor watched as Azimir and Derrek rolled together away from Jared's body.

Then he saw the flash of steel and heard Azimir grunt as the blade went home.

For a moment, everything seemed frozen in stillness. Then Azimir crumpled, and he saw Derrek shove his body aside like so much garbage.

Derrek pushed himself to his feet and wiped the blade of the knife on his thigh. He moved quickly back to Jared's side, and the circle reformed. As soon as he was gone, Katarina dragged herself across the sanctuary floor toward Azimir's fallen body.

The chanting began again, low and chill. Derrek dropped to his knees beside Jared and the edge of the knife glinted in the dying light.

Suddenly, with an inhuman cry, a shambling form burst from the shadows behind the circle. His eyes were wild, and his robe fluttered around his emaciated body. But his fury gave him inhuman strength, and two members of the Order went down under the man's knife before they had a chance to cry out. The rest edged away from him, swinging in an arc to leave him exposed to the leveled weapons of Derrek's guards.

Oblivious to the danger, the man faced Derrek, knife at the ready.

"Let him go!" the man shouted.

His voice was thin and weak, but Deor would have known it anywhere. It was Rafe.

Deor gripped the stone until his knuckles turned white. *Get out of there, Rafe,* he pleaded silently. *Get the hell out of there!*

Derrek lifted his head and locked eyes with the captain of his guards. He jerked his head toward Rafe. Deor sucked in breath to shout, but before he could form the sound, the rapid tattoo of gunfire dropped Rafe to his knees. The knife clattered from his hand as he collapsed.

"NO!"

The shriek rang out from behind the tumbled stones across from him, and Deor's eyes snapped to the spot. He could barely make out Brytnoth, struggling to hold someone behind cover. He didn't need to see clearly to know that it was Sahara.

Deor felt the panic begin to clench his chest. Rafe was dead, as far as he could tell, and Jared was about to be, and he knew that if Brytnoth couldn't hold Sahara down, she would be next on the casualty list. And there was nothing, nothing at all, that he could do about any of it.

He had no time to dwell on it. Derrek's voice echoed through the sanctuary, low at first, then rising in intensity.

"We have waited, brothers. We have bided our time. But the Slayer has been delivered into our hands, and the time for our rising has come. He holds our power within, and we will release it. It is time, brothers. It is time."

Eight curved knifes flashed in the hands of the men surrounding Jared and they knelt around his body.

"Slay the Slayer," Derrek cried suddenly, his voice like thunder, "and become the new Collective!"

The chanting swelled like an avalanche in the mountains.

Nine daggers came up, ready to plunge into Jared's chest.

And then Jared opened his eyes.

FORTY-SEVEN

DEOR'S BREATH caught in his throat.

Jared seemed to be staring straight at him, and his eyes were wide with fear. Jared, not the Dragon, lay in the center of that circle, and those cruel knives were poised to rob him of his life.

Something must have happened to him when I knocked Sahara out of the way and Jared blasted us with that zanthos ring.

He didn't know what had happened, or why, but Jared had slipped out from under the influence of the Dragon, even if it was just for a moment.

A sudden movement on the far side of the sanctuary caught Deor's eye. Azimir, a dribble of blood running down his chin, was dragging himself across the floor toward Derrek.

"Stop, you idiots!" Azimir gasped. "You're going to ruin everything! You can't kill him. Stop, damn it!"

He scrabbled weakly, trying to propel himself faster, but his right leg was a deadweight. He was fumbling with the curved knife that he wore at his waist, trying to draw it. Derrek ignored him, his eyes riveted on Jared, his lips moving in some chanted prayer that Deor couldn't understand.

But Azimir wouldn't give up. He left off the knife and pulled himself along the floor, a blood trail oozing behind him.

"He's mine!" Azimir choked. "Get away from him! I'm not finished with him yet!"

Now Derrek did turn, and Deor saw the flash of his teeth in the lurid glow of the burned-out *zanthos* stones.

"You are finished," Derrek said. "Your men are killed or scattered or just too scared to defend you. Your rule is in shambles. And your life is seeping out of you. You are finished."

Azimir had reached the circle now, and he pushed himself onto his hands and knees. "There is still time!" he choked. "The Hazad...there is still time!"

Derrek kicked Azimir viciously in the stomach and Azimir collapsed, wheezing out his life.

"You thought you could double-cross me," Derrek grated, kicking Azimir again. "You lured us here to destroy us and keep the power for yourself." Another kick. "You never intended to keep your end of the bargain...and so I have decided not to keep mine."

Azimir rolled onto his back, his body racked with broken coughing that brought more blood bubbling from his mouth. He stared up at the shattered ceiling. "You've failed," he said, mustering enough breath to speak. "Your time is up."

He's gone mad at the end, Deor thought as Derrek turned away.

And yet, there was something changed in the air already. The darkness was lessening. Deor could feel the chill easing out of the air, and where the ceiling had caved in, he could see the light growing steadily greater.

The darkness was passing. Azimir had distracted Derrek for just long enough.

Then Deor's blood froze in horror. Sahara, a blur of fury and tears, sprang out of cover and slid across the stone floor. She collided with Rafe's lifeless body and crouched over it, lifting Rafe's head in her arms.

Derrek's men leveled their weapons at her and advanced,

shouting at her to get back. She glared at them and held Rafe tighter. Her matted hair fell across her eyes, brilliant with grief. The captain raised his arm and his men halted, weapons at the ready.

A string of curses choked Deor. Another moment and his sister would be dead, and Jared too.

He glanced around, frantic. He had no weapon. There was nothing he could use within his reach. And alone against eight armed men, he wouldn't be able to stop Derrek, and he couldn't take down a squad of men with machine guns.

Something cold burned into his thigh, arresting his attention. He frowned, then shoved his hand into his pocket. His fingers closed around something.

A sphere.

His eyes widened.

Zanthos.

How could he have missed it? When they had deactivated Derrek's store of *zanthos*, he had completely forgotten to add his little souvenir from Silesia to the stockpile.

That meant that it was still weaponized.

His hand spasmed around it, and he felt the sudden surge of dark energy that had tempted him so strongly on Silesia. Something whispered to him from the shadows, silken assurances that it wasn't too late. He could still destroy Derrek...and Askalon would be his.

Askalon?

He stared across the expanse of stone at his sister, gathered over Rafe's dead body like a cornered animal. Then he shifted his gaze to Jared's face.

Deor. It was Jared's voice in his head...Jared's, not the Dragon's. *Don't.*

The captain's hand lifted higher. "Get the hell back, girl!" he shouted. "Or we open fire!"

Sahara shook her head, and her arms circled Rafe's neck. "Go ahead," she shouted back. "You've destroyed everything else!"

Don't.

Deor launched himself into the clear, pulling the stone out of his pocket. He hit the ground hard, and the impact knocked him breathless. His eyes locked with Jared's.

"Jared!" he shouted. "Now!"

And he flung the stone, sending it spinning across the floor. The light sprang suddenly into Jared's eyes, and the *zanthos* stone began to glow even before it slammed into Jared's waiting palm.

With a roar, Deor pushed himself to his feet and launched himself into the firing squad. At the same moment, he heard Derrek's cry of startled surprise as Jared rolled suddenly, lifting the stone in his closed fist.

With a shuddering yell, Jared opened his hand.

There was a blinding flash, and the shockwave that followed flattened everyone in the sanctuary. As it flowed through the temple, the rest of the ceiling in the nave toppled down with a roar and an explosion of dust and mortar. Sunlight poured through the ruin, sending the shadows into oblivion.

For a long moment, Deor lay on the ground, his cheek pressed into the cold stone, watching the rays of sunlight filter through the motes of dust. Dizzily, he began to realize that everything was quiet. There was no sound of chanting. No sound of gunfire. No sound even of weeping.

With a great effort, he pushed himself to his knees and turned to look at Jared.

He was standing, head bowed, in the center of the sanctuary. Derrek and the Order were utterly gone.

Only their shadows remained, burned into the stones of the floor.

FORTY-EIGHT

SAHARA'S EYES FLUTTERED OPEN. She still clutched Rafe's body in her arms, his cold face pressed to her own. Stunned, she lifted her gaze to the center of the sanctuary and saw Jared standing silently, clenching and unclenching his fists. Dark shadows surrounded him, scorched onto the floor. Eight of them.

She heaved a shuddering breath.

"Jared," she called, her voice sounding thin in the awful stillness of the place.

For a moment, he didn't move. Then, like a man coming out of a dream, he stirred. He raised his eyes to meet hers, but there was no light of joy or recognition in their depths.

"Sahara!"

Brytnoth bounded across the sanctuary and dropped to his knees beside her. She turned and threw an arm around his neck, shattering sobs racking her body. His arms slipped around her, holding her tight against grief.

"I know," he mumbled. "I know."

Then he released her, drawing back, and she turned to see why. Deor stood behind her, his face drawn and pale.

"I'm...sorry," he said, his voice almost bewildered. "I'm so sorry. I couldn't..."

He crouched beside her, smoothing her tangled hair away from her face. She stared at him through her tears for a moment, and then he pulled her to his chest, burying his face in her hair as she clutched his jacket in her fist.

"He's gone," she whispered. "Deor...he's gone. I couldn't...there wasn't anything..."

"He died for me."

Startled, Sahara pulled away from Deor and looked up. Jared stood there, his face a mask.

"Jared," Sahara mumbled.

He met her gaze for a moment, then dropped his eyes again to his friend's still face. Then he knelt, taking Rafe's hand in both his own.

"All that power," he said. His brows drew together and a tear slid down his cheek. "All that power in my hands...and...I couldn't save him. I told him I would save him, Sahara." His anguished eyes met hers again. "I lied."

He bent his head and wept.

A racking cough from the center of the sanctuary made Sahara jump. She turned to see Katarina kneeling beside the body of her son, cradling his head in her lap.

She laid Rafe's head gently on the stone floor and wiped her face with the palms of her hands. Then she rose, and she and Deor and Brytnoth moved to Katarina's side.

"Mother," Azimir was saying. His eyes were wide and staring, and Sahara knew he could no longer see. "Mother...forgive...forgive..."

Katarina laid her cheek on Azimir's forehead. "I love you, my son. I love you."

Azimir heaved a shuddering sigh and lay still. Katarina raised her eyes to heaven, tears streaming down her cheeks, lips moving in a broken prayer.

Sahara pulled Katarina into her arms, as the older woman dissolved into sobs.

"Why didn't you tell me?" Sahara mumbled, not really expecting an answer.

For a long while, Katarina said nothing at all. But finally, her tears spent, she sat up and took a deep breath. She glanced up at Deor and Brytnoth, who stood behind Sahara with bowed heads.

"He accepted the terms," Katarina told them.

Brytnoth's brow furrowed. "What terms?"

"For Askalon's debt. The terms you came here to offer all those months ago." She smiled weakly, and added to Sahara, "And he has vowed to let the Hazad live in peace."

"But who heard him say so?" Sahara protested. "Who will carry the order?"

Katarina turned and glanced over her shoulder. Three men stepped forward out of the half-light, and Sahara immediately recognized Ribbadi as one of them. He saluted his fallen lord with a touch of his hand to his breast, and then he addressed Sahara.

"We shall see it done," he said.

"And the drone strikes?" Sahara asked. "Against the other lords?"

Ribbadi shook his head. "There were never any strikes planned," he said. Then he added, with the glint of a hard smile in his voice, "And since you disposed of Lord Dracor for us, we need not trouble about any coup for the present."

Sahara sat back cross-legged on the floor, staring across the sanctuary at Jared's broken form. He was still once more, grief utterly spent.

Jared. She tried to reach out to him, and met only with the whirl of her own thoughts. *Jared.*

Brytnoth and Ribbadi clasped hands at the wrists. "We will send payment," Brytnoth said. "Once I right the ruin Derrek has caused on Askalon, we will make good on our promise."

Ribbadi cocked his head at Brytnoth, then studied Jared's bowed head and Rafe's lifeless body.

"You know," he said softly, "I think you have paid price enough." He glanced back at Brytnoth and gripped his hand tighter. "The debt is forgiven," he said. "Go back to Askalon and make things right with your own people."

Brytnoth gaped at him, and Ribbadi turned away with a smile.

"I guess people can always surprise you," Deor remarked, watching the men pick their way through the ruined temple, summoning what remained of their men as they went.

A moment later, they heard Ribbadi's voice pronouncing something in the square outside the temple, and then a wild eruption of cheering brightened the heavy stillness within the temple.

"Sahara!" a young voice called from the western end of the temple. "Katarina? Are you alive? Are you here?"

Sahara struggled to stand, and Deor reached down and helped her to her feet. She peered through the dusty sunlight and saw Rigel struggling over the wreckage toward them. In his wake came Jessup and Yasmin. As soon as he was in the clear, Rigel looked up and saw Sahara watching him, and he broke into a run, a huge grin spreading across his face. He vaulted up the sanctuary steps and seized her in a mighty embrace. She heard Deor and Brytnoth chuckling behind her.

"You're alive," Rigel breathed, unable to keep the grin off his face. "I thought for sure you had died...but..." His eyes shifted over her shoulder. "He saved you?"

Sahara followed his glance. "Deor," she said, beckoning him forward. Then, to Rigel, she explained, "My brother."

"Brother!" Jessup panted, finally at the base of the sanctuary steps. "Then he is son to us, Zelie Sahara."

As Yasmin embraced Deor and Brytnoth and Jessup wrung their hands, Sahara slipped quietly back to Jared's side. She came within a few paces of his silent form, then hesitated.

Jared? She tried once more to reach out to him, but her voice died at the edge of her own thoughts.

Biting her lips, she edged forward and dropped to her knees beside him.

"Jared?" she whispered.

And now at last he turned, his dark eyes an abyss of grief.

"I did this, Sahara," he said softly. "I'm so sorry."

Sahara dropped her gaze to Jared's strong hands, clasped still around Rafe's limp fingers. "No," she said finally. "You didn't do this." She fought for a moment against the rush of tears, and met his gaze once more. "Jared, he gave his life to save you. He wanted to save you..."

"We've been brothers as long as I can remember, Sahara," Jared said, his voice breaking. "How will I ever go on without him now?"

The hot tears spilled down Sahara's cheeks. "He wouldn't want you to linger with him here," she said softly. "He wanted you to live...he gave his own life so that you could live."

Jared dropped his head again, silent sobs racking him. And then, so suddenly that it took her breath away, he let Rafe's hand go and seized her in his arms. She could feel him shaking, and she slowly wrapped her arms around him, laying her head against his.

"I love you," he mumbled, his voice muffled. "I love you."

Sahara couldn't say anything. There was so much she wanted to say, so many things she needed to say. And there were no words for any of them. So she just held him tighter and hoped that he understood.

"Children," came a gentle voice, and Sahara glanced up to see Jessup standing nearby. "Give over your grief now for a while," he said. "Our people are preparing a great feast against the coming night, in celebration of the end of our persecution and the banishing of the Dragon. Come and refresh your spirits."

Sahara got to her feet and stretched down a hand to Jared. He took it and stood slowly, facing Jessup with a meekness that Sahara had never seen in him before.

"I am no one that you should welcome me into your midst," he said. "Your daughter..." He choked and paused to collect himself. "Sir, your daughter...I...she died because of me. I didn't mean for her to die. I never wanted her life."

Jessup's face eased into a gentle smile, and he stepped forward to grip Jared's shoulders in his wrinkled hands. "And if my forgiveness will ease the terrible burden you bear," he said, "please know that you have it. She gave her life to keep you from the clutches of the Drag-on...and that was for all our sakes, not just for yours."

"How do you know that?" Jared asked.

Jessup's smile broadened. "I know my daughter," he said. "She sacrificed herself once already...she offered herself to Azimir in exchange for our safety." He glanced up at the crumbling ceiling and then winked at Sahara. "It runs in the family, I guess."

FORTY-NINE

AS THEY STEPPED through the rubble out into the open, Sahara stopped in sudden surprise. In the pale, waning sunlight, an impromptu street festival had begun. Fires in giant braziers glowed at the edges of the square, and on a makeshift platform on the far side of the square, a band was playing.

Sahara saw Isis stamping furiously in the center of the whirling dancers in the square. A look of fierce triumph was on her face, and as she tossed her dark head, she reminded Sahara of a wild horse just set free—and she had never looked lovelier.

"Come on!" Rigel called, scrambling down the ruined steps of the temple. "Let's dance!"

Sahara smiled at him and waved him into the crowd. She couldn't shake the heaviness of Rafe's death, and she had no intention of dancing in any case. She glanced sidelong at Jared, but his face was a mask again.

She felt suddenly lost as she studied his face, and she realized how much she had relied on her ability to read his thoughts. She had never really paid much attention to reading him—he'd always been an open book.

Not always, she reminded herself.

When they'd battled against the Triumvirate on Askalon, Jared had figured out how to guard his thoughts from her, and she'd been the vulnerable one. Her fear had made her turn on Jared. Thinking back on that now, she almost laughed.

I was such a fool. How could I ever have doubted him?

But not so very long ago, he had nearly destroyed her with his ability to penetrate her thoughts. She glanced at him again. There was such calm in his bearing. And his guarded expression gave no hint of what he was truly feeling.

Sahara swallowed. Her heart was racing, and as the music swelled and the dancing became more frenzied, she had a sudden desire to run back into the silent temple tomb behind her. Surely Rafe shouldn't be left alone...surely someone should stay. Surely she should stay.

She must have made some kind of motion, because Jared suddenly glanced down at her.

"What's wrong?" he asked. His voice was husky with the raw emotions of the day, but she saw at last the tiny flicker of the old flame in his eyes.

"Nothing."

He arched an eyebrow at her, and the strength of his hand around hers was suddenly at once an anchor and a beacon, keeping her steady and guiding her safely to harbor. A smile blossomed on her face, and she shook her head at him.

"It's nothing."

He regarded her for another moment, then turned his attention back to the crowd. Sahara followed his gaze and saw with surprise that Deor and Brytnoth had both followed Rigel into the crowd of dancers.

"I didn't know he could dance," she muttered, watching Deor abandon himself to the music.

"You sound jealous," Jared observed. "You're a fine dancer your-self, as I recall."

Sahara felt the heat rise to her face. The one and only time she had ever danced was ages ago, at the summer festival on Silesia. She'd vowed never to do it again.

"I can't let go like that," she said, gesturing to Deor and Brytnoth. "It's..."

"Frightening?" Jared asked.

Sahara's eyes snapped to his face. "What? No! Of course not!"

Jared leaned close to her and whispered, "Liar."

Then, with a gentle squeeze of her hand, he joined Deor and Brytnoth in the crowd. Sahara gaped, and beside her she heard Katarina chuckle.

"Let's get something to eat," she said, slipping her arm through Sahara's. "Sooner or later they'll be hungry."

Together, they made their way around the edges of the crowd to where the cookfires were burning. The rich, savory scent of roasting meat made Sahara's mouth water, and she realized suddenly how hungry she was. Four women were pulling small, round, golden loaves out of the ashes of the fire and heaping them on the boards. As fast as they drew the finished loaves out, other women set new loaves to bake. Four spits rotated slowly over the fires, the goats dripping juices into the flame as they roasted.

"How did they get this started so quickly?" Sahara asked.

"The preparations were all done this morning," Katarina answered, helping herself to a bun and several strips of juicy meat. "We always feast after the ceremony...we just have more reason to celebrate tonight."

They made their way through the line to the next set of boards, where an assortment of all the season's bounty was heaped for their enjoyment. Dried fruits, nuts, candied *borracha* flowers and rich cream cakes loaded the table. She took one of the knives to cut a cake, then hesitated. It was lovely, sparkling with rough sugar and pressed flowers.

"It's so pretty," she said to Katarina. "I don't dare cut it!"

Katarina's scream shattered the dusk, and the band fumbled into discord. Sahara turned slowly and saw Brig, eyes wild, holding Katarina around the waist. He pressed a dagger's edge into the creamy flesh at her throat.

"You had a job to do," he growled at Sahara.

"Brig!" she gasped. "No!"

"You had one job to do. One. And you didn't do it."

"I told you she wasn't a threat!"

Brig threw back his head and laughed. "As if I could believe you," he snapped, "when she had you eating out of her hand. But I had my own spies at work, and I know the truth."

"What truth? What are you talking about, Brig? You're crazy!"

Brig's face hardened. "Crazy? No. She's working for Azimir, just as I always thought. Working to sell us out. And any minute now, those drones are going to come over the border from Perl and wipe us out. It's all been arranged."

"Brig! You damned liar! It's not true!" Katarina cried. "And my son is dead!"

"Is he?" Brig's face creased in a grin. "Well, check that off my list, then."

Sahara felt the weight of the knife in her hand, measured it, calculated. She kept her eyes fixed on Brig's. "You've misjudged the situation, Brig," she said quietly. "You're making a mistake."

"Am I? Am I?" Another maniacal laugh. "Don't you hear the engines? They're coming, I tell you! They're coming!"

Everyone around Sahara froze, turning terrified faces up toward the sky. A little girl nearest to Sahara tugged on her mother's sleeve, trying to drag her toward the houses beyond the square.

"Let's go hide," she whispered. "I hear them!"

And for an instant, Sahara felt certain that she heard them too.

What if Ribbadi was lying? What if it was all just to lure us into the open...to finish the work Azimir began?

She felt a touch on her elbow. Deor was standing beside her, and he folded his arms across his chest.

"Drones in Perl?" he asked. "You sure?"

Brig nodded. "Tell your stupid girlfriend—"

"Sister, actually."

Confusion arrested Brig for a moment, but then he dismissed the matter and swept on, "Tell her. They're there. And they're coming to destroy us all. It is time to rise up!" His voice rose to a shout. "Rise up! It is time for—"

"No, they aren't." Deor's calm, cold voice cut over Brig's hysteria, and he stopped.

Sahara glanced at Deor as Brig snapped, "What?"

"Oh, there were drones there all right," he said. "But we knew about those." He winked at Sahara. "We got good intel on that point. So I sent a team to check it out. Those drones won't be going anywhere ever again, I'm afraid." He gestured to Katarina. "So you can let her go now. And you can hang up the revolutionary jacket. Not necessary."

"She never betrayed us, Brig," Sahara said. "And even if she did, it's Jessup's place to bring her to justice, not yours."

Brig hesitated for a moment, then flung Katarina away from him. She stumbled into Deor's arms, and Sahara relaxed her grip on the knife. Brig saw the action, and he jerked his head toward the knife.

"You were going to kill me with a cake knife?" he said.

"If I had to," Sahara answered with a shrug. "But I'm glad I didn't have to. There's been enough blood and enough death today."

She set the knife on the board and turned away. But before she could take a step, Brig was on her. He tackled her to the ground and pinned her arms behind her.

"Guess you really aren't so fierce after all," he hissed in her ear.

"What are you doing?"

"I've been working for years to get our people to rise up against the Zharib," he growled, his voice low. "Years. And now...it's all been taken from me. So I will have this at least."

As suddenly as he had tackled her, his weight was gone. Sahara rolled over and saw him sprawled on the pavement five feet away. Jared stood over him, fists clenched.

"Get. Out." Jared's voice was hard as steel, sharper than the edge of a knife. "Or I will kill you."

Brig scrambled to his feet, his face red with the shame of his humiliation.

"I won't forget this," he said as he backed away.

"I hope not," Jared said.

Brig turned and fled, and a moment later Sahara heard the sound of a horse galloping down the cobbled street. Katarina crouched beside her as she picked herself up.

"Are you hurt?" she asked.

"No." Sahara dusted herself off and managed a smile. "No." Then, as Jared rejoined them, she nodded her thanks. "What did you do, fling him?" she asked.

"Pretty much." Jared grinned then. "He looked incredibly like a frog as he flew through the air, legs all splayed every which way. Quite satisfying."

Sahara moved back to the sweets table as the band resumed its playing. She picked up the knife and turned it over in her hands. "And I didn't have to kill him," she said. "I'm grateful for that."

Jared gestured to the lovely cake. "Cut me a slice too, won't you?"

She smiled at him. "With pleasure."

They carried their heaping trenchers to the seating area on the far side of the square. They settled around the rough-hewn table and Deor joined them a moment later, balancing five glasses of some kind of delightfully fizzy beverage in mugs.

Sahara took a sip and smiled. "Reminds me of something," she said.

"What?" Deor asked, tasting his.

"*Estevalia.*" Her eyes met Jared's over the rim of the mug as she sipped again.

Then she turned and looked out over the crowd. She felt suddenly wistful. She suddenly missed the warmth of the Silesian sun and the courtesy of Arnauld's hall in Albadir. But her eyes caught sight of Jessup dancing with little Tessa. Her cheeks were pink with excitement and her dark curls bounced as she stepped lightly with her grandfather.

I miss Silesia. But how am I ever going to leave?

FIFTY

AS NIGHT finally fell on the city of Telon, the people of the Hazad retreated outside the city walls to their campgrounds and tents to sleep.

"You can stay with me!" Rigel said to Jared, Deor and Brytnoth as they moved with the crowds out of the city gates.

"You haven't room in that tent for all of them!" Katarina chided, laughing. "I am sure Jessup will have quarters for them."

"But..." Rigel's protest died on his lips. "Not everyday I get to hang out with heroes," Sahara heard him mutter under his breath. Even though he wouldn't have been able to see it in the dark, she stifled a smile.

Jessup's tribe had the choice campground nearest the city gates, so they reached the tent lines within a few minutes. Nestled beneath trees shrouded in lichens, the tents seemed almost to huddle away from the furtive night winds out of the north. Sahara turned her face to the sky. In Azimir's dining hall, she had seen metal sconces punched with elaborate floral scrollwork and tiny holes. Above her, the night sky spread out like a sheet of dark metal, cold stars burned through like tiny points of white flame.

A sudden breeze from the north made her shiver, and she thought of Rafe, still lying in the temple. Jessup had tasked several of his men to watch over the bodies of the dead until they could be laid to rest.

She stopped in front of her own tent, and Jared lingered beside her. The others drifted away from her, and the night wind caught up their voices and laughter and left them in the dark and the quiet.

"Sahara," Jared said finally, once the others were out of earshot.

She didn't look at him, but looked up again at the stars. "What?"

"Now that this is all over..." He stopped, then started again, "We'll have to decide what to do next."

"I know."

"Sahara." He took her shoulders gently and turned her to face him. "Look at me."

She lifted her eyes to his and saw the ghost of a smile touch his lips. "I know," she said, even though she didn't.

He shook his head, his hands warm on her shoulders. "We'll talk it over in the morning. But I just wanted you to know that I will be content with whatever you decide."

He placed a gentle kiss on her forehead and followed the others.

Sahara watched him go, her throat tight with tears.

It isn't fair. How am I supposed to know what to do now?

She hesitated outside the tent for a long time, but the chill in the air finally drove her inside. She didn't bother with lighting a fire, but snuggled under the fur coverlet and shut her eyes. Sleep wouldn't come, and she struggled desperately against the memories replaying themselves in her mind.

Rafe was dead. And shouldn't he be returned to his people? Shouldn't he be buried on Silesia, in the warm sunshine, beside the sparkling river Alba that he loved so much?

And wouldn't Jared have to take him home? And once he was home, would he ever come back?

Sahara opened her eyes, staring up at the dark, sloped ceiling of her tent.

Should I go with him?

She'd been homesick for Silesia, hadn't she? But then she thought of Katarina, and Jessup, and Tessa, and Rigel. Even Isis. They had adopted her, given her a name. She was back with her own people at last.

But what about Deor? Her brother had a life on Askalon, and now that Derrek had been disposed of, there was a good chance he would be promoted to head up Askalon's military force, not just the militia. When she had found Deor on K'ilenfir, all she had wanted was to be with him, to keep their family together.

And now?

A tear slipped down Sahara's cheek. Finally overwhelmed by exhaustion, she slipped into troubled dreams.

———

It was late morning when she ducked out of the tent, and she saw the others gathered over a hot breakfast not far away. Several makeshift tables and benches had been set up under the sheltering branches of the trees, and after a moment's hesitation, she made for them. She caught Jared's eye as she approached, and he smiled at her.

"We saved you a spot and some breakfast," he said, holding out a trencher and patting the seat beside him.

"Thanks."

She slipped quietly into the seat and tore off a piece of the hot, sweet bread. It was loaded with dried fruits and nuts. A wooden bowl with some creamy goat cheese sweetened with honey sat in the center of table, and Deor sent it spinning toward her.

"Try this stuff," he said. "It's delicious. I tried to eat it right out of the bowl, but Katarina scowled at me."

Sahara glanced at Katarina, who was smiling fondly at Deor across the table.

"I told her that you can't expect great manners from a rough guy like me," Deor continued, "but she doesnt consider that a valid excuse."

Sahara tried to smile, but tears were threatening to overwhelm her fragile state of calm, so she focused intently on spreading some of the cheese on her bread.

A tense silence grew as she worked, until finally Brytnoth cleared his throat.

"I know we don't want to discuss this, he said, but we need to make our plans. I'm heading for Askalon with what's left of Derrek's men..."

"Did they surrender to you?" Rigel asked, his eyes alight. "Did they fall down and beg for mercy?"

Brytnoth's mouth quirked in a smile. "Sort of." He turned to Deor. "And are you coming with me? A promotion's waiting for you., remember?"

"Yeah." Deor's laugh died too quickly, and Sahara felt his steady gaze on her.

She swallowed hard and set down the wooden spreading spoon. Then she raised her eyes to meet her brother's across the table. "If that's where you need to be," she said slowly, "then that's where you need to be." She managed a smile through the mist of tears. "Just promise you'll visit me once in a while."

Deor's grin swept all her doubts aside, and the heaviness that lingered in her soul lifted just a bit.

"What about you, Jared?" Brytnoth asked. "Where will you go now?"

Jared rotated his mug thoughtfully on the rough wood boards of the table. "I need to take Rafe home," he said, then stopped abruptly, sucking in a deep breath. It was another minute before he trusted himself to speak. "And after that, I really don't know."

Sahara reached out suddenly and laid her hand over his. All the previous night's doubts and fears resolved in that moment in a flash of clarity. She knew what she had to do.

"I'm coming with you to Silesia," she said. "You don't have to go alone."

FIFTY-ONE

THEY BURIED Rafe under a stunning blue sky, in a spot drenched in warm sunshine. Lazy bees hummed in the orchards, and the gentle ripple of the river cooled the shimmering heat.

It felt so good to be warm again.

Sahara, kneeling in the grass beside the freshly-covered grave, lifted her face and closed her eyes, letting the light bathe her. She could feel the shadows of grief burning away, and a strange sense of peace lay like a cooling balm on her spirit. Rafe had given his life for the friend he loved best in the world...and there was no grief that could rob him now of blessedness.

The city of Albadir was buzzing with activity in preparation for the Summer Festival. As Sahara and Jared walked along the river path back toward the city, they stopped on the bridge and stared down into the sparkling water below.

"A whole year," Sahara said softly. "It feels like...weeks."

Jared glanced at her. His eyes were that familiar silver, and she felt a strange thrill as she looked into them. So many memories of their first meeting, of those first weeks and months in Albadir, came rushing back to her.

"I forgot," Jared said softly. He reached behind his back and drew out a dagger in a worn sheath. He ran his thumb over the hilt for a moment, then held it out to her. "This belongs to you."

Sahara glanced at it, then leaned over the balustrade and tossed a stone into the water. "Keep it," she said, then, grinning at him, she said, "You don't want me to wear it to the party later, do you?"

Jared laughed then. "No. No need for that."

"Then keep it. And you can make me another bird or something with it. Something clever. Actually..." She held out her hand and gestured for him to give it to her. "I've got a better idea."

Jared placed the dagger in her hand, eyebrow cocked. She grinned at him again, then drew her arm back and launched the dagger, watching with satisfaction as it cycled end over end and landed with a splash in the middle of the river.

"So much for that," she said, dusting off her hands. "Are you coming?"

"I can't believe you just did that," Jared said. "What if—"

"What if what? What if I ever need to assassinate someone?" Sahara laughed and took his hand in both her own. "Don't you know by now that I don't need a dagger for that kind of thing? And with what I have planned, I don't intend to need it again."

"That sounds ominous, actually," Jared said.

Sahara shook her head and tugged his hand. "Let's go. I don't want to miss the party."

"I thought you hated these things," Jared said. "I practically had to drag you last year, remember?"

"Well, people change, don't they?"

Jared stopped her and drew her near, brushing her cheek with his thumb. His warm smile made her breath catch in her throat. "Yes, I guess they do," he said softly.

She pulled out of his grasp and headed down the other side of the bridge. "I'll meet you at the fountain tonight," she called. "Don't be late!"

As the sun went down, the thrum of music filled the air. The fountain behind her sparkled and plashed, and Sahara perched on the stone edge, her stomach fluttering with nervousness. She hadn't wanted to tell Jared her plans until tonight, and she was suddenly terrified that he wouldn't understand.

She smoothed her hands over the folds of her skirt. She'd found it packed away in the drawer in her old quarters—the same dress she'd worn last year. It was simple, not like the jewel-crusted gown she wore in Aquila, and as she shifted her feet, the silver bangles around her ankle jingled softly. It was at once familiar and utterly strange, coming home like this...like trying to slip back into the rhythm of a dance that she'd never really known.

Where is he? she wondered, rearranging her skirt for the tenth time. *I told him not to be late!*

She was staring out over the crowd so intently that when someone suddenly sat down beside her, she jumped. It was Kirin, holding two glasses of *estevalia* in his hands.

"Kirin!" she gasped, smiling in spite of herself. "It's been ages!"

"Feels like ages, anyway," Kirin agreed, holding out one of the glasses. "You looked thirsty. Thought I'd bring you a drink."

She accepted the glass with a grateful smile. "Thank you."

Kirin sipped his drink thoughtfully, his eyes traveling over the crowd. "Last time we sat here, the Drakkin ruined the party," he said matter-of-factly.

Sahara glanced at him quickly, swallowing her sip of *estevalia* all at once. "We've come full circle, I guess."

"Well, mostly," Kirin said. "I wanted to throw you in the fountain back then, and I kind of still do." He grinned at her and winked.

She laughed and gave him a playful push. He almost lost his balance and that made her laugh even harder.

"Sorry," Jared said, shouldering his way through the crowd. "If someone's going to push him in the fountain, it really should be me."

Kirin stood and shook Jared's hand. "It's good to see you," he said. Then, glancing at Sahara, he winked at her again. "I can tell when I'm not wanted," he said. "That's my cue."

He disappeared into the swirl of people around them and Jared stood for a moment, studying her. Sahara felt warmth rising to her cheeks and she tried to hide her nerves behind her glass, only to find it empty already.

"I remember that dress," he said finally. "It suits you better this time."

"It fits exactly the same."

"Not what I meant." His mouth turned up in a crooked smile. "And if I tried to explain, I'd end up sounding like an idiot."

Sahara set her empty glass carefully beside her on the stones. *I don't know how to tell him what I have to say. I don't even know how to start.*

Jared hesitated for a moment, then said suddenly, "You need to tell me something, don't you?"

A sudden jolt of suspicion rocked Sahara, and her head snapped up. "Can't you hear my thoughts, Jared?" she asked, the words out before she could find a better way to ask.

"No, actually." The sudden realization of the fact made his brows draw together in a frown. "I haven't heard your thoughts since...since what happened on Halcyon. Not since we banished the Dragon." He sat down beside her and smiled at her. "It's just written all over your face, that's all. Something's on your mind, I can tell."

"Jared..." She stopped, then took a breath and began again. "Jared, I need to go home again. Back to my people. After this, I mean." She couldn't bear to meet his gaze, so she studied the flagstones at her feet.

"I figured as much. So I'm going with you."

At first, she didn't register what he'd said. Then, as the words sank in, she frowned and glanced up at him. "What did you say?"

"I'm going with you." He smiled at her. "Your family is my family...or, I'd like to hope they will be, anyway." He took her hand in both of his and studied it for a moment, then pressed it to his lips. "But...maybe we can spend winters here?"

Sahara laughed then and threw her arms around his neck. "It sounds wonderful," she murmured.

Jared detached her arms from around his neck and leaned back to look at her. And she didn't need to read his thoughts to see the love in his eyes.

"It's a nice night," he said. "Would you like to dance?"

Sahara smiled slowly, the sudden overwhelming rush of joy robbing her of her voice.

"Remember," Jared said, "I can't read your mind anymore. Is that a yes or a no?" He held out a hand, a deeper question in his eyes.

Sahara's smile widened, and she placed her hand in his.

"I'd love to."

WANT EVEN MORE ADVENTURE?

You already know that Sahara is an extraordinary and fearless warrior. But that's not how her story begins.

I can't wait for you to discover Sahara's origin story in *The Shift — A Silesia Story*...and best of all, it's yours for free!

Tap the cover or head to shannonblakebooks.com to pick up your copy today!

AUTHOR'S NOTE

Dear reader,

From the bottom of my heart, thank you. Thank you for coming along on this adventure with me, and for the gift of your attention and your time. It truly means the world to me.

I'd like to ask you for one more gift for me and for your fellow readers. You know how much a good review can help you decide which adventure to choose next, so please help other readers by sharing your rating and review on your favorite store and on Goodreads.

You can find all of my books on Amazon at amazon.com/author/shannonblakebooks.

See you on our next adventure!

Shannon

ABOUT THE AUTHOR

Shannon has been dreaming up stories and writing them down for almost as long as she can remember. She's insatiably curious and loves science fiction for giving her the excuse to research the most random things — and for giving her the freedom to explore galaxies.

In addition to penning novels, Shannon is an award-winning screenwriter managed by Art/Work Entertainment in Hollywood. She loves giving back to the writing community through coaching and teaching, and she also works as a ghostwriter and creative entrepreneur.

When she's not writing, she loves running, dancing, obstacle course racing, and hanging out with her family and friends. And she has never been known to turn down chocolate or a chai latte.

You can find more about her upcoming projects and author appearances at shannonblakebooks.com or follow her on Instagram @shannonblakebooks.

You can follow all her latest projects on Facebook, Instagram, and on her blog over at skvalenzuela.com.

ALSO BY SHANNON BLAKE